WINTER GAMES

John Lacombe

authorHOUSE®

AuthorHouse™
1663 Liberty Drive, Suite 200
Bloomington, IN 47403
www.authorhouse.com
Phone: 1-800-839-8640

First published by AuthorHouse 4/4/2008

ISBN: 978-1-4343-6475-3 (sc)
ISBN: 978-1-4343-6476-0 (hc)

Library of Congress Control Number: 2008901467

Printed in the United States of America
Bloomington, Indiana

This book is printed on acid-free paper.

For my parents

PROLOGUE

MANCHESTER

Manchester Airport was a ghost town.

It was a Tuesday night, in February. There were no college kids coming home to see the folks, no holiday travelers, no weekend skiing crowd. There was only darkness, and snow; the lazy descent of fat sticky flakes seemed to drape the whole scene in a cool calm.

It was nice, Jeff Hutchins thought. He didn't see airports like this very often. DC sure as hell wasn't like this.

The white Ford Focus rolled to a stop in front of the departures terminal. Agent Weathers cut the engine. He and Agent Farrior turned to face Hutchins, who was wedged uncomfortably in the car's "economy-sized" back seat. Weathers looked at his watch.

"The kid's supposed to come in at 10:45?"

Hutchins nodded. "Flight 190, from Newark. It took off on time."

"Well, we've got about twenty minutes, then. Jeff, we'll leave the car here. Hop up front, make sure we don't get towed. We'd better get in there, in case he lands early."

Weathers put the car in park, and he and Farrior hopped out. The two tall, athletic men briskly made their way towards the airport's slowly spinning turnstile entrance. Hutchins scrambled out of the backseat.

"Wait!" he called. "If it's alright with you guys, I'm going to park. I'd like to be there when he comes off the plane."

The two FBI field agents looked at one another. To them, intercepting some college kid in a sleepy New England airport was a great way to waste an evening. But it was probably different for this guy; Jeff Hutchins, some pencil-pusher from the Financial Crimes Section. He was probably salivating over the chance to hold up that shiny badge and say "Son? Agent Hutchins, Federal Bureau of Investigation." Whatever.

Weathers and Farrior shrugged. "Sure," Farrior said detachedly. "See you in a few minutes." And then Hutchins and the Focus were alone.

The small car's headlights cut a lonely path through the falling snow as Hutchins made his way to the airport's cavernous parking garage. Hutchins scanned the concrete structure from top to bottom. The garage was massive; it looked bigger than the terminal. But he couldn't see more than a dozen cars, scattered like modern art about the garage's lowest level. The snow, the quiet, the wide open spaces; it was a scene from some musical, inviting Hutchins to dance up a lamp post and start singing like Gene Kelly.

On any other day, it would have all been relaxing. But not today. Hutchins was here on business. He was following a hunch. If he was right, it might make his career.

Hutchins took a ticket from the automatic dispenser, parked the Focus in the garage's first available space, and jogged back toward the terminal. He was nearly 6'3", but his disheveled brown mop of a haircut, pale skin and un-athletic frame took away any shot he had at being imposing.

Brain, not brawn, had gotten him into the Bureau. Hutchins knew math, knew economics, knew money. At 29 years old, he was a young but seasoned agent. A certified accountant, Hutchins had earned his stripes fighting white-collar crime; he'd done key database research in several major money-laundering investigations. Hutchins had proven himself to be a man with a nose for dirty money. Which, in a roundabout way, was why he was now stepping out of an automatic rotating entrance into an airport in Manchester, New Hampshire.

The lower floor of the small airport held both the check-in counters and the baggage claim. Both were nearly vacant; the metal statue of a moose guarding the airport entrance seemed to be Hutchins' only company. Hutchins cast a sideways glance at the towering, authentically- scaled mammal as he passed it.

If we need any back-up, pal, I'll let you know. Hutchins rode the terminal's single escalator to the airport's upper floor.

The airport's upstairs security checkpoint was surrounded by what looked like a miniature shopping mall. There was a small McDonald's, an enclosed airport lounge, a news kiosk, and a gift shop.

All were vacant, with the exception of the McDonald's. Agent Farrior was at the counter, putting a plastic lid on a Styrofoam cup of coffee. Agent Weathers had seated himself on one of the benches adjacent to the security checkpoint, and was reading a newspaper he had grabbed off the flat top of a trashcan. Aside from the two agents and himself, Hutchins counted a total of eight people in the area.

There were two high-school-aged townies running the fast-food joint. An elderly uniformed gentleman and his younger female partner were manning the luggage scanner at the checkpoint. A short, red-haired young woman leaned against a concrete pole, the headphones from her I-Pod in her ears. A middle-aged man and woman, probably someone's parents, stood by the checkpoint awaiting his or her arrival.

And sitting alone in the center of the room was a twenty-something kid with neat brown hair wearing a Dartmouth College sweatshirt. In his lap sat what looked like a pile of comic books.

The brother.

Hutchins studied the kid for a second, then turned towards Weathers. Should he go sit next to the imposing field agent, or would that be too conspicuous? Hutchins decided against it, and he ambled over to the checkpoint. He awkwardly avoided the gaze of the elderly security guard, who seemed to be trying to decide what a city boy in a nice suit with no luggage was doing here in the middle of the night.

"Don't stand here." The voice came from over Hutchins' shoulder. It was Farrior.

"Don't wait for a target in plain view like this. It gives him something to think about. This kid of yours might be some white-collar pussy, but the bottom line is, he sees us waiting for him, he thinks about running. And I ain't chasing some kid around this airport. I've got coffee now."

Hutchins followed Farrior over to Weathers' bench. "Just wait till he comes out," Farrior said sternly. "Then come from the side and seize command of the situation. Quick, strong, painless."

Without looking up from his paper, Weathers cracked a smile.

"We'll make an agent out of you yet, Jeff." Lowering his voice, he lifted his gaze and leaned toward Hutchins. "Does the brother go to Dartmouth? I saw his shirt."

"No." Hutchins answered. "He owns a comic book store." *It was in the briefing I e-mailed you, moron. Did you miss the stack of comics he's carrying?* Hutchins held his tongue.

"Huh," Weathers offered. "Little young, isn't he?"

"Maybe, but he's a smart kid." Hutchins paused.

"It runs in the family."

"Look." Farrior pointed upward, at the blinking words "FLIGHT 190: DEBOARDING" on the wide flat-screen display suspended above the checkpoint. "Get ready. He's coming out."

All of the airport's gates were a stone's throw from the checkpoint; within seconds of Farrior's announcement, Hutchins watched the first of Flight 190's passengers round the corner and exit to the left of the baggage scanners. First came an old man in a navy New England Patriots parka, followed by a couple of salesmen dressed in leather coats, golf shirts and khakis. Next a teenage girl; she was greeted with hugs from the couple who had been waiting by the checkpoint. Then the terminal was quiet again.

Hutchins could feel his pulse quickening. He tried to remain calm. *Some granny probably caused a traffic jam on the way out of the plane. Keep cool, be patient. . .*

A minute passed. Now Hutchins was worried. *I checked the damn flight manifest. I called Newark. He was on the damn plane.*

"You boys aren't waitin' for someone, are ya?" The gruff, condescending voice rang out from across the room and startled Hutchins. It was the old security guard.

"Yes, sir," Farrior replied. "We have a friend coming off Flight 190."

"Son, that flight's empty. There ain't ever more than five or ten folks on 190, not this time of year."

"Shit!" Weathers muttered, and he and Farrior turned angrily toward Hutchins.

"Hold on!" Hutchins said defensively. "He was on this goddamn flight! I checked multiple times. He must be here!"

"Look," he added. "Why don't you guys just go check the plane?"

"Because," Farrior gritted through his teeth, "going through a goddamned airport checkpoint is a pain in the ass since 9/11. Even if they let us through, we'll have a hundred forms to fill out tomorrow explaining why we had to run airport security to clean up your mess."

Hutchins ignored that last comment. "Sir," he called to the old guard. "Is there any way you can check, maybe on your radio, to see if the plane is completely empty?"

For a moment, the grizzled New Englander stared hard at Hutchins, as if he could scare this young city boy into rescinding his request. Then he rolled his eyes, dug his walky-talky out of his belt, and made a call. In a moment he had his answer.

"Empty," he said gruffly. The guard now clearly considered the matter closed.

Weathers put his elbows on his knees, cast a pissed-off look down at his shoes, and swore again. He took a deep breath and stood up.

"Fuck it," he said to Farrior. "Let's just go take care of this so we can get the fuck out of here."

Farrior nodded. "Who knows," he added quietly, "maybe we can wow Grandpa with the badge, slide in and out, and no one will ever be the wiser. No paperwork." He shot an icy glare at Hutchins. "Right?"

Hutchins nodded.

"Then here," Farrior commanded. "Take this, and this." He handed Hutchins a 2-way radio and his coffee. "We'll go check it out. We'll call you and let you know what's up. If, for some reason he shows up here, call us before you try to collar him."

With that, Farrior and Weather headed over to the checkpoint. Hutchins watched them take out their identification and converse in hushed tones with the elderly guard. Hutchins expected the old codger to continue to be a pain in the ass, but the man seemed to grasp the weight of the situation. In moments, the two field agents had passed through the checkpoint and disappeared into the gate area.

Hutchins was now alone. He looked over toward the McDonald's counter. The two kids were engrossed in conversation. They hadn't noticed a thing. So things were still....

Oh, shit.

Hutchins stared at the ground for a second. Then, with a subtlety that was foolishly useless, he slowly turned to his left. Fifteen feet away, the kid in the Dartmouth shirt was staring, wide-eyed, right back at him. He obviously knew something was going on; if the kid had any doubts, Hutchins knew, they had been erased when this idiot agent had looked directly at him, and quickly turned away.

Farrior's radio, turned up to a healthy volume, suddenly crackled from Hutchins' lap.

"He was here."

"What?" Hutchins attempted to whisper his reply into the radio. Not that it mattered. Between the brother and the airport security guards, this was going to be a conference call whether Hutchins liked it or not.

"Your boy was here," Weathers repeated. "His luggage is sitting in the tunnel. He's gone, though. He must have exited the tunnel through the door by the jetway controls. He's outside somewhere. We're checking it out."

Silence again. Everyone, including the McDonalds kids, was all ears now. Hutchins stared at the ground, red-faced. The whole thing was turning into a complete mess.

Focus. Stay calm. You've done a lot of legwork to get here. Don't blow it now.

"Footprints." It was Weathers again. "In the snow. He went under the terminal. Get to the baggage claim."

Hutchins raced from his seat. In ten seconds, he bolted across the room, shot down the escalator, and slid to a halt, panting, in the baggage area.

His mind spun with equal parts relief and fear; he had escaped that horrible situation upstairs, but what if this kid suddenly sprinted out in front of him?

Maybe he would need the moose's help after all.

Hutchins tried to smile.

That's it. Get a grip. Deep, slow breaths. Just be ready. Chances are, they've already got him.

Hutchins fidgeted back and forth, his eyes transfixed on the six small holes that marked the entrances and exits of the baggage claim's three conveyor belts. His eyes darted from one, to the next, to the next… nothing.

Minutes passed in silence. Now Hutchins shifted his eyes to his radio, as if he could somehow will Weathers to give him an update, the agents' location, anything at all. A look back to the conveyor belts, then at the radio…

Hutchins raised the radio to his ear and pressed the talk button.

"Weathers? Status report." Hutchins tried to sound as cool and professional as possible.

No answer.

"You moron," Hutchins muttered to himself. "You probably just gave away their location." He lowered the radio and returned to staring at the belts.

Then he heard it.

From somewhere under the terminal, beyond the six small, carwash-like gateways, a jarring sound rang out.

It sounded like a gunshot.

Hutchins was now reaching a state of panic.

"Weathers!" He shouted into the radio. "Farrior! Status report! What is your status?"

"Hey," a pale-skinned young man called to Hutchins from the Hertz car rental counter. "Was that a gun-shot?"

Hutchins was now operating entirely on instinct. His hand shot into his pants pocket and produced his badge.

"FBI!" he shouted at the Hertz man. "Stay where you are! Do not move!"

Hutchins spun around and charged like a maniac toward the motionless conveyor belts. He quickly reached the farthest opening to the right and dove into it.

The hanging black rubber strips blocking the hole were heavier than they looked; Hutchins' heroic lunge only succeeded in getting his head and neck through the hole. The sudden stop in momentum blessed Hutchins with a second to address his total lack of a plan.

First, Hutchins realized, he had no sidearm; it had never occurred to him to ask for one.   Second, he didn't begin to know how to navigate the bowels of an airport; from his current prone position, Hutchins was looking at a diner-sized enclosure centered around the three belts, which clearly snaked out to the runway area. But to his left and right were well-lit, taupe-colored hallways that wove around corners and disappeared out of view. God knows where they led.

Hutchins suddenly remembered his radio.   It was still in the terminal, along with most of his body. Rather than wiggle the rest of the way through the hole, Hutchins awkwardly pulled his arm up to his ear and tried his radio again.

"Weathers?"

What was that?

Hutchins' ears perked up. He had heard something, as he had spoken. Not a sound from his radio, but a noise somewhere under the terminal.

"Weathers? Come in."

That noise again.

Hutchins had an epiphany. He held the radio as far away as possible, and pushed the talk button. Off to his right, he heard a crackle. He pushed the button again, and the sound repeated.

The other radio.

Hutchins wiggled with all his might, and finally managed to squirm his lanky frame completely through the hole. He pressed the button. Again, the crackle. It emanated from the hallway to his right.

Hutchins slid off of the conveyor belt and jogged into the passage's white light. He could only see about ten yards of the hallway; after that, it took a 45- degree turn to the left. As he reached the corner, Hutchins stopped. For the first time, he made a full assessment of the situation, and tried to calm down.

Seriously, Jeff... what could possibly be waiting for you around this corner?

Hutchins had shown up at a small airport, in the middle of the frigid, snowy night, to get a young kid. The kid had vanished. Now Hutchins had heard what sounded like a single gunshot. But Hutchins had two burly, well-trained field agents on his side. If, in some ridiculous chain of events, a terrified young man had wrestled a gun from Weathers or Farrior and had gotten off a shot, he would still have had to confront the other, unwounded agent.

See? It was probably just a warning shot. Calm down, take a deep breath, focus, do your damn job.

Hutchins inhaled for a full five seconds, then slowly let the breath out. He wheeled around the corner.

The hallway was long; it appeared to run under the entire terminal, at least 50 yards. Hutchins had jogged about ten of those yards when he realized that Farrior and Weathers were resting at the far end of the tunnel.

"Hey!" he called out, speeding up his run. Remembering he still had the radio, he brought it up to his ear again.

The crackle startled him. Lying on the ground, less than ten feet away, was the other radio. It was angled aimlessly on the hallway's pink-and-white checkered floor. Next to it, smack in the middle of the hallway, was an FBI-issue pistol.

"What the…hey!" Hutchins reached down and picked up the gun and the radio. He called out to Weathers and Farrior.

"Why the heck did you leave…."

Weathers and Farrior didn't answer.

They didn't move.

The two agents were seated on the floor, their backs resting against the right wall of the hallway. Hutchins began to jog toward them.

"Hey! What's going on? Are you guys alright?"

Now he was twenty yards away.

Something is wrong, something is wrong, something is wrong.

Now Hutchins could see the blood.

Two streams of crimson fluid were forming a neat pool between Farrior and Weathers. The rivers of blood snaked onto the men's spread legs, over their crisp black pants, up over their matching blazers, starched white shirts and bold scarlet ties.

The agents' throats had been slashed wide open. Their eyes and faces were contorted, frozen in gruesome displays of pain and shock.

Oh my God. Oh my God. Oh my God.

Hutchins' senses abandoned him. His eyes rolled back in his head as his feet gave way.

And then all was black.

PART 1
DOWN THE RABBITHOLE

CHAPTER 1

UNITES STATES ARMY OPERATION ORDER
(U) OPORD #9905
(U) TASK ORGANIZATION: JSOC, USSOCOM

(S) A) **SWIPE (Silent Warrior Intrusion Protection Exercise): Test course created to assess state-of-the-art automated infrared imaging system for detecting stealthy human intruders in winter environment.**

(S) Terrain: Rural open field in Northern New England adjacent to river. Flanked by 3m security fencing. Includes course obstacles (razor wire, ditches, etc.) barriers.

(U) 1) SITUATION

    (U) A) ENEMY FORCES: Training OPFOR-US Army Corps of Engrs.
    1) SWIPE Test Director: William Sutton.

(S) B) FRIENDLY FORCES: Special Ops Unit, 75th Ranger Brigade
    1) Four-man Ranger team led by SSGT James Sariani

(U) 2) **MISSION: Infiltrate length of course without triggering IR surveillance system.**

(S) 3) EXECUTION: Utilize slow-crawl techniques in combination with CFBI (Composite Flexible Blanket Insulation).

(U) 4) INTENT:
    (U) A) Document efficacy of IR surveillance system.
(S) B) Evaluate CFBI as IR signature countermeasure.
(S) C) Assess Ranger team wintertime CCM and infiltration against simulated high-level threat.

(U) END OPERATION ORDER
--SECRET--

****

    Sarah stared though her night-vision goggles at the S.W.I.P.E. course.

    Rural Vermont could be brutally cold in February, and this frigid Sunday night was no exception.

    Somewhere in the snowy clearing below Sarah's perch, four U.S. Army Rangers were braving the elements beneath insulated blankets. These Rangers, Sarah knew, were about to be deployed to South Korea. Before leaving, though, they had journeyed up from Ft. Benning, Georgia to test this remote infrared security perimeter: The Silent Warrior Intrusion Protection Exercise—S.W.I.P.E. for short.

    Tonight, S.W.I.P.E. was on high alert, and the course was crowded with four of America's most elite soldiers. Sarah would also have to contend with the impervious cold knifing its way through her charcoal windbreaker.

    It was perfect.

Sarah inched along the pine tree's flimsy limb. As she crawled forward, snow quietly cascaded from the branch to the powdery forest floor, twenty feet below. The limb itself wanted to give way beneath her small frame; it was a delicate balancing act most people would never have attempted.

Sarah was not most people.

Reaching a point on the limb with an unobstructed view of the course, Sarah examined the landscape. Hours earlier, she had watched the Rangers, led by Staff Sergeant Jim Sariani, cocoon themselves in insulated blankets and painstakingly slither their way onto the course. Sarah had intentionally masked her eyes as soon as they had begun their assault. Now, she aimed to find them on the course.

Sarah calculated the distance each soldier would have most likely traveled along the probable routes he would have chosen. Like a hawk hunting mice, her sharp eyes searched the area, eventually zeroing in on twenty mounds of snow. These represented potential Rangers. Sarah's quick synapse scanned for movement in any of the mounds. Moments later, she knew the exact location of all four rangers. It was almost too easy.

Satisfied, Sarah nodded to herself. It was a solid way to begin her evening.

Sarah raised her right hand, and purposefully smacked the branch below her. As a great wash of snow fell, Sarah grabbed the branch with two hands, nimbly swinging herself down into a hanging position. As soon as her momentum stopped, Sarah let go of the limb.

Obscured by the powdery flurry she had created, Sarah flew downward. She landed on the ground in a powerful yet delicate maneuver, like a giant spider leaping from its web. Quickly gaining her balance, Sarah headed toward the banks of Vermont's White River.

Reaching the frozen bank, Sarah grabbed the insulated blanket she had hidden in the snow. Without shaking it, Sarah examined the blanket.

There was no doubt, Sarah thought: this new blanket—made of state-of-the-art C.F.B.I. (Composite Flexible Blanket Insulation)—represented the cutting edge of technology. Tightly sheathed in one of these, a Ranger might actually have a chance to become the first person to defeat the S.W.I.P.E. course this year.

The first man, anyway.

Sarah crouched next to the river, and dipped her hand into the icy water. The liquid attacked her fingers like a million tiny daggers of cold.

Sarah removed her hand.

Good.

S.W.I.P.E.'s crown jewel—a hypersensitive infrared camera—was mounted on the side of an olive-green cargo trailer at the far end of the course. Since S.W.I.P.E's creation five year earlier, the camera had detected every member of every special forces unit who had tried to sneak past it—including Sariani's Rangers, who were making their third attempt in three years.

This was Sarah's third trip to S.W.I.P.E. as well. Unlike the Rangers, however, her challenge wasn't in breaching the perimeter.

She'd already done that. Twice.

Sarah was at S.W.I.P.E. to defeat it more quickly. With the new C.F.B.I. blankets, she knew she would almost certainly better her previous times.

Sarah dropped the blanket back down onto the river bank. Then she turned and waded into the river.

The following seconds were the kind that drove Sarah's existence. They were the latest leg in an eternal journey to the limits of her own potential.

First came the pain. It was discussed in hushed circles by unlucky ice fisherman and Navy S.E.A.L.S.--those unfortunate enough to have experienced the icy electrocution of one's flesh. Every inch of the body. Over and over and over again. For most people, simply remaining sane was a victory.

Sarah, however, had been trained long ago to ignore pain, to shut it out. This was merely the latest test of her self-discipline. For her, the mentally taxing part of the experience immediately followed the pain. Her body slowly began to shut itself down.

First, Sarah's limbs began to numb. Then, as her core temperature dropped, her strength weakened. Moments later came the early stages of hypothermia. At this point, Sarah mechanically ambled out of the river and up onto the snow.

Sarah's mission, right now, was to suppress her survival instinct while keeping a meticulous mental record of her body's vital signs.

She grabbed the blanket and staggered over to the edge of the perimeter. Sarah dropped the blanket, unrolled it, and gingerly lowered her tiny, frozen frame on top of it. Then she rolled herself up in the blanket. Fully encased by its insulation, Sarah directed her left hand over to her right arm, and clicked a button on the digital stopwatch she had strapped to her right wrist. Then she inched her way onto the course.

Sarah's extremely low body temperature now drastically reduced the infrared signature she presented to S.W.I.P.E., even without the blanket. This, she knew, would allow her to be less cautious while moving, which meant she could advance more quickly. To Sarah, intense pain or damage to life and limb were willing sacrifices for speed.

Methodically, she slithered up the frozen course. While the Rangers' movements consisted of delicate crawls and wiggles, Sarah's moves were infinitely more graceful. Repeating the same uniquely fluid movements, she glided with such stealth that a person standing next to her in broad daylight would be unaware of her movements. She made no sudden twitches, nothing that deviated from her routine. No visual ripples were detected by the security system. Sarah was effectively invisible.

Sarah was so efficient that, after an hour-and-a-half of wormlike maneuvering, she had pulled to within ten yards of one of the Rangers. Through the blackness, she could detect the faint scratching of his hands and feet from within his blanket. Sarah, for her own part, made no noise at all.

Despite her own silence, Sarah knew she could only get so close to such an elite soldier before he became aware of her presence.

Sarah didn't plan on being discovered by anyone.

The Rangers had been invited to S.W.I.P.E. She had not.

As Sarah swiftly calculated a safe route around the Ranger, her ears perked up. Off to her right, at the fence-line, she heard a noise.

Sarah smoothly slid in the direction of the noise. Next, without exposing her frost-bitten face to the S.W.I.P.E. camera, she peered out from her blanket. Under the light of a full moon, Sarah immediately detected its source. A small, dark shape, set against the uniform stretch of fence, was just inside the course.

Sarah's quick processing of the situation produced informational outputs. First, the shape was a small rabbit. Second, the security system was almost certainly aware of the rabbit's presence. Third, the rabbit was heading directly into the path of Sergeant Sariani, the forward hidden Ranger.

Moments later, Sarah heard the patter of tiny feet as the terrified rabbit scurried back into the woods.

An older man's laughing voice rang out from the green trailer.

"Hey! Straight out! Thirty yards! By the wooden wall and the ditch! Where the bunny was!"

Seconds after that, a flurry of falling snow was accompanied by a plethora of bellowed profanity as Sergeant Sariani rose from the ground.

"I've been moving up from that fucking river for four fucking hours!" Sariani roared. "I've taken your little course to school! I brought my A-Game this year! A better fucking heat shield, better fucking technique, better fucking patience…and I get fucked because a fucking bunny rabbit lands on top of me! You better have some warm food, coffee and booze in there, or I'm going to find that goddamn bunny, rip his head off, cook him and eat him!"

The older voice that Sarah knew belonged to Army Engineer Will Sutton issued an amused reply.

"Not to worry, Sergeant. I've got coffee, apple cider, whiskey, you name it. And I think I can rustle up some food…but you won't find the rabbit."

"Oh, I won't?"

"Nah. He's union. Find one Ranger, go home. It's in his contract."

There was a brief pause before Sariani exploded in laughter. He called back in Sarah's direction.

"I would have beaten it, you fucks! I would have been the first one!"

Directly ahead of her, Sarah heard a small chuckle from the nearest Ranger. The laugh struck her as undisciplined and weak. This man was already moving too slowly, and too awkwardly, for his own good. He would be the next to go. Sarah glided toward the center of the course, to distance herself from the Ranger team's weak link.

As Sarah moved, she listened while Sariani and Sutton continued to talk.

Sarah's ears suddenly perked up again.

Sutton was introducing Sariani to third man.

A younger man. A man Sarah knew all too well.

A man more important to her than any human on the planet.

"Sergeant, I'd like you to meet my son, Tim. Tim, meet Staff Sergeant Jim Sariani."

"Nice to meet you, Sergeant!" Tim Sutton offered.

"Howdy," Sariani returned. "Nice sweatshirt. What, do you go to Dartmouth?"

"No…actually, I run a comic book store."

"A comic book store? No shit? I always liked Wolverine. That guy's a fucking badass…"

Will Sutton interrupted the conversation.

"Excuse me, gents. Is this a conversation that, perhaps, could be conducted from within my cozy, fully-heated trailer? I'm sure Sergeant Sariani wouldn't mind a little warmth."

Sariani apparently agreed.

"Fuckin' A. Let's go in there and get me drunk."

****

Twenty minutes later, Sarah heard the trailer door swing open. Will Sutton called out toward the Ranger Sarah had caught laughing to himself. Soon, the man rose and dejectedly trudged up the course.

That left two Rangers. Sarah knew, from her tree-limb scan, that the two soldiers were shadowing, respectively, the left and right fence-lines. They had probably fashioned this plan ahead of time, to see if one of them could successfully flank the camera.

Sarah doubted it would work. The camera's eye saw everything in its path with clarity. It was the individual, not where he or she was hidden, that determined success. Sarah wasn't about to hug a fence-line. She intended to head right down the middle of the course.

"Right fenceline! Thirty yards out! Just beyond the ditch!"

Will Sutton's voice rang out once again. Three Rangers down. One left.

As the second-to-last Ranger trudged past her toward the trailer, Sarah snaked her way forward. She was now about twenty yards from the camera. She couldn't be anything less than perfect from this point on. For another half-hour, Sarah advanced at a snail's pace. She was within spitting distance of the trailer when she felt the spasm.

Sarah had completely lost all feeling in her right arm in the river, and she had been dragging it throughout the entire length of her crawl. Now, right under the lens of the S.W.I.P.E. camera, her arm suddenly spasmed. In an attempt to jumpstart itself, the deathly-cold limb kicked itself a few inches away from Sarah's body.

Sarah held her breath. She hadn't expected this. She hadn't secured the limb to her body with a rope or cord.

She had made a mistake.

Splayed out on her stomach, shrouded under the snow-covered blanket, Sarah waited expectantly.

If she were discovered, Sarah had less than a minute to control the situation. In her weakened physical state, Sarah doubted she could incapacitate four Army Rangers in hand-to-hand combat. Her strategic move would be to rush Will Sutton as he emerged from the trailer, render him unconscious, seal the trailer door shut, and flee into the woods.

Sarah frowned. She was certain she could escape, but her trip to the course would be a failure. And certain people would find out that she had been here—people Sarah had been running from for a long time...

Above her to the right, not more than twenty feet away, Sarah heard the trailer door swing open. Her body coiled like a rattlesnake as she prepared to spring into action. Even in her frozen condition, Sarah knew she'd be on Will Sutton in less than ten seconds.

"Opposite side, left fence-line!" Sutton called out. "Thirty yards down! Come on in and join us in a toast to the S.W.I.P.E. system! Still undefeated!"

The frown disappeared from Sarah's face. The camera hadn't caught the twitch, which had probably been less pronounced than she had assumed. Still, it had been a mistake to leave the arm free to flail around. She wouldn't make the same error next time. Sarah crawled onward.

Twenty minutes later, her head reached the overhang of the trailer. The camera was five feet away, directly above her on the wall. So close to the end of her assault, Sarah maintained absolute discipline. She continued the same measured, fluid motions until her toes had finally slid under the trailer and out of the view of the camera. Sarah had once again bested S.W.I.P.E.

Sarah's left arm whipped over to the stopwatch wrapped around her limp right wrist. The watch's flashing digits read 2:43:58.

Sarah had defeated the course in less than three hours. It was her best time yet, but she had nearly paid for her carelessness with the rogue arm spasm.

Sarah mechanically rotated toward the course and carefully surveyed the path she had taken.

Next time, she would make no mistakes. Next time, she would be perfect.

****

Sarah crawled out into the parking lot, and stiffly stood up.

Tim Sutton, Will Sutton, and the four Rangers had all left for the night. The S.W.I.P.E. course, and the trailer, were vacant.

Still wrapped in her blanket, Sarah inched her frozen body over to the trailer door and up the stairs.

A rush of much-needed warmth engulfed Sarah as she entered the trailer. She quickly shed the snow-caked blanket and pulled off her clothes. The trailer was almost completely dark. Sarah's curvaceous naked figure was illuminated only by the light provided by a black-and-white monitor that was connected to the S.W.I.P.E. camera.

As she draped her icy garments on a chair near the trailer's heater, Sarah's mind turned to the next day's agenda.

As so many of her days did, tomorrow would revolve around a certain young comic book store owner.

Tim Sutton. The man who held the key to Sarah's destiny.

Years earlier, on a night much like this one, Sarah had come face-to-face with that destiny—only to see it pulled from her grasp and hidden from her sight.

Every minute of her life since that wintry evening, Sarah had been questing for the answers that would reveal her providence once again.

Answers that could only be found through Tim Sutton.

In Sarah's robotic, brilliant mind, no one mattered more.

Right now, however, Tim Sutton was tomorrow's business. Tonight, Sarah would recuperate in the trailer and regain her strength. Then, before dawn, she would vanish, on the hunt once again.

As Sarah's eyes scanned the trailer, they came to rest on a coffee maker two feet to the left of the monitor. Sarah brushed her hand against its glass pot. It was piping hot. She clutched its handle and delicately tipped it toward her mouth.

The scalding liquid seemed to recharge her chilled body the moment it touched her lips. The rush of long-forgotten warmth and feeling returning to Sarah's interior was enough to make a normal person grin from ear to ear.

But Sarah's expression didn't change.

She never smiled.

CHAPTER 2

"The damn delivery truck is bigger than my store."

Blinded by a harsh winter sun that bounced off the snow and into his sleepy eyes, Tim squinted, dumbstruck, as the massive brown vehicle rolled away from Dragon Comics.

Just off of the north end of Main Street in Ruston, New Hampshire, in a tiny strip mall wedged between a small river and the city post office, 24-year-old Tim Sutton sold comic books.

Ruston had once been a thriving mill-town, serving America's textile needs from the banks of the Connecticut River. But those days were long gone. The pavement covering the town's Main Street was a crusty grey mess of cracks and frost heaves. At any given time, nearly half of the street's storefronts were vacant. But Ruston, with its 30,000 rugged, stubborn residents, soldiered on.

Dragon Comics was a tiny store, about twice as wide and half as long as the olive-green S.W.I.P.E. trailer Tim had been sitting in with his father not 12 hours earlier. The front and side walls of the store were lined with six-level shelves of comics. Down the middle of the store was a line of tables on and under which were open boxes of catalogued comics. Dragon was thus divided into two cramped walkways that led back to the sales counter at the rear of the store.

The storefront directly to Dragon's left was vacant. The former occupant, Bragg's Paintball Supply, hadn't made any money (in a gun-happy town, no less).

Dragon Comics, on the other hand, had survived for five years and counting. This was testament to two things.

First, Dragon was well-located. It sat between Quarry Hill—a massive, disheveled mound where much of Ruston's population made its home—and Ruston High School, Ruston Junior High, and Ruston Elementary. To boys of all ages making the trek to and from school each day, Dragon was hard to resist.

Second, Tim Sutton was an absolute genius.

Tim had the innate ability to maintain a mental record of the purchasing habits of every single customer who walked into Dragon; his supply of comics always matched his demand.

And Tim didn't just know comics; he knew all comics, from the first issue of Superman to the latest releases from edgy labels like Vertigo. He would scan his new releases, taking studious notes on what kids were buying. Then he would multiply his profits by bringing in older similarly themed comics he knew his clientele would sponge up. Tim had made a killing buying up surplus, outdated comic supplies.

Tim's intelligence was well established in Ruston: He and his younger brother Eric were said to be the two smartest boys ever to graduate from Ruston High. This status, mixed with Tim's easygoing, affable manner, carried weight with his youthful clientele. It also made him something of a role-model in the eyes of local parents. They didn't mind if their kids lingered at Dragon en route to a night of sitcoms and Playstation.

Dragon wasn't raking in money by any means. But Tim was turning a safe profit, to the point that he had begun to eye an expansion into the still vacant storefront that had formerly sold paint-shooting guns.

Tim loved his job. The comics stimulated his imagination, and the rigors of running a small business kept his brain occupied. Tim's life was one long, comfortable routine. He was content.

Tim's zeal fueled each marathon, never-ending workweek. If Dragon was open, Tim was working. His store had a work force of one.

Technically.

"I was wondering when you were going to fucking get here," Leon muttered as Tim pushed his lanky frame through Dragon's poster-covered door. Leon was leaning lazily against the wall behind the register at the rear of the store. Not coincidentally, this was the farthest point in the store from the massive pile of cardboard boxes that had just arrived at the front door.

"Don't strain yourself, Leon," Tim replied as he stepped awkwardly around the boxes blocking his entrance. "You've got a long day ahead of you, sitting on your ass and bothering my customers. Make yourself useful and help me with these boxes, will ya?"

"Fuck you, carrot-cuffer," Leon replied, his eyes never leaving the comic book he was perusing. "I don't work here."

"Fuck you, I don't work here," was Leon's M.O. And, technically, he was right.

Leon was an 18-year-old, freckle-faced, Death-metal t-shirt, combat-boot wearing, 6-foot, 2-inch monument to teen rebellion. Ever since he'd dropped out of school at 16, Leon had been spending his days at Dragon Comics. While he tended to scare Dragon's younger clients, he understood the workings of Tim's business surprisingly well. Leon could often be pressed to open the store, ring out the odd customer or perform a comic book sorting task for free. Tim had tried to hire him as a part-time employee several times, but Leon wasn't interested.

Tim lived alone in a small second-story apartment. He had always wanted to have a girlfriend, but each of his prior attempts to get one had ended in disaster. Tim's brain malfunctioned around attractive members of the opposite sex, and it didn't help that Dragon Comics, where Tim spent nearly all of his time, wasn't exactly Dating Central. Real women walked through Dragon's front door about as often as real dragons did.

Leon didn't buy any of this. The problem, he assured anyone who'd listen, was Tim's constant masturbating—or, in this particular day's parlance, "carrot-cuffing." Pushing Leon's verbal jabs from his mind, Tim spent the next couple of hours going through his new shipment. When he was finished, he carted the now-empty shipping boxes out to the dumpster in the cramped parking lot in front of his store.

Walking back through the front door, Tim heard a crunch under his right foot. Looking down, he saw a small manila envelope. Tim picked up the package and examined it. The envelope was addressed to "Tim Sutton, Dragon Comics." There was no return address. Tim looked up at Leon.

"Hey," he called to the back of the store. "Did UPS bring this?"

Leon looked over from a conversation he was having with an oily thirty-something in an AC/DC T-shirt.

"Dude, do I fucking know?"

Tim looked down at the envelope, puzzled. He slit open one end with his box cutter, and tilted it downward. Out fell a comic book.

At least, it was about the same size as a comic book, made with the same kind of paper, but...

What the hell is this thing?

Tim brought the item back to his register, dropped it onto his clear glass display counter, and studied it intently. Leon noticed Tim's expression, and he and the AC/DC fan ambled over to inspect it for themselves. Leon peered down at the comic.

"What the fuck...what is that, Japanimation or some shit?"

"Beats me..." Tim replied. The cover of the comic featured two young Asian children. The children were wearing school uniforms and staring skyward with large, cartoonish grins. The rest of the cover was covered with an Asian language Tim didn't recognize. There was no English on the cover.

Flipping open the book, Tim scanned from page to page. It was more of the same: laughing school children, smiling parents, etc. There was no English to be found anywhere in the comic. Tim furrowed his eyebrows.

"This looks..."

"Really fucking boring?" Leon offered. "That weak shit might fly in Tokyo, but someone needs to tell Bob Nintendo that no one here gives a shit about school kids."

"Brilliant analysis," Tim responded sarcastically. "What I'm wondering, though, is why 'Bob Nintendo' didn't translate his comic. I mean, look," he said, pointing to a line of Japanese comics to the right of the counter. "Even the most obscure Manga we get are fully translated, no matter how good or bad the translation."

"Maybe you were shipped this by mistake," the AC/DC fan offered. "Don't you sometimes get comics you aren't supposed to?"

"Sometimes," said Tim, "but not in little envelopes with no return address. This is really strange..."

"Too bad it isn't porn." It was Leon again. "Those Japanese porn comics have some crazy shit. I saw this one where--" With that, Leon and the AC/DC man resumed their expletive-laced conversation, leaving Tim alone with his new arrival. He flipped again through the pages, examining the unintelligible cartoon word bubbles above the relentlessly happy groups of children and adults. Tim couldn't help but feel that something, aside from the lack of English words and the bland subject matter, was strange about the comic. Exactly what, he wasn't sure.

Tim made one last, quick flip through the comic, and dropped it back onto the counter. He was a half-step toward a shelf of new comics when a small alarm went off in his head.

I saw an English word.

Tim paused. Had he actually seen something? He had scanned the comic several times now, and had only seen foreign language characters. Perhaps his peripheral vision had subconsciously picked up an English word or phrase. Tim flipped open the comic again. He moved slowly from page to page, scanning closely.

On the third page, he saw it.

The page featured both a large group of school children and a bewildering array of foreign word bubbles. But there, in the bottom right corner of the page, in one of several bubbles attributed to a chubby, sedentary child, was a single, English word. It was a name.

Eric.

Tim's eyes went wide.

In a flash, his frantic mind envisioned the only other Ruston High graduate whose intellect had ever equaled his own. A young man who'd shared Tim's brilliance, but had been neither affable, nor easygoing, nor content. A man, gone five years, remembered in Ruston as brooding, dangerous, and cruel.

His brother.

****

Tim sat anxiously at a wide wooden desk in the middle of the expansive reference room in Dartmouth College's Baker-Berry library.

After drafting a resistant Leon as Dragon Comics' emergency steward, Tim had driven his ancient, Columbia-blue Ford Taurus twenty minutes north to Hanover, New Hampshire, comic book in hand, in search of answers. He stared down at a massive tome marked "Korean/ English Character Dictionary."

Moments earlier, he had discovered that neither Japanese nor Chinese translation dictionaries matched up with the characters in his comic book. Upon opening the Korean book, however, Tim realized it was the one he needed.

The comic is in Korean? Who reads Korean comics other than Koreans?

Tim looked at the cover, with its smiling children, and began to translate. When he had finished, he leaned back, and let out a very low whistle.

The title of the comic, emblazoned across the top of the cover in bold red characters, read:

"The Sunshine Of Our Great General!"

Smaller characters, underneath the main title, read:

"Keeping Us Warm From The Coldness Of America!"

"Jeez," Tim muttered. "It's a damn North Korean propaganda comic."

He opened the book and flipped through it again. Now it was obvious. A smiling, robust, bespectacled adult was present on every page. Presumably, the North Korean dictator, Kim-Jong Il. Children and adults (some of whom wore army uniforms, Tim now realized) were always looking in "The Great General's" direction, always with smiles, always happy. There was no doubt: This was communist propaganda targeting North Korean children.

As Tim perused, the hairs on the back of his neck suddenly stood up.

It took Tim a second to realize that this nervous manifestation had nothing to do with the comic book.

Someone is watching me.

Tim's head snapped up from the desk. Abruptly pushing back from his seat, he uneasily surveyed the reference room.

The room was quiet, but packed with students. At the table to Tim's right, a bespectacled young lady was absorbed in her studies. To his left, a slightly older redhead, probably a graduate student, stared down at a periodical. Ten feet from his desk, a throng of collegians did internet research at a row of computer terminals. No one seemed to be showing the least bit of interest in Tim.

Calm down, buddy. Focus...

Shaking his head at his own paranoia, Tim restlessly continued translating. The name "Eric", he had discovered, wasn't the comic's only irregularity...

During his first look at the comic back in Ruston, Tim had spied something that only a true aficionado would notice.

Comic books were mass-produced items, and this propaganda comic was no exception. The comic's original art, as well as its original text, had been copied electronically again and again using a matrix of tiny colored dots that were only individually discernable when examined extremely closely.

What Tim had discovered was that a large number of text bubbles, including the initial one with the name "Eric", had no such dots. These bubbles were original additions to this comic book, and this comic book only. Someone had hand-drawn them in. Someone who had wanted Tim to read what he/she had written.

With a chilling mix of fear and anxiety, Tim began to work. He quickly translated the characters in the first bubble.

The translated bubble read:

> *Big Brother, this is Eric. I am in great danger.*
> *I need your help. Save me!*

CHAPTER 3

Tim's grip on the steering wheel was the only thing that kept his hands from shaking. He navigated the Taurus up the winding, steep, snow-covered dirt road that led to his father's single-story log-cabin house. The grade made driving difficult even in the summer months, let alone at night in the middle of the winter.

His mind was still spinning from the sketchy revelations in the fully-translated comic:

> Big Brother, this is Eric. I am in great danger. I need your help. Save me!
>
> I am trapped in North Korea.
>
> Hiding my message in this comic book was the only way to ensure that it would make its way to your eyes, and your eyes alone. You are the only one I trust, the only person who can rescue me.
>
> I'm sorry to put you in this situation, and I'm sorry I don't have the time or space to explain how I ended up in this place. All I can do is tell you how to save me:
>
> 1. In the nearby capital, there is a school that is wealthy, where a man you know is made wealthy to teach children to be wealthy.
>
> Get help from this man, and only from this man. Tell him that what happened at the airport was not my fault. Others were

*involved. He will know what you mean,
and he will want to help you. He will want
to know the truth. Tell no one but this man
about what you are doing.*

*2. Go to Chicago, to the Maxwell Lee
Homes, and ask for a man named T.C.
Tell him 'Shadow' sent you. Ask for the
name of a city, the name of a boat, and the
name of a shipping container.*

*3. Travel to the new city, find the boat,
and stow yourself within the container.
You will travel across the ocean to China,
then across land to North Korea. When
the container reaches its final destination,
leave the container. There will be a single
road leading downhill. Follow this road
for a quarter of a mile until a path appears
on your left, leading into the forest. This
path will take you to me.*

*Help me, Tim! Without you, I have
no hope.*

What had Eric done?   And why, after all this time, was he
contacting Tim for help? How the hell was Tim going to travel across
the globe and pull off some bizarre rescue mission?

Tim reached the top of the driveway and pulled up next to his
father's pickup truck. The cherry-red door of the cabin was framed
by aged, almost black logs. This venerable wood marked the humble
original cabin, the cabin of Tim's childhood. Extending off the left side
of the older structure was a large, grand addition that had only recently
been completed. Those logs were much lighter in color, and the cabin
had an old/new feel to it.

Not bothering to knock, Tim opened the door and moved
directly into the cabin's square, spacious living room, with its mix of civil
war paintings (a passion of his father's) and books of all kinds.

Tim made a quick scan, didn't see his father, and hustled back
out, securely closing the red door behind him. Tim jogged past his

Taurus and down the small, sloping yard behind the cabin to a structure best described as a glorified woodshed.

In this small brown building Will Sutton fiddled with systems related to S.W.I.P.E., or whatever other project the Defense Advanced Research Projects Agency (D.A.R.P.A.) was willing to sponsor. The poorly insulated shed was heated by a tiny woodstove. But this was sufficient, when fully roaring, to keep the shed pleasantly warm. On a cold winter night, Tim thought the shed, with its single glowing overhead lamp and smoking, stove-pipe chimney, actually looked inviting, in a quaint, New England sort of way.

Right now, however, nothing seemed inviting to Tim. Consumed by graver fare, he did his best to mask his emotions as he entered the shed.

"Howdy, Bunny Man. What's cracking in the infrared world?"

Will Sutton, a balding, potbellied 57-year old, was standing over a chipped, paint-spattered workbench, fooling with some sort of mobile tripod. Tim presumed he was searching for a better way to mount his fancy camera equipment at ground level. Will smiled.

"Evening Comic Boy. Good to see you. What brings you to my neck of the woods?"

Tim dodged the question. "Are you still babysitting Rangers, or have they headed off to fight the global war on terror?"

"It's funny you mention that," Will replied. "Because there have been some strange goings on out at the course."

"What do you mean?" Tim raised his eyebrows.

"Well," Will began, "As you know, S.W.I.P.E. batted a thousand Sunday night. The system detected every one the Rangers on the course. None of them, with the exception of Sergeant Sariani, even came close to succeeding."

Tim smiled faintly in recollection of Sariani. The short, darkly-tanned fireplug of a soldier he'd met two nights earlier had a thunderous voice, a fondness for swear words—and a gregarious, warm personality. Tim had enjoyed describing the intricacies of his business to Sariani as the intrigued Ranger swigged down a bottle of Jack Daniel's.

"So," Tim prodded his father, "What's the problem, Pops?"

"Okay," Will continued. "So the next day, the five of us planned to meet to review the routes the Rangers took, problems they had, areas where they were able to maximize the effectiveness of their insulation, etc., etc. When I got there, I began my usual morning ritual of brewing a fresh pot of coffee. But when I went to rinse the pot, I discovered that it was empty."

"So?"

"Well, when I left the night before, there was at least a half-pot of coffee left. I'm sure of it, because I brewed a full pot for Sariani, and remember being somewhat surprised that he only drank one cup. None of the other Rangers drank any; they were all detected in quick succession, and immediately headed out to a bar to drink and warm up shortly afterwards. So who drank my coffee?"

"You're sure there was half a pot...did you lock the front gate to the facility?"

"Absolutely. And I have the only key to that padlock, and it was most certainly on the gate overnight."

Will looked at his son with a wide smile.

"You see where I'm going with this, right? The only other way up to that trailer is from the river, through S.W.I.P.E. Central. And my infrared system was on all night, but it didn't detect a thing."

A few days earlier, Tim would have laughed off the incident as proof of the dangers that highly-intelligent bunnies posed to Will's infrared system, or as proof of his father's faulty memory. Yesterday's events, however, had left him far less inclined to humor.

"So," he said, eyebrows raised, "Maybe they sent a second team in after you left? Maybe they were watching the first group, learned from their mistakes, went in, and beat the course."

"Maybe," Will replied, "But would that help me much? I can't build a better system if I don't know how they beat it."

Will sighed.

"Or maybe the pot was empty when I left that night. Your Old Man ain't as sharp as he once was."

Tim managed a grin.

"Hey, as long as the rabbit community keeps picking up your slack, you'll be fine." Tim's smile faded as he formed the next words in his mind.

"Anyway...I dropped by to tell you I'm going to be leaving town for a little while. I had to feed that kid Leon a made-up story about going to care for my sick aunt in Massachusetts…but I finally managed to hire him to watch over Dragon for a week."

Will stopped working on his tripod and turned to face his son.

"Where are you headed?"

For a few seconds, Tim was silent, looking away from his father, at the tiny, crackling black stove.

"Well…if anyone asks, tell them I went to a comic book convention in Boston."

Will was no longer smiling. He took a small step in Tim's direction, and stared hard at his son.

"Where are you really going?"

"I just…I have to do something," Tim looked back at his father, his eyes betraying his emotions. "Something important. I have to help someone. I don't know how long it's going to take, but…I might be gone a while."

Will stared into his son's eyes for a moment. Then he took a deep breath, turned back to his bench and focused intently on his tripod.

"This is about Eric, isn't it," he said softly.

Tim was silent. Will began fooling with his tripod, but it was obvious to Tim that his father was just looking for a way to gather his thoughts. Finally, Will continued.

"Look, I know that, since the whole deal three years ago, we haven't talked much about your brother. When he didn't show up at the airport that night…"

Will turned back to Tim.

"You two were the smartest kids to every pass through Ruston High. But few people in this town really understood Eric. His teachers were worried about what he would do after high school, but after he left, they buried their concerns." Will paused.

"…And then there are the two of us. You and I…" Will's voice trailed off.

"You and I know that Eric was running that night," Will said with grim finality. "Running from the law. Running from who knows what else. I'm afraid to think about why he was running, or how he got away. In any case…he's contacted you?"

Tim nodded slowly.

"And," Will continued, his tone becoming incredulous, "You're going to help him?"

Tim paused. It was a question that he'd never bothered to consider.

Eric had abandoned Tim and Will five years earlier. In the years before his departure, Eric had always been cold and indifferent to his father. Will clearly didn't think he or Tim needed to aid Eric now.

Will, Tim knew, had never understood the special bond his two sons had shared.

"Yeah, Pops," Tim replied finally. "I have to help Eric."

Will's faced settled into a grim frown.

"Well. . .alright," he finally conceded. "Do what you need to do. I'll cover for you if anyone asks. Just…"

Tim looked back at his father.

"What, Dad?

Will stepped forward and grasped his son's right shoulder.

"I've already lost one son, Tim. I don't want to lose my only other."

CHAPTER 4

In the nearby capital, there is a school
that is wealthy, where a man you know
is made wealthy to teach children to be
wealthy.

Tim stood in a wide, quiet, wood-floored hallway on the second floor of a schoolhouse northwest of Concord, NH. As he readied himself near the doorway to a particular classroom, Tim gathered his thoughts.

A man you know.

Tim had no idea what that meant. He had deciphered the rest of the message pretty quickly though, with the help of the internet. Tim had known where to go, in any case. He even knew the name, he thought, of the man he was trying to track down. But Tim didn't remember having ever heard the name before, and he wasn't one to forget anything. The message was troubling, almost foreboding.

Tim wrapped his thoughts tightly around the words, as two larger realities undermined his confidence. First, this was merely the initial task on the comic book's long list of instructions. Second, it was certainly the easiest.

Tim's quest to save Eric, it seemed, would begin on the sprawling campus of one of the richest prep schools in the country.

St. Paul's, one of America's foremost boarding schools, counted among its alumni publisher William Randolph Hearst; and, more recently, 2004 Presidential candidate John Kerry. The school enrolled fewer than 600 students. Its endowment of over 350 million dollars was higher per pupil than many of America's colleges.

Outside, on the torn passenger seat of Tim's Taurus, sat a weathered, dark green JanSport backpack holding some toiletries, a second pair of jeans, a few t-shirts, socks, and underwear. Though the message hadn't specified, Tim packed as few belongings as possible; he had no way of knowing where, or for how long, he would have to carry them.

The goofy red "Spiderman" wallet that Tim had tucked into the right front pocket of his jeans was unusually fat. The comic hadn't mentioned anything about money either, but Tim had withdrawn two thousand dollars (the bulk of his savings account). It was the largest sum of money he'd ever had on his person at one time. He was constantly conscious of it, and thinking of perilous ways he might have to spend it...

A chill suddenly ran down Tim's spine.

It was the same feeling he'd received in the library at Dartmouth two days earlier.

Someone is watching me.

Tim whirled to the right, then back to his left, anxiously staring down the length of the vacant hallway. He saw no one.

Minutes earlier, the three o'clock bell had rung and a throng of students had exited the building. If the schedule at St. Paul's was similar to that of the Ruston school system, the students here were probably done for the day. Save for a few teachers, the building was empty.

Get a grip, Tim. No one is watching you. There's no one here TO watch you.

Attempting to calm himself, Tim fixed his eyes on the classroom entrance in front of him. A small metal nameplate attached to the wall to the left of the doorway read: "Room 203. Finance. Mr. Hutchins."

Tim stared at the name for a second, then shifted his eyes back to the door. He took a deep, slow breath.

Well, Pal, your journey begins here. Let's get to it.

Tim exhaled, and walked into the classroom.

The room was small, with classic proportions. The wooden desks, although new, had an antique style. The far wall consisted of floor-to-ceiling meticulously cleaned windows, through which sunlight streamed, making the long, fluorescent lights on the ceiling of the room scarcely necessary. At the front of the room was a long, green chalkboard.

A tall, thirty-something, gangly man in black dress pants, a neat white shirt and a dark red tie was erasing a series of financial equations from the board. He looked over as Tim walked in.

"Yes, can I help--"

The man froze. The eraser slipped slowly from his hand and clattered to the floor.

For a full five seconds, the two men stared at each other in mutual shock. Finally, it was Tim who managed the first words.

"I...I know you! You were in the airport that night! You were there to apprehend my brother!"

Jeff Hutchins continued to stare at Tim. The young man whose image had been seared into his memory, along with his pile of comics and Dartmouth sweatshirt, had suddenly come back to haunt him.

"W--what the hell are you doing here?" he managed.

"I was...instructed. . . to find you," Tim said slowly. "By my brother. He's in danger. In North Korea. And he specifically told me to seek your help."

"What?" Hutchins remained in a state of shock. "What the hell? Your brother...told you...to contact me? North Korea? I mean," he managed. "Do you have any idea who I am? Or what I was?"

Hutchins shook his head in disbelief.

"This is absolutely ridiculous! I mean...there's no way he could ever contact you. Not without someone finding out. And he wouldn't have any reason to contact me. So why the hell are you doing this? Do you hold some grudge against me, because I was there that night?"

Tim's brain was spinning.

"Look," Tim said slowly. "I know this whole thing seems crazy. I don't know exactly who you are, or who you were, but I do know you were at Manchester airport with those two agents that night, to apprehend my brother. The two agents went out to the plane, you ran off, and that was the last I saw of any of you."

Tim managed to collect himself, and remembered a specific message the comic had provided, to address this exact situation. "But the...the message I got from my brother said I'm supposed to tell you this: What happened at the airport that night wasn't his fault. Others were involved. He said you'd know what that meant."

Hutchins' eyes widened even more. His jaw dropped, and he simply stood there staring, dumbfounded, at Tim. Finally, Hutchins went to the wooden chair behind his spacious desk and slumped into it.

"When did he contact you?" he asked softly.

"Earlier this week," Tim responded. He moved slowly to a desk directly opposite Hutchins and sat down. "He sent me a message in a manila envelope with no return address. He said he's in North Korea, in danger, and that I'm supposed to get your help, and only your help to save him. He said you would want to help me. He said you would want to know the truth."

At the word "truth" Hutchins' head shot up, and he eyed Tim briefly before looking back down at his desk. Tim leaned back and took another deep breath. Both collected their thoughts and attempted to grab hold of the situation. Finally, Hutchins rose gingerly from his desk, walked to the door of his classroom, closed and locked it. Then he walked to a student's chair next to Tim, pulled it close, sat down, and stared Tim directly in the eyes.

"I want you to understand something, Tim," he said. Tim had never mentioned his name, but the fact that Hutchins knew it didn't surprise him.

"Until the minute you walked in that door," Hutchins continued, "I believed, beyond a shadow of a doubt, that your brother murdered two Federal Agents in that airport three years ago."

Now it was Tim's turn to be wide-eyed.

"Murdered?" Tim pulled himself together and leaned forward. "Hold on, back up!" he commanded. "What the hell are you talking about, and what the hell were you doing at that airport, anyway? Why were you after my brother?"

Hutchins shifted his gaze from Tim to his desk, then nervously to the locked classroom door, back to the desk, and finally back to Tim.

"Look," Hutchins began. "I've been teaching at this school for going on three years now. I teach finance, white collar crime, a few other miscellaneous classes; the kind of classes only taught at a high school like this. But before I joined the St. Paul's faculty, I was in the F.B.I., working in the Financial Crimes Section. I was still pretty young, not much older than you are now, when I was tabbed to help track down some Humanitarian Aid money that went missing in Africa."

Tim stared back at Hutchins. He remained silent but his brain was screaming. *Eric was in Africa!*

"Do you know who Pierre Mangara is?" Hutchins asked.

Tim nodded. "The Warlord in Mali, in Western Africa. I've heard of him."

"Well," Hutchins continued. "At that time, he and his army of thugs controlled almost all of northern Mali. They were squeezing the Malian Government, making all kinds of demands. There were rumors of a possible coup. Anyway, Mangara was a typical warlord, diverting humanitarian food and other resources away from the Malian people and toward his army. Innocent people were starving because of him."

"The U.S. had sent hundreds of thousands of dollars in humanitarian aid to help combat the crisis Mangara had created. Money for food, medical supplies, etc. Money to save the people of northern Mali. Long story short, around $500,000 of the money was stolen. At the time, the CIA was unable to figure out who took it. A while later, as a sort of mopping-up exercise, they made one last attempt to track it down. There'd been a big increase in CIA/FBI inter-agency cooperation following 9/11, so this time, they called up the FBI for help, which is how I got involved."

"After I was put on the case," Hutchins went on, "I simply tried to follow the money, looking for spending influxes in the neighborhood of $500,000. I was trying to find something to pin the theft directly on Mangara's army, or on a terrorist organization."

Hutchins paused.

"But one other thing I did," he continued, "was something that no one else had thought to do. I looked for obscure targets, non-affiliated individuals who might have simply stolen the cash for themselves. Amidst a sea of names, I came across your brother. Did you know he was in Mali?"

Tim nodded slowly. "Yes," he said evenly. "He was working at an orphanage in Tauodenni, in the north."

"Yes, the 'Spirit of Hope Orphanage,'" Hutchins replied. "Initially, I doubted your brother's involvement in the theft. But, I made a call to the orphanage to check him out. They claimed they hadn't seen him in weeks. Out of the blue, he just up and flew back to the 'States. I tracked down his flight, and discovered that it had departed for the U.S. shortly after the money went missing. Then I checked domestic records to track his spending and other personal activities following his return. Know what I found?"

Tim shook his head.

"Nothing," Hutchins leveled. "Your brother is at an orphanage in Africa. Suddenly, he just buys a plane ticket, flies home, and effectively vanishes from the face of the earth. No records of credit expenses, rent payments, car registration, school attendance; or as far as I can tell, any official employment. He just disappears."

"This was all very strange, so I checked into your brother's personal background and found out he was a small-town teenage genius who could have had his pick of colleges. Instead, without any prior public-service record, he decided to fly to Africa to work at an orphanage? It didn't add up."

"Then, out of the blue, within days of my discovering all this, your brother popped back up on the grid for the first time in two years. He was registered on a late-night flight from Newark to Manchester. So I headed to Manchester with a couple of field agents to pick him up for questioning. The rest of the story, I think, you know."

Tim shook his head angrily.

"Except for the part where my brother kills two agents!"

"Look," Hutchins said, "the last time you saw me, I was running off to find them. Well, I found them alright, with both their throats slashed. We cleaned it up that night, kept it out of the papers, but trust me, those two agents were murdered. And your brother was somehow involved."

"Your brother is suspected of committing a double homicide to protect himself and the money he stole. And that conclusion made perfect sense until right now."

Hutchins' voice trailed off and silence filled the classroom once again. Tim studied the laminated surface of his desk, as if a proper response to the bewildering story he had just heard could be found in its wood grain.

"Look," Tim said quietly, "I know my brother. And I can see you've done your homework. I don't think either of us knows exactly what Eric has done. He very well may have taken that money--he certainly could have pulled off such a stunt."

Hutchins nodded. Exhausted from the effort of divulging all of this information, he was grateful for the frank response. Tim continued.

"But…he didn't kill those agents. I know because he told me he wasn't responsible for what happened that night and my brother and I would never lie to each other. I know he's not a murderer. But I do believe he's in danger, and that he needs our help."

Tim paused.

"Mr. Hutchins, I need to get to North Korea, find Eric, and bring him home."

Hutchins took a long, slow, breath, and managed to find some strength. He locked eyes with Tim once again.

"Tim," he said coldly. "Your brother robbed me of my career at the FBI. I was a special agent on a fast track for promotion before Eric came along and wrecked things. Now, I'm nothing more than a glorified high school instructor on a career path to nowhere."

Hutchins continued.

"But that's not even what really matters here. Even if he's not a murderer, your brother stole a lot of money from Uncle Sam. And he's going to pay the consequences for that. If I help you rescue Eric from whatever predicament he's in, you need to assure me he's going to turn himself in to the authorities. End of story."

Tim sighed, and slowly nodded his head.

"You help me, and Eric does whatever time is coming to him. I'm okay with that."

Hutchins studied Tim's pale features for a moment, his mouth spreading slightly into a barely-detectable smile.

"Okay, then. I'll help you. Now…this communiqué from your brother…it told you he's in North Korea? Why the hell North Korea?"

Tim shrugged his shoulders. "I have no idea. The message didn't explain why."

"And so," Hutchins said, raising his eyebrows. "You expect to just go over to North Korea, alone, and get him?"

Tim nodded.

"I'm supposed to stow away on board a cargo ship—I'm not sure which one—headed to China. I'm supposed to travel inside a specific cargo container, which will then travel by land to some spot in North

Korea. When the container arrives at its final destination, I'm to get out and somehow travel to the location where my brother is hiding."

Hutchins frowned.

"Look, Tim, I know you're a smart kid, but…you do know that the China/North Korean border is rigidly patrolled, right? I mean, North Korea is one of the most difficult countries in the world to access. And, if you're a North Korean, escape is next to impossible. They will almost certainly conduct a detailed search of the shipping container's contents at the border."

Tim nodded.

"I know, I know. But my brother seems to think that if I'm in this particular container, I'll make it across. I don't know why."

Hutchins shook his head incredulously.

"Okay, fine. Let's say you manage a safe crossing of the China/North Korea border. What about the rest of your plan? Do you speak any Chinese or Korean?"

Tim shook his head.

"Then," Hutchins continued, "you're in some serious trouble. Although that probably won't matter. Once you're discovered, you'll probably be shot on sight. You're going to need help."

Tim managed a smile.

"Yeah, obviously," he said. "I figured that's why I was sent here."

Hutchins smiled back. It was, Tim realized, the first time since the two men had met that they had shared a positive exchange of any kind. Hutchins grabbed a piece of paper from his desk, scrawled 10 digits onto it with a red grading pen, and handed the paper to Tim.

"Back when I was cooperating with the CIA probe, I associated with people who had some, shall we say, international connections. When you get to the West Coast, call this number. I'll phone ahead on your behalf and work a few things out. We should be able to give you the kind of help you're obviously going to need."

"What," Tim replied suspiciously, "are you owed a favor or something?"

"Tim," Hutchins responded, "we aren't the only ones who want to know what happened to your brother."

Hutchins could see the anxiety creep into Tim's facial expression.

"Look," he said, "I know you want to keep a lid on this. Don't worry, your secret is safe for the time being. I owe no special favors to the Feds when it comes to Eric Sutton, and neither does anyone else who'll be helping you. I'm mostly doing this because I want to know the truth about your brother. I'll do my best to keep this whole thing off the FBI's radar screen, until we get your brother out of whatever trouble he's in."

"But remember our agreement," Hutchins added, the iciness creeping back into his voice. "If I help you rescue Eric, your brother has to eventually answer for his crimes. And if he doesn't..." Hutchins paused. "I'll still want answers. And I'll track your brother down myself if I have to."

Tim looked back down at the desk.

"I understand," he said quietly.

Hutchins nodded with satisfaction, then abruptly furrowed his brow.

"Wait a second...This message from your brother—it told you that you're supposed to get to China on some secret boat?"

Tim nodded.

"Well," Hutchins queried, "how the heck are you supposed to find this boat?"

CHAPTER 5

Go to Chicago, to the Maxwell Lee
Homes, and ask for a man named T.C.
Tell him 'Shadow' sent you.

Tim wished his flight reflex had an off switch.

At the moment, that reflex was trying everything in its power to get Tim to countermand what he was now doing: Driving a tiny station-wagon the color of a baby boy's shirt smack into the center of a Chicago housing project.

When Tim had first seen the name in the comic book, he had dared to think that, perhaps, it was going to be in one of the Windy City's brighter spots; on the city's famed Gold Coast, perhaps, or nestled amongst the skyscrapers in downtown Chicago. But deep down, he knew the truth. Following in Eric's footsteps was going to mean getting his feet dirty. Just how dirty, he was now beginning to realize.

Minutes earlier, Tim had turned off an avenue on Chicago's South Side onto a stretch of weathered pavement that looked like it hadn't seen a resurfacing in ages. Tim drove under a rusty archway inscribed with the phrase "Maxwell Lee Homes." To Tim, the word "Homes" sounded euphemistic, like the wishful thinking of some city official.

The Maxwell Lee Homes complex consisted of four monolithic towers that were as bleak in appearance as they were imposing in height and length. Each building had a similar blend of boarded up windows, death-trap fire escapes, and walls that hadn't been cleaned in decades. The thick gray clouds blocking out the mid-day sun magnified the gloom of the complex.

The "street" Tim was on dissolved into a wide circle of barren ground in the center of the complex. Once, Tim thought, the area might have been a park. Now, the circle's only ornaments were the stripped steel frames of three cars abandoned long ago.

The towers, grounds, and automobile hulks were all sprinkled with dirty snow. The temperature outside was freezing, at least as cold as it had been in Ruston when Tim had departed two days earlier. The cold weather was apparently keeping Maxwell Lee's residents indoors--except, Tim saw, for about thirty shivering people bravely standing in the openness of the snowy circle. As his car inched slowly toward them, Tim ventured a guess. . .they were buying and selling drugs.

"Hey!"

The deep, booming voice was accompanied by the rapping of knuckles against Tim's driver's side window. Color drained from his already-paled complexion as Tim turned fearfully to his left. Standing next to his car was an imposing black man, at least six-and-a-half feet tall, with the physique of an NFL linebacker. An uncontrolled voice in Tim's head assigned the man the name "Kong."

Kong was wearing a thick, oversized Chicago White Sox parka, baggy jeans, and a black knit hat with the red Chicago Bulls logo on the front. His right hand held what looked like a communication radio.

"Hey!" Kong repeated. "Somethin' I can help you with, man?" The phrase wasn't so much a question as a statement: Tim was not welcome here.

With a trembling hand, Tim cranked down his window, and looked up at the towering figure.

"I'm here to see T.C. Um, I was told to come here and see him."

"What?" Kong responded angrily. "Boy, you best get the fuck out of here before--" The man stopped, realizing, apparently, that he didn't yet have a read on exactly who Tim was.

"I don't know anyone with that name," he said finally. "You should just turn your ass right around and drive on out of here."

"No," Tim began, immediately realizing his poor choice of words. "Uh, I mean, I'm supposed to see T.C. I'm supposed to tell him that 'Shadow' sent me. Believe me," he added, managing a weak smile, "I want to be out of here as soon as possible. I'll just see T.C., and then be gone."

Kong didn't return Tim's smile. Instead, he glared menacingly for a few seconds. Then, slowly, he backed away from the car, turned around, and began talking into his hand-held radio. After a few long minutes, he returned to the Taurus.

"Wait here," Kong commanded. He turned around, and walked north, past Tim's car, back toward the project's arched entrance.

Tim rolled up his window, leaned back against his seat, and attempted to slow his rapid breathing. This foray into ProjectLand U.S.A. had exacerbated his already highly stressed emotional state. His past two days had consisted of white-knuckle driving on snow-swept highways, and sleepless nights in cheap motels. Tim was bleary-eyed and unshaven, feeling both queasy and frightened. The search for his brother was off to a roaring start.

None of the people at the center of the complex seemed to pay Tim much mind, which was a small relief. In his rearview mirror, however, Tim could see Kong standing under the metal archway, staring coldly at his car.

After an agonizingly-long fifteen minutes, a black Cadillac Escalade sport utility vehicle with tinted windows and glistening silver wheels pulled up to the entrance of the complex. Tim watched in his rearview mirror as Kong shuffled over to the SUV. The passenger's side window lowered, and the giant began to converse with someone inside.

Suddenly, Tim saw a hand pass an object through the open window to Kong. It was small, and gray, and...Tim froze.

Was it a gun?

Tim began to panic. Was it really a gun? If it was, were they going to shoot him, or just tell him to leave? Should he stay, or should he go tearing south, past the throng of people and out the exit of the complex? Paralyzed by fear, Tim remained motionless as Kong headed back to the Taurus.

He pounded his fist on Tim's window and pointed at the glass.

"Roll it down," he commanded. Trembling, Tim slowly cranked open the window.

Kong reached into the same pocket Tim had seen him place the object from the SUV...and pulled out, to Tim's relief, a digital camera. He leaned his wide frame down into the window.

"Look at me. Stay still." Kong clicked several photos with the camera.

"Turn to the side," the giant man commanded. Tim robotically complied, and the Kong snapped a few more photos.

"Wait here." He trudged back toward the Escalade, and handed the camera through the passenger-side window. After a few minutes, the window rolled back up. Kong hopped up onto the step-up rail on the side of the vehicle, and grabbed one of the door handles. Then the Escalade, with the giant man hanging off of the side, slowly rolled toward Tim. When the Escalade pulled up alongside Tim's ancient Taurus, Kong hopped off, and leaned into Tim's window a second time.

"Get out," he said. Tim cautiously opened his door, and hesitantly stepped into the shadow of the massive figure next to him. Kong walked over to the right rear Escalade door, pulling it open.

"Get in." Tim climbed into the vehicle. Kong, remaining outside, closed the door behind him.

The interior of the Escalade was dark, but lavish. The seats were made of expensive black leather. The backs of the two front seats had digital television screens, while a third screen hung from the ceiling of the vehicle. A booming sound-system reverberated rap music throughout the Escalade. The volume of the music slowly decreased, and it eventually became nearly silent inside the vehicle. Then the man in the passenger seat turned around to face Tim.

He was a slender African-American who looked to be about 40 years old. He wore a black coat over a black suit, a black shirt, and a dark red tie. On his head were wire-rimmed glasses and an ivy cap, both of which matched his tie in color.

"You know," the man said, in a low, measured tone. "You look just like him."

Tim was silent.

"Except for the hair," the man continued, "you could be twins. You ain't twins, though....right?"

Tim realized after a second that he was supposed to provide a response.

"Uh, no," he managed meekly. "I'm older by two years."

"Huh," the man responded. He looked down at the camera in his hand, then back at Tim.

"So," he continued, in an almost amused tone. "Shadow told you to find me. You know, kid, that don't make too much sense. You see, Shadow don't need no one's help to find me. Or to find anyone else, far as I know. So why are you here? I figure," he added, "that this ain't really your scene, or I 'spose you and I would already be acquaintances. I can see you ain't exactly thrilled to be here."

Tim paused for a second before answering. This didn't seem like the kind of man one ought to interrupt.

"Sir," he began, "Shadow is in trouble, and I'm trying to get him out of it. He sent me a message, and told me to come to you for help. I'm supposed to get the location of a specific shipping container on a specific ship. I'm supposed to travel in this container to a place where I can save my brother. That's all I was instructed to tell you. I mean," Tim added hastily, "that's all I know. I suspect you know more about this stuff than I do."

The amused look on the man's face shifted into one of contemplation. He studied Tim for a few seconds, then looked off to the side, momentarily lost in his own thoughts.

"So, Shadow is in trouble..." he said slowly. "That's the thing about ghosts, you know."

Tim kept silent.

"They walk around," the man went on, "all invisible and shit, doin' different things for different people. And some people, well, they're content with that, they thank the ghosts, and life goes on. But eventually, other people gon' wonder how Mr. Ghost gets himself so invisible, and how he does the wonderful things he does, and they gon' try to find out. And then, that ghost has a problem. I 'spose it was only a matter of time."

The man continued to stare off into space.

"You know," he said, almost absentmindedly, "your ass should have got itself shot today."

Frozen with fear, Tim could muster no response.

"And I could have shot you, too," the man murmured, still half-lost in thought. "Ain't that some funny shit? A clean-cut white boy drives up in here, smack in the middle of the day, right out in the open, and I rub his ass out! And no one asks questions, no one raids the premises.

No police even comin' by sayin' 'Y'all seen a little white boy up in here?' Nothin.'"

The man emerged from his trance, and he looked back at Tim.

"You know what every business man wants?" he asked. "People think it's money, and, I mean, shit, don't nobody hate money, right?" The man grinned, and Tim tried to smile in return. He wasn't sure if he succeeded or not.

"But you know what it really is?" the man continued. "Security. A man wants to go to bed at night knowing his shit is wired tight. His head is sleepin' on that pillow, 'cuz he got all answers, and no questions. I mean, someone like you show up at the wrong place at the wrong time in a lot of places, you gon' get shot. But then whoever shoots you, his head might be on that pillow that night…but he ain't sleepin'. Now he got more questions, less answers, you feel me?"

Tim had no clue what the man meant, but he nodded anyway.

"But here," the man said. "Your ass could get shot today, and my head would be sound asleep on that pillow tonight. But that," he added, "is precisely why you didn't get shot: Security."

Lost for words, Tim dumbly nodded again.

Silent, the man continued to stare at Tim. Then he turned back around to the front of the vehicle, and opened the glove box. The man produced a pen and a notepad, and scribbled on it. After a minute, he tore a slip of paper from the pad, and turned back to face Tim.

"Here," he said, handing Tim the paper. "Take this, and go help Little Brother. And when you do, tell him to come back around some time, and visit this humble entrepreneur. Tell him not to forget the Little People."

The man motioned toward the door, and Tim scrambled out as quickly as he could. Kong was still waiting outside. He watched unblinkingly as Tim climbed back into his Taurus, turned around, and drove back out the way he had come.

Tim headed north, and drove until he reached Interstate I-90. Once on the Interstate, Tim cruised northwest toward Wisconsin. He watched as the Chicago skyline faded from his rear-view mirror, and the suburbs morphed into open, expansive farmland. Finally, at the first rest area he spotted, Tim pulled over.

He eased the Taurus into a vacant parking space and put the car in neutral, staring vacantly at its streaked windshield. Then he threw open the driver's side door and vomited.

When Tim managed to pull himself up he stumbled into the men's room, washed his face, and rinsed his mouth. Back at the car, Tim fumbled with his cell phone.

"Dragon Comics," the uninterested voice on the other end answered.

"Leon, this is Tim,"

"Dude, I'm glad you called. This little fat fucker came in today, and he was trying to tell me that you told him the Pokemon cards were buy one, get one free."

"Really?" Tim asked with a relieved smile. "I definitely never told anyone that."

"Good," Leon responded. "Because I told the ballsy little marshmallow exactly what he could do with his free fucking Pokemon..."

"Glad to see you're maintaining law and order, Leon."

Tim's breathing slowed. For a brief moment, his mind wandered from the day's trauma, away from the long journey ahead. He was back in Ruston, running his little store, and life was, once again, simple.

CHAPTER 6

Travel to the new city, find the boat,
and stow yourself within the container.
You will travel across the ocean to China,
then across land to North Korea.

Mesmerized by the Seattle Skyline, Tim steered his Taurus toward the Pacific Ocean.

It wasn't the size of the Emerald City that was having an effect on Tim; Chicago had taller buildings, and more of them. It was the fact that Seattle had tall buildings in the first place, and that the city did not have any snow.

Tim had spent the better part of three days driving through Wisconsin, Minnesota, South Dakota, Wyoming, Montana, Idaho, and Washington. Tim, used to hilly, wooded terrain, had seen enough wide-open snowy spaces to last a lifetime, and as far as he was concerned, the light drizzle of rain accumulating on his windshield was a marvelous thing.

In the shadows of Seahawks Stadium and Safeco Field, Tim finally bid farewell to Interstate 90, and drove west, passing under Route 99. Finally, Elliot Bay was before him, and for the first time, Tim saw the ocean.

Tim understood that the bay wasn't exactly the ocean; it led to Puget Sound, which led to the Juan de Fuca Straight, which led, finally, to the ocean. But Tim was a small-town guy from New England; he had rarely ventured outside of New Hampshire and Vermont, and had seen the Atlantic Ocean only five times. As far as Tim was concerned, the saltwater body in front of him qualified as the Pacific.

The monotony of Tim's I-90 odyssey had, in a way, been a blessing. The numbing journey had afforded him time to recover from the first near-death experience of his life. Now, the fresh, enticing topography kick-started his emotions once again. Excitement, anxiety, fear, and a sense of purpose all flooded Tim's head, and, for the first time since Chicago, his brain was on high alert. It was time to get back to business. Tim turned south, and drove into shipping country.

Seattle and its neighboring city, Tacoma, handled roughly four million containers of cargo each year. The two cities combined to form America's third-busiest port, after Greater Los Angeles and the New York/New Jersey area. Looking to his right, Tim saw a series of concrete lots that extended along the harbor for miles. Neatly stacked in the lots were rows and rows of twenty-foot-long, eight-foot-wide, eight-foot-tall shipping containers. The containers were myriad colors and shades, akin to a set of building blocks for some mountain-sized infant.

Beyond the lots, to the west, was a narrow shipping channel, where the three biggest vessels Tim had ever seen were docked. Each of the ships looked to be nearly a quarter-mile long, and they were stacked so high with cargo containers that Tim couldn't imagine how they could sail without tipping over (Tim had a hard time believing boats that big could move without cargo). Beyond the shipping channel was Tim's destination: Seattle's Harbor Island.

Sitting at the southern end of Elliot Bay, Harbor Island looked like the world's largest outdoor warehouse. The 400-acre island was the point at which most of Seattle's shipping cargo was moved to and from boats and on and off trains and trucks. There wasn't a space on the island that wasn't accounted for. The eastern and southern portions of the island were crammed with stacks of cargo containers. Eight gargantuan cranes stood waiting next to the water, ready to load or off-load containers. Most of the island that wasn't jammed full of cargo was filled with paved roadway or railroad tracks.

Tim crossed onto Harbor Island at its southern tip, the only point on the island that could be accessed from the mainland. He turned north and began to navigate his way through the island's great supply-chain fields, attempting to find a suitable spot to park his car.

The task was much more difficult than Tim had assumed. There were thousands of available spaces, but which ones were reserved for parking? Tim didn't want his Taurus to be accidentally loaded onto a freighter bound for Taiwan.

Finally, at the northernmost end of the island, Tim found what could actually be described as a parking lot, stocked with actual cars. He parked his Taurus, climbed out, stretched his legs, and took in the view.

Across the bay, to the northeast, were the football and baseball stadiums he had passed earlier. North of those were Seattle's downtown skyscrapers, an impressive group dominated by the giant black Bank of America Tower. To the north of the skyscrapers, standing alone, was the unmistakable pointed spire of the famous Space Needle.

Even under grey skies, Tim found the view inspiring. But nothing he saw across the bay interested him as much as the navy-colored, town-sized cargo vessel moored directly to his east. The ship, at least as large as the three vessels Tim had passed earlier, was the only cargo ship docked on the island's east side. Pulling the hood of his red jacket over his head, Tim walked toward the ship through the huge maze of cargo containers.

The part of the island surrounding the ship was bustling with activity. Two giant four-legged cranes were extended over the ship's gaping cargo hold, neatly stacking cargo containers inside of it. Hard-hat wearing harbor employees hustled about, making sure the right containers were being loaded, and that they were loaded in the correct order.

No one seemed to notice him, but Tim realized he looked out of place without a hard hat. If someone asked him what he was doing, he didn't have a good answer prepared. Luckily, he was able to get within 50 yards of the boat without being stopped, which was as close as he needed to go; Tim's goal, for now, was to determine the name painted in white on the front of the ship's right side.

In bold white strokes, Chinese characters were painted towards the bow of the ship. Just below the characters was a word written in smaller, western letters that Tim could just barely make out: "Haihu."

Tim reached into his pocket and pulled out the piece of paper T.C. had given him. The name matched. This was the ship he was going to ride to the other side of the world.

Tim had found the Haihu, but the second part of his mission would be much more difficult. How the hell was he going to find the correct container? Tim hadn't given the task a second thought until he had actually seen Harbor Island. Now, he realized, it might take hours, or longer, for him to find the right container. And he was going to look pretty damn conspicuous doing it.

"Crap," Tim muttered. This was as far as he was going to make it on his own.

Tim pulled a second piece of paper out of his pocket. It was the number Jeff Hutchins had given him. The ten red digits made Tim nervous. He didn't know who would be waiting for him when he dialed, and he was reluctant to bring anyone other than Hutchins into the fold. But Eric had told him to contact Hutchins, so he must have been expecting this. Tim pulled his cell-phone from his pocket and began to dial the number.

"Hey." Tim jumped as he heard a woman's voice behind him. A lump grew in Tim's throat as he lowered his cell-phone.

Damn it, moron, what are you going to tell this lady when she asks you what you're doing here?

Tim turned around, expecting to see a harbor security official. The woman standing before him, however, didn't resemble any of the other harbor employees Tim had seen thus far.

The woman looked to be about 30 years old. She was short, 5'3" at the tallest, with a slightly stocky but athletic build. From the top of the woman's freckled face sprang shoulder-length, bright red hair. The woman was wearing baggy work jeans, dirty white tennis shoes and a black windbreaker. She stared at Tim with unblinking brown eyes.

"You're Tim Sutton," she said evenly.

Tim was completely caught by surprise. How could this young, moderately attractive member of the opposite sex possibly know who he was?

"My name is Sarah," she explained. "I'm Jeff Hutchins' contact. I'm here to help you get your brother."

Tim looked at the small woman in shock, then down at his cell-phone.

"B-but. . .I didn't...I didn't even call you, yet! I mean, how did you know I would be here? How did you even know I was going to be in Seattle?"

The woman's expression remained even.

"Jeff contacted me right after he met with you and explained the situation. I know the west coast/Asian shipping routes, and I knew you'd be leaving out of Seattle. And the Haihu is the only boat leaving port with a Chinese destination. I knew you'd end up here. I couldn't afford to wait for your call. There's work to be done."

"Whoa..." Tim began. "This is...this is all happening a tad fast for me. I mean, how do you know Jeff? And what, exactly, are you guys planning to do to help me?"

The woman stared past Tim at the Haihu.

"How I know Jeff isn't a concern of yours. What you need to be concerned with is buying food, batteries and reading material, A.S.A.P. This boat leaves in approximately eight hours, and if we're going to be on it we need to..."

"The boat is leaving in eight hours? Wait a minute, we?" Tim mouthed in disbelief. "You're coming with me?"

"Yes," the woman replied, still staring calmly past Tim at the boat. "From what Jeff has explained, you're going to need a lot of help, and you won't get it unless I come with you. I speak Chinese and Korean, and, should something go wrong when we reach our destination, I know people who can come to our aid."

"I mean, that's fantastic!" Tim began, wide-eyed. "But why would you want to come with me? Is Eric really that big a deal to you guys?"

The woman returned her gaze to Tim.

"Tim, look at me and focus," she said. "You will get all the answers you need in due time. But right now the information most valuable to you is as follows: This boat leaves for Dalian, China, in eight hours. It's going to take us 10 days to get there, and for you, those days will be spent, in their entirety, inside a shipping container. You need provisions, a sleeping bag, a source of light, and a way to occupy yourself for this period of time."

"Ten days? Just to get there? Oh my God..." Tim realized as he spoke, however, that this timetable made perfect sense. If anything, a week-and-a-half was probably as fast as a cargo ship could travel from the United States to China. He simply hadn't given the matter any thought until now.

"Look...Sarah?" Tim began. "I don't know if Jeff told you, but I run a-"

"A comic book store, I know," Sarah finished. "And I assume you have people filling in for you on a temporary basis. You need to contact these people within the next couple of hours and inform them that you will be occupied for at least two more weeks. Once we are on the boat, you will not be able to make any more phone calls."

"However," Sarah added, "I will be bringing a laptop with a satellite receiver onboard the ship. Once a day, I will contact Jeff via email to keep him apprised of our situation. You will have a limited opportunity at this time to exchange e-mail with your temporary employees. This should be sufficient to stay abreast of the transactions at your store. Do you understand all of this?" Sarah stared at Tim expectantly.

"Uh, I think so," Tim managed, still dealing with the latest crazy turn his journey to find Eric had taken. "But how am I going to explain to Leon--to my employee, that I can only contact him through e-mail?"

"It's simple," Sarah replied distractedly. She was now staring at the Haihu again. "Just tell him your aunt's condition has worsened, and you have moved into the hospital to care for her. There are strict rules regarding the use of phones, so you plan to send e-mail, instead."

"My aunt? Wait a minute, how do you know that--"

"Tim," Sarah said forcefully, her rugged gaze shifting back to him. "Time is of the essence here. Drive out the way you came in. Get on interstate I-5, and drive ten miles north. Exit at Northgate Way. There's a large shopping mall there. You will need to purchase lots of water, food, batteries, a pillow, and blankets. And get things that will keep you occupied--books, comic books, etc. But you must be back here within three hours, do you understand? Go, now."

"But," Tim managed, "what about the container? I have the labeling information, but how are we going to find it?"

"Don't worry," Sarah said, again eyeing the boat. "I've already found it. Now, go."

****

Two and a half hours later, just before 5 p.m., Tim re-crossed onto Harbor Island. Piled on the backseat of his vehicle were two black sleeping bags, two rolled-up, manila-colored foam mattresses, two large goose-feather pillows with dark green pillowcases, ten gallons of water, a giant plastic bag teeming with granola and energy bars, a flashlight, and ten spare sets of batteries. Tim had also purchased the entire "Lord of the Rings" trilogy, as well as several books by fantasy author David Eddings. He hadn't bought any comic books; Tim read comics so quickly that he would have had to purchase hundreds. The novels would suffice.

Stocking up on provisions had been the easy part of Tim's trip. The hard part had been his phone call to Leon. Tim hadn't had any difficulty maintaining his "sick aunt" ruse during the call, but that hadn't helped matters much. Amidst the hurricane of profanity he had weathered, it had been hard for Tim to discern what infuriated Leon more; learning that his work detail had been extended by several weeks (albeit with a hefty raise), or learning that—thanks to the daily e-mail Tim would be sending him—he would actually be forced to type.

To Tim's surprise, Sarah was waiting for him on the side of the road at the southern end of Harbor Island. Tim pulled over his Taurus. Without looking at Tim, Sarah strolled over to the left rear door of the car and peered inside. After a few seconds she opened up the passenger's side door. Tim moved his green backpack out of the way, and Sarah hopped in.

"I don't need a pillow, sleeping bag, or mattress," Sarah began, "and the amount of food you bought may be too much for you—if you stuff yourself, you're going to have to make a lot of bowel movements, and you'll need to minimize those."

Tim blanched. Until now, the problem of relieving himself hadn't crossed his mind. He pushed the thought out of his head for a second.

"Sarah, I thought I was buying for two people! What are you going to…"

"I'll be fine," Sarah interrupted. "I don't need the sleeping gear. And I can get food on the ship."

"The ship?" Tim was confused. "But aren't we going to be locked into the box?"

Sarah ignored Tim's question.

"Drive north," she commanded. "We're going to the container now."

Tim stifled his urge to ask more questions and complied. Under what was now an overcast night sky, Tim drove across the island. Harbor Island, ironically, seemed more brightly lit at night than during the day. Thousands and thousands of lights, on poles, buildings and even the massive loading cranes, painted the island in white and orange hues. The place looked festive, as though island officials had decided to leave Christmas lights up an extra few months.

Sarah silently directed Tim with her finger, pointing this way and that until they finally reached a small cluster of seven black containers near the northern coast of the island. Tim frowned. These containers were nowhere near the Haihu, and no one seemed to be paying any attention to them. In fact, as far as Tim could tell, there wasn't anyone within 100 yards of the containers.

"Park in front of this one," Sarah instructed, pointing to a lone container that sat beside the other six, which were stacked in sets of three. "Leave your lights on." Tim drove in front of the container, and watched though the misty glow of his headlights as Sarah briskly hopped out and strode up to it.

The box's two entrance doors were fastened shut with a cylindrical locking mechanism that ran vertically down the middle of the container's entrance. At the bottom of the cylinder, just above the ground, a thick steel padlock was fastened to lock the door. Before Tim could ponder how they were going to get past this new glitch, Sarah produced a small key, unlocked the padlock, and swung the right-side door of the container wide open. She walked over to Tim's door and opened it.

"Do you need to urinate?"

"What?"

"You're going in the container now, and it's going to be a while before you can pee, so..."

"I'm going in now? Wait a minute, what about..."

"Tim," Sarah said in a measured yet forceful tone. "Go to the bathroom. Take your things. Load them on the container, and get in. I'll join you on the ship. This will all make sense to you in a few hours."

Tim took a deep breath. From the start, he reasoned, this whole trip had required a suspension of disbelief. Why should he start being skeptical now?

"Okay," He said. "Should I just pee...anywhere?"

"I don't care," Sarah returned. She was already grabbing Tim's provisions out of the rear of his car.

"Uh, okay," Tim offered meekly. "So, I'll just walk around the side here..."

By the time Tim had relieved himself, Sarah had carried all of his items, including his backpack, into the box. Tim ambled over to the entrance of the container, and peered inside. The container was completely empty, save for Tim's items, and was surprisingly clean. It almost looked cozy. Tim managed a smile. If his old man could stand to sit in a metal box all day, so could he.

"Tim," Sarah called from behind him. "I'm going to lock you in. Then I'll park your car in a safe spot. You will be loaded onto the ship in about an hour. After we leave port, sometime tonight, I will join you in the container. Questions?"

"Um," Tim started, "should I use my flashlight yet, or save the batteries?"

"You won't need your flashlight, not yet. You'll see."

"Well," Tim asked, "if this container is being loaded in an hour, why isn't anyone near here?"

"This container will be the last one loaded onto the Haihu," Sarah responded. She began to not-so-lightly shove Tim into the box. "And this container is special. Almost all of the workers on this island aren't even aware it's going on the boat. Those who do know are doing their best to pretend like it's not even here."

Sarah pushed Tim into the container. Claustrophobia suddenly gripped Tim, and he began searching his brain for more questions to ask, in vain hope of delaying the inevitable.

"Wait, what about, how will...what if I have to go to the bathroom? What if I have to poop?"

"See you in a few hours, Tim."

Sarah swung the door shut with a dull thud, and clanked the padlock back into place. And then Tim was alone.

CHAPTER 7

Tim's eyes began to adjust. Looking up, he saw that at least 100 quarter sized holes had been cut into the roof of the container, allowing the bright lights of Harbor Island to illuminate the box.

Seattle had thus far been a blur, and Tim's mind raced, expecting another crazy, frantic-paced development. After a moment in his silent, twenty-foot-long residence, however, Tim calmed down. Despite all that had transpired since he reached the Emerald City, absolutely nothing was happening right now.

Tim surveyed his new home. Barren except for Tim's small pile of provisions in its center, the container felt like an unfurnished miniature apartment. Tim arbitrarily chose the rear left corner as his personal living area, and slid his belongings into it. He unrolled his foam mattress, took his sleeping bag out of its plastic container, and plopped his pillow at the head of his makeshift bed. Tim realized he hadn't eaten since breakfast, so he grabbed a granola bar from his food bag. He ate it in seconds and quickly grabbed another. Tim swallowed the second bar, reached for a third, then caught himself. He had a ton of food, but who knew how hungry he'd get during a week and a half of solitary confinement? Better to eat sparingly now and see how his rations held up over the long haul.

Tim sat down on his sleeping bag. After making his "bed", there were no additional chores. It was a dose of the sparse reality he would face on his voyage across the Pacific. Tim pulled out his new copy of "The Fellowship of the Ring" and attempted to read. After a few minutes, he put the book down and stood up.

"Tim," he said aloud to himself. "You have just been locked into a metal crate that is less than four times long as you are tall."

Tim's solitary tones bounced off of the lonely walls of the container, magnifying his feeling of isolation.

"Furthermore," Tim continued, his voice rising, "You are about to be loaded onto a ship bound for China, crewed by people who don't know you're on board. Your only company is a scary CIA chick who says she's going to join you later. You can't do anything but read books, you can't see or talk to anyone, you don't know how you're supposed to go to the bathroom, and a frigging week ago, you were minding your own business at Dragon Comics in Ruston fucking New Hampshire!"

Tim sighed, and plopped back down on his sleeping bag. In the solitude of the square box, he cracked a sarcastic smile.

"Thanks, Eric! Thanks, Little Brother! This is a real hoot!"

Tim picked his book up and, for about twenty minutes, actually managed to lose himself in its pages. Soon, however, he was startled by voices.

At least three men had arrived and were standing next to the crate, talking to one another. Tim could clearly hear the men through the wall of the container, but he couldn't understand what they were saying. The men were speaking in Chinese, or possibly, Korean.

Fear swept his consciousness. What if the men opened up the box? Would he be arrested? Worse, what if these men were the same kind of "businessmen" Tim had encountered in Chicago? Tim grew pale.

For a few minutes, Tim listened anxiously, as if he could will himself to understand the men. Then the voices stopped, and Tim braced himself for what he feared could be an untimely death in a metal box. Again, there was silence.

In a few minutes, the rumble of a truck engine could be heard approaching. The noise got closer and louder until it overwhelmed the crate. Above the din of the engine, Tim could barely make out several voices yelling to each other.

Suddenly, the whole container began to elevate. Tim was jolted from the comfort of his sleeping bag and into the center of the crate. Aware of his belongings clamoring across the container floor, Tim scrambled to gather everything and return to his makeshift bed.

With a thud, the container set down on what Tim assumed was the bed of a large truck. Then the vehicle's engine revved, and Tim figured he was now headed for the Haihu. After about ten minutes, the truck's momentum was suddenly arrested.

Tim remembered the holes in the roof of the container. Above him appeared a complex collage of lights and orange metal. A giant chunk of steel at least as long as the container descended toward Tim. The metal appendage finally impacted on the surface of the crate, covering up the ceiling holes, and shrouding Tim in darkness. The crate rose quickly but smoothly, as it was loaded onto the Haihu.

With a dull clang, the container was set down. Light returned as the crane released its cargo and withdrew into the space above. Tim breathed a sigh of relief. If this container was last to be loaded, then Tim was sitting high atop a huge stack of multicolored boxes. No one would be opening up his crate now.

But how was Sarah going to join him? Could she climb up here? And if she didn't, Tim realized in shock, how would he ever get out? The crate didn't open from the inside! If Sarah didn't show up, he surmised, the situation would unfold as follows: In a week and a half, some nefarious gang would open the container and discover the stench of excrement and urine, as well as Tim's sickly body or corpse.

Wonderful.

Over the next several hours, Tim pondered a number of "untimely death in the back of a metal crate" scenarios. Once again, nothing was happening, yet attempts to read his book were futile. Tim was consumed by a sense of resignation regarding events over which he had no control.

Suddenly, Tim heard the clanging of machinery. He looked up and saw the skeleton of the huge crane withdrawing toward the shore. When the baritone of the Haihu's horn thundered, Tim covered his ears. He looked skyward again. He could detect movement in the lights on Harbor Island. Though Tim couldn't actually feel the boat moving, it was now setting sail. His journey across the Pacific had begun.

Gradually, the lights from Harbor Island waned, and the container went dark. Tim pawed the area around him until he found his flashlight. He was grimly happy to see that its beam was more than sufficient to light up the entire container

The Haihu's launch had calmed Tim slightly, and he was reaching for his book when he detected a bang on the roof of his container. Tim pointed his flashlight toward the ceiling. The flashlight beam exposed a three-foot wide circle that he hadn't noticed before.

"Turn the light off."

Relief washed over Tim as he heard Sarah's voice outside his container. He was so relieved he forgot the command.

"Tim, turn the light off now."

Tim came to his senses and switched off his flashlight. Moments later, he heard the sound of metal scraping against metal where the cylindrical hole had been cut into the container. With a soft patter Sarah dropped down inside.

"Okay," she commanded. "Switch the flashlight back on. But do not point it at the roof of the container."

Tim clicked on the light. Sarah was dressed as she had been earlier, but she was now carrying a small white cloth sack. Sarah dumped the bag in the center of the container. Out spilled a hot water bottle, a screwdriver, several lengths of bungee cord, a roll of toilet paper, and a long sheet of clear plastic.

"First," she began, pointing to metal rings on the side of the crate, "secure all of your items against the side of the container with these cords. The boat is going to yaw tremendously on the open sea, and anything not secured will slide all over the place. This includes you; you will need to secure yourself to the wall when you sleep, and when the weather gets rough."

"You will also," Sarah continued, "most likely get sick. There is no avoiding this. Look here."

Sarah moved to a two-foot square of sheet metal that had been fastened with four screws to the floor of the container. She unscrewed the sheet and removed it, exposing a circular hole a foot wide in diameter.

"This hole leads into the container below. If you need to throw up, do it here. This is also the hole you will use to go to the bathroom."

Tim stared uncomfortably at the hole, then at Sarah. Sarah continued.

"If going to the bathroom in my presence is a problem, you can go when I am outside the container. When you have finished, immediately slide the sheet back onto the hole and re-screw it."

Tim nodded, uncomfortable with the whole "going-to-the-bathroom in a metal hole" scenario. He grimaced. The person he truly didn't envy was the guy opening the excrement-filled container below his in a week and a half.

"Another major problem will be the weather," Sarah went on. "In the event of precipitation, use the plastic sheet to cover yourself, your belongings, and your sleeping bag. I will alert you if precipitation is imminent."

"As far as the cold," she continued. "You're going to have to get used to a lower temperature. However," she added, "I will refill this hot water bottle as often as possible, at least once each night. Place the bottle inside your sleeping bag, and zip yourself up tight. It should provide you with a degree of warmth."

Tim nodded. His anticipation of pending discomfort was offset by his relief at Sarah's thorough preparation. Whoever this woman was, she certainly knew her stuff. Tim gestured to the various container modifications.

"So," he asked, looking at Sarah, "you did all of this?"

"Yes," Sarah replied. "After reaching the Haihu initially, I determined the location of the crate and made the necessary modifications."

"But," Tim interjected. "How did you find the container?"

"It required nothing more than a simple monitoring of the ship's crew," Sarah returned. "There are about 25 men aboard this vessel. Some of these men have no job other than to guard and manage this container and others like it. While these men never approached this container directly when the Haihu was docked, it was easy to see from their movements that they were protecting it."

"Is it drugs?" Tim asked. "I mean, is that what this container is used for?"

"Yes," Sarah said. "In effect, we are stowing away on a heroin caravan."

Tim nodded. He had assumed as much.

"So, was this container loaded with heroin when it reached the U.S.? Is that why it's going to North Korea?"

Sarah ignored Tim's other questions. She reached behind her back, and pulled an ultra-thin laptop from under her jacket. Tim hadn't been aware that Sarah had the laptop on her person, somehow strapped to her back.

"Tim, I'm about to leave the container," Sarah said, handing the laptop to Tim. "I will send Jeff Hutchins an e-mail. If you need to contact your place of business, use the notepad application on this computer to type correspondence. Include the necessary address. I will then cut and paste it into an e-mail, and use the address you have provided to send it."

"Uh," Tim responded, surprised, "I guess I really don't need to send an e-mail, yet. Tomorrow, I guess, will be fine."

"Good," Sarah said curtly. She grabbed the laptop and the water bottle, moving back toward her ceiling hole. "I'm leaving. Remember, do not shine your flashlight toward the roof, especially when I leave the container. The light escaping is visible to those on the boat. I will be back in several hours. If you need to go to the bathroom, do it now. If you are able to sleep, do so."

Tim shined his flashlight at the floor, and watched in the ambient light as Sarah moved to the front of the container. He saw that the circular sheet was aligned slightly to the left of the hole Sarah had cut.

Sarah bent her knees, and, with acrobatic strength that caught Tim completely off-guard, she sprang upward. Sarah shot her fingers through the curved slit in the roof. Dangling by one arm, Sarah used her free hand to loosen a screw in the ceiling of the container. Then she slid the circle out of the way, and pulled herself up out of the crate. She slid the circle back into place, retightened the screw, and vanished into the darkness. Tim was alone again.

****

The following ten days played out in a grim routine.

Tim rarely "slept" during the night. He attempted to, but was rarely successful in getting more than a few hours at a time. Since he wasn't required to actually do anything during the day, however, he spent most of his time in a catatonic state, drifting in and out of half-sleep. When he could, he read.

Shortly after the Haihu left Seattle, Tim descended into seasickness, a pain he had never known. The ocean rocked the boat so much that the container shifted, constantly, from one 45-angle extreme to the other. Tim's stomach immediately twisted itself into knots. At first, keeping his food down was all but impossible. Tim had spent much of his time huddled next to his small "toilet", even when he wasn't going to the bathroom.

Fortunately, about halfway through the journey, Tim's body seemed to have raised a white flag to the elements; he still felt sick, but at least he wasn't throwing up. This was fortunate, since the mounting stench below his "toilet" made hanging his head over it unbearable.

The cold was difficult, but it didn't rival the seasickness. Sarah usually refilled his hot water bottle several times a day, so he was never in danger of freezing to death. It was far from comfortable, though, and the weather was one more battle in the relentless attack of insomnia.

Sometimes, Sarah was present in the container, other times, not. She was almost never around at night. When she was in the crate, she would strap herself against the side and rest silently, her eyes closed. She rarely spoke to Tim, except to notify him that she was leaving the crate or sending an e-mail. She would often command him to get up and attempt to walk around, to prevent his muscles from cramping.

Tim couldn't fathom how Sarah was able to move about the ship with ease, undetected. Any attempt he made to find out hit a brick wall. Tim found, in fact, that attempts to initiate any conversation with Sarah failed. Asking her about her connection to Jeff Hutchins brought no response. Asking her personal, "Who are you, where are you from?" questions brought no response. Even offering a bite of one of his PowerBars brought no response. Tim felt alone whether Sarah was in the crate or not.

Life in the container was exhausting. Sick and isolated, Tim now looked back fondly on his cross-country, somewhat numbing car trip. The car was bearable. As the days passed and his destination loomed closer, Tim's spirits rose slightly. There would surely be new challenges and brushes with disaster when they reached Dalian.

But at least he would be off this damn boat.

****

The bellowing horn of the Haihu jolted Tim from rare slumber. He looked upward. A dark blue dawn was scarcely visible through the roof of the container. Sarah was seated against the wall, eyeing him intently.

"Tim, we are about to dock in Dalian. Pay attention."

Tim rocketed into a sitting position, bleary-eyed but fully alert.

"Okay," he said. "I'm ready."

"The Haihu will dock at Dalian in thirty minutes," Sarah began. "This container will be the first removed. It will immediately be loaded onto a truck. Then it will head northeast."

"Is it going to be loaded with heroin, now?" Tim queried.

"No," Sarah replied dismissively. "That's not how it works. Anyway, if what your brother says is correct, this container will head northeast toward the North Korean border, where it will be offloaded. At that point, you will wait for my arrival. When I arrive, I will open the container and we will-"

"Wait, what?" Tim interrupted. "You're leaving again?"

"Yes," Sarah replied. "I have things I need to take care of in Dalian. I will follow the crate to the offloading site, where I will open it and let you out. We will then continue on, using the directions Jeff tells me you have been given. Do you understand?"

"Uh, I think so," Tim managed. "But how long will it be before I see you again?"

"Not more than a day after you arrive in North Korea," Sarah replied. "Probably sooner."

"How do you know that?" Tim pressed. "How do you know any of this?"

"You know what you need to know," Sarah returned authoritatively. She stood up, and, in the acrobatic fashion that continued to stun Tim, Sarah shot up through the container's ceiling hole.

A half-hour and several blares of the Haihu's horn later, the boat finally came to a stop. Overhead, the skeleton of a dark green loading crane materialized in the blue sky. Its giant clamp descended, plunging Tim into blackness once again. Tim felt himself being lifted, then lowered. He heard the rumble of another truck engine. With a loud clank, the crane set the container down. No sooner had the crane retracted, returning daylight to the container, when the truck's engine roared. As the crane above him disappeared from view, Tim realized he had been placed directly onto the back of a departing truck.

Tim was now in China. And he was on the move again.

CHAPTER 8

For hours, the truck rumbled on.

Tim peered through the holes in the roof of the container, his ears numbed by the never-ending drone of the vehicle's engine. The power lines and bridges eventually disappeared.

Dalian, one of China's busiest ports, was a huge city. But Tim was well beyond Dalian now, and he didn't expect cities, or even towns, where he was headed. On the maps he had studied at Baker-Berry Library eons ago, the Chinese/North Korean border had appeared as a rugged abyss of mountains and forest. The whole area seemed to scream, "Keep out!" If you were doing something you didn't want anyone to know about, Tim figured, it was an impressive place to hide.

Tim was surprised that the truck never stopped. From what Tim had gathered, long-distance automobile travel in China was fraught with difficulty. Depending on the destination, one had to pass through checkpoints, submit to inspections, present proper authorization…and that was just for cars. Tim had no idea how a truck toting a twenty- foot long crate could negotiate all of these regulations. Perhaps, he guessed, the wheels on this particular operation had been greased.

Tim watched as the sky above him slowly darkened. After careful consideration, Tim decided not to turn on his flashlight. In such close proximity to other people, it was best not to risk drawing attention to the crate. In any case, at this point, he wouldn't get any reading done. Those days were over.

It was extremely cold in the crate, and Tim no longer had the luxury of a hot water bottle. He enveloped himself in his sleeping bag as the night wore on. But the bitter cold fought its way through, and Tim was soon shivering uncontrollably.

At some point, the truck shifted permanently to low gear, and the rear of the container tilted upward. Tim could feel the truck climbing now, into what he assumed were the mountains that stretched along the Chinese/Korean border. He was now officially in the middle of nowhere.

Finally, late into the night, the vehicle came to a stop beneath a single yellow overhead lamp. Under the glow of the first light source Tim had seen in hours, he realized that it was snowing. Large flakes lazily descended through the holes in the container, magnifying Tim's chill.

As the truck's engine idled, Tim heard the swinging of a metal gate. Then the vehicle was moving again, and the crate went dark. Within minutes, however, light returned in the form of a brightly-lit ceiling, at least twenty feet overhead, and the truck's engine stopped. Tim could clearly hear two men talking to each other, but the voices soon disappeared into the distance. Again, silence. Abruptly, the lights overhead were shut off, and Tim was shrouded in darkness.

The truck's arrival at its destination was so unexpected that Tim had no time to worry about being discovered. Regardless, Tim had more faith, now, than before. Sarah had protected him across the ocean; surely she wouldn't let him get captured now.

Tim lay back on his sleeping bag, his head comfortably on the pillow. Five seconds later, he was dreaming. In the absence of a 90-degree yaw, seasickness, and a truck's roaring engine, Tim fell into the best sleep he'd had since America.

****

Tim awoke with a start.

What was that noise?

Tim couldn't think straight. He felt as if he had just emerged from a coma, and nothing was making sense.

Tim couldn't see anything. It was five minutes before he remembered there ought to be a flashlight nearby. Tim felt around in the darkness clumsily until he found it, and flipped it on.

Tim's brain slowly resumed function. Yes, he was still in a crate. Yes, it was still dark. Yes, he was still alone. But how long had Tim been asleep? Hours? It felt like longer, and every joint in Tim's body ached. And if it was still dark, why had he awakened?

There was a noise.

Tim paused. Had he actually heard something, or was it a dream? Tim couldn't say for sure; the minutes since his waking seemed infinite. But he could have sworn he heard...

Was it gunshots?

Maybe, maybe not. The bottom line was, awake, Tim hadn't heard anything, since the two voices had faded long ago. If memory served, there was a ceiling somewhere in the darkness above the crate. The ceiling was part of a building, and the building was probably part of a facility. There were sure to be dangerous men lurking. And yet, cocooned in his 20-foot home, Tim felt alone. Until he heard the footsteps.

They began as a barely audible sound, a tiny crunch. Then the noise grew louder, until it became the distinct sound of feet stomping through snow. Soon, it was clear that a single set of footsteps were approaching the container.

Tim was fully awake now.

The footsteps were right next to the container--below it, actually. Tim had forgotten about the truck. Suddenly, toward the head of the container, there was the loud thud of weight landing on wood. The lock on the crate began to rattle.

For a moment, Tim was completely disoriented. He had forgotten the container even had a door, or a lock. Tim was acutely aware that, for better or worse, his stay in the container was coming to an end. Fear swarmed in his head, paralyzing him once again. Tim remained frozen in his sleeping bag, as the container's left door swung open.

When Sarah's tiny figure materialized at the entrance, Tim couldn't offer up a reaction. His mind had reached its fear threshold, and Tim felt little more than alive.

Sarah, in any case, didn't care.

"Get up," she said curtly. "We're leaving."

Tim slowly rose, staring vacantly at Sarah. He took a few awkward steps toward the entrance. Looking back, Tim felt surprisingly attached to the crate's furnishings, and to the crate itself. It had been, for better or worse, his home.

Sarah had no patience for Tim's zombie-like affection.

"Tim, we are moving now. Take your backpack. Leave the rest. Move."

Sarah yelled the last word, and succeeded, finally, in pulling Tim together. For the first time since he had awoke, Tim thought about Eric, North Korea, and the Big Picture. He blinked, shook his head, grabbed his backpack, and headed out the door.

Vertigo set in as Tim, cooped up for nearly two weeks, was confronted with a vast, open area. Standing on the elevated wooden platform of a flatbed hauling truck, Tim stared out the bay of a wide loading hangar. After swaying dizzily for a few seconds, Tim realized he was still holding his flashlight, but that Sarah no longer seemed to care. He pointed it at the ceiling.

Tim guided the light's beam toward the entrance of the hangar until he reached a gaping opening that was wide enough to allow loading trucks to drive in three abreast. Looking around, Tim noted six such vehicles in the hangar, each with a crate identical to his stacked on its bed.

Tim directed his flashlight at the blackness beyond the hangar opening. An acre of open space was covered by a half-foot of snow that extended into in all directions. Sarah's footprints looked out of place in the uniform, opaque landscape.

As Tim attempted to readjust to open space, Sarah exited the container the way she had come in. Without looking back, she began shouting information. Her commanding tone yanked Tim off the truck like a leash, and he was soon trudging in her wake.

"Tim, we are at a small base in the mountains along the North Korean/Chinese border."

Sarah pointed to Tim's right. Tim could just make out a single white light about thirty yards away, illuminating a steel door.

"Off to your right are barracks. Ahead of you, fifty yards out, is the gated entrance to this facility. There is only one entrance to this base, via a paved one-lane road that snakes up from the west. With the exception of that road, we are surrounded on all sides by mountains and thick forest. The facility itself is surrounded by a perimeter of eight-foot high security fence. Does this information give you sufficient bearings?"

Bearings. Of course.

The shipping container had reached its "final destination." Tim was now supposed to use the information from the comic book to guide him the rest of the way. Tim squinted and looked out into the darkness, directly ahead.

"Wait, ok...so the gate is somewhere out that way?"

Sarah nodded, continuing to trudge forward.

"Ok, and you said there's only one road leading in?"

"Yes."

"Ok, then, I think we're supposed to head out of the main entrance and back down that road."

Sarah turned around and stared, hard, at Tim.

"Are you sure?" she demanded.

"I--I think...yes. If that road is the only way in here, then yes."

Sarah nodded.

"Good. We will leave shortly. Before we do, head to your right. Enter the barracks through the illuminated door. Turn right, walk through the open door, where you will find a bathroom facility with toiletries. You can shave and shower, but do it quickly. I will wait for you outside."

Tim promptly felt around his face, groping the healthy beard. Tim didn't grow facial hair quickly, but it had been nearly two weeks since he had last shaved. It was the first time in his life that facial hair had accumulated.

Tim and Sarah slowly navigated the blanket of snow that covered the premises and trudged toward the barrack's single white lamp. Tim, as always, had questions.

"Sarah, how long have I been here?"

"About 24 hours," Sarah replied, her eyes on the approaching barracks' door.

That meant, Tim realized, that he'd been asleep for almost a full day. And even then, he only awoke because...

"Sarah, when I awoke earlier, I thought I might have heard gunshots.

Were shots fired?"

Sarah stopped and turned, studying his inquisitive expression thoroughly.

"There isn't anyone here. They've all left. The facility, for the moment, is vacant."

The pair reached the barracks door. Tim looked around. To the far right of the front facing wall, a white light hung over the doorway of a drab, grey, single-floored concrete building that was perhaps 100 feet long. Tim assumed that entering and turning left would take him down a long row of empty bunk-beds, like the kind he had seen in army movies.

"Go ahead," Sarah said, gesturing toward the entrance. "I'll wait. Be quick."

Tim grabbed the handle of the heavy, reinforced door and, with considerable effort, swung it open. He was stepping into the facility when Sarah issued him a final command.

"Tim, do not open any other doors or visit any other parts of this barracks besides that bathroom. Clean, shave, and get out. Do you understand?"

Tim was surprised by Sarah's edict, but he nodded, and continued inside.

Inside the barracks, Tim found himself surrounded by doors. Ahead was a single wooden door, on which hung a white sign with bold Korean characters. To his left were broad double doors, each with a thick plastic window at eye level. Tim assumed these doors led to the bunks. To Tim's right was an open door that led to the bathroom; the only opening Tim had been "authorized" to pass through.

Tim walked into a brightly lit bathroom. The room was sparse, but clean. There were three toilet stalls, two mirrored sinks, and a communal shower with three heads.

Tim was surprised to find a single red towel draped next to the showers, and a bar of soap in the dish under one of the showerheads. In addition, a razor and can of shaving cream sat on one of the sinks. Tim didn't know why someone would have left these items, but he didn't care. He happily jumped into the shower, recoiling as icy water sprayed from the showerhead.

The water quickly warmed, though, and Tim enjoyed the best shower he'd ever taken. Two week's worth of sweat, dirt, and stink were finally scrubbed away. It took all of his resolve to tear himself away from the blissful water wonderland.

As he toweled off, Tim felt human again. The young comic book store owner, having finally arrived in Korea, felt reborn—at least, until he looked into the mirror.

His face was barely recognizable. Tim, already a skinny man, had lost weight over the course of his journey, and his face looked gaunt and unhealthy. Tim's sickly features, coupled with his new beard, gave him a weather-beaten, ragged appearance. Were his father to see him now, Tim thought, Will Sutton would probably faint.

Tim examined the can of shaving cream. It was a red cylinder covered with white Korean characters, including a bold phrase across the middle of the can that ended in an exclamation point. The can was very captivating. Although Tim had traveled through China to Korea, he had yet to see anything distinctly "Asian." If not for this can, Tim could have been at a facility on the outskirts of Ruston.

Tim quickly shaved. He was glad to be rid of his beard, but the face he uncovered looked sunken and pale. It was a price he had paid to save his brother.

The moment of truth was rapidly approaching. If the comic book had been correct, he wasn't more than a few hours from reaching Eric! Perhaps then, finally, Tim would learn exactly why been summoned to the other side of the Earth.

Why had Eric ended up here? Clearly, drugs were somehow involved. But what part had Eric played in this international heroin operation? T.C., back in Chicago, had spoken of Eric like a friend or partner. And those cryptic words about ghosts...what did it all mean? Had Eric, pulled deep into a big-time drug ring, pissed off the wrong people? And if so, why was Tim the only one who could come to his rescue?

Other questions lingered. What would his brother look like? It had been over five years since Tim had seen Eric. Would he seem older? Would Tim find a man in the body of the eighteen-year-old who had departed for Africa?

These were questions Tim had pondered long ago, at a moment not unlike this one.

A moment when Tim had nervously awaited a reunion with his long lost brother.

CHAPTER 9

Hello, Mr. Moose.

His arms burdened by a stack of comic books, Tim shuffled past the towering mammal. The giant metal creature was the highlight of Tim's trips to Manchester Airport.

Not that Tim spent much time in airports. This marked, by his count, the fourth time he had been here. On his most recent trip two years earlier, Tim had bid farewell to the same person whose arrival Tim was now anticipating: Eric, his brother.

Why Tim was at the airport alone was no mystery. He was the only one who wanted to come. Tim's father became animated when he heard that Eric was returning home, but his mood was quickly tempered by anger and skepticism. Why, Will Sutton reasoned, should he be happy to see the son who had always been indifferent to him? The son who hadn't bothered to inform his father and brother of his whereabouts for two full years?

Will doubted that his younger son would even show up at the airport. He cautioned Tim not to get his hopes up: Eric didn't care much about his family.

Except, Tim knew, where he was concerned. True, he hadn't heard from Eric since his younger brother had departed for Africa. But Tim and Eric shared a special bond.

As young children, the two had been mirror images of each other. Minor differences between them were obscured by the extraordinary intellect they shared. The young Sutton children could learn and comprehend things that many of their classmates would struggle to understand later as adults.

Tim and Eric had been inseparable, spending their early years exploring the woods around their cabin and defending ragged wooden forts from imaginary invaders. As they grew, the boys adopted a myriad of intellectual, "nerdish" pursuits: role-playing, computer, and trivia games. They read scores of comic books and novels; anything that would satiate their mental acuity. Since none of their peers in Ruston had comparable intellects, they branded Eric and Tim "geeks." Neither boy cared. Socially accepted or not, each knew he had the other to return mental serve.

And yet, over time, they had begun to travel down different paths.

The catalyst for this separation was the death of their mother.

Karen Sutton had been a short, pleasant woman with light-brown hair and rosy cheeks. She was a warm and intelligent woman who had understood her boys' unique gifts from the very beginning.

Karen had made it her mission to impress upon her children how special they truly were. It was a fervor that surpassed simple mothering. Karen expected big things of Tim and Eric, and had felt that it was her duty to help them harness the powerful minds that would lead them to great success as adults.

Tim's earliest fond memories were spending nights seated between Karen and Eric on the family's weathered couch, watching "Jeopardy" on the Suttons' tiny television. As his mother earnestly prodded them on, he and his blond sibling would struggle to come up with questions to the answers intended for people five times their age.

When they were stumped, Karen was always there, eager to help. She was flanked by stacks of dictionaries, almanacs, atlases and thesauri, items she would use to educate the boys on the subjects covered during that evening's show.

Tim and his brother would hang on Karen's every word as she unlocked the mysteries of the world for them. They soaked up every bit of knowledge she provided, forgetting nothing. It was heaven.

When Tim was nine years old, however, these wonderful moments came to a tragic end.

Karen Sutton was diagnosed with an aggressive form of breast cancer. She succumbed within three months and Will Sutton was left alone to raise his two boys.

Tim coped with his mother's passing far better than Eric did. Tim was aided by the fact that his own personality mirrored that of his father. As long as Tim was helping Will tinker with his surveillance equipment, compiling lists of his favorite comics or otherwise keeping his mind occupied, he was content and happy.

The same was not true for Eric. He was rarely content or happy. Eric had only been seven at the time of his mother's death, and had clung more tightly than his brother to her grand vision of his future. Eric felt entitled, bound to future greatness by his intellectual strengths. As he grew older, and this "greatness" failed to materialize, Eric bitterly pulled away from the world around him.

By the time both boys were enrolled at Ruston High School, Eric was known as the impatient, darkly brilliant younger brother of the comic book enthusiast everyone loved.

Aside from the excellent grades both boys earned at Ruston High, teachers noted few similarities between the two. Unlike his brother, Eric rarely applied himself in class, taking scant interest in courses, sports, or extracurricular activities. He was also subtly mean to his teachers. Eric never swore, fought or was overtly disrespectful. He just treated them with distracted disdain.

Eventually, Eric began treating everyone in the same cold fashion, especially the female students at Ruston High. The same girls who left Tim tongue-tied filled Eric with loathing.

As far as Tim had been able to tell, Eric viewed Ruston's entire populace as a series of painfully average, two-dimensional cut-out figures that ought be ignored. Attractive women posed a problem, however, because any young man, Eric included, was forced to pay attention to them whether he wanted to or not.

As a result, Tim was often forced to listen to Eric's lurid descriptions of the depraved sex acts he wished to perform on various Ruston High coeds, were he only given the chance. Conversing with these girls, as Tim longed to do, was never part of Eric's plan.

In spite of their pronounced differences, the Sutton boys remained as close in adolescence as they had been in childhood. This came naturally to Tim. A guy who was friendly to pretty much everyone would naturally have an ironclad bond with his own blood. From Eric's perspective, the relationship was more complicated. Eric's feelings for Tim were as much driven by intellectual respect as brotherly love.

Of course, the two had their sibling clashes. Eric was usually at odds with Tim's perceived state of contentment. With disdain, he compared Tim to their father, whom Eric viewed as little more than a U.S. Government tool. Eric had initially berated his brother's intent to open Dragon Comics. Ultimately, however, he had extended a verbal olive-branch; the kind of words he could only offer to Tim.

"Understand, Big Brother, that you will own the greatest comic book store in history," Eric had asserted with conviction.

For his part, Eric's dreams were as nebulous as they were grand. He had no discernable career plan. His father, teachers, and guidance counselors had presented a plethora of options. None of them interested Eric. None were challenging enough for his intellect.

During a period when disaffected teenagers with high IQ's were firing guns in schools across America, Ruston's most brilliant and brooding student made people nervous. Eric was considered by many to be a ticking time bomb. With graduation approaching, administrators braced themselves for an explosion.

In the final weeks of his senior year, however, Eric's demeanor suddenly changed. When Tim's brother periodically visited Dragon Comics, Tim sensed a quiet focus.

After graduation, Eric abruptly announced his plans to go to Africa and work in an orphanage. Will Sutton reacted with shock, then with skepticism. He had a hard time believing Eric had any interest in helping others.

In contrast, Tim was intensely curious. Like his father, he questioned Eric's motives for travel to a remote city in Mali. Tim, suspected, however, that a complex and lofty scheme hid behind Eric's stated intentions.

Then, after leaving for Africa, Eric had vanished, severing all contact with his family. After many failed attempts to contact the orphanage in Taoudenni, a livid Will finally succeeded, only to be informed that Eric had just flown back to America. Will obtained a record of Eric's flight, but no further clues to his whereabouts.

Tim's father felt betrayed by the son with whom he had never connected. Tim had simply remained curious.

That curiosity mounted as Tim rode the escalator up to Manchester Airport's security gate. In his arms was a stack of edgy adult comic books, the kind that had been Eric's favorites. Tim planned to offer the comics to his brother as a token of. . .well. . . brotherhood. He meant to demonstrate that, regardless of what his father thought, Tim held no grudge. He just wanted answers.

Tim plopped himself down on one of the benches in the waiting area opposite the security checkpoint. Eric's flight was due to arrive from Newark in about 20 minutes. Tim scanned the people around him. There were a couple of kids running the small McDonald's, a handful of security guards, and several people waiting. Nothing out of the ordinary...

Suddenly, Tim saw two hulking, well-dressed men in crisp black suits. They seemed out of place. Having stepped off the escalator, the men looked around authoritatively, slowly studying each face. Both men stared directly at Tim for several seconds. Uneasy, Tim had the fleeting perception that they were after him. But then the men looked away, and fanned out in different directions. One went over to the McDonald's to get coffee, while the other grabbed a newspaper off the top of a trash can and sat down.

Tim now noticed a third man. He was tall, and his style of dress indicated that he was an associate of the others. Unlike the first two men, however, this one was skinny and gangly. He looked around uncomfortably, before ambling to a random spot near the security checkpoint. He fidgeted continuously. Soon, one of the other two men approached and said something. Next, both men sat next to the third man. Tim was now thoroughly interested.

A nearby monitor indicated that Flight 190, Eric's flight, had begun to de-plane. Nagged by anxiety, Tim clutched the comic books as he awaited his brother's arrival. The three suits appeared to be waiting for someone as well...was it Eric?

Over the next few minutes, passengers exited through the security gate. At most, ten emerged and soon, the tiny rush of people through the airport's upper level was over. No Eric. And the suits were still here. Tim's eyes darted back and forth between the security checkpoint and the men. They seemed agitated, restless. They were expecting someone who had not arrived. Now Tim was certain that they were after his brother.

The two larger men were conversing in angry, hushed tones with the thinner man. Then one of the big men handed the third guy a radio. The two large men got up from their seats, moving rapidly to the checkpoint, where one of them produced a badge and flashed it at the guard.

Uh oh. These guys are the law. And they're here to get Eric.

The big men disappeared beyond the checkpoint. Tim sat frozen, staring intently at the remaining man. This guy seemed to be as nervous as Tim, and he kept staring at his radio, as if to will some sort of response.

Then, out of the blue, the man whipped around and stared directly at Tim, who reacted with silent shock. As soon as Tim made eye contact, the man quickly turned away and studied his radio.

My God, this guy knows who I am!

The radio sputtered loudly.

Tim clearly heard the radio broadcast the phrase "he was here." Then Tim heard something about "footprints in the snow," followed by the words "baggage claim." At that, the skinny man jumped up, sprinted to the escalator, and disappeared.

Tim remained in his seat, dumbly staring at the escalator. His adrenaline was pumping, his mind was spinning, and he had no idea what to do. As far as he could tell, the three men were in pursuit of his brother. And judging by the expression Tim had seen on the skinny man's face, Eric's capture was a big deal to these guys. Whatever Eric had done the past two years, it was something serious! Things didn't look good.

Tim heard a barely audible sound—a faint popping noise— somewhere below him in the airport. He would have dismissed it, but the security guards at the checkpoint reacted to it as well. One of the two guards, a woman, moved briskly to the escalator and descended. The fast food employees also reacted. Without any customers, and obviously curious, the two kids abandoned their post at the McDonald's, moseyed over to the escalator, and went down as well. Tim and the elderly male were the only ones remaining on the airport's upper level.

A few minutes later, the radio hanging from the elderly guard's belt hissed. After responding to the message, the guard grew tense and disturbed. He jumped up from his seat and, without looking at Tim, hustled over to the escalator as quickly as a man his age could manage.

Tim was now totally distressed. He nervously fingered the pile of comics still piled neatly on his lap. What did one do when one's brother was apparently on the run from menacing lawmen? Help? Help whom? Tim didn't want to help anyone. He didn't want to leave, either, making the two-hour drive home just to tell his father that Eric was a no-show. He didn't want to do anything. He just wanted his brother to appear at the security checkpoint, and for them to leave Manchester together.

But Eric never arrived.

As one brother waited for the other, the minutes turned into hours.

The hours became days.

The days became years.

CHAPTER 10

Tim stumbled through the deep snow that blanketed the mountain facility. He pulled the hood of his jacket as tight as he could, in a vain attempt to ward off the bitterly cold mountain air. Ahead of him, Sarah marched forward, leading Tim toward the gate through which he had arrived via delivery truck a day earlier.

Sarah ordered Tim to stow the flashlight in his backpack. Since the sky was shrouded in clouds, Tim's only guidance was the sound made by Sarah's confident stride.

The lonely light that Tim had spied from the shipping container slowly materialized in front of him. It hung from a pole fifteen feet in the air, illuminating the wall of deadly, barb-wired fence that extended from both sides of a ten-foot wire gate. An enormous piece of tortuous steel, the sliding gate looked like the entrance to a maximum security prison.

The fence melted into the darkness. The gate itself was opened slightly, with just enough room for a person to slide in or out. Tim assumed that Sarah had come in though this slit, though he didn't know how she had managed to open it.

Wait a minute. How did she even get up here?

Tim squeezed through the tiny opening and out into the cloak of the darkened wilderness. Moving away from the solitary lamp, Tim detected a giant object, barely visible on the narrow road in front of him.

Tim recoiled instinctively when he realized that the shape was a large truck parked directly in the middle of the road. He recovered and followed Sarah toward the vehicle. The truck's lights were off, with the passenger's-side door swung wide open.

"What is this?" Tim called ahead to Sarah, who strode through the darkness ten feet ahead of him. "Is this how you got here?"

"Yes," Sarah responded, without stopping or looking back. She trekked past the driver's side door, and Tim dutifully followed. The cab of the vehicle had the standard frame of a shipping truck, but the body appeared to be a hulking military transport vehicle. Tim imagined soldiers piling into the back, which was covered with a high ceiling of reinforced canvas. Right now, apparently, it was empty.

"You drove this thing all the way up here?" Tim queried.

"Keep moving," was Sarah's only response.

Tim made his way past the truck, and soon the facility, with its lone lamp, vanished into the blackness. He followed the sound of Sarah's footsteps down a steep grade of paved, snow-covered road for several minutes. Abruptly, the noise of Sarah's movement ceased. A few seconds later, her voice materialized next to Tim. He stopped moving.

"Okay, Tim," Sarah instructed. "Tell me where we're going."

Tim paused, trying to visualize a road he couldn't actually see with his eyes.

"Okay, according to what I was told...a quarter-mile down the road, on the left, is a path into the woods. But...I don't know how we're going to see it in the pitch black. I mean, even with a flashlight, do you think we can find it?"

Sarah didn't answer, turned around, and continued her march down the road. Tim hustled to keep up.

"Sarah, this place we're going...do you think it will be guarded? I mean, what if it's some sort of prison? Shouldn't we have, I don't know, guns or something?"

Tim received no response. Sarah had switched back into her "no talking" mode.

As he followed Sarah along the switchback turns of the steeply sloped road, visibility improved slightly. At first, Tim assumed his eyes were simply adjusting to the blackness. Then, looking upward at the now barely-detectable blanket of clouds above him, he realized that dawn was on its way.

Now, Sarah's petite figure could be seen, and Tim's eyes finally had something to grasp and follow. Eventually, after a half-hour of walking, the brightness of Sarah's red mop of hair came into focus.

The topography of Tim's exotic new locale, heretofore a mystery, finally began to reveal itself. On both sides of Tim was dense coniferous forest. The trees were so thick that Tim couldn't believe someone had actually been able to build a road. Beyond its thickness, however, the landscape was a letdown. If Tim had wanted to see pine trees, he could have stayed at home.

Get over it, moron. You didn't come here to sightsee.

After an hour of walking in the thin light of dawn, Sarah halted at the side of the road. She turned to her left and stared into the forest for a second, then jogged ten yards into the woods. Sarah paused again before disappearing into the trees. A minute later, she emerged.

"This is it," she stated.

"What is?"

"The trail. The path we're looking for. It's through here."

"It is?" Tim looked at the thick layer of foliage surrounding Sarah. If there was a trail where she was standing, he couldn't see it. Sarah wasn't inclined to offer insight.

"Let's go," she commanded. Tim had no choice but to once again put his faith in Sarah as he followed her into the brush.

Once Tim was actually in the forest, he found that it was pretty easy to move around. The forest was surprisingly sparse, with nothing but snow, tall trees, and the occasional boulder to avoid. Still, it took another half hour of plodding in Sarah's footsteps before Tim began to discern a trail.

Though there were no footprints of any kind, Tim began to see other nuances. Nearby trees were missing branches that would have hung in Tim's way. Other trees had dark red blazes painted on their trunks, blazes that were easily spotted once Tim realized they were there. To Sarah, these markings must have stood out like neon. Tim shook his head. How would he have ever achieved any of this without this amazing woman's help?

For another hour, the two trekked through the wilderness. Daylight finally permeated the clouds overhead. To Tim, everything turned from black to gray, scantly more appealing, but at least he could now see.

Ahead of him, Sarah suddenly raised her right hand.

"Stop," she commanded, in a hushed, urgent tone that surprised Tim and grabbed his attention.

Tim stood still as Sarah slowly backtracked to his position, never once taking her eyes off of the trail ahead. When she reached Tim, Sarah pointed forward into the distance.

"There," she said softly.

It took Tim a second before he saw what she was pointing at. Fifty yards ahead of them, he realized, the trail stopped at the steep side of a looming mountain wall; an apparent dead end. But as Tim stared at the mountain, he saw a camouflaged tarp that hung from a wooden crossbeam about ten feet off the ground. The tarp appeared to be concealing a mineshaft-like passage into the mountain.

Sarah was clearly on high alert now. Without blinking or speaking, she stared off into the woods in all directions. Finally, deciding the area was safe, she signaled for Tim to proceed to the opening.

When she reached the mountain wall, Sarah motioned for Tim to stop. She grabbed the side of tarp, ducked around it, and disappeared into the side of the mountain. As had become the custom, Tim waited anxiously while his all-knowing counterpart scouted out the terrain. Finally, Sarah reappeared from under the tarp.

On Sarah's face was an expression Tim had never seen before. It was a sharp departure from the staid alertness Tim was used to. Sarah looked, almost…excited.

"Tim," Sarah asked, shooting an intense gaze into his eyes. "Your message only described a single way into this area?"

Tim nodded, tensing at the steely tone of Sarah's voice.

"Then this is it," Sarah stated. "This is the route that will lead you to your brother. Head through here."

Tim waited in silence for Sarah to continue. When she didn't, he blinked.

"Wait a minute…you're not coming?"

Sarah looked up at the mountain wall in front of her.

"No," she said. "I have to secure this area. I'll meet you on the other side."

"Other side?" Tim mouthed. "Of what, the mountain? What's on the other side? Aren't there going to be soldiers there?"

"Tim!" Sarah shot him a fiery look. "You will be fine. Now, go get your brother. I will find you."

Tim was thoroughly confused. If the outside of the area needed securing, then what about the inside of the area? He wished, for once, that things would make some goddamned sense to him. From the moment he had met Sarah in Seattle, she had been leading him like a puppy on a leash.

Focus, Tim. Focus on your brother. You're too damn close to lose a grip now. Let's go.

Tim took a deep breath, and grabbed for the tarp. Sarah put her hand on his shoulder and stopped him.

"Take out your flashlight. You'll need it."

Tim dug into his backpack, pulled out the light, and moved under the tarp. As he lowered it back into place, he cast a look back at Sarah.

"Ok, well…I'll see you on the other side."

Sarah, studying the side of the mountain, said nothing.

Having lowered the tarp, Tim was surrounded by darkness once again.

He clicked on his flashlight, expecting to see a gold-rush era collage of rotting crossbeams and dirt. Instead, Tim was greeted with bright, clean concrete.

Tim was in a tunnel. Nearly twice as tall as he was, the tunnel was composed of huge cylindrical segments. It was as wide as it was high, and it extended farther than the light of his flashlight. The massive tube seemed like the kind of system a major city would build underground to protect a network of sewer pipes or electrical wiring.

But this tube was empty. With one notable exception.

Leaning against the tunnel directly to Tim's right was a shiny, bright yellow bicycle. The machine was sleek and light, and featured spoke-less wheels made of space-age plastic. It resembled an exotic cycle Lance Armstrong might design for the Tour de France.

Tim studied the bike for a second. Randomly, the words of T.C., the Chicago "entrepreneur," popped into his head: "More questions, less answers." This bike was yet another question to which Tim didn't have the answer. Luckily, common sense prevailed, and Tim put two and two together.

It's to ride through the tunnel, genius. Hop on.

Tim climbed aboard the bicycle and began to pedal. Awkwardly, he held his flashlight in his left hand as he attempted to steer the bike with his right. It was difficult to keep the bike straight at first, especially considering the curvature of the handlebars, but Tim managed to keep the bike from careening into the side of the tunnel. He took off down the endless, uniform tube, pedaling faster and faster.

The ride down the tunnel was eerie, to say the least. The tube was almost perfectly level, with a smooth surface that seemed to invite Tim to pedal as quickly as possible. But he couldn't see more than twenty-five or thirty feet in front of him, and he had no idea what lay on the other end. If a concrete wall jumped out of the blackness, his round-the-world travels were going to end with an ignominious splat. That said, Tim was excited and anxious, and he shot down the tunnel as fast as he could.

The ride was so monotonous that, when Tim did reach the other side of the tunnel, it came as a shock. He had been riding for about twenty minutes when a tarp, identical to the first one, emerged in front of him. Tim jammed on his breaks, screeching to a halt directly in front of the covering. He found himself parked next to a second bicycle, identical to his own. Tim climbed off his bike, and stared at the second cycle.

Whatever kind of place this is, someone is home.

Tim gingerly lifted up the tarp, half-expecting to see some uniformed Korean yell "Intruder!" and then open fire. To his relief, the only thing waiting for him on the other side of the tunnel was more forest.

The new woods were the same blend of pines and snow that Tim had seen before. But this time, the path at his feet was clearly marked; a trail of dirt extended away from the tarp and down into the trees. Propelled by his mounting excitement, Tim briskly hiked down the path. He hadn't gone more than fifty feet when he saw the building.

Tucked under several huge pines was a tiny, square, concrete structure. It looked like a single-story, one-room rock hut. Unlike the tunnel through which Tim had just cycled, this concrete was caked with a mixture of dirt and snow. Tim tensed at the sight of a man-made structure placed so randomly in the wilderness. Compelled by anxious curiosity, he tiptoed toward the building.

By the time Tim reached the hut, however, he had spotted three more identical buildings within twenty feet of it. When Tim stopped to examine those buildings, he noticed at least four more. Fixing his eyes on the snowy distance, Tim realized there were still more huts, more than he could count. Tim had stumbled upon a hidden concrete city.

Tim crept around the side of the first hut. The structure had no windows, but the front of the building was adorned with a rusted steel mesh door that hung half-open from its hinges. Tim inched himself over to the doorway, and peeked around the corner.

The building was completely empty. There were no people, no beds, no furniture; just an empty, dirty floor that was devoid of footprints.

Tim moved to the next concrete hut. This one was empty, too. So were the others nearby. It occurred to Tim that, although he was standing in the midst of some kind of mountain village, he could hear nothing. The place was a ghost town.

Tim continued down the dirt path, passing so many of the tiny, identical square structures that he quickly lost count. All were empty, but the well-worn trail at Tim's feet told him that someone was lurking in the area. The whole thing was creepy, and Tim's nerves were fully charged.

A hundred feet down the trail, the scenery suddenly changed. Tim was still surrounded by frosted pines, but the huts had given way to a series of dirt circles.

Tim counted at least fifteen such clearings. They ranged from thirty to perhaps seventy feet in diameter, and were laid out in neat rows on either side of the path. They looked like miniature, snow-dotted arenas, although the odd sprout or bit of brush growing in the circles told Tim they hadn't seen any use in a long time.

The circles fascinated Tim. Soon, however, his senses were redirected a hundred feet down the path.

Straight ahead was another single-story concrete structure. But this building was at least twenty times larger than any of the buildings Tim had passed thus far. And this building was dotted with clear, square-shaped windows. Shining out of the windows, in the pale dawn, were lights.

Someone was inside.

Chilled by a mix of temperature and fear, Tim trembled as he tiptoed toward the enormous building. Like the other structures, this one had a metal mesh door at its entrance, though this door appeared to be cleaner than the others, and was free of rust. Crouching down until he was below the level of the windows, Tim ambled over to the door and peered inside.

Tim found an interior exactly the same as that of the other huts; a tiny, empty square room. At the rear of this room, though, was a wooden sliding door. The door's construction seemed starkly out of place; it looked heavy and thick, with a rich, lavish brown hue. The door belonged in a Hollywood mansion, not a North Korean hovel.

Tim gingerly pulled open the metal door and slid into the small room. He crept up to the fancy sliding door, and gently put his hands upon it. To Tim's surprise, the door, unlike just about every object he had felt in the past two weeks, was warm to the touch. Tim pressed his left ear against the door. Despite his best efforts, he couldn't detect any noise emanating from within.

Tim took a deep, slow breath. Then, as delicately as he could, he slid the door open just wide enough to squeeze himself through. Jolted by a rush of toasty, room-temperature air, Tim closed the door behind him and stared in shock at the scene in front of him.

He had just stepped into another world.

Tim gazed at the single, massive room that appeared to make up the building's entirety. The huge open space was best described as a cross between a modern apartment and a high-tech office building.

Directly to Tim's left was a messy, but fully stocked, kitchen. A cafeteria-sized bag of rice sat next to a sink stacked with pots. Empty beer bottles dotted a wide island of countertop that also contained a range with four heating coils. Near the sliding door was an imposing steel refrigerator.

To Tim's right was an epic, sprawling workstation. Five state-of-the-art flat-screen monitors were arranged in a semi-circle on a chestnut-colored wood grain desk, likely constructed for this exact computer set-up. A black luxury office chair sat opposite the arrangement, ready to swivel from machine to machine. Electrical wiring and computer cables were messily strewn about the entire area.

Behind the chair was a circular table about ten feet in diameter. The table was awash with paper, beer bottles, pens, and pencils, and there wasn't a single portion of its surface that was visible. Against the wall near the table was a row of five three-level black filing cabinets.

Down the left side of the room, past the kitchen, was a king-sized bed flanked by two mammoth wooden dressers. The red sheets on the bed were scattered haphazardly, and the drawers of the dressers were half-open, overflowing with clothes. More clothes covered the floor around the bed. The area was awash with men's apparel: T-shirts, jeans, boxer shorts, and dirty socks.

With one glaring exception. A gaudy, colorful collection of bras, panties and other exotic women's lingerie hung from a wire strung along the wall above the bed.

Opposite the bedroom, on the right side of the building, was a bathroom area. There was a wide, white, porcelain sink affixed under a chrome oval mirror. To the right of the sink was a red medicine cabinet, attached to the wall at head level. To the left of the sink was an enclosed shower, ringed by a vertical cylinder of opaque glass.

The back two corners of the room were an electronic scrap yard. Flat-screen televisions, laptop computers, DVD players, and a host of other high-end equipment were distractedly piled against the walls, seemingly forgotten.

Directly down the middle of the building was a wide walkway. Like the rest of the room, this walkway was covered with thick, burgundy-colored carpet. The walkway ended at a long black conference table that was a third as long as the room itself. It extended backward, ending at the rear wall.

The table was surrounded by twelve chairs, all of which were empty.

Except for one.

At the far end of the table, leaning over a laptop computer and a mess of paperwork, sat a single man. When he saw Tim standing at the far end of the room, the man jumped up from his chair in shock. Frozen, his eyes focused on Tim.

The man was about five-feet, ten-inches tall. He was Caucasian, with a slender, unimposing frame and pale-white skin. The man's cleanly-shaven, brown-eyed face was capped with a crop of short, neatly cut blond hair.

Tim exhaled. A cornucopia of emotions flew through his head: joy, satisfaction, fear, trepidation, validation, and, of course, curiosity. Tim's legs seemed ready to buckle beneath him as he slowly approached the conference table. The man opposite him remained still, speechless at Tim's approach. When Tim reached the table, the two men stared at one another in silence.

Then, with the best smile he could muster, Tim spoke.

"I'm here," he said. "Little Brother, I'm here."

Eric Sutton, staring back at Tim, opened his mouth as if to say something, but no words came out. He simply continued to stare, unblinkingly, back at his brother.

"I got your message," Tim continued breathlessly. "I've come a long way, and it's been quite a trip, let me tell you...but I'm here. I'm here to help you."

For a moment, Eric continued his paralyzed gaze. Then, suddenly, he blinked. Eric's eyes shot past Tim to the door, then at the windows to his left and right. Tim, a tad uneasy, tried again.

"Eric, I'm here. I got your message."

Eric's eyes whipped back to meet his brother's. Finally, he spoke.

"What?"

"Your message. I-"

"Tim, how did you find me?" Eric mouthed in shock. "How the hell did you get past--how did you get in here?"

"I-I followed your instructions!" Tim stammered. "I did everything you told me to do, and it all worked. I'm here!"

"Instructions?" Eric repeated, white-faced. "What instructions?"

"The message you sent. I--"

"I never sent you any message!"

"What?"

Eric bounded around the table and clasped Tim's left shoulder, shooting a steely gaze into his brother's eyes.

"Big Brother," he began. "What the hell are you doing here?"

PART 2
THE CRACKED CEILING

CHAPTER 11

--TOP SECRET—

21 February 2008, 06:30Z

From: Davidson, Sam 3RD RADIO BN., USMC
[sam.davidson@mbch.usmc.smil.mil]

To:**Archer, Jeff** CEILING[jeff.archer@specproj.
sgov.gov];
Danielson, Percy CIA[percy.danielson@cia.
sgov.gov]

(S)Subject: **Coded messages from China-bound
cargo ship.**

(TS)Intelligence Scanning, 3RD Radio BN., MBCH
Hawaii, report **embedded code words in email
from cargo ship *HAIHU*, traveling Seattle—
Dalian.**

(S)Said messages addressed to **Jeff Hutchins**,
St. Paul's School, Concord, New Hampshire,
USA.

(S)Speculation **code was intentionally simple to ensure interception.**

(TS)Embedded code words: **CEILING; APPLE**

(S)Messages intended to **mislead recipient (Hutchins) that writer is in California, not onboard *HAIHU*.**

(S)**Additional messages sent to Dragon Comics, Ruston, NH.** Business owner: **Timothy Sutton,** age 24. Messages do not have embedded code and appear benign.

(S)Daily message transmissions from *HAIHU* span last 1-1/2 weeks. Message decoding only accomplished during the last 24 hours.

(S)Haihu scheduled to dock in Dalian Thursday, 23 February, 07:30Z.

--TOP SECRET—

****

Jeff Archer roused himself from slumber. The cell-phone to the left of his Manassas, Virginia bed was ringing. Jeff groggily raised his slender, muscular, grey-haired 48-year-old frame and picked up the receiver.

"This is Archer. Go ahead."

"Sorry for the late night phone call, sir. This is Percy Danielson over at Intelligence. I just wanted to know if you'd care to tag along with us tomorrow. We'll be heading up to New Hampshire to question a guy in connection with those Haihu messages. I thought you might be interested."

Archer was interested. He also had no idea what the man on the line was talking about.

"Haihu messages? Is that supposed to mean something to me? What are you talking about?"

There was a pause before Danielson continued.

"Sir…I thought you had already been briefed. The message was addressed to you as well as myself…"

"What? What message? What are you talking about?" Jeff shouted into the phone. He was fully awake now. "I was in Richmond watching my son in the high school basketball playoffs all day. I haven't been briefed on any of this!"

"Sir, I apologize. The message came out of MBCH in Hawaii, and was addressed both to you and to the CIA. The information therein refers peripherally to persons we were tracking in an investigation that dead-ended several years ago. At one point, your program was involved: at an airport in New Hampshire."

"What?" Archer bolted up from his bed. "What else?"

"Well…not much, except for the persons mentioned. The information makes reference to several coded words that would seem to involve you."

"What?" Archer repeated. "What words?" His eyes widened. "Was the Ceiling Program mentioned?"

There was another pause on the other end of the line.

"Uh…sir, I'm not sure I can…perhaps it's better if we didn't talk on the phone."

"Goddamn it!" Archer rushed over to the dresser opposite his bed and began pulling out clothes as fast as he could. "I'm coming in! Right now! And when I get to Langley, you better have some goddamn answers!"

Archer slammed the phone down on the hook. His wife Ann, rudely awakened from her own slumber, stared at him angrily.

"What was that about? Where are you going?"

"I'm sorry, honey," Archer replied hurriedly. "I've got something I have to take care of. I don't know when I'll be back."

"What? Where are you...what about the state finals tomorrow?"

Archer stopped for a second. He had momentarily forgotten about his son's upcoming basketball game.

"Tell...tell Ryan I'm sorry. This is something I have to do."

****

Jeff Archer stared at the transcripts spread out across the long wooden conference table. His face was tense, his nerves on edge. Next to him stood the short, baldheaded, sweaty, bespectacled 50-year-old CIA agent Percy Danielson. Danielson looked questioningly at Archer.

"We don't have much of an Agency presence in Dalian right now...but I might be able to get some agents over to the Haihu by the time it docks," he offered.

Archer continued to study the messages.

"That's a great idea," he replied derisively, "if you're looking to assassinate a couple of CIA agents. They wouldn't stand a chance."

Danielson, defeated, stared at the table. Archer continued.

"I want you to get on the phone with Fort Benning. They've got Rangers operating somewhere in the Korean DMZ right now. Tell them to pull their team out and send their asses down to Dalian as quickly as possible. They won't beat the boat there, but they'll get there before we do."

Danielson looked back at Archer in surprise.

"We're going to Dalian? When?"

"As soon as we see your man up in New Hampshire," Archer responded coldly, "I want us on a plane to China. I want to be looking at the Haihu by Friday morning."

Archer looked at his watch. It was nearly six-o'clock in the morning. He turned to Danielson.

"We're wasting time. Get me to New Hampshire."

CHAPTER 12

As America's future tycoons and senators filed out of his classroom, Jeff Hutchins ambled over to the spotless windows. He gazed at the grey winter sky, eyes focused on nothing, his mind in a trance.

It had been nearly two weeks since Eric Sutton re-entered his life. Between the e-mails he received each day and his own mental images of Tim's quest, Hutchins struggled to focus on his curriculum. Students hadn't noticed, but a few colleagues had raised their eyebrows at Hutchins' recent detachment. To many of them, Hutchins was an outsider with an undeserved salary, and they didn't appreciate his daydreams about FBI glory days.

As Hutchins' mind wandered, he caught something out of the corner of his eye.

A tan Crown Victoria had just pulled into the main parking lot. Four men in suits climbed out of the Ford and were heading towards his building.

Hutchins froze. He didn't know the men. But he knew what they were about. And he knew they were coming for him.

Hutchins wasn't surprised. He was a former FBI agent, having once drawn paychecks from organizations with titles like "Intelligence" and "Investigation." He knew that guys like these had carte blanche access to anyone's personnel file since 9/11. His whereabouts wouldn't have been a secret.

Minutes later, a nervous Hutchins received a knock on his open classroom door.

"Mr. Hutchins? Percy Danielson, Central Intelligence Agency. We need to have a word with you."

Hutchins nodded silently from his desk, and the four men entered the room. Two of the men, tall and imposing, closed the door and stood like silent sentries in front of it. The short, balding, bespectacled man who had introduced himself as Percy Danielson pulled a student desk over to Hutchins' desk and squeezed into it.

A fourth man, tall, with chiseled features and distinguished grey hair, shifted to the right of Danielson and remained standing.

"Uh, what can I do for you, gentlemen?" Hutchins offered, realizing how stupid the question sounded. He knew exactly why the men were here.

"Mr. Hutchins," Danielson began. "We want you to know up front that we are fully aware of your communication with the Haihu."

Hutchins frowned. As soon as he saw the four suits emerge from that sparkling government vehicle, he knew he'd be required to spill his guts about Tim, Eric and the whole plan. He hadn't, however, expected to be confused.

"The Haihu?" he questioned. "What are you talking about?"

Danielson smirked impatiently.

"Mr. Hutchins, we don't have time for the runaround here. Trust me when I say we know about your--."

"Percy!" The commanding tone came from the grey-haired man. Danielson stopped, cowering slightly.

"I've read Mr. Hutchins' file, Percy," the grey-haired man continued. "I know about his role in Manchester and about the fallout. I know how Intelligence saw to it that the boys at the Bureau washed their hands of him, even though he was a straight arrow--a company boy and potential high climber."

The grey-haired man turned his attention to Jeff.

"Mr. Hutchins, my name is Jeff Archer. Who I represent isn't important; suffice it to say, I understand what kind of man you are. I know you're going to cooperate with us. And I can tell, from the look on your face, that you honestly don't know what the Haihu is. But I suspect, given a moment's time, you'll understand what we're talking about."

Hutchins eyed Archer for a second. Then he grasped Archer's meaning, quickly realizing that it was pointless to be anything but forthright.

"It's the ship," he deduced slowly. "The ship Tim Sutton is traveling on."

Archer nodded silently. Danielson took the moment of silence as an opportunity to resume speaking.

"Correct, Mr. Hutchins. Now, understand that we have no interest in investigating your failure to properly report the goings-on of the past several weeks—provided that you produce all of the information we require. Do you understand?"

Hutchins nodded.

"Good," Danielson continued. "First question: When did Tim Sutton first contact you?"

"Two weeks ago this coming Wednesday," Hutchins sighed. "Sutton came to my classroom and sat down exactly where you are sitting now. He told me his brother Eric was in danger, and that he needed my help to save him."

"And when he said Eric," Danielson, replied, "You knew who he was talking about?"

Archer interrupted Danielson a second time.

"I suspect, Percy, that Mr. Hutchins knows more about Eric Sutton than anyone in America. I'm interested in specific pieces of that information."

Danielson paused. He was clearly bristling at Archer's weakening of his attempts to strong-arm Hutchins.

"But we already have a full file on Eric Sutton!" he offered, looking up at Archer. Danielson turned back to Hutchins. "What I want to find out is why Tim Sutton saw fit to contact you, Mr. Hutchins, and what you know about Eric's whereabouts."

"Well," Hutchins began. "Tim Sutton told me that he had received a communiqué from his brother in a manila envelope with no return address. It instructed him to enlist my help in rescuing Eric. I can only assume that Eric Sutton knew I would have a personal interest in locating him, and that I had the means to make Tim's trip to North Korea feasible."

"And by means," Danielson continued, "you mean contacts you made while employed by the FBI?"

"Correct."

"And did Tim Sutton provide you with specifics on the exact North Korean location of his brother?"

"No," Hutchins answered. "Actually, there didn't seem to be much he did know. Tim told me he had to travel to Chicago, where someone would give him the name of a ship and the location of a specific cargo container on that ship. He was supposed to stow away in this container on its trip across the ocean, and then across the border from China into North Korea. Once he was there, he would follow a set of directions to the location of his brother."

"And did you request to see these directions?" Danielson queried.

"No," Hutchins returned. "Honestly, I don't think they amounted to more than a few rights and lefts. I think the directions depended entirely on Tim's arriving with the container at an exact location in North Korea. Frankly, the whole thing was a long-shot. Although it seems to be going well so far..."

"And you know this," Danielson prodded, "Because of the communications you've received from the Haihu, correct?"

"Yes," Hutchins replied, "with the help of an old CIA contact who's been relaying Tim's communications from the ship. I just didn't know which ship."

"Look," Hutchins offered, "I was hoping to use this development as an opportunity to bring Eric Sutton to justice. As far as not requesting outside help, well..."

Hutchins glanced up at Archer, sighed, and continued.

"Mr. Archer is correct; I was booted out of my old job. But I'm no idiot. No novice high school teacher draws my salary, private or otherwise. I know I was given a very generous offer. The government had a mess on its hands, and wanted it covered up. That meant locking me out. And I played ball. But that doesn't mean I don't have questions. And the last thing I want is to be shut out again before I can apprehend Eric Sutton and finally get some answers!"

"Rest assured," Danielson returned. "We want to apprehend Eric Sutton as much as you do. The more help you give us, the easier it will be for us to determine his location, and get him out of there and into a court of law here in the States."

"This is bullshit!"

Jeff Archer's outburst startled everyone in the room. Even the two agents guarding the door widened their eyes. Danielson's own face registered a mix of shock, fear, and frustration. He turned to Archer in anger.

"Damn it, Jeff, you're going completely against protocol here! The Agency has interests here that you need to fully consid—"

Archer ignored Danielson's words. He stepped forward, put his palms flat on Hutchins' desk, and leaned down until his face was directly in front of Jeff's.

"Mr. Hutchins, how do you suppose Tim Sutton is sending e-mail from the Haihu?"

Hutchins was taken aback. It was a question he had never considered.

"Um…I guess he must have some sort of satellite link."

"And how do you think he's getting access to this equipment?" Archer responded. "Who gave it to him? How does he know how to use it?"

Hutchins, confused, was silent. Danielson, at a loss for a way to rein Archer in, was also speechless. Archer continued.

"For that matter, how is young Tim staying alive on this boat? Is he hiding in the shipping container? How is he feeding himself? How is going to the bathroom? Did your contact make all of this possible?" Archer paused. "Mr. Hutchins, I know you're a smart man. You understand where I'm going here."

Hutchins did. In retrospect, he couldn't believe that none of these questions had ever popped into his mind. But what Archer was now implying really disturbed him.

"Wait a minute," he stammered. "What are you not telling me, that the communications I've been getting every day telling me Tim is fine aren't true?"

Archer looked at Hutchins for a moment. Then he turned and glared at Danielson, ensuring that what he was about to say would go uninterrupted. Archer turned back to Hutchins.

"Yes, Mr. Hutchins, you are being lied to. But not in the way you think."

"What do you mean?"

"I mean," Archer explained, "that, in one sense, you are correct. Tim Sutton is fine. To explain further, I'll first need one more piece on information, the name of your CIA contact."

Hutchins was silent.

"Look," Archer offered, "you don't even have to give me a full name. Just a first name."

Hutchins, determined to avoid revealing the name, kept his mouth shut. Archer stared into Hutchins' eyes. A small smile crept onto his face.

"Mr. Hutchins, I don't even care if you give me a real name. Just give me a name."

Hutchins leaned back in his chair, eyebrows furrowed. The whole situation was getting more confusing by the second. Finally, he offered up a name.

"Michael. Michael Smith."

Archer nodded.

"And this 'Michael Smith'...he lives in California, correct? And he's been sending you these e-mails from California?"

"OK, yes," Hutchins allowed guardedly.

"Mr. Hutchins," Archer explained. "The e-mail you have been receiving isn't coming from California. It's being sent from someone on board the Haihu. And the messages aren't being sent by 'Michael Smith'. Or, for that matter, by Tim Sutton."

Hutchins blinked.

"What? What are you talking about?"

"In short," Archer said. "Someone with no connection to you is piggybacking Tim Sutton on his journey. Someone with the guile to impersonate this 'Michael Smith' and possessing the skills necessary for keeping Tim Sutton alive."

"B-but," Hutchins stammered. "I've been receiving e-mail every day! If I'm getting a fake set of messages, then how are the real ones being diverted?"

Archer looked down at the desk. With a hint of sadness in his voice, he replied.

"I doubt there are two sets of e-mail. Frankly, I would say the well-being of 'Michael Smith' is in serious doubt."

Hutchins collapsed against the back of his chair, aghast. He managed to summon the wherewithal for another question.

"But, if my contact is...and I'm receiving bogus emails...then what has happened to Tim Sutton?"

Archer looked back at Hutchins.

"Actually, I imagine he's fine. At this very instant, he's probably marveling at his good fortune. Someone has, in effect, made an impossible journey possible for him. Someone who will ultimately deliver him to his brother."

"W. . .Why?" Hutchins stuttered. "Why would he be okay if my contact isn't?"

"Because," Archer explained. "I believe Eric Sutton has planned all of this. I think he expected someone to intercept 'Michael Smith' and take his place. He appears to have used his own brother as a smokescreen to confuse you--a ruse made all the more effective because Tim didn't realize he was being used."

Hutchins slumped in his chair, utterly dismayed. It briefly occurred to him that Archer might be making this up, in an attempt to squeeze information out of him. But those thoughts were pushed to the back of his mind by the unstoppable realization that Eric Sutton had managed to screw him over a second time.

"I...I don't know what to say," he offered weakly. "I guess it's beginning to look as though I may have been duped. I'm sorry."

Danielson seemed unconvinced by Hutchins' resigned tone.

"Mr. Hutchins, you may very well be telling us the whole truth. But the CIA is not about to let Eric Sutton simply disappear a second time because you claim you were outwitted. We know he is in North Korea, and we aim to bring him to justice. Now, if I find in the course of the upcoming days, weeks or months that you are withholding information, rest assured that you will be prosecuted to the full extent..."

Archer cut Danielson off a final time.

"Yes, fine, great. I don't have time for this. We need to be leaving--Now." He backed away from Hutchins' desk and, looking downward, silently commanded Danielson to do the same.

"Wait a second!" Danielson protested. "I'm not finished questioning Mr. Hutchins, and there are still some things I need to..."

"He's told you all he knows about Eric Sutton's whereabouts," Archer stated. "This man wants to find Eric Sutton as badly as you do, Percy. Anyway, there's no need to waste any more time here. Mr. Hutchins is coming with us."

Hutchins and Danielson registered identical expressions of complete shock.

"What?" they exclaimed in unison.

"Percy," Archer stated authoritatively, "Mr. Hutchins is of no more value to you. But he is valuable to me. And unlike you, I'm not going to waste time here when I can learn what I need to know during our flight over the Pacific."

Archer turned to Hutchins.

"Mr. Hutchins, I know that you believe you have given us all the help you can," he offered. "But there is a great deal about this situation you don't understand, and a great deal more that I can learn from you."

Danielson visibly tensed. There were details he clearly didn't think Hutchins needed to hear. Archer seemed to acknowledge this.

"Most important, Mr. Hutchins," Archer continued, "You need to be aware that Mr. Danielson and I have different objectives here. Percy's goal is to apprehend Eric Sutton. My interests extend to another individual. A person who is much, much more threatening than Eric Sutton. A person we've wanted for a long, long time."

Hutchins stared back at Archer.

"The piggy-backer!" he surmised, aloud. "You know the person with Tim Sutton! Is he a rogue agent? Some guy who got pissed at the CIA, flipped, and is helping Eric Sutton, North Korea, or both?"

Archer was moving toward the classroom door. He motioned for Hutchins and Danielson to follow him.

"I do know who is with Tim Sutton," he answered. "And that person is far more dangerous, far more deadly, than any rogue agent could ever be."

Archer opened the classroom door, turned around, and stared hard at Hutchins.

"And she isn't a guy."

CHAPTER 13

Sarah looked around at the small, dirty, nearly pitch-black room.

A dead rat lay under a boarded-up window, next to an electric heater that looked like it hadn't worked in a decade. Old newspapers, food crumbs, and a few used drug needles were littered about the room. There was no furniture or appliances--only a rusted, non-working range in the tiny corner of the room masquerading as a kitchen. The place reeked. Its former tenants, whoever they were, had lived a brutally-hard, bare-bones existence.

Sarah didn't care. For her purposes, the room was perfect.

The room had two windows. Both were covered with cracking sheets of plywood. Sarah advanced to the window above the electric heater. After inspecting the plywood for a moment, she grabbed the sheet with two hands and ripped it from the window. Drab sunlight filtered in from an overcast sky. Sarah stared out the open window, momentarily adjusting her eyes to the light. She surveyed every inch of the landscape.

This room would be just fine.

Sarah moved from the window to the room's "kitchen", where she grabbed the metal range, and pulled it away from the wall. She pushed the rusty metal square against the wall opposite the open window, then tipped it on its side. Sarah hopped up on the range and looked back at the window.

Excellent. Time to go to work.

Sarah kneeled down on the range and reached for the dusty floor. She retrieved a long, black case, deftly removing a Marine Corps M40A3 Sniper Rifle.

Sarah mechanically loaded five rounds of state-of-the-art M118LR ammunition into the rifle. Then she stood back up on the range. She hefted the giant weapon into firing position, and leaned her body back against the room's dirty wall.

Sarah guided the rifle's powerful scope to her eye. Then she stared out the open window at the Maxwell Lee Housing Projects.

This was as still as Sarah had been in over a week. She'd been busy. Her frequent visits to Ruston, New Hampshire had finally yielded the information she had long sought.

As she so often did, Sarah had gone to Ruston to shadow Tim Sutton. She checked on bugs she had previously placed in his comic book store, tracked his movements, discreetly followed him about his daily routine...and was finally rewarded for her efforts.

The tiny surveillance cameras Sarah had installed in Dragon Comics revealed that Tim had received some sort of mysterious package on the Monday after Sarah's successful penetration of the S.W.I.P.E. perimeter. The package had clearly affected Sutton, who left his store immediately. Sarah followed Sutton to the Baker-Berry Library. She stealthily posed as a nearby student while he pored over a Korean dictionary. Most important, she had watched from afar as he used a nearby computer to search the Internet, and spied his retrieval of the name "Jeff Hutchins."

Sarah had raced to St. Paul's School, arriving a full day ahead of Sutton. She snuck into Hutchins' classroom in the middle of the night, lacing the room with micro-miniature audio and video monitoring devices. The following day, Sarah had covertly watched from a far-off doorway as Sutton entered Hutchins' room for the first time.

Sutton's conversation with Hutchins was an absolute bonanza, as was Hutchins' e-mail to a contact from his FBI days—John Kenninger, a former CIA agent who now lived in Los Angeles—that Sarah's surveillance camera captured on an exposed computer screen.

In the 36 hours since St. Paul's, Sarah's movements had been a blur.

She had smuggled herself onboard a cargo plane traveling from Hartford, Connecticut, to Los Angeles. Arriving in L.A., Sarah had infiltrated John Kenninger's house and knocked him out. From that point, Sarah had assumed Kenninger's identity and had begun sending fabricated e-mail to Hutchins.

After ensuring that Kenninger would neither escape nor die for weeks, Sarah snuck onboard a second cargo flight, this one bound for Chicago's Midway airport. Once she arrived in Chicago, things had taken an unexpected turn.

Sarah flew into Midway on a Thursday night. After leaving the airport, she quickly secured a pair of high-grade night-vision goggles and a 9MM pistol with silencer. Getting this equipment was easy; the Ceiling program had equipment caches in unmarked storage containers in nearly every major city in the world. It wasn't until Sarah visited the Maxwell Lee Homes that she ran into trouble.

To the lay observer, Maxwell Lee looked no different than other housing units in the neighborhood. Sarah, however, immediately knew better. She had quickly discovered that the entire perimeter of Maxwell Lee was guarded like Fort Knox.

Peering through her night vision goggles, Sarah spotted hundreds of motion sensors, placed at every possible entrance to the complex. There were also dozens of infrared surveillance cameras watching the surrounding area from every angle. She could also tell, from the four towers' many strategically-placed, un-boarded windows, that nearly every entryway into the complex was physically guarded by a person.

Sarah had backed away from Maxwell Lee and surveyed the blocks surrounding it. In a few hours, she unearthed what amounted to a giant net of high-grade surveillance equipment protecting the entire Maxwell Lee Complex. In the midst of a barren urban landscape, apparently, stood four towers protected by more security than most army bases.

Sarah hadn't expected this strange development, but wasn't completely surprised by it, either. This new wrinkle had, however, forced her to alter her plan. She had no time to scheme a way to enter Maxwell Lee undetected, so she improvised. She had returned to the equipment cache, taken the sniper rifle, and gone in search of a far-away perch. In the wee hours of Friday morning, Sarah found another project tower a block away that offered an expansive view of the Maxwell Lee Complex.

Of course, the same people who had installed the security system at Maxwell Lee were aware of the far-away tower's prime viewing location. This building was also watched. But it wasn't nearly as well protected as Maxwell Lee itself, and Sarah had had no problem sneaking her way in. Once inside, she climbed to the highest vacant room, knocked out a window, and waited for Tim Sutton's imminent arrival at Maxwell Lee.

Now, Sarah focused the M40A3's scope on the roof of one of the towers.

Twenty stories above the ground, a young man in a thick winter parka surveyed the complex's perimeter with binoculars. A few minutes after Sarah began watching the man, he suddenly spotted something below in his binoculars, and communicated the sighting into a walkie-talkie he was carrying.

Expectantly, Sarah tracked the scope down the tower and over to the entrance of the complex. Sure enough, there was Tim Sutton's small, light blue Taurus rolling slowly into the heart of Maxwell Lee.

Sarah steadied the rifle as a giant, menacing figure approached the driver's side of Sutton's vehicle. She slid her finger across the M40A3's trigger. If all went according to the instructions Sutton had been given, Sutton would be fine. But if Maxwell Lee foot-soldiers like this behemoth didn't follow the chain of command, things could get violent. Sarah might have to lend Sutton a lethal helping hand.

At first, the large man appeared to angrily motion for Sutton to turn his vehicle around and leave. A few moments later, however, he motioned for Sutton to remain where he was. Then the man walked back to the entrance of the complex and talked on a cell-phone.

Shortly thereafter, a Cadillac Escalade with tinted windows arrived at the entrance to the complex. The vehicle came to a stop between Sarah and the giant man, partially obscuring her view. The giant man began conversing with someone in the passenger's side of the vehicle. A moment later, he was handed an object that he put in his pocket. Then the behemoth turned and trudged back to Sutton's car.

Because of her obscured view, Sarah hadn't been able to tell what the object was. She doubted it was a gun. The giant was almost certainly carrying at least one firearm already. If it was a gun, however, Tim Sutton's trip to Maxwell Lee was about to take a dangerous turn.

Sarah set the giant man's torso between the crosshairs of her scope. She couldn't afford to take any chances. If the man pulled a gun out of his jacket, she wouldn't wait to see if he fired. A millisecond after the man produced his firearm, a high-caliber sniper round would rip through his chest.

Of course, if this happened, Sarah knew, the men in the Escalade would assume Sutton had fired the shot. They would have to be dealt with, too. The glass on the vehicle was tinted, but it wasn't bulletproof--not against these bullets. And Sarah had enough ammunition to make sure that no one got out of the Escalade alive...

Thankfully, the giant man unwittingly decided to spare his own life. He pulled a digital camera out of his pocket, snapped a few photos of Sutton, and returned to the Escalade, which, in turn, rolled up alongside Sutton's vehicle. The giant man motioned for Sutton to climb out of his vehicle and into the SUV. Sutton did as he was told. Sarah couldn't see inside of the SUV. She could only hope Sutton remained unharmed and wait for him to reemerge.

Ten minutes after he climbed into the Escalade, Sutton hopped out. He was visibly shaken, but physically unharmed. More importantly, Sarah watched him slip a piece of paper into the pocket of his jeans. This paper had the information Sarah needed.

Sarah watched as Sutton slowly turned his car around and drove out of the complex. She then she trained the rifle on the Escalade, in case it decided to follow Sutton. Finally, satisfied that the whole scenario had run its course, Sarah slowly lowered her weapon. On to the next item of business.

****

As Sarah drove a stolen silver Acura TL west on Interstate 90, she glanced over at the laptop sitting on the vehicle's passenger seat.

A wire ran from the laptop out the Acura's passenger's-side window, and fed into a Global Positioning System antenna that Sarah had attached to the roof of the vehicle. On the laptop's screen was a map with a small red beacon. The beacon corresponded with a transmitter that Sarah had attached to Tim Sutton's Taurus while he had been talking to Jeff Hutchins at St. Paul's.

Sutton had left Chicago a full 90 minutes ahead of Sarah, but with the GPS tracking system, it had been easy for her to follow his trail. Now, Sarah could see that Tim had stopped at a hotel just outside of Sioux Falls, South Dakota.

A half-hour later, Sarah pulled the Acura into the parking lot of a Super-8 Motel. She took a parking space four cars down from Sutton's. Sarah hopped out into the frigid night air and approached the Taurus. After a brief inspection of the vehicle, she could see that the piece of paper wasn't anywhere to be seen. Most likely, the paper was still in the pocket of Sutton's jeans.

Sarah scanned the two-story unit of rooms directly in front of Sutton's car. Figuring out which room he inhabited would take time. Sarah would make a quick sight-check of the rooms on the first floor by walking by and peeking through the darkened windows using her night-vision goggles. To scan the second floor windows, however, she would need to scale the hotel wall. It was a risky proposition, even for someone of Sarah's guile. A hotel parking lot could be a busy venue, even in the middle of the night.

If Sarah couldn't determine Tim's room number by sight, she would have to sneak into the hotel lobby and get a look at the registry. She most likely had to sneak into the lobby anyway, in order to steal an electronic room key.

Once Sarah had determined Sutton's room and secured a key-card, she had to wait within earshot of his room until the next morning. If, upon waking, Sutton took a shower, Sarah could silently enter his room while he lathered and get a look at the piece of paper in his jeans. If he didn't shower, Sarah would be forced to wait for another opportunity. Unless...

Approaching the first floor, Sarah saw that only a single room was lit. She approached the window and saw that the room's thick burgundy curtain was only drawn three-quarters closed. Crouching down, Sarah slowly raised her eyes to the window, peering in. Tim Sutton was passed out on the room's queen-sized bed.

Wearing only boxer shorts and a white t-shirt, Sutton had dozed off without drawing back any of the bed coverings. The TV was still on, as were most of the lights in the room. Sarah could see Sutton's blue jeans, along with his Dartmouth sweatshirt, piled messily to the left of his bed. She would still have to enter the room to get into the jeans...

Or not.

On the table directly in front of the window, less than two feet away from Sarah, sat a small pile of miscellanea. A pair of keys attached to an "X-Men" key chain lay to the left of a red "Spiderman" wallet. To the right of the wallet was a scratched gray cell phone surrounded by scattered loose change. And just to the right of the cell-phone sat two pieces of paper.

On the first scrap of paper was a phone number. From the 626 area code Sarah determined that it was John Kenninger's number, given to Sutton by Jeff Hutchins.

The second piece of paper was folded in half. On the left, visible side of the paper, above a set of numbers that Sarah ignored, were the halves of two words.

"Sea-"
"Ha-"

Three minutes later, Sarah was back on the Interstate, heading Northwest.

CHAPTER 14

As the Lear jet soared west, Jeff Hutchins gazed out the small oval window next to his seat. Far below, the sprawling Pacific Ocean sparkled under the midday sun. As Hutchins took in the spectacular view, he shook his head and allowed himself a smile of disbelief.

He sure hadn't seen any of this coming.

"Mr. Hutchins." Jeff Archer's voice pulled Hutchins from his thoughts.

Hutchins spun his head away from the window. Archer was making his way from the cockpit down the nearly-empty plane's narrow aisle. He reached the seat opposite Hutchins, directly behind a napping Percy Danielson, and sat down.

"Mr. Hutchins," Archer continued, "I've got good news and bad news. The bad news is that, as I feared, we can't fly directly into Dalian. We'll have to land in Beijing under diplomatic cover, then travel over land from there. Unfortunately, this is going to cost us an additional day of travel time. The Haihu will get to Dalian a full 24 hours before we do."

Hutchins nodded slowly.

"And the good news?"

"We found John Kenninger, and he's okay."

Hutchins blinked.

"John Kenninger? But how-"

"After you confirmed that your 'Michael Smith' lived in California," Archer interrupted, "We scanned our list of all ex-agents living in the state. Kenninger fit the profile: he's 56 years old, has plenty of connections in the Asian theater, and he worked with you in the past. He'd also had a number of run-ins with his superiors and had been passed over for promotion several times prior to his retirement. We figured he was your contact."

Hutchins sighed. In hindsight, withholding Kenninger's name when he was questioned at St. Paul's seemed pretty stupid.

"But, he's okay?"

"Yes...for the most part," Archer returned. "Physically, he's fine. But his last two weeks haven't exactly been a walk in the park."

"What do you mean?"

"Well," Archer continued, "CIA agents broke into his house this morning, and found him restrained, gagged, and tied down to his bed. Apparently, he hadn't moved from that position since the Thursday before last; nearly two full weeks."

"But, I don't understand!" Hutchins replied, aghast. "How could he have survived if he's been tied to his bed, let alone be 'okay'?"

"Because," Archer said, "An intravenous drip unit was attached to his arm, apparently as well prepared as anything you'd find at a top hospital. He's understandably shaken up, but otherwise fine."

Hutchins frowned. Archer's tone seemed almost like that of a proud parent.

"That doesn't make any sense! Why would someone break into Kenninger's house, incapacitate him, yet keep him alive?" Hutchins raised his eyebrows. "Was this the work of your lethal mystery woman?"

The question caught Archer off guard. He quickly recovered and shot Hutchins a glare.

"Mr. Hutchins," Archer commanded icily, "Before I go any further, we need to make some things absolutely clear."

"Please, call me Jeff," Hutchins managed, attempting to pump a little levity into Archer's sudden change in demeanor.

"Jeff," Archer continued, his tone unwavering. "As I mentioned back in New Hampshire, I have a thorough understanding of you as an individual. I respect you as a former agent, and I have no doubt that, had your career not taken a downward spiral, you would have ridden the Bureau's fast-track a long way. Why am I saying all of this? Because I think you're a man who understands the sanctity of certain institutions."

Hutchins nodded knowingly.

"And when I say 'institutions,'" Archer went on, "You know I don't mean the FBI, the CIA, or the NSA. I mean other organizations; those that conduct their business behind enemy lines with no record.of their operations being kept. Organizations whose members do not exist. Are you following me?"

Hutchins nodded a second time.

"Now," Archer proceeded, never diverting his eyes from Hutchins, "The fact that the existence of these 'shadow' groups' is kept off the record underscores the absolute sanctity of the secrets they keep. Secrets, however dark, that encompass an unyielding effort to protect the American people. Secrets that are exempt from the boundaries of law."

Archer leaned toward Hutchins, his eyes glazed with an expression of intense calm.

"Jeff, if an American civilian were entrusted with, let's say, top-secret CIA or FBI information, and he let this information slip, that civilian might find himself sitting in a federal courtroom, on trial for treason against these United States. But with these other groups...there would be no courtroom. There would be no trial. There would only be justice--swift and vicious. Are we clear? Nod your head and tell me that you understand exactly what I'm saying to you right now."

Hutchins gulped, then deliberately moved his head up and down a final time.

"I will take whatever information you impart to my grave," he asserted. "I will never repeat or so much as hint at knowing about any of this information. I know that doing otherwise would prove, at best, fatal. Mr. Archer, I understand completely."

Archer nodded, and leaned back in his seat. He allowed a tiny smile.

"Please, call me Jeff."

Hutchins exhaled forcefully and tried to return Archer's smile.

"Okay, Jeff. So...who is this girl?"

Archer's serious expression returned. He took a slow, deliberate breath.

"Her name is Sarah. The last name isn't important. What is important is that she was the lead operator in the Ceiling Program.

The details of this program are outside your need to know. Suffice it to say, Ceiling's operations were global in scope, classified in nature, and specialized to the extent that only a select few individuals could carry them out. Sarah was one of these individuals."

"We found her," Archer continued, "in Marine Corps basic training at Parris Island. At the time, we were secretly videotaping military recruits, and studying the tapes to find individuals who fit a particular profile."

"We weren't expecting to find someone like Sarah. She didn't fit our 'mold': she's a small woman, not imposing in the least, with freckles and bright red hair. She doesn't resemble a soldier, let alone a Ceiling operator. We wouldn't have even noticed her, except..."

Archer paused.

"A few weeks into her time at boot camp, she was cornered in her bunk by five male recruits. Whatever they were planning to do, the poor bastards probably thought she wouldn't put up much of a fight..."

"The things she did to those guys..."

Archer shook his head in disbelief.

"We ended up having to fabricate a press release about five recruits who were blown up in an ordinance disaster, just to ensure that the caskets would be closed!"

"Attempted rape or not, Sarah would have faced a serious psychological evaluation after a slaughter like that, and landed her tight little ass in a military prison."

"But that year," Archer continued, "Ceiling was there. When we saw what she'd done, and the total absence of remorse or emotional affect, we made sure that she remained in boot camp. And we began to watch her. Once we'd seen her in action, we realized this was the person who would open new doors for our program, allow us to infiltrate--"

Archer cut himself off.

"In any case," he continued, "Once in the Ceiling program, Sarah evolved into the ultimate special ops combatant. Her size belies an unbelievable strength-to-body-weight ratio that allows her a nearly unlimited range of movement. She is proficient in every weapon that can be shot, and every form of combat that can be taught. She speaks several languages. She knows computers, electronics, and combat communication systems. She has been taught how to maximize her unassuming appearance to blend into any populated environment. In wilderness settings, she is virtually invisible. Sarah is, for lack of a better term, perfect."

Hutchins nodded. "But?" he returned.

"But," Archer proceeded, "there were problems. Under our tutelage, Sarah became fully aware of how singular her abilities truly were. And the more aware she became, the more eager she was to singularly test her own potential."

"How so?" Hutchins was leaning forward with increasing curiosity.

"For example," Archer replied, "we conducted an exercise in Alaska midway through Sarah's indoctrination into Ceiling. Sarah was deposited into the wilderness with no supplies of any kind and directed to fend for herself for a period of weeks. Of course, we had established multiple monitoring points to observe her actions and study her decision making process."

"Predictably, Sarah immediately surveyed her surroundings, investigated signs of wildlife, and set traps to catch her food. What happened next was, well…bizarre."

"Within a day, Sarah had managed to trap herself a large buck. She advanced on the struggling animal with a wooden shank she had fashioned, fatally puncturing the animal's throat. Then…she didn't do anything. She dragged the massive creature out into the open, climbed up a pine tree, and waited. Every half-day or so she would descend to drink some water from a nearby brook. The rest of the time, she just sat in that tree like a robot."

"After four days, a grizzly bear the size of a small car showed up to sniff the deer carcass. As soon as the bear arrived, Sarah sprung into action. She dropped out of the tree, directly in front of the bear, making sure it knew she was there. Then she attacked it. After going four days without food, she went straight at the bear."

"We scrapped the whole exercise immediately and drove into the site as fast as we could. We found Sarah lying in an ocean of blood between a deer and a bear carcass. Her right arm was broken in three places. She had cuts on her thighs so deep it was a miracle she wasn't paralyzed from the waist down. She was soaked with blood. But she was fully conscious. And her mental state was nothing other than simple satisfaction. She had wanted to pit herself against the best nature had to offer, and come out on top. And she had succeeded."

"Upon her eventual activation as a Ceiling agent," Archer continued, "Sarah had a perfect operational record. There was no task she couldn't accomplish. But her behavior outside of the operating environment became more and more detached, increasingly aloof, until, eventually...she went A.W.O.L. One day, she just vanished, and we haven't seen or heard from her in years. Until she started sending us messages from the Haihu."

Hutchins let out a low whistle, and leaned back against the cushion of his seat.

"Wow...and you're sure those messages were sent by her?"

Archer nodded.

"I'm positive. Not only did Sarah send the messages, she wanted us to see them. Sarah possesses a full understanding of military intelligence. She knew her satellite transmissions would be intercepted, so she secretly inserted the name Ceiling into her communications, along with her Ceiling operator code name, 'Apple'. Sarah used the most basic code, knowing our intelligence people would crack it and would notify me."

Hutchins was puzzled.

"But, why? Why would she contact you after so long? And how the hell is she connected to Eric Sutton?"

Archer nodded; he and Hutchins were now on the same page.

"That," Archer replied, "Is what you are going to help me figure out. Now, as Mr. Danielson intimated yesterday, I have read everything the CIA has on file regarding Eric Sutton, most of it information you gathered. What I need from you, now, are theories about his motivations. You know this guy: What is Eric Sutton doing in North Korea? How does he know Sarah? If he's in danger, why would he go to Sarah for help? Does he know she's contacting us? If, as I believe, he isn't in danger, why does he contact Sarah at all? And why is he involving his brother in any of this?"

Hutchins took a moment to digest Archer's questions. He turned and stared out at the brilliant blue sea, lost in contemplation. After ten seconds, he turned back to Archer.

"Well…the one possibility that keeps going through my mind, that would answer some of our questions, is drugs."

Archer nodded. Both he and Hutchins were well aware of North Korea's involvement in international drug trafficking.

"Go on."

"Okay," Hutchins proceeded, "We know Sutton is incredibly smart. So, he concocts a plan to fly to Africa to steal over five hundred-thousand dollars in cash, and get himself back to America in relative obscurity. So let's say this genius kid uses his new cash as seed money for a burgeoning drug business. Business is good, so he expands the scope of his operations."

"Okay," Archer nodded again, understanding where Hutchins was going. "So at some point, he makes a connection with a North Korean supply line. North Korea is producing a huge supply of heroin, opium and God knows what else. Sutton manages to plug himself into that supply. That would explain the container that Sarah, and Tim Sutton, are tracking."

Hutchins nodded, and continued.

"Then, possibly, he betrays his supplier, leading to his abduction. Or, more likely, he actually moves there on his own to get himself higher up the supply chain. Heck, the Koreans might have recruited his services, if he were talented enough."

Hutchins frowned.

"A bunch of things still don't wash, though. For starters, five hundred-grand in seed money doesn't exactly make Eric Sutton into Pablo Escobar. He would have had to have moved a bunch of product over a period of years to generate the reputation to be noticed by the North Koreans. It doesn't match the timeline we're working with. In addition, this kid should have been on the CIA watch list before he even began his career as a drug lord. In all that time, he never pops up on the DEA mainframe, not once? He manages all of this alleged drug running, without anyone putting two and two together until now?"

Archer looked down at his lap and cracked a small smile.

"I think your theory makes more sense than you realize, Jeff," he said softly. Archer looked up at the seat in front of him. "Wouldn't you agree, Percy?"

Hutchins' eyes darted to the seat in front of Archer's. Danielson had apparently awoken from his nap and rotated his stout body 90 degrees, silently but intently following their conversation. Now, his only response to Archer's question was a determined stare that Archer returned in kind. Hutchins uncomfortably shifted his eyes back and forth between the two men.

"In any case," he offered quickly, "I have no idea what any of this has to do with Sarah."

Archer turned back to Hutchins.

"Actually," he replied, "Your drug theory has raised a fair possibility for her involvement: Sarah may be trying to work her way back into the fold of the Ceiling program."

Hutchins raised his eyebrows.

"Really? After all this time?"

Archer nodded.

"It's possible. Someone like Sarah thinks outside the box. She may have simply decided that she is ready to come back to work. And, in doing so, she has decided to offer us an olive branch of sorts: the capture of Eric Sutton. This would explain why she contacted us intentionally."

Danielson, whose expression had softened somewhat, threw his own two cents into the pot.

"It would explain her connection to Eric Sutton," he offered, looking earnestly at Hutchins. "She may have contacted him somehow, and gained his trust with the idea of getting close enough to capture him."

"You're right," Hutchins concurred. "She might have even told him she could arrange for his older brother's safe passage into North Korea. That would obviously get her to Eric. So she alerts you guys to her intent. Then she goes in, gets Eric, brings him out, and delivers him into your custody. Makes sense to me."

Archer and Danielson nodded in unison. Hutchins was satisfied. After years chasing and subsequently trying to forget about the shady Eric Sutton, he was finally learning something new.

"There's just one thing I'm still curious about," he added. "Why would Sarah choose Eric Sutton as the collar that would get her back into your good graces? I mean, after all this time, is he really that big of a deal? There's a long list of people who have killed a few government employees, or stolen a lot more than a couple hundred grand from the Feds. Why Eric Sutton?"

Danielson silently eyed Hutchins. Then he shot a glance at Archer, rotated his body back around into his seat, and resumed his nap. Archer looked back over at Hutchins.

"Who knows?" he returned. "The bottom line is, we've managed to get a few of our questions answered."

"Hopefully, the rest of the answers are waiting for us in Dalian."

CHAPTER 15

"Christ," Jeff Archer muttered. "Thank God the damn boat is so big."

He took his eye away from the telescope and stared back in frustration at Percy Danielson.

"Percy, are you telling me this is as close as the CIA could get us? We must be ten goddamned miles away from that thing!"

Archer, Danielson, Hutchins and five China-based CIA operatives were staring from a British-owned penthouse, thirty floors above the bustling city of Dalian, China, population five million. It was near midday on Friday. The Haihu, the distant target of Archer's gaze, had been in port over 24 hours. The CIA didn't have many established hide sites in Dalian—at least none suitable for spying on the Haihu in her current berth. So Archer and Danielson had been forced to set up shop in the Dalian Development Zone, or DDZ-- the city's district open to foreign investment.

Unfortunately, the DDZ was located at the northernmost tip of Dalian Wan Bay, while Dalian Harbor, where the Haihu was docked, sat at the southern end of the bay. Archer turned to an agent who was fiddling with a radio receiver situated next to three high powered telescopes.

"How are we coming on that link-up with Sergeant Sariani?" he demanded.

"We'll be ready in one minute, sir," the agent replied. "We received intel from Sariani's team at 0530 this morning. They're in place, waiting for our go."

As Archer impatiently waited for his radio link, Hutchins peered through one of the telescopes. The powerful lens was focused on a target so distant, that any nudge of the scope sent the Haihu careening from view.

Good Lord, that's a big ship!

Hutchins never ceased to be amazed at the size of today's modern cargo ships. Equally impressive was the towering stack of multicolored cargo containers that soared high above the ship's main deck. Hutchins figured hundreds of dockworkers were probably scrambling about the Haihu; he was just too far way to see them.

"Okay, sir, we're up."

The agent next to Archer handed him a headset with an attached microphone. Hutchins, Danielson, and the other agents were given ear-pieces. As Archer, Danielson and Hutchins stared through their respective telescopes at the Haihu, Archer spoke into his headset.

"Squirrel, this is Tree, over,"

Immediately, a grainy response crackled through the receiver.

"Tree, this is Squirrel. I read you loud and clear, over."

"Good," Archer responded. "Squirrel, I can barely see the ship from our location. You'll have to be my eyes, over."

"Copy. Over."

"What's the situation down there, over?"

"Not much activity to report," the voice in the radio returned. "We've been here all morning; they've off-loaded and loaded a few crates, but that's it. This was supposed to be a brief stop before continuing down the coast and back to the US. Something seems to be holding things up. Over."

"Anything else? Over?"

"I have a group of eight crew members talking to some soldiers from the Dalian Port Authority," the voice continued. "Judging from the language, the crew appears to be Korean. The DPA guys seem to want the boat out of Dalian A.S.A.P., but the eight are protesting; one of the men has gestured several times, as if he's waiting for a required phone call. Over."

Hutchins raised his eyebrows. The agent was so close to the Haihu that he was actually listening to conversations taking place on the docks! Whoever this guy was, he was good.

"Squirrel," Archer continued, "does this look like a drug exchange to you? Over."

"That's a possibility," the voice confirmed. "These guys may have a drug container that they don't want to place on board until they get the proper OK from above. The DPA guys must be players, though; otherwise, they would have drawn guns and forced this ship to leave hours ago. But they're clearly becoming impatient. Over."

Archer pulled away from his scope and looked down in contemplation. Hatching an idea, he returned to the lens.

"Squirrel, do you have an idea where that questionable container might be located on the dock, over?"

"Tree, I'm looking at a cluster of probable containers sitting in a row not more than fifty feet from the ship, but until they make a move, I won't know which one it is, over."

"Squirrel," Archer replied, "Do you have a thermal imager with you, over?"

"Affirmative, I came in with thermal goggles, over."

"Squirrel, put your goggles on and take a look at those containers. Over."

"Roger that."

Archer, Hutchins, and the others waited in silence. Thirty seconds later, the voice chattered in their headphones again.

"Tree, we have a positive ID on your container, over."

"Squirrel," Archer immediately replied, "You have a 100 percent positive ID on the box in question? Over?"

"Affirmative. Someone used an Infrared Marker to draw 'Apple' in giant letters on the front and side of one of the boxes. I'd say your operator was definitely here to tag the drug box for us, over."

Archer covered the headset microphone as he glanced over at Hutchins.

"Looks like you were right about the drug angle. Sarah even tagged the outgoing drug shipment so we'd be certain what we were de-"

Archer was interrupted by the voice in his headset.

"Tree, we've got a second set of infrared markings on another container. I almost missed them because they aren't anywhere near the first set of containers. Over."

"What have you got, Squirrel? Over."

"Tree, the second tagged container is off in the stacks, about 100 meters from the ship. If it's part of a drug shipment, it's not going out today. I'm reading the same word on the side: 'Apple'. And it looks like...an arrow pointed down is drawn on the side of the container, as well. Over."

"Squirrel," Archer replied, a hint of excitement in his voice, "What's the traffic like by that second crate? Can you get one of your guys over there to check it out? I want to know if there's anything underneath that crate. Over."

"Tree, there's nothing going on by the second crate. I'm pretty well dug in here, but I can put a man there in less than ten...Tree, we have another discussion taking place between the Koreans and the Port Authority. Stand by."

During the pause that followed, Hutchins cast a curious glance at Archer, who remained glued to his telescope. What was the significance of the second cargo container? Before Hutchins could think, the voice crackled through his headset once again.

"Tree, it looks like the Koreans have given up on waiting for word on that marked container. A few of them are getting on the ship. The rest are taking off, along with the DPA guys. The dock around the Haihu is clearing out; looks like the Haihu may be heading out to sea without that container, over."

"Copy that, Squirrel," Archer returned. "Sit tight for now. When the Haihu is gone and that place is quiet, see if you can get me an up-close description of those containers, over."

"Copy that. Squirrel out."

In the ensuing half-hour, the men watched the massive Haihu slowly pull away from its moorings in Dalian Harbor.

"Well," Danielson offered, "we were right on the drug angle, apparently."

"Looks that way," Archer acknowledged. "I think we've stumbled on an international drug-smuggling ring."

"I agree," Hutchins concurred. "My thought process might be jet-lagged to hell, but...I've got a theory on how it works."

Archer and Danielson listened silently.

"It looks," Hutchins began, "Like the Chinese and North Koreans are in cahoots, shuttling containers and drug shipments across the Korean/Chinese order to the US market."

"I figure when a cargo ship docks in Dalian," Hutchins continued, "an empty container is offloaded and shipped back to the border for reloading. At the same time, a full container recently arrived from the border is loaded onto the ship."

"If that's true," Danielson replied, "why is this container of drugs just languishing out in the open on the docks?"

"I know why," Archer stated. "This drug-running system requires the cooperation of the Chinese government, at least on a local or provincial level. But there's no way the Koreans are going to fully trust their Chinese partners, right?"

Hutchins and Danielson nodded in agreement.

"So," Archer continued, "they have a safeguard in place. When a boat docks, there's a middle-man on board whose job it is to broker the deal between the U.S. drug dealers and the Koreans and Chinese. He hops off the boat with a big briefcase full of cash and waits for the container full of drugs to arrive from the border. When that occurs, money is exchanged, the Chinese get their cut, and the remaining cash heads to North Korea."

"But," Archer concluded, "The container isn't loaded on the boat until the Koreans know that their money is safe in North Korea. Think about it: it puts pressure on the Chinese. The longer the system takes, the longer that crate sits on the dock, out in the open. If the drugs are discovered, it's the Chinese who are left holding the bag. The Koreans disavow involvement. Basically, it gives the Chinese a reason to ensure that the briefcase arrives at the North Korean border ASAP."

"Then why is this container still sitting on the dock?" Danielson persisted. "If they're supposed to get a signal, why didn't they get it?"

"Oh," Archer offered quietly, "I think I know why..."

The voice on the radio interrupted further questions.

"Tree, this is Squirrel, over."

"Squirrel, this is Tree," Archer replied. "Go ahead. Over."

"We're taking an up-close look at your containers. There's nothing at the first container. It's just sitting there by itself, locked shut. I think we'll have to take your operator at her word that it's full of drugs…but we found something at the second container. Over."

"What have you got, Squirrel? Over."

"Underneath the second crate there's a foot-wide depression in the concrete creating a cavity; that's what that big arrow was pointing to. We looked in the cavity and found a laptop computer wrapped in plastic. We booted up the laptop. There's a file on the desktop addressed to…well, to you, Tree. Over."

"Squirrel, give me the gist of the message! Over."

"Tree, it says that if we enlist the right Korean personnel, we should be able to haul that drug container off this dock without the Chinese batting an eyelash. The message also says that a GPS transmitter is attached to the money headed to the Korean border, and that the receiver connected to this laptop will pinpoint its location. The message closes with this sentence, and I quote: 'Get rid of the evidence, and make it his fault'. Over."

"Copy that, Squirrel. Bag up that laptop and pull your team out of there. Well done. Over."

"Roger that. Squirrel, over and out."

Archer pulled off his headset and stared down at the penthouse's plush red carpet.

"I know what she's doing," he said softly.

"So do I," Danielson cut in. "She's giving us a way to set Eric Sutton up."

Hutchins was confused.

"What do you mean?" he asked.

Danielson turned to Hutchins.

"Think about it. Using her instructions, we go down to the dock and steal those drugs. Then we sneak over the Korean border and take the cash. Assuming no one knows we're here, the Koreans will have a very short list of suspects-"

"Which points to Eric Sutton," Hutchins finished. "Sarah knows he's plugged into the drug ring, so she's giving us a way to use that against him!"

"Exactly," Danielson replied. "All we have to do is drop word of his involvement into North Korean backchannels. If they think he's taken their cash and drugs, they'll kill him. Basically, Sarah has provided us with a back-up plan."

"A back-up plan?" Hutchins asked, suddenly confused. "What do you mean, a back-up plan? Why would a back-up plan to Sutton's arrest be his execution by the North Koreans? That won't bring him to justice! And why would Sarah go to all of this effort? Just to offer an 'Olive Branch' to her former employers?"

Danielson was suddenly uncomfortable. Looking for an escape route, he turned to Archer. Hutchins looked at Archer, too, and realized that the silver-haired man had been silent for some time. Archer was still staring at the penthouse's carpet, deep in thought.

"Well, Commander?" Danielson demanded. "What's your take on the situation?"

Archer didn't respond.

"Jeff, why would Sarah do all of this?" It was Hutchins this time. "Why would she go to all this trouble to provide an elaborate back-up plan? What the hell is so important about Eric Sutton?"

Archer was silent for a few more seconds, before slowly raising his head to face Hutchins and Danielson.

"There's an issue here that neither of you are considering," Archer said coldly. "Sarah has decided to enter North Korea to find Eric Sutton after earning his trust by safely transporting his older brother across the Pacific. But before leaving for the border, she apparently thought to launch this elaborate back-up plan. Don't you realize what that means?"

Archer stared hard at the two men across from him.

"It means," Archer finished, "She thinks she might not make it back."

CHAPTER 16

Sarah slid the metal disc across the opening in the roof of the cargo container.

Today would be a busy day.

Lying flat on top of the container, she scanned the bay. Dalian Harbor and the sprawling city beyond were beginning to emerge in the pale light of dawn. Sarah nimbly jumped into a crouching position, preparing to move.

The containers on the Haihu were stacked four high and packed tightly, forming a massive rectangular block of steel. Sarah was 200 feet above the ocean, on one of the top-most containers, exposed to a strong and cold north wind. She faced the stern where, stretching from starboard to port, loomed the tall white superstructure that quartered the crew. Sarah had become intimately familiar with this section of the ship. It held, among other things, the kitchen she had raided each day, and the bathroom faucet she used to fill Tim Sutton's water bottle.

Sarah scrambled along the edge of the container. It was the last to be loaded onto the Haihu; therefore, it sat on the outer edge, one side fully exposed to the elements.

Sarah deftly slid off the exposed side and clung to the edge of the container with both hands, hanging from the side like a rock climber.

Then, with a maneuver she had perfected over the past 10 days, Sarah swung from container to container, hand over hand, with the agility of a tree monkey, toward the stern of the ship. The grip of a single hand was all that kept Sarah from plummeting hundreds of feet to a watery grave.

Within minutes, Sarah reached the stern. Still dangling, she peeked around the last container and inspected the white superstructure. Confident that no one was watching, she sprang onto a fixed ladder on the side of the superstructure and climbed to its top, where several large antennas were clustered. As she had done at least once every day, she slid her hands under a harness strapped beneath her black windbreaker and removed the laptop. Producing a series of wires, Sarah methodically used them to connect the laptop to one of the antennas. Then she powered up the laptop, and began to type.

At this stage of the voyage there was little need to continue sending e-mail. Her messages had almost certainly been decoded by now, and Commander Archer was probably hot on her trail. But Sarah was far too disciplined to break from the routine she had established; Jeff Hutchins would get a final e-mail from "John Kenninger", whether he read it or not.

A few minutes later, Sarah finished typing, and sent her message, along with Tim's final note to Dragon Comics. She disconnected the laptop from the antenna, and reached behind her back and produced the silenced 9mm pistol acquired in Chicago, along with the clear plastic she had stowed in the cargo container. She carefully sealed the laptop and pistol in plastic, and secured the package to her back.

As the Haihu neared the towering green cranes of Dalian Harbor, Sarah returned to the ladder. She deftly descended past the stacks of containers until she reached the main deck, then crept to the side of the ship farthest from the long approaching concrete dock. As the giant vessel sidled up to a dock bustling with workers, Sarah crouched above the water far below. Her 10-day voyage was about to come to an end.

When the Haihu finally eased to a stop alongside the dock, Sarah stealthily plunged into Dalian Wan Bay. The frigid water tried to consume her mind and body, but Sarah barely noticed. Thirty seconds after her plunge, Sarah pulled her shivering frame to the wall of the dock.

Using crude handholds in the pock-marked concrete, she yanked her small frame upward. Pressed tightly against the wall, she surveyed her surroundings.

Wearing orange hard hats, about 100 Chinese longshoremen were variously handling cargo. Sarah watched as one of the loading cranes slid out over the Haihu to grab a container. As she had suspected, her container was the first to be offloaded.

Several longshoremen guided the crane operator in placing the container onto the bed of the cargo truck. As soon as the container was in place, the truck rumbled away from the dock. Tim Sutton was on his way to North Korea.

Concurrently, Sarah knew, an identical truck was departing from the North Korean border en route to Dalian, where it would arrive in the late afternoon. Until then, Sarah would hide and wait.

As the sun rose in the sky, Sarah crept onto the dock and away from the Haihu. When she was sure that all of the harbor employees were sufficiently absorbed in daily tasks, Sarah bolted across fifty yards of open concrete. Hidden amidst hundreds of candy-colored containers, Sarah stared back at the cargo ship. It was time to think like a Ranger.

Sarah knew that the CIA had agents near Dalian. But Commander Archer was too smart to allow the CIA to apprehend or locate Sarah. She was sure he would opt instead for Sergeant Jim Sariani's Ranger team, currently stationed in the Korean DMZ--the same Ranger team which, coincidentally, had been on the S.W.I.P.E. perimeter 18 days earlier.

The Rangers hadn't arrived yet. In the dead of night, Sarah had pinpointed these four men in a snow covered field. If they were hiding on the dock now, in daylight, she would have known. When they did arrive, however, Sarah knew that Sariani would hide his men as close to the Haihu as possible to best assess the situation…but where?

Sarah scanned the dock area directly in front of the ship. There were a few loose containers, but the wide open space was teeming with dockworkers. There was no place to hide.

Sariani's best option, Sarah realized, would be to crawl up the side of the dock from the water, and peer over as she had done. Using a fiber-optic cable or mirror on a stick, Sariani could survey the dock without exposing himself. He could then get close enough to possibly pick up any conversations taking place near the ship. Sergeant Sariani was a smart soldier. This was the move he would make.

Sarah crept back into the container stacks. Looking for a suitable place to hide her laptop, she spied a small depression in the concrete below one of the containers. Removing the package from underneath her ocean-soaked windbreaker, she pulled out the pistol. Then she rewrapped the package and approached the container.

The box was out in the open, exposed. That meant that Sariani would see it from his hiding space...assuming that Commander Archer told him what to look for.

The container's exposed position also meant, of course, that Sarah might be spotted by someone. But the crate was well removed from the present dock activities. As long as Sarah didn't linger in front of it, she shouldn't be seen.

Sarah knelt in front of the small concrete depression and quickly slipped the laptop snuggly beneath the container. When she was satisfied that the laptop was sufficiently concealed, Sarah stood up.

Sarah produced a fat, silver marking pen from the pocket of her windbreaker. After momentarily studying the side of the container, she went to work.

****

One, two, three, four, five, six, seven, eight...

Sarah had been taught this technique long ago in the Ceiling program. Repeating the numbers over and over in her head, she established an internal metronome, a rhythm for her ensuing actions. This allowed her to mentally formulate a series of complex tasks like the one she was about to begin.

From her hiding place amongst the container stacks, Sarah saw the delivery truck from North Korea arrive with the next shipment of drugs. The truck had an escort: a North Korean olive green military troop transport vehicle. As the two trucks rolled to a stop in front of the Haihu, Sarah spotted two soldiers in the cab of the lead vehicle. She guessed that at least eight more armed men sat under the green canvas in the rear.

One, two, three, four...

One of the giant loading cranes plucked the drug-filled container from the bed of the truck, placing it among a row of boxes fifty feet from the Haihu. As the box touched the ground, a group of eleven men approached the military troop transport. Eight of these men, Sarah knew, were Korean and American drug dealers. She had seen each of them as she crept through the bowels of the Haihu. The other three men were Chinese Port Authority officials.

Sarah watched as two Korean soldiers climbed out of the cab. The one who appeared to be in charge yelled to the back of the truck. Ten soldiers, all armed with AK-47 assault rifles, immediately poured out of the rear of the vehicle, encircling the group. It was a typical display of muscle. The North Koreans were reminding the Chinese and their Korean-American associates who was running the show. These were the kind of theatrics Sarah had been awaiting.

Five, six, seven, eight...

There were now 23 men standing 15 feet away from the drug container, all armed. The North Korean soldiers closely watched the Chinese, the Chinese closely watched the Koreans, and drug dealers closely watched both the Chinese and the Korean soldiers. And everyone periodically snatched glances at the black duffle bag carried by one of the Koreans--a bag Sarah knew contained several million American dollars.

None of the men, however, were watching the crate or transport vehicle. Nor were any of the dockworkers near the Haihu. Long ago, they had learned to ignore and avoid the crate and the soldiers if they valued their lives. As the metronome in her head clicked back and forth, Sarah steadied an unblinking stare on the 23 men. She was waiting to see the money.

The drug dealers would hand the duffle bag over to the soldiers, who would deliver it to North Korea. First, however, the Chinese had to get their cut. Crisply-stacked hundred dollar bills would be removed from the bag, and no one would be able to resist staring at so much money.

Sarah withdrew into an almost meditative state, preparing to move.

The drug dealer with the duffle bag addressed the lead soldier. Then he nodded, gesturing toward the Chinese. Now the drug dealer moved toward the Chinese and reached into his bag...

Sarah quietly went into action.

One, two, three, four...

Sarah rocketed across the open concrete. She was perfectly silent, but easily visible. Her stealth depended on speed and timing.

Five, six, seven, eight...

As Sarah reached the crate, she pulled out her marker and began to draw. She was within twenty feet of several of the soldiers. If any of them turned around, or so much as glanced in her direction, she would be spotted.

One, two, three, four...

Sarah swung to the side of the container directly facing the Haihu. For five seconds, anyone glancing at the crate would see her. With blinding, silent speed, Sarah continued marking the box.

Five, six, seven, eight...

Sarah completed without a hint of a pause and bolted toward the troop transport. Diving under the carriage, she inched to the rear of the truck, flattened herself against the concrete and froze. Regulating her body with deep, controlled breaths, she stared at the docks.

The soldiers and drug dealers were silently waiting for the Chinese to finish counting the money, as the dockworkers continued to mind their own business. Sarah had executed the entire task undetected, in less than 30 seconds.

Done counting, the Chinese nodded to the Koreans, and headed away from the Haihu. Next, the drug dealer stepped forward and handed the duffle bag to the lead soldier, who unzipped and checked the contents. He ordered his soldiers to head back to the troop transport.

One two three four five six seven eight...

A new metronome, twice as fast as the original, began in Sarah's skull. As the rhythm pounded, Sarah watched the two soldiers return to the cab of the truck. She waited breathlessly as the other ten soldiers climbed into the back, directly over her head.

One two three four five six seven eight...

This truck, Sarah knew, would head back to the Korean border as quickly as possible. No stops, no checkpoints, no inspections. No one would look in the back of this truck until it reached its destination.

Sarah reached behind her back and produced the 9mm pistol. As the final soldier piled into the transport, Sarah glanced at the drug dealers. They weren't watching the truck...

Like a ticking time bomb preparing to detonate, Sarah crouched beneath the transport. When the vehicle's engine thundered to life, she shot out from under the truck. In a single, lightning-quick motion, Sarah jumped up into the rear of the transport, pistol raised.

One two three four five six seven eight one two.

****

The transport stopped.

Sarah climbed over the pile of corpses at her feet and hopped out of the truck into blackness. She landed in the deep snow with a crunch, but the sound was lost above the drone of the truck's engine. Pistol at the ready, Sarah crept up along the right side of the truck until she was directly behind the vehicle's passenger's side door.

When the door of the truck swung open, Sarah whipped herself up inside, slamming her tiny body against the soldier before he could exit the vehicle. With deadly poise, Sarah pressed the barrel against the shocked man's temple and executed him. As the stunned driver attempted to open his own door, Sarah shot him in the back of the head.

Lying on top of the dead soldier in the passenger's seat, Sarah holstered her pistol behind her back. She snatched the black duffle bag at the man's feet and slung it over her shoulder. Jumping out of the vehicle, she returned to the rear and grabbed an AK-47 amidst one of the ten bodies in the back of the truck. Then she hustled to the driver's side door, popping it open.

Sarah pushed against the blood-stained body, to keep it from falling out. Reaching across the body, Sarah turned off the vehicle's ignition and headlights. Then she shut the driver's side door, and rushed toward the fence-line ahead.

The gated entrance was open just wide enough for a single person to slide through. Sarah pushed her way through the gate, and jogged out into the open center of the mountain facility. Spying a single lighted building to her left, she sprinted to the structure.

She pushed through the lighted door. To her right was a bathroom. Sarah poked her head inside the room and found it empty, save for a bar of soap sitting under a vacant showerhead and a can of shaving cream perched atop a sink. She was in the soldiers' barracks, exactly where she wanted to be.

Sarah wheeled out of the bathroom. Across from her stood a set of double doors, the entrance to the general quarters where the soldiers lived and slept. Sarah pressed her ear to the doors. She could hear at least five voices on the other side.

To her right Sarah noticed another door marked in Korean: "Commander's Quarters/Communications." Sarah silently pushed open the door and slid her way inside.

She immediately saw a lone soldier, who appeared to be repairing a radio. In utter confusion, the unarmed man froze. Sarah bolted toward him, crushed his larynx with the butt of her rifle, and snapped his neck. As the soldier's limp frame crumpled to the floor, Sarah moved onward.

Sarah poked her head into the adjacent room marked "Commander's Quarters," which was currently unoccupied. She wasn't surprised. The "Commander", Sarah assumed, was the man dripping blood all over the troop transport's passenger's seat. Sarah turned and headed back to the soldiers' quarters.

Outside the double doors, Sarah set the duffle bag down and readied her AK-47. Then she kicked open one of the doors and charged inside.

Sarah immediately came face to face with a naked man. The soldier, brandishing a red towel, was on his way to the shower. With a quick press of her trigger, Sarah fired three rounds into the wide-eyed man's chest. As his lifeless body collapsed, Sarah calmly moved on.

Six soldiers lay on bunks to the left side of the room. Smoothly controlling the recoil of her powerful assault rifle, Sarah methodically executed each man with a controlled three-round burst.

On the right side of the room, three men were seated at a round wooden table, playing cards. As Sarah machine gunned his comrades across the way, one of the three men flipped the table up on its side, dropping behind it.

The other two soldiers failed to react at all. As their bullet-ridden corpses crashed to the floor, Sarah dropped her rifle and charged at the upturned table. She leapt over it, landing on top of the terrified soldier. Before the man could respond, Sarah drove her knee into his chest, grabbed his head, and twisted until she heard a crack.

Sarah leapt up to survey the room. There were no signs of life. She was done.

Sarah mechanically turned and strolled out of the room. She paused at the naked man's body to grab the towel at his side. Sarah walked into the bathroom and placed the towel next to one of the shower heads. Then she returned to the barracks entrance, lifted up the duffle bag, and left.

Outside, Sarah reached behind her back, pulling out a black transmitter the size of CD player. She tossed the transmitter into the duffle bag, then buried the bag under a pile of snow next to the barracks door.

As Sarah trudged across the facility, a loading hangar emerged out of the darkness. Entering the hangar's gaping entrance, she jumped on the back of a cargo truck inside, and pulled a key from the pocket of her windbreaker. She unlocked the cargo container, swung open its door, and stepped inside.

"Get up," she commanded Tim Sutton. "We're leaving."

CHAPTER 17

Jeff Hutchins was sprawled on top of the king-sized bed's satin sheets. This was easily the most comfortable bed on which he had ever lain.

Through squinted, bloodshot eyes, Hutchins watched Archer and Danielson converse by the penthouse window. Hutchins had thus far managed to stave off jet-lag, thanks to the adrenalin generated by his whirlwind, transcontinental adventure. Less than an hour after the Haihu set sail, however, the Sandman finally arrived. And yet, as drowsy and comfortable as Hutchins felt, he could not sleep.

Ten feet away, Archer and Danielson monitored Dalian Wan Bay. Danielson was attempting to conduct two simultaneous cell phone conversations. Every so often, he relayed some tidbit of information to Archer, who offered a terse response or simple nod. Hutchins called to Archer.

"Hey, Jeff? Do you mind if I bug you for a minute?"

Archer ambled to the edge of the bed.

"We're not keeping you awake, are we, Hutchins?" he inquired with a wry smile.

Hutchins managed a sleepy grin.

"Nah," he replied sarcastically. "This trip has been an adventure, but it can't compete with the rigorous life of a private school math teacher."

"Sorry to disappoint you," Archer deadpanned. "What did you want to talk to me about?"

Hutchins was concerned.

"Well," he began, "despite everything we've deduced, there are still some things that just don't make sense."

"Such as?" Archer's smile dissolved.

"Back when I was researching Eric Sutton for the FBI," Hutchins continued, "he struck me as a remarkably brilliant young man. This was a kid who hatched an elaborate plan for a cash heist in Africa and actually pulled it off."

"Now, it looks like he's a big-time drug dealer, and he's plugged himself into a North Korean drug ring. And he's still in his early 20's! With every passing second, the kid looks more like the evil genius."

"So?" Archer countered.

"So…" Hutchins went on, "I don't see him falling into Sarah's trap. I mean, I understand that she's an amazing super-agent, but honestly… would Eric Sutton, rarely seen, let alone caught, put this much trust in a person he doesn't even know? It doesn't compute."

Hutchins stared up at Archer inquisitively, but the gray-haired man didn't respond. Rather, Archer studied the foot of the bed in silence. It was the same hesitant vibe that Hutchins usually got from Danielson, when the latter was intentionally withholding information.

"Well, Jeff," Archer finally offered, eyes locked on the mattress, "maybe he did know her. Maybe he's known her for a long time."

"What?" Hutchins was confused. "What do you mean, 'known her for a long time'? What are you not telling me?"

"They're on the move." Finally lowering the cell phones, Danielson called to Archer from the window. "They're heading northeast out of Dalian, as we speak."

Hutchins shifted his confusion from Archer to Danielson.

"What? Who's heading northeast?"

Danielson turned to Hutchins with a hint of exasperation.

"The Rangers. Sarah's instructions were to bring in some Korean operatives to cart an empty cargo container out of Dalian Harbor. So we did just that, and offloaded it at a secure location. Then Staff Sergeant Sariani and his team climbed inside, and we sent the crate off toward the North Korea border."

Archer finally looked up at Hutchins.

"The truck is driven by federal agents disguised as North Korean soldiers," he clarified. "The container resembles others used to ship drugs, which should prevent the truck from being stopped or inspected. With the help of a GPS beacon Sarah planted in the drug money, the truck will track the signal and reach the border by midnight."

"Wait a minute...they're going up there now?" Hutchins stammered. "Didn't you say Sarah hid the money somewhere? Why the urgency? Why would you risk the lives of U.S. soldiers by shipping them to some enemy army base in a metal box?"

Danielson looked at Archer, expecting him to respond. But Archer had resumed his silent gaze at the bed. Danielson's face twisted into a frustrated scowl.

"Because I don't trust Sarah, that's why!" he snapped, still staring at Archer. "And neither does he."

Danielson rolled his eyes, took a deep breath, returned his angry glance to Hutchins.

"Tell me something, Mr. Hutchins," Danielson demanded. "If you were handed a knife and ordered to slit Commander Archer's throat, would you be able to do it?"

Hutchins' mouth dropped as he scrambled into a sitting position on the bed. Danielson continued.

"Let's say you were trained. Let's say Commander Archer spent a few weeks teaching you the ins and outs of hand-to-hand combat. Then he and another soldier attacked you. Could you slit both of their throats?"

Hutchins could summon no words.

"Could you?" Danielson persisted.

"Uh, n-no, I don't think so!" Hutchins stammered.

"Well," Danielson replied icily, "neither could Eric Sutton."

As Hutchins looked at him in shock, Danielson continued.

"Of course, I understand how you could miss something like that. You were just a money man, tracking Eric's spending habits. You can be forgiven for overlooking the obvious."

"But him..." Danielson whipped his eyes back to Archer. "Although he knows what happened, he's still trying to convince himself that Eric Sutton could successfully brandish a knife."

Danielson glared at Hutchins.

"I don't trust Sarah. She isn't human. Commander Archer was given carte blanche to create a super-soldier, and he managed to fashion a killing machine wrapped in a tiny red-haired package. But somewhere in the master scheme, his machine blew a gasket. People died. Our people. Then, after this lethal robot of his slips off the grid for years doing God knows what, she suddenly resurfaces. And just like that, Archer convinces himself that she's coming back in."

"Well," Danielson continued. "I'm not convinced. Call me skeptical, but I can't help wondering why Sarah is suddenly delivering her buddy Eric Sutton to the Commander she abandoned long ago. I'm wondering if we aren't the ones being set up here."

"At best," Danielson finished angrily, "we have a well-meaning woman who could flip into 'kill' mode at any time. If that happens, I want to get my hands on Eric Sutton before she pops another fuse and dumps his splattered corpse somewhere up in North Korea! Regardless of what Sarah's true intentions are, those Rangers are headed up there to ensure that Sarah and Sutton don't do any more damage!"

Exhausted by the diatribe, Danielson paused to catch his breath. Hutchins delicately cut in.

"What did you mean, 'her buddy Eric Sutton'?" he asked slowly. "Why would she and Eric Sutton be friends?"

"I have no idea," Danielson retorted. He gestured at Archer. "Ask him. She's his machine."

Hutchins turned to Archer, who, inexplicably, had endured Danielson's entire outburst without returning a single word

"Honestly, Jeff," Archer offered, "I don't know either. To tell you the truth, I was hoping you could shed some light on the subject. That was the reason I brought you over here. All of your suppositions about Eric Sutton's drug business appear to be solid."

Archer continued. "And the idea that Sarah is planning to trade Eric Sutton for a pass back into the U.S. Government fold also seems credible. But that isn't the whole story."

"What do you mean?" Hutchins asked.

"Sarah must have had a relationship with Eric Sutton," Archer quietly replied. "And it must have gone back a long way." Archer dropped his eyes to the bed a final time. "I wish I knew otherwise, but…it seems to be the only explanation for what happened in Manchester."

Hutchins's eyes shot wide open.

"What?"

"Manchester Airport, three years ago." Danielson interrupted. "You think you and those two field agents were the only ones waiting for Eric Sutton that night."

"You weren't."

CHAPTER 18

Sarah tapped a button on her stopwatch.

3:32:54.

Sarah frowned. She hadn't expected to take longer than three-and-a-half hours. Nonetheless, she was satisfied. Sarah had traveled to Vermont in pursuit of a goal, which she had attained. On her first attempt, she had penetrated the S.W.I.P.E. perimeter.

Sarah had slithered her way up the right fence-line until she was twenty yards from the drab trailer. Then she had angled her way inward until she finally slid her entire body beyond the range of the S.W.I.P.E. camera. It had almost been too easy.

Now, a loud noise came from directly over Sarah's head, as the trailer's metal door swung open.

Splayed out on her stomach, Sarah watched five men descend the wooden staircase in the darkness two feet from her face. Four of the men wore bulky camouflage pants and black Army boots. They were Army Rangers, and they had faired poorly; the best of the men had only made it halfway up the course.

The fifth man was wearing tight blue jeans and faded brown hiking boots. He was apparently the engineer who had designed the S.W.I.P.E. course. The man did his best to mask his pride in what he thought was an unbeaten system.

"Guys, like I said, your team is the best I've seen since this course went operational. The other Ranger teams were lucky to get a quarter of the way up in before my camera started barking at them. You guys should be happy!"

"Begging your pardon, Sir, but screw that," one of the Rangers returned. "I didn't fly up here to make it a lousy fifty feet. We're Rangers, sir. We aim a little higher than that. The Sergeant is the only one who can hold his head up high. He did alright."

"Please, enough of this 'Sir' business," the engineer chuckled. "I'm not that old, am I? Just call me Will. But you're right. Sergeant Sariani did a heck of a job. That's the farthest anyone has made it yet!"

Another Ranger grunted a dour response.

"Yeah, well, next year I'm going to make it all the goddamn way up there and then piss all over that fuckin' camera!"

"Perhaps, Sergeant, perhaps...I'll see you guys tomorrow."

Sarah watched as the Rangers hopped into a Humvee and drove away. Will, the engineer, followed shortly afterwards in a black pick-up truck. As soon as she was alone, Sarah scrambled from under the trailer into the perimeter's empty parking lot. She jogged up to the entrance of the course and deftly scaled its barb-wired gate. Then Sarah turned right and hustled off into the surrounding thick forest.

Sarah bounded through the icy black wilderness, retracing her steps until she came to a towering pine. She nimbly sprang up the tree's trunk to a particularly wide branch fifteen feet above the forest floor.

Sarah untied the rope around a small green sack that she had secured to the base of the branch. Grabbing the sack in her right hand, Sarah jumped from the limb and gracefully plummeted into the white powder below. As soon as she landed, Sarah trudged out of the woods.

As she marched through the snowy darkness, Sarah opened the sack. Inside were a set of car keys, an Army combat knife, a roll of twenty-dollar bills totaling $480, and a digital satellite communication radio.

The radio, disguised to look like a white Apple Ipod, allowed her to hear radio instructions through the device's headphones. The radio also doubled as a cellular phone, but it wasn't garnering any reception in the remote Vermont countryside.

Reception didn't matter. Sarah wasn't paying attention to the phone, anyway.

From the forest Sarah emerged onto a remote dirt road. She removed the car keys from the sack and unlocked a purple Nissan Altima she had stolen in Boston two days earlier. Sarah turned the ignition and sped out of the wilderness.

A half hour later, on Vermont's Interstate 91, her phone acquired cellular service. The blue display screen flashed, indicating that Sarah had a message waiting.

Sarah picked up the radio and put on its tiny headphones. She pressed a button on the front of the device.

"Operator Apple, do not disregard this message. You have now been AWOL for fifteen days. You have chosen to ignore previous requests to return to base. This is not such a request. Know that you are suspected to be or to have recently been in Vermont. If this is the case, you have an assignment. This assignment is Top Priority. Your instructions are as follows: "

****

As large, wet snowflakes slowly descended to the concrete at her feet, Sarah looked out over Manchester Airport.

Perched atop the highest level of the airport's multi-story garage, Sarah had a clear view of the entire airport complex. The garage was twice as high as the structures that comprised the terminal. Sarah strapped a set of infrared night-vision goggles to her head and slowly scanned the landscape in front of her.

Was she walking into a trap?

Commander Archer was smart enough to guess that Sarah would make a trip to the S.W.I.P.E. course. It was conceivable that he fabricated the radio message to lure her to Manchester. Sarah knew that Commander Archer was one of few people on earth capable of capturing her.

Sarah carefully swept the airport with her goggles. There were no snipers on rooftops, no plainclothes undercover agents, no irregular electronic surveillance equipment. With nothing out of the ordinary, this was just another sleepy winter night at an out-of-the-way airport.

Commander Archer's message seemed authentic. That meant he felt this job really required Sarah's talents. And the Commander didn't unleash the *Ceiling* program unless a mission was extremely important...

Sarah sprinted to the parking garage's narrow stairwell, quickly descending to the bottom floor. She concealed the night-vision goggles beneath her black windbreaker, then produced the disguised radio from the front pocket. With the headphones in place, she calmly strode to the airport's main entrance.

As Sarah emerged from the terminal's automatic rotating door, she noticed the life-size metallic moose sculpture to her right in the terminal lobby. But she immediately shifted her focus to the three conveyor belts in the baggage claim area across the way.

There were two ways that a person on an inbound flight could leave Manchester Airport. One was via the debarkation gate and single security exit point. The other was via a clandestine foray across the airfield tarmac.

If a passenger opted for the latter, he could attempt to run out into the wilderness beyond the airport's runways. But that path had its drawbacks. The entire airfield was surrounded by a 10' high, barbed-wire topped perimeter fence.

The smarter move, Sarah thought, was to sneak from the tarmac into the underbelly of the airport. There the escapee could find an unguarded exit that led to freedom. The baggage claim conveyor belts offered that kind of exit.

After studying the baggage claim area, Sarah ascended an escalator. She strolled into the middle of the waiting area, and leaned her unimposing frame against a concrete pole. Sarah combed the periphery, simultaneously scanning everyone and no one.

It was easy for Sarah to be inconspicuous. As long as Sarah didn't make eye contact with anyone, people assumed she was lost in an aloof world of music.

Aside from a small group waiting to greet arriving passengers, there were two security guards at the checkpoint and a few teenagers manning a fast food counter. No one posed any kind of threat; Sarah had not walked into a trap. If Commander Archer had meant to capture her, this is where he would have done it.

A young man sitting ten feet away caught Sarah's attention. Wearing a Dartmouth College sweatshirt, he had a pile of comic books in his lap. His hair was brown, not blond. Aside from that, however, the man matched the radio message's physical description of Eric Sutton.

A brother, perhaps? The message hadn't mentioned anything about Sutton's family. If this man were Sutton's brother, Sarah would eventually have to deal with him. In the absence of specific instructions, standard procedures pertaining to collateral damage would apply: Sarah would avoid the brother if possible, incapacitate him if beneficial, and kill him if necessary.

A new development ripped Sarah's attention away from the brother. Two Federal Agents had just stepped off the escalator. They were surveying the room.

It occurred to Sarah, however briefly, that someone with monumentally poor judgment had dispatched FBI agents to apprehend her. More likely, the agents were here to get Eric Sutton.

Sarah frowned. The message hadn't included the FBI. This was a problem. Sarah assumed that she, not the FBI, was supposed to capture Eric Sutton. If the Feds grabbed Sutton at the checkpoint, Sarah would have to follow them and wait for a chance to intercept. This was sticky; Sarah hadn't been given the green light to "deal with" FBI agents.

A third agent arrived on the scene a few minutes later. This new man looked anxious and unsure, conspicuously fidgeting back and forth with trepidation. The man clearly had no field experience. This third agent probably had played some role in tracking Sutton down, and no doubt asked to be present at Sutton's apprehension.

A digital sign overhead indicated that Sutton's plane was disembarking. Sarah watched the gate area. If Sutton was corralled by FBI agents, Sarah would discreetly follow them out of the airport. From that point on, she would improvise.

Sarah watched five people exit the gate area. First was a man in a colorful winter jacket. Next were three men in leather coats and khaki pants. The last to pass through the checkpoint was a teenage girl. By the time the girl hugged her parents, Sarah had already retreated to the escalator.

Eric Sutton wasn't coming out.

There were, at most, ten people on this flight. There wouldn't be a hold-up exiting a wide-open plane. All passengers would reach the checkpoint at approximately the same time. Sutton had apparently been spooked, possibly by the presence of FBI agents. He was on the run. Sarah calmly but briskly descended the escalator.

Behind a counter across from the baggage claim sat a bored young man in a yellow Hertz t-shirt. The pale-skinned man appeared to be under hypnosis. Consequently, he didn't notice Sarah creep into one of the baggage claim's conveyor belt entrances.

Deftly separating the hanging rubber flaps with her arms, Sarah slipped through the opening. On the other side, she hopped down and crouched alertly. Sarah's determined, unblinking eyes scanned the area for movement.

If Sutton reached the baggage transfer of the airport, Sarah knew he would be squeezed in her direction by the FBI agents. The agents were doubtlessly on the plane by now, noting Sutton's absence. They would head outside to look for him.

Sarah's eyes darted to her right. Her acute hearing had detected a barely audible noise, coming from a hallway adjacent to the conveyor belts.

She heard the sound of footsteps.

Sarah crept toward the corridor. She could only see ten yards down the taupe passageway. After that, the hallway meandered left and disappeared from view. Sarah slowly proceeded down the hall. As she approached the bend, a voice rang out.

"Eric Sutton! FBI, freeze! Freeze or we will...what the...freeze! Free..."

The voice went mute. Sarah pressed her face against the left wall of the hallway and slowly peeked around the corner.

As her eyes followed the long, pink-and-white-floor, she reacted with confusion. The message hadn't said anything about this!

What is going on here?

Sarah wasn't confused for long. She assessed the situation, made a split-second decision, and reached under her jacket for her combat knife. Brandishing the weapon in her right hand, Sarah rounded the corner and charged down the hallway.

CHAPTER 19

"Sarah had been missing for nearly two weeks when I got the call."

Jeff Archer stared out the penthouse window at the frigid bay, glistening in the dusk. He ran his right hand through his grey hair in resignation.

"A day or so earlier, I heard of a Ranger team's visit to a winter test site in Vermont. Despite many previous attempts, several other elite SOF units had not been able to penetrate some S.W.I.P.E. security perimeter system funded by DARPA. So, I thought of Sarah. It just seemed like the kind of impossible task she'd be drawn to. Sarah would see this course as a new way to assess her potential."

"When Eric Sutton's capture was assigned to Ceiling," Archer continued, "I realized I had a chance to kill two birds with one stone. My best agent was in Vermont. I could send her to Manchester. Capturing Sutton was a challenge she wouldn't be able to resist. I had a way to get her back!"

Hutchins was incredulous.

"So...Sarah was at the airport that night?"

Archer nodded.

"We didn't know for sure until we reviewed the airport security cameras the day after Sutton's flight. She was definitely there. In fact, she was standing in the middle of the airport's waiting-area when you arrived. You probably saw her; you just don't remember it. Even in broad daylight, Sarah has a way of making herself inconspicuous."

"Shortly after Sutton's plane arrived," Archer went on, "Sarah rode the escalator down to the first floor of the terminal. Then she disappeared. We don't know exactly what she did next, but we assume that she did what you did--pushed her way through one of the conveyor belt openings in the baggage claim area. She was only a few minutes ahead of you, but..."

Archer sighed wearily.

"That's all the time Sarah would need," he finished softly.

Stunned, Hutchins slowly shook his head.

"Whoa whoa whoa...you're telling me, after all this time...that Sarah killed those agents? You've got to be kidding me!"

Archer motioned to Percy Danielson, who was standing next to the bed.

"As I said before, Percy is right. Those two FBI agents would have had no problem apprehending Eric Sutton. At best, Sutton might have put up a fight, but there was no sign of a struggle. Apart from their slashed throats, those agents had no wounds, whatsoever. No cuts, no scratches, nothing. They were neatly dispatched in a matter of seconds, before they could even begin to defend themselves. It was Sarah. It had to be."

"And...you have no idea why?" Hutchins mouthed in astonishment. "How is that possible?"

"Don't think I haven't exhausted myself trying to figure it out." Archer turned back to the window. "It could be that Sarah had made a deal with Sutton at some point. Maybe he was bankrolling her, allowing her to be independent, free to chase whatever pursuit struck her fancy. In exchange, maybe she was helping him. So she skips town, knowing I'll think she's in Vermont, so that she'll be sent to Manchester... I know it seems like a complicated scenario. But it's the best I've got; I have no other clue why Sarah would do what she did that night."

"Oh, you don't?" Danielson rolled his eyes sarcastically at Archer. "Well, I can think of a few. She's a killing machine, for starters! Who knows how many people met their end under Sarah's knife while she was under your command? Maybe she just popped a gasket one day and figured, 'Hey, a few more meaningless bodies?' Or maybe she thought taking out a few agents would be an exciting new 'challenge'! 'Hey, let's see how long it takes me to paint the floor red with FBI blo-'"

"Hold it!" Hutchins shouted, raising both of his hands in the air. Danielson halted, surprised by the outburst.

Hutchins' eyes narrowed and he slowly rose from the bed, turning toward Danielson.

"Wait a minute," he began, locking eyes with Danielson. "There's a giant piece of the puzzle missing here. And it's about time that piece was put in its place."

Hutchins glanced over at Archer.

"A few minutes ago, you said you thought that, maybe, Sutton could have reached a business arrangement with Sarah?"

Archer nodded.

"An arrangement based on what?" Hutchins continued. "The money he stole? How long would that bankroll her? A year or two at the most, right?" Archer's mouth cracked a grim smile.

Hutchins turned toward to Danielson.

"The CIA solicits my help to find Eric Sutton," Hutchins continued, his tone intense. "Then, when I do find him, without my knowledge, you send out an emergency bulletin to the Ceiling program. Within hours, Ceiling dispatches the deadliest person on earth to nab Eric Sutton at the Manchester Airport."

"Now," Hutchins proceeded, "years later, Sutton turns up on the CIA's radar. And the CIA rounds up the cavalry, charges halfway round the world, and sends U.S. troops into North Korea. All in a matter of days. And according to you..." Hutchins pointed a bony finger in Danielson's direction. "All of this, because of $500,000 and a double-murder that you know Eric Sutton didn't commit?"

Danielson's demeanor had shifted completely. As he slowly backed away from Hutchins, Danielson's eyes sought Archer for help. Archer maintained his grim smile.

"What, Percy?" Archer murmured sarcastically, "you didn't think he'd figure it out? If it weren't for Jeff Hutchins, you wouldn't have found Eric Sutton the first time, let alone now. You'd still be choking on dust in Mali, chasing dead ends. Without this man, you would have had nothing. After everything he's learned in the past few days, you're still going to hide your cards?"

Danielson's mouth dropped open. He tried to think of a response to Archer's comment, but none came to mind. Danielson stared at the floor for a moment, his face red with frustration. Finally, he uttered a defeated sigh and addressed Hutchins.

"Okay," Danielson offered slowly, "What is it that you think you know?"

Hutchins stared back at the shorter man with unblinking eyes.

"I know that this is about a hell of a lot more than $500,000."

****

Eric Sutton's eyes softened. He loosened the vise-like grip on his brother's shoulder and lowered his arm. Eric guided his haggard-looking sibling to one of the luxury office chairs ringing the room's long conference table. As Tim Sutton collapsed into the cushioned chair, Eric took the seat directly to his left.

"Okay, Tim," Eric said, in a calm, managed tone. "Start from the beginning, and tell me what the fuck is going on here."

Tim, who hadn't taken his eyes off his brother, attempted to regulate his breathing. Suppressing his mounting confusion, he began.

"Eric, a few weeks ago a coded message arrived at my store in a manila envelope. That message appeared to be written by you. It said that you were in North Korea, that you were in grave danger, and that you needed my help."

Eric furrowed his eyebrows in confusion, but nodded for Tim to continue.

"The message told me to contact Jeff Hutchins," Tim went on. "Does that name ring a bell?"

Eric frowned.

"No. Should it?"

Tim shook his head and sighed.

"I don't know. Maybe. He was at Manchester Airport three years ago, the night you were supposed to fly in from Newark. He was there to arrest you, for stealing some money in Africa."

Eric arched his eyebrows.

"I see... So, this Jeff Hutchins...he's alive? If he was at the airport that night, did he go alone?"

Tim shook his head.

"No. He was with two FBI field agents." Trepidation crept into Tim's voice as he stared at his brother. "Both of whom were killed in the airport that night. Did...did you kill those agents, Eric?"

Eric shook his head earnestly.

"No. But I know what you're talking about. In any case, that's not important right now... What happened after you contacted this Jeff Hutchins guy?"

"When I met with Hutchins," Tim continued, "He gave me the phone number of an agent on the West Coast who could help get me into North Korea to..." Tim paused with embarrassment. "...rescue you. Then I left Hutchins, and traveled to Chicago, per the instructions in the message--"

"Wait," Eric interrupted. "Chicago?" He looked inquisitively at his brother. "Did...did you go see T.C. Watson?"

Tim nodded.

"Yeah, T.C., that was his name. I never caught his last name. T.C. gave me the name of a ship and the serial number of a cargo container. After I got that information I headed to Seattle."

Eric's eyes lit up in understanding.

"I see. So you went to Seattle, snuck inside a cargo container, traveled with that container to Dalian, and then over land across the Korean border, right?"

Tim nodded.

"Yes. Then I followed a set of directions included in the message. Those directions led me right to this camp."

Confusion returned to Eric's face.

"You had directions to this place? From where, the holding facility a few miles from here?"

Tim nodded. Eric shook his head.

"That doesn't make any sense. And frankly, Big Brother, I'm amazed you made it even as far as the holding facility."

"Well," Tim replied, "I had help. When I got to Seattle, I was met by Jeff Hutchins' contact. She traveled over here with me. Frankly, without her, I wouldn't have made it onto the boat, much less across the ocean."

Eric froze.

"Wait...she? The agent is a woman?"

Tim nodded. Eric stared back at his brother with mounting alarm.

"This agent...is she, like, a short, red-haired woman?"

"Yes, but how did you-"

"Fuck!" Eric muttered. "It's the girl from the airport!"

"What?"

"That night in Manchester," Eric continued. "She was there. And unlike those FBI agents, she wasn't there to arrest me."

"What?" Tim's overwhelming confusion resurfaced. "Sarah was there that night? Why?"

Eric shrugged.

"Afterward, I figured that the U.S. Government had sent her to apprehend me, and get back the money I took. Those FBI agents at the airport that night...I don't think they'd been given the whole story. If they had, there would have been a lot more than three agents."

"The money you took..." Tim replied, his eyes once again wide with shock. "Hutchins mentioned that. He said that when you were in Mali, you stole $500,000 of human aid money!"

Eric's mouth broke into a small smile of confusion.

"$500,000, huh? Well, that explains why the FBI only sent three agents... Now, this girl, the red-haired girl...Where is she right now?"

Tim shook his head, his eyes delirious with confusion.

"I-I'm not exactly sure. She guided me to that tunnel through the mountain, the one that leads to this camp. Then she told me to go through the tunnel without her. I haven't seen her since." Tim paused. "If...if Sarah was at the airport that night...and she's here now...is she coming here to arrest you? Or worse? I mean..."Tim pleaded, his nervous eyes darting toward the entrance. "Are we in danger right now?"

Eric shrugged his shoulders. He rested his elbows on the surface of the coffee table, put his head in his hands, and stared down at the table.

"I--I have no idea. There's so much about this that doesn't make any fucking sense..."

In the moment of silence that followed, Tim's anxious eyes wandered from his brother. As he surveyed the room, the mounting confusion was briefly replaced by genuine curiosity.

"Eric," Tim queried, looking back at his brother, "the message I got—it sounded like you were some sort of prisoner. Are you a prisoner? I mean…what is this place?"

Eric looked up. A tiny smile crept onto his lips.

"A prisoner? Well…that's an interesting question. I suppose you could say I'm under sort of…house arrest. But that wouldn't really be accurate. As far as this place…well, that would take a little bit of explaining."

Tim's eyes circled the room, taking in its outlandish decor. He looked again at Eric's pale face. The confusion and curiosity that had been welling up inside of Tim exploded in a single question.

"Eric, who the hell are you?"

PART 3
SHADOW

CHAPTER 20

CENTRAL INTELLIGENCE AGENCY OPERATION ORDER

(U) OPORD #10572

(U) TASK ORGANIZATION: NFAC, DD/CIA.

(S) A) Unnamed village 7Km Northwest of Taoudenni, Mali, Africa.

(U) Small desert settlement consisting of several huts. Enclave occasionally used by Malian nomads and salt-trader caravans. Intelligence indicates village is presently vacant.

(U) 1) SITUATION
   (TS) A) PARTICIPATING FORCES: **Rebel forces commanded by Malian General Pierre Mangara.**
      (S) 1) Regional Commander designated to negotiate on Mangara's behalf.
      (S) B) FRIENDLY FORCES: Four-man CIA negotiation unit with attached Malian guide/translator.

(S)1) Unit Coordinator: CIA Agent Anthony Hess.

(TS) 2) MISSION: **Rendezvous with Mangara forces. Lay groundwork for U.S./Mali economic relations under future Mangara regime. Deliver financial incentive package of $20,000,000 American.**

(TS) 3) EXECUTION: Infiltrate Northwest Mali via Mauritania using all-terrain vehicles. Attached guide will provide optimum route to village. Negotiate with Mangara forces and exit using entry route.

(TS) 4) INTENT: Initiate relationship with Mangara that yields privileged access to Malian Petroleum Reserves.

(U) END OPERATION ORDER

--TOP SECRET--

****

"Sir, we appreciate your agreeing to meet with us. We hope today will mark the beginning of a profitable relationship for both of our nations."

Tony Hess gestured across the interior of the thatch-roofed, mud-and-straw hut at the Malian Commander seated opposite him.

The hut was surprisingly spacious inside: Hess, his fellow three CIA agents, their Malian guide Thomas, the Commander and four rebel soldiers were all seated comfortably in a circle along the hut's wall. Three more rebels were stationed directly outside the hut's open door-flap. The hut's interior was lit only by the sunlight that poured through the flap.

"I'm sure it will," the Commander replied. "General Mangara is pleased that America acknowledges the legitimacy of his rule and appreciates the strength of his army."

Hess nodded.

"We recognize that General Mangara is the kind of leader capable of building strong economic relationships between your nation and the outside world—something this country's current ruling party has been unable to do."

"Of course," Hess conditioned, "It would not be appropriate at the present time for the United States to take a public stance in support of General Mangara."

"Of course," the Commander acknowledged, nodding his own head. "But rest assured that once the General gains control of the whole of our nation, he will reward those who have aided him with, shall we say…special trade privileges. Especially with regard to Malian oil."

Hess smiled at the Commander.

"I think we understand each other, sir," he replied.

The Commander looked at the four duffle bags positioned in front of the CIA agents.

"And I see that, as a symbol of your faithful support of General Mangara, you have brought us something?"

Hess issued a subtle instructional nod, and his men responded by hefting their duffle bags and tossing them into the center of the hut. Hess gestured to the bags, looking at the Commander.

"In those bags," he declared, "Are twenty million American dollars. You can use this money as you see fit. Purchase equipment, manpower, or whatever you need, but please, be discreet. If public queries arise over these funds, the United States will flatly deny any knowledge or connection."

The Commander nodded distractedly. He was busy unzipping one of the bags and pawing through the cash inside.

As the Commander's soldiers gawked at the largest amount of money they would ever see, Hess's own eyes became drawn to a small object in the center of the hut.

"Hey," he observed, motioning to his fellow agents, "what is that?"

One of the tossed duffle bags had partially uncovered a metallic item, buried just beneath the dirt surface of the hut's floor. As the soldiers excitedly discussed their army's financial windfall, Hess crawled to the center of the hut. Kneeling above the object, Hess dug around it with his hands. After a minute, he lifted the dusty apparatus.

Hess stared at the toaster-sized silver box. He could see that one side was covered with black metal mesh, and as he lifted the device higher, that a thick red wire extended from the box into the dirt below.

Hess looked up. No one was smiling. As his soldiers hushed, the Commander gruffly pointed at the bizarre metal box.

"What is that?" he demanded.

Hess shook his head angrily.

"You tell me! What is this thing doing in your hut?"

The other soldiers, most of whom understood no English, became agitated at Hess's alarmed tone. Several of the men warily fingered their AK-47s. A nervous sweat collected on Hess's brow. He carefully lowered the box to the ground, and attempted to interject calm into what had quickly become a volatile situation.

"Okay, okay, easy...Look, I honestly have no idea what this thing is. Are you telling me that you don't know either?"

The Commander stopped glaring at the CIA agent and looked again at the device. He silently shook his head, but offered nothing further. Hess could see that the leader wasn't buying Hess's claim of ignorance. Hess slowly turned toward his agents.

"Hey," he whispered, "Do any of you have any idea what this thing is?"

The other CIA men, whose hands had slid down to the pistols holstered at their waists, offered Hess no help. He looked back down at the device in his hands.

"You know," Hess began, his brow furrowed, "It looks like a spea-"

Before he could finish his sentence, the silver contraption abruptly erupted with noise. The entire hut reverberated with the sound of a man yelling at the top of his lungs.

The jarring noise stunned the soldiers, who reflexively sprang back against the wall of the hut. A thoroughly bewildered Hess faced his agents.

"It is a speaker!" he yelled over the din. "What the fuck is going on here? The voice from the box, what's it saying? I can't understand the language!"

Hess shifted his eyes to his African guide, Thomas.

"Thomas! That voice! What is it saying!"

Thomas stared back at Hess in confusion.

"The voice is saying, 'Quick, get in here! Hurry, all of you, get in here, right now!' It's repeating those words over and over again!"

"What?"

As Hess mouthed his startled reply, one of the three soldiers who had been standing outside the tent charged through the open flap, his AK-47 assault rifle at the ready. He pointed his gun at Hess with a mix of fury and confusion. Then, the other two soldiers bolted into the hut. Disarray reigned inside the enclosed area.

As suddenly as it had begun, the broadcast yelling stopped. Everyone in the hut froze, exchanging bug-eyed stares. Hess's eyes shot from the soldiers to the box, then over to the Commander.

Suddenly, Hess had a frightful epiphany.

Oh no...

Hess spun toward the open flap of the hut, then whipped back toward the Commander. Eyes wide, Hess hastily raised his hands.

"Wait-"

His words were cut short as the door flap was suddenly closed shut and the hut plunged into darkness. Then four loud "pops" issued from the floor, followed by a deafening hissing noise as a foreign substance filled the air.

In the ensuing panic, Hess attempted to crawl through the darkness toward the door flap. But it was no use. His thoughts became clouded, the CIA agent's limbs gave way, and he collapsed to the floor.

What the fu. . .

Seconds later, Hess was unconscious.

CHAPTER 21

T.C. Watson gazed out the passenger window of his vintage, emerald green Cadillac. As the golden spoke wheels turned into the expansive parking lot outside of Chicago's United Center, Watson pointed at the Chevy Malibu.

"Is that him, Dom?"

"Yeah," the driver replied. "That's the car. I told him to show up here after dark. He probably been sittin' out here for hours, sweatin' it out."

"Well, then," Watson replied. "Let's pay him a visit."

The classic Fleetwood rolled up beside the idling black Chevrolet; it was parked in an isolated space with its headlights off.

According to Domino, Watson's 6-foot-5-inch, 260-pound sidekick, bodyguard and lieutenant, this same Chevy Malibu had made an appearance outside Maxwell Lee earlier that day.

When Domino had approached the suspicious vehicle, he had confronted a blond, pale-skinned white boy, no more than twenty.

The blond kid had calmly resisted Domino's threats that he leave, and had insisted on meeting with Watson to discuss a business proposal! Watson had no idea how this kid even knew his name.

The most intriguing part of Domino's exchange occurred when Domino assured the white kid that T.C.'s time was too valuable to be wasted on his scrawny ass.

The white boy had reached into a plastic bag, pulled out a stack of $100 bills, and asked Domino, "How much time can I buy with $20,000?"

What the fuck, Watson figured.

For twenty grand, he'd hear the kid out.

"Go get him, Dom," Watson instructed. "Tell him to get in the back."

Domino put the Cadillac in park and climbed out. A minute later, the left rear door opened and a lanky, blond-haired man slid onto the seat. Watson's associate returned to the driver's seat.

"Okay," Watson began, turning to stare at the pale young man,. "You seem to like throwing money around. So tell me: Why shouldn't I just rob you and leave your scrawny ass in the trunk of that Malibu?"

The blond kid took a deep breath.

"Sir, I want to make a business proposal that will astronomically increase your profit margin. In short, I'm offering to make you a rich, rich man."

Watson frowned. He smoothed his tailored suit and red tie.

"Boy, does it look like I ain't rich now? My pockets are already full of paper! Why the fuck would I want to risk doing business with some pasty cracker? For all I know, you a cop!"

The young man cracked a thin smile.

"You're right, sir. You seem to be doing quite well. But I think, in time, I could completely change your concept of 'rich'. But I can do a lot more than make you money. I can give you something more valuable than money."

Watson raised his eyebrows.

"More valuable than money? Shit, boy, what kind of businessman are you? There ain't nothin' more valuable in this world than money!"

"There's one thing," the young man responded. "Security."

Watson had to admit, this skinny kid was beginning to intrigue him.

"Okay," he allowed. "Go on."

The kid nodded and grinned. Clearly he had anticipated getting this far.

"Well," he began. "For the past month and a half, I've been studying the way the Chicago drug business operates. Lately, I've focused on your operation. As far as I can tell, you control the territory in and immediately around the Maxwell Lee housing projects. Your staff includes several hundred teenage dealers, who are overseen at any given time by ten to twenty managers."

Masking his surprise, Watson eyed the enthusiastic young man. How could this kid have figured out his operation so quickly?

The young man continued.

"You've done well for yourself. But life has hardly been a walk in the park. You've got cops coming in to bust your dealers, and you have no way of knowing when they'll arrive and how hard they'll lean on your operation."

"Furthermore," the kid continued, "You have serious territorial issues at the fringes. I've watched arguments take place to the west, between your dealers and those of the neighboring operation. You can expect some serious turf wars soon that are sure to slow your operation and deplete your workforce."

"What *I* can do," the man continued, "Is eliminate these problems. With the right equipment and training, you can have the police working for you, not against you. I can make your territory so technologically secure that the cops will never get the drop on you. I'll also teach you how to use state-of-the-art surveillance systems to eavesdrop on your competition. You can pass that information on to the police. Basically, I can shift all of the heat from you to your competition. Using technology that I will provide, free of charge."

Watson allowed a small smile. He had to admit…the kid had put a lot of thought into this. In any case, Watson lost nothing by hearing the rest of what the young man had to say.

"Son," he returned, "Ain't nothin' free. I can tell from the way you throw around the Benjamins that you ain't hurtin' for green. So what's in it for you?"

"What I'm after," the young man replied, "is 'juice', so to speak. I'm after your respect. I want to be a vital cog in your operation. I want you to grow into a rich, powerful man because of my help. And then I want to move on, leaving you wealthy and secure."

Watson shook his head in disbelief. Where the fuck had this kid come from?

"Boy," Watson grinned, "You are the craziest muthufuckin' white boy I have ever met! Why ain't you in the CIA, or fixin' to be a corporate security or some shit?"

"Because," the kid matter-of-factly returned, "Those jobs suck."

"Okay," Watson allowed, his smile fueled by continuing curiosity. "Besides intel and security…how else you plan to make me rich and powerful?"

"Well," the kid replied without missing a beat, "You are currently following a simple and reasonably effective business model. Your operation is solid, but you can't expand your business without invading the surrounding turf. I can help you implement a more imaginative plan, one that can significantly boost your bottom line."

"For instance," the man continued, "In the state of Illinois, there are hundreds of small towns with completely unstructured drug operations. By employing big-city techniques in these areas, with the high tech security I'll provide, you can expand your sales and increase your profit margin without having to fire a single shot."

"Look," the kid concluded. "The very idea of a young white guy throwing all of this at you in the backseat of your car must seem pretty crazy. But understand…there is no financial risk to you. I'll put up the hardware and cash, and teach you everything you need to know. All I ask at this point is that you carefully consider my proposal. If you're interested, arrange another meeting and I'll lay out the specifics."

The young man finished, staring at Watson expectantly. Watson looked at Domino, who was clearly as stunned by the kid's presentation as Watson.

"Okay," he responded. "I'll think about it. If I decide I want to hear more, I'll let you know. You got a phone number?"

The kid shook his head.

"No, but I have this." Reaching into his pocket, he produced a fat silver marker. "There is a blue mailbox adjacent to the fence against which your large associate was leaning earlier today. If you decide on another meeting, draw an "X" on the front of the mailbox with this marker. I'll meet you the following night at this very spot."

The man handed the marker to Watson, who grabbed it and pulled off the cap. Watson touched the tip of the marker to his pointer finger.

"The marker's out," he concluded, looking at his uncolored finger.

"Don't worry," the kid replied. "It works. Use it."

The young man rotated in the seat toward the door, and Watson nodded.

"Alright, get out. I'll let you know if I want to hear more."

As he climbed out into the cold night, the kid called to Watson before closing the door.

"By the way, how should I address you? As 'Mr. Watson'?"

Watson held his tongue for a moment.

"You can call me T.C.," he offered, finally.

"Great," the kid responded. "Thanks for your time, T.C."

"Wait!" Watson called as the kid swung the door shut. "What's your name?"

The young man smiled. "Call me Shadow."

CHAPTER 22

"But how did you set up surveillance in such a short amount of time? And how did you know the CIA would be delivering that much money to Mangara?"

Tim was struggling to unravel the complexities of Eric's story when it suddenly hit him.

"You didn't know," he mouthed. "You guessed."

Eric Sutton smiled. He hadn't seen his brother in five years, but some things never changed. No one knew Eric better than Tim.

"About three weeks before graduation," Eric confirmed, "I read a few articles about the CIA's funneling of money into northern Iraq prior to the second Gulf War. Large amounts of cash indiscriminately thrown around to curry favor with whomever."

"Then," Eric continued, "I looked at the situation in Mali. Pierre Mangara, an opportunistic warlord on the rise, was strong-arming his way to the top. I figured this was a man with whom unprincipled financial deals could easily be struck. I considered the huge untapped oil reserves of Mali, and the likelihood that Mangara would soon be controlling them. Considering the potential for long term pay off, I reasoned that 'monetary assistance' to his cause would be considered a prudent investment by the petroleum addicted United States."

"The rest, as you correctly surmised, was guesswork. I studied the territory Mangara controls in northern Mali. Taoudenni, the only major city in the region, is where Mangara is often seen publicly. Therefore, it was a probable location for any deal making."

"If the secretive CIA were attempting to buy Mangara's cooperation, however, they wouldn't just roll into Taoudenni to do the deal. They would look for a remote village near Taoudenni."

"I did a little more research and located the orphanage, which I realized offered me a plausible cover for being in Taoudenni. From there I could improvise. So, I went."

Tim shook his head in disbelief.

"So on a hunch, you flew eight thousand miles to Africa, with the hope of ripping off a truckload of cash from the CIA?"

"Hey," Eric replied bluntly, "I didn't have much going on at the time."

Tim frowned incredulously.

"So you get there and discover a group of soldiers who are about to do a deal? It was that easy?"

Tim listened as Eric explained that, in fact, it had been that easy.

Eric had understood that Mangara's army was primarily deployed in the south, pushing toward Bamako, Mali's capital. As a result, there hadn't been that many soldiers stationed in Taoudenni.

A couple of months after Eric had arrived, however, a jeep and a pick-up truck loaded with troops pulled into town. Something was up.

By this point, Eric knew the lay of the land. He figured the CIA would come from the Northwest by way of Mauritania. Eric scouted the main road and found a settlement a few hours' ride northeast of the Taoudenni. He hid and waited.

A couple of days later the goons in the pick-up showed up. They stomped around carrying AK-47's, tossed some nomads out of a cluster of huts and left. Eric made a few inquiries and found out the nomads were told they could come back in three days. He laid his trap in the largest hut and waited. And sure enough...

"And the gas you used. . ." Tim probed further.

Eric nodded.

"Remember a few years back when those Chechen rebels took hostages in that Moscow theater? The Russian military diffused the standoff by pumping in a gas called Carfentanil, a tranquilizer 10,000 more powerful than morphine. The Russians used enough to fill a spacious theater, whereas I only needed enough for a modest-sized hut."

Ruston, Tim's modest hometown, had only a single veterinarian, the venerable Doc McCusker. Upon learning that Carfentanil was sold commercially as an animal tranquilizer , Eric had impersonated McCusker and simply ordered some by phone. He had the gas within a week.

Tim realized that Eric wouldn't have had any trouble smuggling Carfentanil into Africa. U.S. airport luggage scanners were designed to detect explosives, not that kind of material.

Eric had purchased the rest of the items needed for his grand plot—the speaker, a few gel-cell batteries, and tiny charges used to release the gas—in Taoudenni. Wiring everything together, including an mp3 player with the voice recording, had been easy for Tim's brilliant brother. The dirt floor of the hut allowed Eric to easily conceal the entire set-up.

"It wasn't rocket science," Eric concluded with a chuckle. "Using intuition, common sense, a few months of planning and a little luck, I made twenty million dollars!"

Tim wasn't laughing.

"I remember reading about that theater in Moscow. It was a disaster! The gas killed nearly two hundred people, including over a hundred hostages. That stuff is deadly! What happened to everyone in the hut?" Tim tried to suppress the wave of nausea washing over him.

Eric shrugged.

"I'm not really sure. Before I left I stuck each one with a syringe of antidote. The antidote is supposed to be quick and effective; they all probably woke up several hours later with a wicked hangover."

"But do you know that?" Tim persisted. "How can you be sure that they were okay?"

Eric's face darkened. Tim was suddenly confronted with the "other" Eric; the prickly, brooding loner that Ruston's populace had known to steer clear of.

"What?" Eric scowled. "Should I have held their hands until they all woke up? Maybe I should have fixed them a fucking omelet before I made off with their twenty million!"

Dismayed, Tim dropped his head and paused for a few seconds. He had no choice but to trust that Eric was as talented a vaccinator as he was a thief. Tim tried to push the matter from his brain, and pressed onward.

"So you took the money and became a drug dealer?"

"Well, Tim," Eric clarified, "I didn't actually go into the drug business. I provided sound council and technological expertise to an existing drug lord. My services caused his operation to grow and my sphere of influence to expand."

"Really," Eric emphasized, "after Africa my options were limited. There was no way a legitimate business would accept my suspect money. The drug trade was an attractive alternative. First, it's a multi-billion dollar industry. Second, for the most part it's run by uneducated people with only a rudimentary understanding of capitalism! By investing wisely, who knew how far I could climb?"

"And this T.C. guy was the drug lord you were working for?" Tim returned.

Eric flashed a confidant grin and nodded.

"Oh yeah," he replied. "I hit the jackpot with T.C."

"By the end of our second meeting T.C. was hooked. I showed him infrared photos of items his crew had marked with an IR applicator pen I gave him at our initial meeting. This demonstration alone was enough to convince him that I would bring useful technological magic to his operation."

"From then on," Eric continued, "things exploded."

Eric had first set about securing the perimeter of the Maxwell Lee Complex.

He bought second hand laser-based motion detection systems from security firms, and paid a few disgruntled National Guardsmen to steal state-of-the-art night sight equipment. Eric even made a weapons run to a clandestine militia in the Upper Peninsula of Michigan. A wad of cash and some tough talk regarding second Amendment rights was all it took to close that deal. In total, Eric purchased three million dollars worth of gear.

Tim realized that Eric had obviously paid much closer attention to their father's profession than had been apparent. When the Sutton boys were younger, Eric had always spoken of Will Sutton's security perimeters with scorn. And yet, through some surreptitious watching of his father and Eric's own innate brilliance, he had clearly inherited Will's technical wizardry.

That expertise shown through as Eric described the foolproof detection system he had constructed around Maxwell Lee. The system of sensors and infrared cameras surrounding the housing project was so secure, Eric claimed, the T.C. Watson could have built nuclear warheads inside without anyone finding out.

In addition, Maxwell Lee was monitored from the roof and several windows by T.C.'s security team. These men used high powered binoculars and night-vision goggles. It became impossible for anyone to hop a fence and sneak into the complex. Everyone who entered Maxwell Lee was detected immediately and quickly assessed as being a threat or not.

After securing Maxwell Lee, Eric had helped T.C. implement a tagging system to track his clientele Regular customers were labeled 'green,' less frequent visitors 'yellow,' and unknowns, 'red.' Meticulous records of all of this data were maintained on a computer.

Upon arrival, 'red tags' were thoroughly interrogated by T.C.'s security force and generally told, in no uncertain terms, to leave. The possibility of an undercover cop sneaking in was virtually eliminated.

This caught Tim's interest.

"Wait a minute…You kept computer records of everyone who goes in and out of that place? What did you have…a team of analysts?"

Eric responded with a wry laugh.

"Let's just say that I found a 'malleable indigenous workforce' that more than covered my computing needs!"

Eric had surveyed T.C.'s rugged, street-wise mob of 200 youths, and effortlessly plucked the brainy ones from the bunch. The chosen boys had been trained, then put to work at the computers. The end result was highly-skilled labor that cost nothing.

This, Tim knew, was classic Eric. Tim's brother viewed the world through a lens of mental Darwinism. The environment didn't matter. Whether he was standing on Dartmouth's campus or in the middle of the Chicago ghetto, Eric divided those around him into two groups: smart people and idiots.

Tim found it to be an amusingly ironic outlook: free of social stereotypes, yet loaded with prejudice. He listened as Eric described the next phase of his lofty plan.

After securing Maxwell Lee, Eric had gone to work on the surrounding blocks. He showed T.C. how cops could monitor his actions from five blocks away, using the same kinds of imaging equipment Eric had purchased. Eric identified the spots where police could potentially set up surveillance, and had T.C. move families into those vacant apartments. T.C.'s drug dealers were relocated to corners in and outside Maxwell Lee that could not be photographed from afar.

Next, Eric had switched from defense to offense. He laced the entire area with equipment set up to look out at any positions where someone might be looking in. Soon, T.C. had an eye on every street and every sidewalk within a half-mile, all day, all night.

"When cops decided to make a sweep," Eric boasted, "we knew they were coming 45 seconds ahead of time. Do you know how much time that is? You can empty a city block in 45 seconds!"

Tim frowned.

"Didn't the police get suspicious when they found every block vacant?"

"Ah," Eric countered, "but we didn't go that far. Once again, T.C.'s plentiful young workforce was a big asset. Instead of completely vacating the streets, we left enough kids behind to satisfy the police's arrest quota for that day. By continuously rotating sales personnel, we minimized the number of times any one individual got pinched."

"I swear," Eric chuckled, "Maxwell Lee must hold the world record for 'Most First of Second Time Arrests.' None of the kids felt pressure to roll on their boss because none of them ever faced serous jail time! Once a kid was arrested twice, he was taken out of the rotation, allowing fresh faces to be nabbed."

"The funny thing," Eric added, "is that all of the green dealers were begging to get arrested! Getting locked up for the first time is a badge of honor to those kids."

"But still!" Tim persisted. "Wouldn't the cops eventually figure out what you're doing and turn up the heat?"

"I explained that very possibility to T.C.," Eric replied. "What we needed to do, I told him, was to pony up someone else. So, we took our surveillance to the next level; we began to eavesdrop on T.C.'s competitors."

Eric had quickly discovered that it was easy to spy on drug dealers when one was employed by other drug dealers. The drug parlance, method of product import and supply stashing didn't vary from dealer to dealer.

With T.C. at his side, Eric analyzed audio recordings and digital video clips of T.C.'s rivals. T.C. could quickly determine what the dealers were up to. His men would pass along those details to cops on the take, who would push information up the ranks. Occasionally, Eric would have T.C. feed the police a big-time bust. Once, for example, police had raided a warehouse run by one of T.C.'s competitors and had "happened" to find $100,000 worth of heroin.

Eric was well equipped morally, Tim recognized, to embrace one of the smug truths of the ghetto: Often times, the only people who cared about the drugs being dealt in a neighborhood were the people who actually lived in that neighborhood. The police didn't care who they arrested, as long as they were making collars and fulfilling their monthly arrest quota. Eric had simply made sure that that quota was filled by drug dealers who didn't work for T.C.

"Eventually," Eric concluded, "T.C. conducted his day-to-day operations with no need to look over his shoulder. I had delivered exactly what I had promised—security."

Tim's eyes widened with recollection.

"T.C. gave me a big speech about security when I met him in Chicago! At the time, I didn't understand what the hell he was talking about!"

Eric grinned and rolled his eyes.

"Did he give you his 'head on the pillow' speech? During the later stages of my time with T.C., he delivered that speech to his more promising young dealers, acting like a benevolent father figure or something. It was pretty amusing."

"And those minions," Tim returned. "What did they think of you?"

"Nothing," Eric responded. "They never met me. There are only a handful of people in T.C.'s operation who even know I exist. After the initial meetings, I dealt with T.C. and T.C. alone. I provided him with the equipment, and taught him how to set up and operate it. Sometimes I had to painstakingly write step-by-step instructions for him to follow, but by and large T.C. was a good student. I suspect most of his employees think he's a genius. . ."

As Eric's voice trailed off, Tim glanced over at the unkempt pile of hi-tech hardware next to the conference table. Then his eyes wandered back to the large computer workstation near the door of the cavernous room.

"Eric, everything you've described is mind-boggling," Tim began, "but what does any of it have to do with this place?"

Eric nodded in understanding.

"It doesn't make sense yet, does it? Don't worry; there's a lot more to explain."

"First, Eric continued, "I made two promises to T.C. One was to provide him with security. The second was to make him an extremely wealthy man. So, when I had successfully secured T.C.'s turf, I expanded the scope of his operation."

"With so much police involvement, neighboring drug trades were in shambles. We could have easily seized their turf."

"However," Eric conditioned, "we tried to avoid that. The more territory T.C. controlled, the harder it would be to secure that territory. Instead of 'claiming corners' in Chicago, so to speak, I fashioned another plan that was more secure and more lucrative."

By this point, Eric explained, he had completely gained T.C.'s trust. T.C. was willing to confide to Eric that all of his heroin and cocaine came from Mexico and was trucked from the border all the way to Chicago. Eric fashioned a plan that redistributed a chunk of these shipments within the smaller towns of southern and central Illinois.

T.C., in effect, would take his big-city operation to the heartland.

Under the system Eric established, T.C. upped his Mexican purchases by 20 percent. This 20 percent went to a quiet, isolated warehouse in central Illinois. From there, the distribution of drugs fanned out across the state through a supply network of middle managers, men T.C. trusted. Each of these managers controlled a drug marketing territory of 10 to 15 towns.

Eric made sure that T.C. stayed away from Aurora, Rockland and Peoria—large cities with established drug rings. He concentrated, instead, on small communities where the person moving product was some hippy or skinhead pushing heroin out of the back door of his trailer.

Under Eric's guidance, T.C. was careful to avoid bloodshed in claiming this new territory. Instead, Eric used competitive pricing to convince the dealers in those towns to sell T.C.'s drugs. Most of these dealers had been getting ripped off in their previous arrangements; they thought the standard deal T.C. was offering was a great bargain.

Ever the cold pragmatist, Eric had also understood that there was a side benefit to keeping indigenous rural dealers in place. These dealers were white. Had T.C. moved his own people into the heartland, he would have run up against rural police forces looking to arrest the lone black man in town whether he was committing crimes or not.

Eric paused for a moment, giving his sibling a few seconds to digest this information.

Tim's head was swimming. In the past few minutes, he had learned that his little brother had stolen $20 million from the CIA and become the right-hand man of a Chicago drug lord!

Of course, was that it all perfectly believable. Eric, Tim knew, had been born with a brain capable of moving mountains.

The thing that truly unnerved Tim was the fact that his brother had finally found mountains worth moving in such a cold, dark place.

"And, this whole rural drug network…it actually worked?" he managed weakly.

Eric coolly flashed a cocksure smile.

"It worked, alright. Within a few months, T.C. upped his drug shipments to the heartland by 35 percent. Eventually, more than half of his drug supply was sold by dealers outside of Chicago. And, if any of those people were ever pinched, the chances of their product being traced back to T.C. were remote."

"Business was booming," Eric continued. "And this was before we began to dabble in the meth."

"You mean crystal meth?" Tim questioned. "Hillbilly heroin?"

"They used to call it that," Eric corrected. "The nickname doesn't fit anymore, because meth is used everywhere, not just in the boonies.

The meth movement is currently at least as big as crack ever was, and unlike crack, meth isn't confined to cities. Meth use is on the increase."

"The thing about meth," Eric explained, "Is that you can make it yourself. A user just needs an over-the-counter drug that contains ephedrine, like Sudafed, and the right chemicals to mix it with. There are thousands of 'meth labs' all over the country with people cooking this shit up. There are meth dealers, of course, but you don't necessarily need them."

"When I approached T.C. about meth," Eric went on, "he assumed I wanted him to create a bunch of 'meth labs' outside the city. But that was the last thing I wanted him to do. Meth labs are dangerous. The chemicals needed are volatile, and there's no shortage of stories of addicts blowing themselves up or burning their faces off when they eventually screw up. I didn't want any part of that. I told T.C. that the money to be made from meth would come from the drugs used to make it—the nonprescription drugs like Sudafed."

"With meth use reaching epidemic proportions," Eric continued, "drug stores and supermarkets had moved Sudafed behind the counter. The only recourse left was to steal it. But pharmacy stick-ups had proven to be dangerous and unreliable. I figured if we could find a way to purchase mass amounts of the drug, we could sell it at an inflated price to ragged addicts being turned away from the counter at CVS."

"T.C. suggested the idea of obtaining large quantities of nonprescription pseudoephedrine from Mexico, but that didn't pan out. The Mexican government had recently turned up the heat on its drug exporters, and things were dicey for T.C.'s south-of-the-border partners. As a matter of fact, it was beginning to look like his supply of cocaine and heroin would be threatened."

"And so," Eric continued, "I began a search for another drug pipeline. T.C. needed a reliable source of large quantities of pseudoephedrine, as well as coke and H; a source without the danger of government interference."

"And one night," Eric concluded with a telling grin, "I had an epiphany! Can you guess what it was?"

Tim didn't return Eric's smile. He nodded and gravely replied.

"Yes, Eric, I think I can."

CHAPTER 23

Bogged down in Saturday night traffic, the black Escalade inched down L.A.'s Wilshire Boulevard.

The large Avis SUV sadly lacked what T.C. Watson called "the bling factor." The vehicle had factory-issued rims, a standard sound-system and un-tinted windows. Eric Sutton, sitting in the vehicle's passenger's seat, speculated that someone could make a pretty penny renting the kind of "pimped-out rides" that guys like T.C. preferred.

T.C. took one hand off the steering wheel and gestured to the quaint strip malls dotting both sides of the boulevard.

"We're getting close, right?" T.C. guessed, pointing to the Korean characters that accompanied the English in neon above each business.

"Yes," Eric replied. "We're smack-dab in the middle of Koreatown right now. The club is only a few blocks further."

"What's it called again?" T.C. inquired. "Club Canary?"

Eric glanced at the older man to his left. T.C., as usual, was nattily dressed to impress. Tonight he chose a blood red silk suit with leather shoes to match.

"It's Club Kenari," Eric corrected. "It's named after a flower." Eric warily eyed his partner. "Are you sure you're okay with doing this in a nightclub, T.C.?"

T.C. scoffed.

"Bitch, please! I'm straight out of South Chicago, boy! I grew up in clubs! Don't get it twisted!"

"Okay," Eric replied. "But I don't think you've ever seen a club quite like this one..."

"Whatever, Shadow, whatever," T.C. interrupted dismissively. "A club is a club. Anyway...tell me again, how'd you narrow it down to this place?"

Eric shrugged his shoulders.

"Simple logistics. The club's human traffic is far from the norm, considering its rated capacity."

T.C. narrowed his eyes in annoyance.

"You wanna put that in English terms, muthafucka?"

Eric grinned.

"Sorry. What I mean is that, of all the Korean nightclubs on this street, this one stands out, because way more people are entering this place on a Saturday night than should be the case, given the club's size. And that's because the customers aren't staying long. Most go in, then quickly leave. Clearly, they're not coming here for the nightlife."

T.C. was unimpressed.

"I don't know, Shad," he replied. "Seems to me like you just got lucky. I mean, that's what happens at clubs. The dance floor gets packed. Then people go in, see they ain't got no space, and jet. So you got niggas going into a small place, then leavin' quick. So, like I said, you got lucky."

Eric, still smiling, shook his head.

"You'll understand when you see the place," he assured T.C. Eric pointed up ahead of the Escalade. "Get ready. The club is coming up on the right."

"What," T.C. questioned, "Should I start looking for a parking space?"

"No," Eric replied dismissively. "Parking doesn't exist in L.A. on a Saturday night. We'll just use the valet."

A line of predominantly Asian twenty-somethings snaked along the sidewalk to a narrow door jammed between a Korean restaurant and a closed convenience store. Above the door, the words "Club Kenari" were stylishly emblazoned in neon blue letters.

"Mm-mm..." T.C. murmured, his eyes perusing the scantily-clad females waiting to enter the club. "It's been a while since I dipped my wick in some of that Shanghai shit, you feel me? I might have to roll up on one of them 'happy ending' massages when this shit is done..."

"Focus, T.C." Eric advised with a roll of his eyes. "Keep your eyes on the prize. And Shanghai is in China, by the way. We're dealing with Koreans tonight. Big difference. You'll probably want to remember that."

"Bitch, shut the fuck up!" T.C. snapped. "What, you think I don't know business from pleasure! And don't hand me no 'eye on the prize' bullshit. Where were your eyes last week when I scored you that little visit from Candace and Shanquay?"

Eric's mouth widened into a guilty smirk.

"Well, okay...point taken."

Over the past several months, Eric had enjoyed a special perk as T.C. Watson's prized advisor. T.C., who had a financial stake in many of Chicago's strip clubs and houses of ill repute, had begun providing Eric with "female companionship."

Eric had lost his virginity in the backseat of a sport-utility vehicle—courtesy of a surgically-enhanced platinum blond named, fittingly enough, Destiny. Since then, Eric had received more 'visits' than he could count, from similar women eager to please.

Eric didn't have to talk to or even acknowledge these women! They simply showed up to perform the 'services' Eric had envisioned when he was a student at Ruston High. Then the women left.

As he pulled the Escalade up to the curb, T.C. glanced at Eric.

"Are you sure this place even has valet parking?"

"For $100,000," Eric replied, "They'll have valet parking for us."

As the two men climbed out of the Escalade, a slender man in a black suit approached them, scowling.

"Hey! You can't park that here!"

Eric calmly raised his hands in assurance.

"I'm Shadow. We have an appointment with Jason."

The man was quickly apologetic.

"Oh, I'm sorry, gentlemen. We'll take care of your vehicle."

The man yelled in Korean to a second black-suited doorman, who jogged over to the SUV. With a smirk, T.C. tossed the young Korean man his keys.

"Park it somewhere nice, Jimmy."

The first doorman gestured to Eric and T.C. "Please, gentlemen, come with me."

The Korean ushered the two Americans past the long line of club-goers and through the narrow doorway. As they entered Club Kenari, Eric glanced back to the front of the line. A young man, accompanied by a female, flashed a small lime-green card to the muscular bouncer.

Eric's mouth widened into a faint smile as he realized what was going on. It made sense. People coming to Club Kenari for drugs had a special membership card—a card that waived any entrance fee. A cloak-and-dagger application process was probably required for one of those green cards, limiting L.A.P.D. undercover cops from easily obtaining one. Although admirable, the club's security system wasn't nearly as impressive as the "tagging" concept that Eric had installed at Maxwell Lee.

Eric turned to see if his silk-suited drug lord had picked up on the subtle system. Instead, T.C. was staring at the club's interior, totally bewildered.

"Shad," T.C. questioned, "Where the fuck is the club?"

At the far end of the room, a cocktail bar spanned the entire wall. To the left of the bar was a small stage with a microphone stand. Opposite the stage were fifteen round wooden tables, each of them taken by smiling, boisterous Koreans. The room was packed.

To the right of the bar was a long narrow hallway that stretched to the rear of the club. On each side of the hallway were ten doors, all of them shut.

On the small stage, a clearly intoxicated young Korean was slurring his way through a loud rendition of Donna Summer's disco classic, "Hot Stuff."

Eric laughed.

"The club?" he replied. "You're looking at it! What, T.C.? You've never been to a Karaoke bar? People pay to drink and sing. Then they either sit out here in the club or rent one of the private rooms down the hallway. Then they sing, sing, sing the night away!"

T.C. stared in revulsion at the raucous crowd cheering on the disco reveler.

"We're doing this thing," T.C. stated flatly, "And then we're getting the fuck out of here."

Eric and T.C. followed their Korean guide down the narrow hallway. Eric watched, mildly amused, as T.C. listened in disgust to the show-tunes and bell-bottom standards that emanated from the rooms.

T.C.'s misery ended when they reached the final four doors. The music was absent here, but not the human traffic.

Young men and women, all of whom carried lime green cards, steadily streamed in and out of three of the rooms. Eric glanced at T.C., who nodded in understanding. Business that had nothing to do with singing was booming at Club Kenari.

The suited Korean gestured to the last door on the left.

"Please, gentlemen, go in. Jason is waiting for you." Eric followed an edgy T.C. through the door. The Korean man, remaining outside, shut the door behind them.

The circular room was festive. Neon-yellow cushions sat atop benches lining powder blue walls. A silver disco-ball hung from the ceiling in the center of the room. Directly under the sparkling ball was a coffee table, also neon yellow, on which a thick, bright pink directory of Karaoke songs was placed.

A large plasma screen television was attached to one wall, and two microphone cords extended from a black console below the television. The microphones lay on a yellow bench, alongside a short, fortyish Korean man.

The man had a mature, angular face, and a thick patch of black hair sprinkled with gray. He wore expensive tan   dress pants and a buttoned dress-shirt that, oddly enough, matched the deep red of T.C.'s ensemble. The man rose to his feet.

"Gentlemen, thank you for coming," he offered with a thin smile. "My name is Jason. Please. Have a seat."

The man extended a handshake to Eric, then T.C., who couldn't mask his discomfort as he took a seat beside Eric on the yellow bench.

"Before we begin, gentlemen" Jason stated formally, "Please understand that your generous payment to me did not 'buy' you this meeting. While I—we—appreciated the gesture, you're here because of the extremely lucrative business deal my suppliers anticipate making with you."

T.C.'s eyes narrowed. Jason continued.

"I want you to know, however, that I only operate a small drug business out of this Karaoke club, and that my future involvement in this matter will be limited. Since you approached me initially, I have been authorized to serve as my suppliers' representative."

"When I shared your proposal with them, they were intrigued enough to investigate your operation in Chicago. They were quite impressed, and would now like to hear more details about the arrangement you seek to establish."

Eric looked over at T.C., who recognized that the floor was now his.

"Well, J," T.C. began "As you know, I run a booming business back east. H, Coke, Crack...We own Chicago, and pretty much the whole state of Illinois. I've got two reasons for being here. Up till now, I've been getting my goods from some cats—from some gentlemen, in Mexico. But the heat's been turned up down there, and I'm startin' to worry that my supply is going to be cut off."

"And two," T.C. continued, "I'm looking to expand into meth."

Jason nodded.

"And the purchases you are seeking to make..." Jason interrupted, "are on the order of three to five million dollars?"

T.C. flashed a confidant grin.

"At first," he replied. "If the shit is good, I'll start spendin' some real money."

Jason nodded a second time.

"My suppliers are interested in such a relationship. You will find that doing business with them is vastly superior to dealing with the Mexicans."

"The Mexicans," Jason continued, "have to elude their own federal drug enforcement agency, which they accomplish through substantial payments of bribes to local politicians and law-enforcement officials. These costs are passed directly onto you."

"In contrast, my supplier," Jason went on, "is the federal government."

"Now, I do pay a mark-up on the goods I purchase. But that money is nothing more than a modest tax the government extracts, which I gladly pay because I know my suppliers are in no danger of being shut down. They cannot be shut down."

Eric was smiling. This was why he wanted to do business with the North Koreans. No supply of illegal drugs was more stable than one operated by a military dictator.

"We understand," Eric assured.

Jason continued, "Business with my suppliers is done on their terms. If you are prompt and efficient, you will have no problems. If you conduct yourselves otherwise, the consequences will be swift and merciless. Do you understand?"

Eric nodded. T.C. was visibly annoyed by the harsh warnings from the diminutive Korean, but he kept his mouth shut. Jason went on.

"Now, although my suppliers can provide you with the large quantities of heroin and cocaine you need, they are more interested in helping you to expand your rural crystal methamphetamine operations in Illinois, and the potential such expansion holds."

"We hoped as much," Eric responded. "The future of the American market exists in this area. We know that North Kor—that your suppliers have access to large quantities of the prescription drugs used to make meth. We would like to purchase these drugs and distribute them in our network."

"Ah," Jason replied, his thin smile returning to his lips. "You are correct, in that my suppliers do possess vast quantities of the drugs you seek. But they have no interest in selling you those drugs. They use those drugs, in giant state-run laboratories, where massive quantities of crystal methamphetamine are manufactured."

"My suppliers," Jason finished, "are ready to ship you truckloads of product. But that product won't be prescription ephedrine. It will be refined, market-ready crystal meth. Do you understand?"

T.C.'s eyes widened, and he anxiously turned to Eric. The dapper dealer had been caught off-guard by Jason's proposal for selling meth in bulk form.

Eric hadn't considered this either, but he quickly made sense of it in his head. There was a bumper crop of meth across the Pacific that needed to be carted into America's heartland. North Korea had the crop. T.C. would provide the cart.

Both sides would get filthy, stinking rich.

Eric shifted his eyes toward T.C. as his mouth widened into a telling grin. Eric turned back to Jason.

"We understand perfectly," Eric asserted. "We're in."

CHAPTER 24

Eric Sutton leaned towards his older brother.

"When you traveled cross-country," he began, "You drove, right?"

Still reeling from his brother's narrative, Tim nodded slowly.

"Okay," Eric continued. "Let's say you're a strung-out meth addict. Are you still driving that piece-of-shit blue Taurus? Because that thing has 'drug addict' written all over it! Anyway," Eric went on, "Let's say you're driving west from New Hampshire, looking to score a hit along the way. When you cross from Pennsylvania into Ohio, you enter T.C. Watson's drug territory, and you don't leave it 'till you leave the state of South Dakota!"

Tim's eyes widened.

"Are you're saying, that after collaborating with the North Koreans, you expanded T.C.'s territory to include the entire Midwest?"

"Pretty much," Eric confirmed, smiling. "At least, with respect to meth. Now, I'm not suggesting that we cornered the market. We certainly couldn't force all of the addicts cooking up their own meth in the sticks to start buying ours. And, we were careful to stay out of the big cities like Cleveland, Columbus, and Indianapolis."

"But in the rural center of America," Eric assured, "T.C. is king. Local dealers push pure, reasonably-priced crystal methamphetamine, trucked into the heartland by one T.C. Watson. Those bags of meth might as well be labeled 'Made in North Korea.'"

Tim Sutton rested his elbows on the surface of the conference table, head in hands.

"Good Lord," he managed, rubbing his temples.

It was pointless, Tim knew, to question a business relationship that was so quintessentially "Eric." The whole scheme was completely unethical, yet undeniably logical.

His brother's partnership with North Korea was illegal and immoral—but totally free of hypocrisy. Tim knew, as Eric obviously did, that the United States did business every day with dozens of countries that denied their citizens basic human rights. Eric no doubt relished the idea that he was dealing with the Koreans because of their lack of scruples, not in spite of them.

Tim also recognized that there were much more concrete benefits to dealing with the North Koreans.

Most of the western world saw North Korea as a prickly dictatorship with a nuclear arsenal—a nation to be avoided at all costs. As long as Kim-Jong-Il wasn't lobbing warheads at Japan, the United States and its allies intended to leave him alone.

This was obviously a huge advantage for Eric. Tim realized that North Korea could hang banners at its borders saying "We're making boatloads of drugs here!" without the fear of global reprisal. The nation was as secure a drug pipeline as Eric's benefactor, T.C. Watson, could have ever hoped to have.

"Two weeks after our meeting at Club Kenari," Eric continued, "T.C. returned to Chicago, and I headed to Long Beach. There I visited a vessel known as the Haihu." Eric grinned. "A ship you're familiar with. Jason, my Korean contact, explained their system for smuggling drugs out of North Korea."

"Drug-filled shipping containers are trucked from North Korea to Dalian, loaded along with legitimate cargo onto freighters like the Haihu, and shipped all over the world. Thanks to the deal I brokered with the North Koreans, the number of containers bound for L.A. and Seattle was about to increase substantially."

Eric had spent the rest of that month traveling up and down the West Coast. He met illicit dockworkers, Korean-American drug-runners, and people serving as official liaisons to the North Korean government. Once Eric was completely familiar with the North Korean drug trade system, he had T.C. send him $2,000,000, which he used to close a deal on top quality heroin. Meth acquisition was left for later.

Next, Eric had headed back east, to reorganize T.C.'s Midwest network and to prepare for the distribution of meth. He established a series of hubs, where inbound truckloads of North Korean drugs could be stored prior to sale in the surrounding area. These were painstakingly scrutinized low-profile locations, which Eric guarded with a plethora of electronic surveillance accoutrements.

Months later, satisfied that he had put together an extensive, efficient, and sufficiently secure network, Eric had returned to Seattle. On a rain-soaked dock on Harbor Island, he shook hands with the Koreans and closed a $50,000,000 methamphetamine deal.

Tim's eyes widened with amazement, then narrowed with curiosity.

"When was that day you brokered your monumental meth deal?"

"A little over three years ago," Eric casually replied.

"Three years?" Tim gasped. "Then that means…"

"That's right," Eric interrupted, "I did it all in two years. Before my twenty-first birthday, I stole $20,000,000 from the CIA, redefined the operations of a Chicago drug kingpin, and cut a $50,000,000 deal with the North Koreans. Not too bad, if I do say so myself."

"And on top of that," Eric added. "Because of our carefully selected locations, trained personal and high-grade security equipment, none of T.C.'s warehouses have ever been raided. As long as they remain secure, T.C.'s operation is safe."

"It probably helps you," Tim added gravely, "That you're dealing in meth, as opposed to crack or heroin."

Heroin, cocaine, and crack, Tim grasped, were perceived as imported, then networked, drugs. To combat their proliferation, the DEA caught little fish and subsequently used them to catch bigger fish. Eventually, they might get their hands on a guy like T.C. Watson.

Meth, on the other hand, was seen as a drug that sprung up at the grass roots level. The DEA tried to coordinate a national response to the meth epidemic, but primarily addressed it at the local level. So if a dealer was pinched in Iowa with a few kilos of T.C.'s meth, the cops were likely to assume that the stuff was cooked up locally. T.C.'s hands were clean.

Eric flashed a mischievous grin and winked at Tim.

"Ahhh...Exactly! I knew you'd catch on, Big Brother!"

"T.C.'s ass is also protected" Eric continued, "By the degree to which he stays on top of his operation. Every sale in every town is logged into a computer database in Maxwell Lee--a database maintained by the same ghetto prodigies who cut their computer teeth operating my 'tagging' system. Although Maxwell Lee is still the center of T.C.'s Chicago operation, its main function, now, is to serve as the ultra-secure nerve center for T.C.'s entire operation."

"Thanks to me," Eric concluded, "every aspect of T.C.'s business is digitally wired. As long as it remains so, he stays one step ahead of the law."

Tim nodded slowly, but his confusion refused to settle.

"But Eric, I still don't understand! How does all of this--"

"Get us here, to this building in North Korea?" Eric finished. "The answer to that question stems from the final promise I made to T.C. Watson."

"I knew from the beginning," Eric began, "That I wouldn't remain at T.C.'s side forever. I told him that I'd make him rich and powerful and then move on. I made it clear to T.C. that eventually I'd leave. I had no idea what kinds of opportunities would open up, given the illicit nature of my technical wizardry. I simply knew that I would leverage them when they did occur, to secure as much power and influence as possible. It wasn't long before another opportunity came along."

"The North Koreans had made a mint selling drugs to T.C. They were impressed with our operation and could see who was responsible for its success; not T.C., of course, but yours truly."

"They decided that I was an intellectual and creative asset they had to 'recruit'. So, while I was managing T.C.'s business, the North Koreans were conspiring how to acquire me. Ultimately, they succeeded."

"With one major twist. When the North Koreans want something, they don't buy it. They just take it."

CHAPTER 25

You're driving through a tunnel.

Wrapped in a drug-induced cocoon, Eric tried to pry open his weary eyelids.

As sometimes happens in a dream, things briefly made perfect sense.

You hear that rhythmic bumping? That's the sound of tires rolling over regularly spaced gaps in the concrete, like when you drive over a bridge. But there's a roof over your head, and there isn't any water. You must be driving through a tunnel.

But wasn't this long, dark, perfectly-round tunnel too narrow for an automobile?

Uhh...of course! This must be a special tunnel, reserved for small vehicles. You must be riding a motorcycle.

But where were all the other vehicles? Why wasn't this "motorcycle" making any noise and where were its handlebars? Did Eric even know how to ride a motorcycle? And who was the guy sitting next to him in the military uniform?

Eric's brain advised him to quit asking so many questions.

You're riding your motorcycle through a tunnel. See that man, standing up ahead in the light? He's waiting for someone to pick him up, so that he can travel through the tunnel, too. See? It makes perfect sense.

For about five more seconds, this completely empty logic made perfect sense to Eric.

Then the fog of confusion cleared.

I'm not dreaming.

Eric blinked, looked down at the pair of strong arms pressed against his body, and whipped his head to the right.

The North Korean soldier noticed that his charge had awoken. "Stay still!" the uniformed man commanded.

Eric instinctively tried to disobey the order. He quickly realized, however, that his doped-up body was unresponsive to his mental directives. After feeble attempts to pry himself from the soldier's clutches, Eric slumped back against the bench.

The bench that was somehow propelling itself forward.

Whatever he was riding on, it certainly wasn't a motorcycle.

Eric slowly rotated his head and discovered that he was propped on the front end of a human-powered rickshaw.

The vehicle had a spoked wheel on each side and a bicycle attached to the rear, with a second uniformed Korean man perched on its pedals. While the first soldier kept Eric's drugged frame from falling out of the vehicle, the second soldier powered the contraption along.

In his earlier confused state, Eric had gotten one detail right: He was in a tunnel. They were pedaling down a long, white, concrete tube about fifteen feet in diameter.

Although the tunnel had no lighting, the area immediately in front of the rickshaw was illuminated by the bicycling soldier's helmet-mounted lamp. As the vehicle approached the end of the tunnel, the soldier's headlamp illumination became less and less necessary, due to the sunlight pouring through the gaping opening.

Silhouetted against the light, a lone figure awaited the rickshaw's arrival.

As it rolled to a stop, the grey-haired, smartly dressed North Korean military officer strode forward.

At his approach, both soldiers jumped from the rickshaw and snapped to attention. Eric, suddenly robbed of his human counterweight, nearly toppled from the vehicle. After reestablishing his tenuous perch on the rickshaw, he trained his bleary eyes on the Korean officer.

The man was about 5'10," somewhere between 50 and 70 years old. His lined and grizzled facial features and nearly white coif seemed like the product of age and challenging life experiences.

An imposing collection of pins and medals were pinned to the breast of his crisp uniform, and he wore a wide-brimmed military cap.

Although Eric could not make out the officer's insignia, he could tell from his commanding demeanor that he held a high rank. The two soldiers remained at attention.

The officer distractedly acknowledged them before turning his black eyes on Eric. Immediately noticing the young man's lethargy, the officer motioned to the two soldiers. The men sprinted to Eric's side, hoisting him up into a standing position. As Eric dangled weakly from their arms, the officer approached until he and Eric were eye-to-eye.

"So. . .you. . . are the brilliant young American," he stated slowly, in heavily accented English.

The officer surveyed every inch of Eric's body, as if doing so would provide insight into Eric's mind.

"Very well," he gruffly concluded. He motioned to the soldiers supporting Eric. They abruptly did an about-face, roughly dragging Eric through the tunnel exit into the open outdoors.

Eric could see that the area was surrounded by towering pine trees caked with sticky white snow. Overhead, a bright midday sun lit the sparse winter landscape, briefly robbing Eric of his sight.

As his breath crystallized in the frosty air, Eric feared he would blindly lurch into a snowdrift when his captors released their grasp. Fortunately, this didn't happen; Eric's motor control function seemed to have finally returned.

The glistening snow cover was nearly a foot deep, with a narrow shoveled pathway leading from the tunnel exit to the woods. The stately officer briskly strode down this trail, with Eric and his minders in tow.

With each step, Eric became more alert and self-aware of his current situation. Questions that had been suppressed by days and days of heavy sedation crashed into his consciousness.

Where am I? Why was I kidnapped? Am I going to be tortured? Killed? What the fuck is going on here?

A scene that exacerbated his confusion materialized in the wilderness: The entire forest was a maze of miniature concrete huts!

A bewildered Eric was escorted past the huts deeper into the woods. A veritable ghost town of small, uniformly square, window-less concrete buildings emerged beneath the trees. There were hundreds of them, many connected by well-worn paths.

The whole place was eerily vacant.

Minutes later, the scenery changed. The huts fell away, revealing an open snow-covered plain. Eric was able to quickly discern that this expanse contained about fifteen circular clearings in the snow. Each seemed to have a different diameter, the largest being perhaps 70 feet. While contemplating the purpose of these strange circles, Eric's eyes were drawn to a large concrete structure another several hundred feet down the trail—a structure teeming with North Korean soldiers.

The soldiers weren't carrying weapons, and the men appeared to be moving a large quantity of furniture and computer equipment into the building.

When Eric, along with his guards, reached the sizable edifice, the officer wheeled around to face him. Behind the officer, several of the soldiers stole glances at the pale-skinned, blond-haired new arrival. The officer stared at Eric with cold eyes.

"Eric Sutton," the officer barked, "I am Colonel Pak. I have been in charge of this facility for more than 30 years. Now, I am in charge of you. Follow me."

Colonel Pak quickly spun around and strode through the building's metal mesh door. Eric expected to be propelled in the Colonel's wake, but his two guards stepped away. Realizing that he could now fully support himself, Eric hustled after the Colonel.

Beyond the mesh door was a tiny room, roughly the size of the huts Eric had passed earlier. At the far end of this room, an open wooden sliding door revealed a cavernous space beyond.

Eric felt a rush of warm air pouring from this area as he followed Colonel Pak through the sliding door.

The huge room was apparently in the early stages of mass remodeling. To Eric's left, two soldiers were installing a refrigerator. To the right, three others sorted through a mass of electric cables as they assembled a computer workstation. The rest of the room was a jumble of furniture, wall and bathroom fixtures, and electronics. Without turning to face Eric, Colonel Pak began to robotically point to various areas of the room.

"That will be your kitchen," he began, motioning to the left. "Your food supply will be replenished each month. To the right is your workstation. You will have several computers, each corresponding to a specific project. You will also be provided with a file system containing hard copies of all the documents that you require."

"This facility has been hardwired for high-speed internet access through the existing electrical grid, so you will have a reliable communication link with Pyongyang."

"Ahead, to the right, is your bathroom area. To the left is where you will sleep. A conference area with a large table will be established at the far end of the room. In this area, at least once per month, you will brief key government officials on the state of your operations."

The Colonel turned toward Eric.

"Do you understand?" he mechanically inquired.

Eric's jaw dropped open. His face turned bright red as he stared back at the grizzled officer.

"Dude!" Eric finally exploded. "Are you fucking insane? I have no fucking clue what's going on here! A couple of weeks ago I was minding my own fucking business in the U.S. of A! Since then, I've been kidnapped, drugged unconscious with enough dope to kill a fucking horse, and been taken God knows where. And I don't have a fucking clue as to why you crazy Korean motherfucks did any of this!"

"So, no!" Eric forcefully concluded, "I'm a little fucking short on understanding right now!"

Colonel Pak absorbed the outburst without a hint of emotion. As a thoroughly winded Eric struggled to recover from his tirade, the Colonel matter-of-factly replied.

"From this site," he began, "You will gradually assume direction of our nation's international drug exportation. You will also provide us with insight on drug production, electronic security measures, and any other domestic or international logistical questions that we see fit to present."

"The location of this facility is hidden, secure, and heavily guarded. Escape is impossible. You will remain here permanently, conducting assigned business. If you resist, you will be tortured. If you continue to resist, you will be eliminated."

"Now," the Colonel finished. "Do you understand?"

Eric's crimson face turned white with shock. He staggered for a few seconds before spying a black computer chair placed aimlessly near the doorway. Eric stumbled to the chair, collapsed on it, rested his elbows on his knees, and put his head in his hands. Eric spent the next few minutes in stunned silence.

Then, oddly enough, he began to laugh.

It began as a faint, exhausted chuckle, but soon grew into a hearty guffaw that surprised not only Colonel Pak, but every other soldier in the room. Still laughing, Eric finally looked at the Colonel. Shaking his head in disbelief, Eric stared at the icy soldier with a wide grin.

"Jesus Christ!" Eric laughed. "You fuckers want me to work for you?"

Colonel Pak's expression didn't change, but he slowly nodded a single time. Eric, still chuckling, ran his hand through his blond hair in fatigued amusement.

"You know," he managed finally. "All you had to do was ask."

CHAPTER 26

"So," Tim concluded, "You really are a prisoner here!"

Eric flashed a smug smile.

"C'mon big brother," he chastised. "I'm no prisoner. I would expect you, of all people, to understand."

"Understand what?" Tim protested. "The North Koreans abducted you and stuck you here to do their dirty work! How, exactly, are you not a prisoner?"

Eric shook his head.

"Tim, this isn't a prison."

Eric's smile shifted to an icy grimace.

"Ruston was a prison," he continued coldly. "Prison is knowing that you're exceptionally brilliant—and coming to the realization that your intelligence means absolutely nothing to the people around you."

Tim understood his brother's meaning.

When their mother had died, Eric had lost the one person who validated his destiny. In the years that followed, his mom's loving encouragement was replaced by the numbingly standard expectations of his teachers, classmates, and even his father.

Ruston's townsfolk had assumed that Eric would do what smart, ambitious kids always did. He would graduate high school at the top of his class, matriculate to college, then on to business, medical or law school. Then Eric would settle into a white collar, respectable job.

The kind of life that Eric despised.

Eric looked at the room around him and forced a deep laugh.

"Prison?" he chuckled. "Here? Shit, Tim, do you know what I do here?"

"Well, I-I guess..." Tim stammered, "...Drug stuff?"

Eric rolled his eyes.

"Drug stuff?" he repeated sarcastically.

Eric pointed to his cluttered workstation across the room.

"I've got data on every poppy field in North Korea, every location where heroin is processed and packaged, every crystal meth factory, and every single Korean citizen who sets foot in any of those places!"

"I control the production, timetable and shipments worldwide. I study the drug-purchasing potential of every region on the globe, and establish new networks. All of the techniques I developed for T.C. are now being practiced in southeast Asia and parts of Europe."

"And no more of this Michigan militia shit," Eric boasted. "I work for a nation now. Let's say I want to build a crystal meth warehouse in Bangkok. All I have to do is tell the Koreans where the building should be located and the required square footage. Then I simply compose a technological grocery list. Infrared cameras? Done. Motion sensors? Done. In-house computer database? Of course. Trained professionals? Absolutely. It's carte blanche."

"But you can't leave!" Tim protested. "I mean, aside from obvious challenge and apparent gratification . . . you're stuck here! Forever!"

Eric leaned back in his chair and shrugged his shoulders.

"So?" he smirked. "Who gives a shit? There aren't many places I'd rather be than right here."

Eric pointed across the room at the gaudy array of lingerie in his messy bedroom area.

"Tim," he asked with a hint of curiosity, tilting his head toward his brother. "I don't suppose you've gotten laid in the five years since I left?"

Tim's pale face reddened slightly, but he remained silent.

"Don't answer that," Eric hastily proceeded. "I don't mean to be condescending. It's not like I'm 'Don Juan' or anything. However..."

Eric slyly winked at his older brother.

"I have," he continued, "demonstrated my own worth to the extent that willing and capable people reward me with plenty of, shall we say, 'feminine companionship.'"

"Back in Chicago, T.C. demonstrated his gratitude by delivering vacuous high-end escorts to satisfy my sexual needs. The North Koreans are equally generous."

Eric gestured again, to his collection of undergarments.

"The supply of women is endless. They're brought in, they perform, they leave. Sometimes they're Chinese, sometimes they're Korean, and sometimes they come in groups! At my signal, they're taken away. Their panties, however, stay with me."

"Lord..." Tim muttered. "And I don't imagine you actually talk to these women..."

"Nope," Eric assured. "I never even try. None of them speak English. It's better than Chicago, really. Occasionally, one of T.C.'s bimbos wanted to talk, so I had to ignore her until she stopped. No such problems here."

As Tim attempted to suppress his disgust, Eric swiveled his chair, rotating toward the pile of high-tech gadgets amassed in the rear corner.

"Women, obviously, aren't the only entity I collect."

Eric reached for a brightly colored piece of equipment near the top of the pile. As Eric set the device on the conference table, Tim realized that it was the Nintendo Corporation's latest, state-of-the-art video game system.

"Look at this thing," Eric commanded, gesturing proudly at the neon yellow box. "You know how long I've had this? 13 months! Shit, it's only been on store shelves in Japan for seven."

Eric looked at Tim with a pompous grin.

"Know why I have that? Because I asked for it. I simply wrote a note that said, 'Boy, I'd sure like to see the latest game system the Japanese are developing!' Two days later, that thing 'fell off' the back of a truck in Tokyo."

"It was the same with all of that stuff," Eric added, gesturing casually at the pile of wires and metal. "None of that crap has anything to do with my work here. I just wanted it. And I got it, no questions asked."

Eric rolled his chair toward Tim's, as close as possible to his brother's face to drive his point home.

"It's not about the women, Tim, or about all of this stuff. It's not about what I have. It's about why I have it. I'm a goddamned Faberge Egg to these people. They need me, and they know it. Screw freedom. I have power."

Tim leaned back in his chair, stared down at the conference table and let out a dejected sigh.

"I know," Tim admitted softly. "Eric, I know. You've got everything you always wanted. But to get it, you had to provide a steady stream of deadly drugs to thousands of addicts around the world."

Eric pursed his lips and shrugged a second time.

"Hey," he replied evenly, "That was the path that presented itself. And it's not like I'm Hitler or anything. Addicts are always going to need their fix. If they weren't getting their junk from T.C. Watson and North Korea, they'd be getting it from somewhere else."

Tim issued an exhausted sigh.

"I'm not sure how to feel about all of this, Eric," Tim mumbled. "But you're right: Hitler, you're not. I have to admit, though: I feel a little like Eva Braun right now. I'm stuck in a small room with you as enemies close in around us. And I'm wondering if I'm going to make it out alive."

Eric's mouth opened slightly. He'd become so entrenched in justifying his actions that he'd forgotten the circumstances that had brought his brother halfway around the world. Eric spent the next few seconds in silence. When he finally spoke, his tone was tinged with regret.

"Tim," Eric sighed, "I…I never meant for anything bad to happen to you. All of those years without contact…it wasn't just about staying off the grid. I didn't want you, of all people, to be vulnerable to the folks I've had to befriend, or to their enemies."

"I know," Tim admitted. "But here I am, just the same. And so is Sarah."

Eric's eyes narrowed inquisitively.

"Sarah? You mean the red-haired girl…"

Tim nodded.

"For reasons I can't begin to understand, she's here to capture, or worse, kill you. And from what I've seen of this woman, I doubt she's just going to let me go. Eric, how the hell are either of us going to get out of this situation alive?"

Eric leaned forward, raised both of his arms, and clasped the shoulders of his only sibling, his only true friend.

"Don't worry," he stated, firmly. "We'll figure it out. For starters, let's figure out why you were brought here."

CHAPTER 27

"Two minutes, Sergeant, over."

"In two, copy."

Jim Sariani slid infrared goggles down over his white baklava and addressed Paul Wallin, Tevin Davidson, and Jordan Wood—the three U.S. Army Rangers who were crouching inside the cargo container.

"You heard him, guys. Gear up."

The four men pulled the drawstrings of their white camouflage hoods tight around their faces. Then they hefted their M-4 Carbine assault rifles, each covered with a black-and-white camouflage wrap. Completely encased in white with their eyes obscured by black infrared goggles, the Rangers resembled "Star Wars" soldiers preparing for a futuristic battle.

A moment later, Sariani's radio headset received a second report.

"Sergeant, we have a problem. The facility is completely fenced-in. It looks quiet, but there's a large troop transport vehicle blocking the entrance, over."

Sariani frowned.

"Do you see any movement, over?"

"Negative, Sergeant. The vehicle's passenger side door is open, but there doesn't appear to be any movement or response to our arrival, over."

"Alright," Sariani replied into the tiny microphone. "We'll offload here. Get us out of this box, over."

"Roger that."

The rumbling sound of the truck's idling engine ceased and two Korean CIA operatives, disguised as North Korean soldiers, swung open the back door.

With rifles drawn, the four white-suited men peeled out into the cold mountain night to survey the area.

Without acknowledging their Korean comrades, the Rangers crept toward the troop transport truck. Sariani signaled for Davidson to approach the driver's side, and for Wallin and Wood to inspect the rear.

Sariani crept along the right side of the truck, his rifle trained on its open door. When he reached the door, he deftly swung his rifle into the cab. Sariani discovered, however, that this particular threat had already been eliminated. He issued a radio report to his fellow Rangers, who were also wearing headsets.

"I've got two dead bodies in the front of the vehicle. Looks like they were executed at close range with a single shot to the head. The guy on the passenger's side appears to be an officer."

Wallin's report immediately followed from the back of the truck.

"Sarge, it's a damn bloodbath back here. We're looking at ten dead North Korean soldiers, each killed the same way, one gun-shot to the head, over."

Sariani nodded to himself.

"Alright. Sang-Ki, Du-Ho," he directed the CIA operatives, "Hop back in the truck while we secure the facility, over."

"Roger," the two men replied in unison over the radio.

The four camouflaged soldiers hustled through the deep snow toward the facility's metal gate. Sliding through the narrow opening one-by-one, the men were briefly illuminated as they jogged under the single yellow lamp before disappearing into the darkened compound.

Thirty feet beyond the gate, Sariani silently raised his hand, commanding his team to stop. He scanned the facility.

"Sang-Ki," Sariani whispered into his headset. "Give me a location on that beacon."

Sang-Ki, the Korean operative, sat in the cargo truck staring at a laptop connected to a satellite receiver. The computer's display showed a blinking icon on a detailed map of the North Korean facility that had been developed from U2 spy plane imagery. The icon, a bright red dot, represented the tracking beacon Sarah had attached to the drug money.

"From where I'm sitting, Sergeant, the beacon looks to be situated 50 to 70 yards ahead and to the left of the main gate, over."

Sariani looked to his left. If Sang-Ki was correct, the beacon was currently in the smaller of the facility's two buildings.

The Barracks.

Sariani turned to his men.

"Paul," he commanded, "Check out the hangar on the right. It looks quiet over there, but stay sharp. I want a report of everything that's in that building. See if there are any signs of Sarah or Tim Sutton. Tevin, Jordan and I will secure the barracks and find the money. Go!"

As Wallin broke to the right, the other three soldiers crept toward the compound's barracks, their M-4 rifles trained on its door and windows. When the Rangers had reached the building's single illuminated door, they crouched down, paused, and listened. The men exchanged knowing looks.

No sound.

As Sariani gingerly swung the door open, he and his men tip-toed into the building. Sariani immediately issued Jordan a silent command.

Right side. Bathroom. Go.

Jordan swung into the room, emerging ten seconds later with a mouthed report of "all clear."

Sariani nodded. He signaled for Jordan to turn towards the door identified in Korean letters as "Commander's Quarters/ Communications." Sariani and Davidson would enter the barracks' main room to the left, while Jordan would deal with anyone coming through the other door. As Jordan watched out of the corner of his eye, Sariani pressed his ear against the double doors.

Still no sound.

Sariani took a deep breath, looked at Davidson, and silently mouthed the word "go." As the Rangers exploded through the double doors, prepared to fire, Sariani's jaw dropped.

"Jesus Christ…" he muttered. "One woman did all of this?"

With rifles pointed down, the soldiers stepped carefully from corpse to corpse. They detected no movement.

"Clear," Sariani mouthed to Wood, who nodded. With Sariani in the lead, the men sprang through the door Jordan was guarding. Inside they discovered one additional corpse. The three men quickly returned to the front door.

"Barracks, clear," Sariani reported into his headset. "Multiple corpses. The officer in charge was likely the guy out in the passenger's seat of that troop transport. Paul, what's your situation, over?"

"Sergeant, the hangar is secure," Wallin returned. "We've got six flatbed trucks, each with a shipping container on it. The one nearest to the entrance is open. I found food, water, sleeping bags, and a few books inside. They were definitely here, over."

"Copy that," Sariani replied. "Facility is secure. Paul, back-track to the front gate, and open it. Sang-Ki, Du-Ho, you drive the cargo truck and the troop transport into that hangar. Paul, close the gate behind them and meet us at the barracks. The rest of us will look for the money, over."

Sariani turned to Davidson and Wood.

"Alright," he ordered. "Everyone take a room."

Sariani hopped over and around the bloody Korean soldiers in the main room. The men's faces, including that of a naked soldier lying a few feet from the double doors, were frozen with shock.

A few minutes later, Davidson and Wood joined Sariani.

"Anything?" Sariani inquired.

The Rangers shook their heads.

"Me neither," Sariani returned. "Fuck! What are we missing? She wouldn't make it this difficult. She wants us to find the cash!"

A light-bulb went off in Sariani's head.

"Follow me, boys."

The soldiers retreated from the barracks. Two trucks were now rumbling into the facility's hangar, and Wallin, having just shut the gate, jogged toward his comrades. Sariani eyed a pile of snow to the left of the door.

"A case of Jack Daniel's says its right there, boys..."

Sariani dug his hand into the powder, quickly retrieving a black duffle bag. Kneeling, he set the bag on the ground and unzipped it.

"We're in business, boys," Sariani reported into his headset. "Sang-Ki and Du-Ho, I'm coming in with the cash. Find a gassed up truck, and get ready to roll."

"Copy that."

As Sariani swung the duffle bag over his shoulder and trudged through the snow toward the hangar, he caught a faint glimmer of light out of the corner of his eye.

Headlights!

"Shit!" Sariani barked. "We've got company! Everyone take cover!"

Sariani sprinted into the hangar, taking cover beneath one of the cargo trucks. The other Rangers dove into the deep snow surrounding the barracks.

The CIA agents swiftly hopped out their trucks and dropped to the cement floor next to Sariani, who assessed the situation through his infrared scope.

"We've got a cargo truck and troop transport coming through the front gate." Sariani quickly fashioned a plan.

"Okay," he began. "As soon as these guys find their dead comrades, they will alert Pyongyang. We take them out or we're fucked."

"Paul, Jordan," Sariani commanded. "Circle right, get behind the vehicles, and set up flanking positions in the snow. Tevin, come 15 yards towards me, and cover the vehicle from the side. Wait until everyone is out of the rear of that transport, and then open fire. I'll handle the cargo truck. Move!"

Sariani turned to the Korean operatives and ordered them to hide in the rear of the hangar.

The vehicles came to a stop just outside the hangar. Two North Korean soldiers hopped out of the front of the truck, and slowly advanced. As Sariani listened to the two soldiers converse in Korean, he quickly deduced that they were confused by the presence of extra vehicles in the hangar.

According to the two bewildered men, at least one cargo truck had been scheduled to head east to refill its shipping container with drugs. Moreover, troop transport vehicles were normally parked next to the barracks, not inside the hangar.

One of the North Korean soldiers waved at the arriving transport vehicle and motioned for its occupants to come forward. As their cohorts poured out of the vehicle, the two men ambled into the hangar. They were less than 15 feet from Sariani, but the disciplined Ranger remained calm, coolly waiting for the sound of gunshots.

One of the men stood directly in front of Sariani's truck, gesturing to the open cargo container. He continued to voice confusion. The men were now so close to Sariani that he could have reached out and grabbed their ankles. Instead, the sergeant lay prone, waiting. . .

The crack of M-4 rifle fire abruptly rang out through the cold winter night.

Astonished, the two men above Sariani spun around and gaped out into the blackness beyond the hangar door. As they did, Sariani deftly rolled out from under the truck, assumed a firing stance, and executed the two men with controlled bursts from his M-4.

Sariani scrambled to the opening and crouched down on one knee. Directly ahead of him was the newly-arrived troop transport. Two shocked soldiers were staring back toward the rear of their truck. Apparently, they hadn't heard Sariani's shots over the din of the other Rangers' weapons.

Sariani steadied his rifle, focused on the man to the left of the truck, and squeezed off another burst. A split-second later, he shot the second soldier as well.

Then, only seconds after the firefight had begun, the shooting stopped.

"Clear here!" Sariani reported. "What's your status, over?"

"Clear!"

"Clear!"

"Clear!"

Each of the other Rangers reported that the soldiers at the rear of the transport had been eliminated. After confirming that the soldiers he himself had shot were dead, Sariani sprinted to the rear of the hangar.

"Get up," he yelled to the two CIA operatives, "and back one of these trucks out of the hangar. We're getting you guys out of here, now! Hopefully, we'll see you in Dalian."

Sariani tossed the black duffle-bag to Du-Ho, turned, and jogged towards the front of the hangar.

"Tevin," he commanded Davidson, "Move that cargo truck out of the way, over."

"Copy that, Sarge."

"Paul, Jordan," Sariani continued. "Get those bodies out of the way, and pull the troop transport vehicle to the side. How many bodies we got back there, over?"

Sariani hustled out of the hangar toward the transport.

"I say again!" he repeated, a tad irritated. "How many bodies, over?"

There was no response.

Sariani froze. Something was wrong.

"Tevin!" he anxiously ordered. "Give me a status report on Paul and Jordan, over!"

Through infrared lenses, Sariani stared back toward the compound's gate.

Two bright human shapes lay splayed on the ground, lifeless forms contrasting vividly with the dark surface beneath them.

Paul and Jordan!

Sariani's instincts kicked in. He sprinted to the front of the troop transport and took cover against the vehicle's engine grill. There was still no response from Davidson. Readying his M-4, Sariani warily pivoted toward the opposite side of the vehicle, and scanned the barracks.

Tevin!

Davidson's motionless corpse lay face down in the snow, halfway between the hangar and the barracks.

And a short, combat-knife-wielding figure scampered towards the hangar.

Jesus Christ!

As a shocked Sariani aimed his rifle, the figure reversed course with blinding speed and rocketed toward the barracks. Sariani fired several times, but was unable to score a hit before the figure disappeared behind the structure.

Seconds later, the figure reemerged in the distance. Sariani sprinted five feet to the right of the truck, dropped to one knee, and began to fire again at the diminutive shape. Sariani was a crack shot, but the figure was moving so fast...

As the bright shape in his infrared goggles streaked toward the gate, Sariani's supply of ammunition, already depleted from his assault on the troop transport, ran out. He vainly clicked the trigger of his M-4.

As the sergeant worked frantically to load another clip, the fleeing individual reached the gate, stopped, and turned for a moment to stare at the remaining Ranger.

By the time Sariani lifted his weapon to fire again, the figure had disappeared into the forest.

CHAPTER 28

"Sarah is probably a weapon of the United States government. I fucked them over and now they want revenge."

"Okay," Tim replied. "But how did Sarah know where to find you? The North Koreans have obviously gone to great lengths to keep you hidden. How many people in this country truly know who you are and why you're here?"

Eric shrugged.

"It can't be more than 20 or 30 bigwigs and a few other officers. I'm top secret. All of those soldiers who moved my furniture and equipment don't have a clue what this whole operation is about. Shit, it wouldn't surprise me if they were all shot, just to make sure they didn't reveal anything! As for my 'female companions'...they're brought in with sacks over their heads. They don't have a clue where they are."

Tim shook his head in revulsion, but remained focused on the task at hand.

"So it's hard to believe that the feds would know your location," he returned. "But even if they did know, why would they risk sending someone here? The United States is spending two hundred and fifty million dollars a day in Iraq. They wouldn't risk pissing off the North Koreans over a lousy twenty million."

"It's not just the cash," Eric countered. "It's what I know. In Mali, I witnessed the U.S. Government ass-kissing a mass-murderer. I can detail the time, place, and amount of money involved in their gluttonous quest for cheaper oil."

"Maybe," Tim returned. "But you're not a threat to reveal U.S. secrets to anyone while you're stuck in here. Again, why would they risk it?"

"Let's assume for a minute," Tim went on, "that the feds engineered my trip around the world as a way to get their secret operative into North Korea. Sarah is sneaking around a country with which the US doesn't even have official diplomatic relations!"

"If Sarah were captured, what's to prevent Kim-Jong-II from retaliating with some provocative act, maybe even a nuclear strike, against South Korea or the US! Are you really worth that much of a risk?"

"I know," Eric agreed. "It doesn't make much sense. There has to be something we're not seeing."

"Well," Tim offered, "what about T.C.? Could he be trying to spring your release?"

Eric shook his head with a smile.

"No," he scoffed. "Not T.C. He's happy as a clam. His network is huge, and he understands it well enough to operate it on his own. He doesn't need me. Does he know the Koreans kidnapped me? Probably, but he couldn't care less about my well-being. He only cares about maintaining his current business relationship and making shitloads of cash."

"In any case," Eric added, "How could he know Sarah? And what good would T.C. do her? It's not like he knows where I am."

Tim nodded. "How about the North Koreans? Would they have political motivation for selling you out to America?"

"Maybe," Eric returned. "It's possible, I suppose. Maybe some rogue official is looking to arrange a back-alley deal with the U.S., exchanging me for a fucking condo in Boca. But I doubt it. The few people who know about my work are devoted, banner waving Communist Party members who despise the U.S."

"Still," Tim replied, "How would the U.S. know your location without collusion by someone on this side of the border?"

"Look," Eric flatly stated. "The Koreans would not give me up without getting something major in return. And what could the U.S possibly give them?"

Tim leaned back in his chair and stared down at the table in thought.

Eric rolled his eyes.

"Look, none of these ridiculous scenarios would have been necessary to get Sarah in the country. She probably just came on her own. She wouldn't need to receive a fake message designed to lead her to my location, or baby-sit you on an ocean adventure. She'd just hop on a plane and sneak across the border. Give it a rest, Big Brother. The North Koreans aren't in on this one."

Tim looked back up at Eric.

"Actually," he replied, "I was just thinking about Jeff Hutchins."

Eric narrowed his eyes inquisitively.

"Who?"

"Jeff Hutchins," Tim continued. "That agent who was at the Manchester Airport to arrest you that night."

"Oh," Eric nodded. "What about him?"

"Well," Tim proceeded, "he wasn't just randomly assigned the job. He was the guy who tracked you down in the first place."

"The CIA enlisted the FBI's Financial Crimes Department to figure out who stole their money. They assigned Hutchins and fed him a bogus report about $500,000 of stolen foreign-aid money. In the course of his investigation, Hutchins eventually dug up your name."

"Okay," Eric allowed. "So what?"

"I was thinking," Tim went on, "About the way he found your name."

"A bright young agent is tasked with sorting out potential thieves in a war-torn African nation surrounded by other war-torn African nations. I mean, who knows how many people could have taken that money, right? You've got warlords, radical Islamic groups, a corrupt government, and no shortage of local criminals. So Hutchins pores over countless names, looking for opportunity, motive, and large purchases made after the time of the theft."

"But at some point," Tim noted, "He considered a far simpler scenario: That a foreigner, someone who just happened to be in Mali, executed the heist for himself. And that led him to you."

"What if," Tim supposed, "there's a similarly simple explanation for our predicament?"

Eric nodded slowly.

"Huh," he replied, leaning back in his own chair. The room went silent as the two men pondered unseen solutions to the riddle that confronted them.

Then, slowly, Eric's eyes narrowed.

Somewhere in the recesses of his mind, a tiny light began to glow.

Tim watched in silence as his brother rolled something over and over in his head. Eric's eyes were blazing with intensity when he finally spoke

"Tim!" Eric urgently inquired. "The message you got--the one that told you I was in trouble! Was it in a comic book?"

Tim was taken aback.

"Uh, yeah! But how did you know—"

"Oh, Jesus fucking Christ!" Eric exploded. "Manchester Airport!"

Tim was stunned.

"W-what?" he stuttered.

Eric slapped his hand to his forehead.

"How did I not see this? It's so obvious!"

"What is?"

"The simplest answer!" Eric replied. "You were right!"

"What do you mean?" Tim stammered. "What is the simplest answer?"

Eric removed his hand from his forehead and shook his head in amazement.

"Tim," he proclaimed. "I know exactly what's going on here! And it doesn't have anything to do with either of us!"

CHAPTER 29

"More peanuts, sir?"

Eric spun his head away from the plane's window toward the flight attendant standing in the aisle.

"What?"

"Sorry to disturb you, sir. I was just wondering if you'd like more-"

"Oh," Eric interrupted. "No, thank you."

The 30-something brunette nodded. With mild interest, Eric watched her shapely backside as she attended to other passengers.

It had been a while, Eric realized, since he'd had sex with a white girl. T.C.'s recent delivery of "gifts" had consisted entirely of dark-skinned beauties. Eric chuckled under his breath.

A few years back, you weren't getting any action. Now, you're picky!

The sexual diversion helped to calm Eric's nervous mind. For the first time since he left the Malian orphanage two years ago, Eric was back on the grid. He had purchased a plane ticket home in his own name.

Technically, Eric knew, he had nothing to worry about. As far as the United States government was concerned, Eric's only transgression was failure to file income tax returns for the past two years. And Eric seriously doubted that the IRS would be waiting for him when he touched down in New Hampshire.

There was, of course, the extremely remote chance that the CIA had somehow linked Eric to the stolen money...

No, he convinced himself, his plan had been flawlessly and perfectly executed. He wouldn't have bought the ticket from Los Angeles to Manchester—with a layover in Newark—if he had had any doubts. Still, in light of the fact that he was known in some circles as "Shadow," stepping back into the light had been unsettling.

"Hi folks, from the cockpit," the pilot of Flight 190 announced. "We are beginning our final descent into Manchester. We should be touching down in about fifteen minutes."

As Eric listened to the pilot, he silently surveyed the aircraft.

The plane was a relatively small twin-prop, with only three seats in each row, two to the left of the aisle and one to the right. Seated in the last row of the plane, Eric had a window seat and an aisle seat rolled into one. There were only five other passengers, each of whom had opted to sit opposite Eric on the left side of the plane.

Three rows ahead, a teenage girl was reading a romance novel with a cheesy pink cover. Reading supposedly made you smarter, but Eric doubted that reading about shirtless men with mullets would boost this girl's IQ.

Two rows ahead of her, a trio of men wore nearly identical outfits: Leather coats, polo shirts, and khaki pants. Two were seated in the same row, while the third man sat in the next row forward. He was rotated to face the other two. The three men were engrossed in an annoyingly loud conversation.

Salesmen. Eric sneered. Western society was full of parasites like these, badgering others into buying things they didn't really want or need. Eric shook his head in disgust. Men like these cluttered Ruston's City Council, making self-serving decisions that adversely affected everyone else.

The plane's only other passenger was a man in a New England Patriots jacket, sitting in the second row. Eric was never much of a sports fan, but seeing the jacket still made him feel a touch nostalgic. As much as he hated to admit it, there were aspects of New England, and even Ruston, that Eric missed.

At the top of that list was his brother.

Despite his extensive travels, Eric had never met anyone he truly loved and respected. The only person to elicit those emotions ran a tiny comic book store in Ruston.

Tim.

Tim was the reason Eric was returning to Ruston. He wanted to spend time with his brother. Seeing his father meant little, since Will Sutton had turned his back on Eric long ago. Eric doubted that Will would even make the trip to Manchester to pick him up.

But Tim would. Tim, Eric knew, would be standing outside the airport's security checkpoint with a big smile on his face, happy to see his long-lost younger brother. He'd probably present Eric with a stack of comic books from his store—smart, edgy stuff that he knew Eric would like. Eric would walk out of the terminal, hug his brother, and for a while...it would be just like old times.

After a few days, of course, as Ruston's little idiosyncrasies lost their charm, Eric would emotionally regress. Unable to shake the constant reminders of the frustration he experienced as a teenager, he would turn sullen, or what his brother termed "perpetually pissed off."

And so, Eric's trip to Ruston would adhere to a short, neat schedule.

Eric would meet Tim in Manchester. He would then drive back to Ruston and exchange uncomfortable greetings with his dad. He would answer Will's "where have you been?" questions with a story about a remote village in Africa where he had tirelessly helped sick children, but was unable to communicate with the outside world. Perhaps his father would try to believe the story, perhaps he wouldn't.

After an hour of bullshit with his dad, Eric would finally get some time alone with Tim. And they would just talk.

They would talk about Tim's store, about life in Ruston, about politics, pop culture, and trivia. The two would reminisce about an imaginative childhood spent in the woods of Ruston, and fondly recall teenage days of role-playing games and reading comic books.

Maybe Eric would share some of what he had accomplished since leaving Ruston, and maybe he wouldn't. Either way, Eric would get one last dose of brilliant repartee.

After an entire day spent alone with his brother, Eric would give Tim a hug and say goodbye for the last time.

And then Eric would leave Ruston, and Tim, forever.

With a thud, the landing gear of Flight 190 touched down on the frozen tarmac of Manchester International Airport.

Eric fidgeted in his seat as the plane taxied through the darkness toward the modest terminal. Finally, the aircraft docked at its gate, and a docile tone sounded to indicate that it was okay to move about the cabin.

Eric sprang from his seat, snatching his single black suitcase from the overhead compartment. He turned and eagerly strode down the aisle. Eric's spirits were so high that he actually returned the smile of the flight attendant bidding farewell as he exited the aircraft.

Eric followed his fellow passengers up the long, empty, telescoping tunnel that stretched from the plane to the terminal. He watched as the New England Patriots fan reached the end of the tunnel and disappeared to the left. The three salesmen, still flapping their jaws incessantly, were next to round the corner.

Ten feet ahead of Eric, the teenage girl stuffed her pink novel into a large black purse. She was exiting the tunnel when a strange feeling came over Eric.

He detected tiny irregularities—the flicker of a shadow, a footstep against the tunnel's carpeted floor. In unison, his senses reported a message that Eric might otherwise have ignored.

Someone is behind you.

As the teenager disappeared into the terminal, Eric instinctively turned.

Then the kick smashed into his leg.

In less than a second, Eric's body was rocked by twin blasts directly behind each knee. Eric's suitcase flew from his hands as his legs buckled. The strikes came so quickly that Eric was kneeling before his mind registered an attack.

Before Eric could utter a sound, a small, pale hand whipped around the right side of his face and clasped his mouth with startling strength. From Eric's left side came another hand. This one held a long black combat knife.

Eric felt the deadly steel on his throat.

"Eric Sutton," an even voice commanded. "Do not attempt to speak or move. If you do so, I will kill you."

It was a man's voice.

Eric, profoundly shaken by the sudden assault, robotically complied with the order. For several seconds, he knelt in silent terror.

Then slowly, the hand covering his mouth was removed. The knife remained at his throat, but the hand holding it began to rotate. Slowly and smoothly, with the knife never leaving Eric's neck, Eric's captor stepped around Eric's left side until the two were face-to-face.

The man was Asian.

He was about 5'4" tall and looked to be in his early thirties. A long-sleeved black shirt, black pants, and nondescript set of black sneakers covered his small frame.

His chin had a thin layer of black stubble, as though it had been recently shaved. The man's ears stuck out abnormally, accentuated by his nearly-bald scalp.

The man's face was gaunt and rugged, but not unhealthy. Above an expressionless mouth and small nose sat the blackest, most unyielding pair of eyes Eric had ever encountered.

The man slowly removed the knife from Eric's throat.

Without blinking, he issued commands in heavily-accented English.

"Stand up, Eric Sutton."

"You are coming with me."

PART 4
CROCODILE TEARS

CHAPTER 30

UNITED STATES ARMY

OPERATION REPORT

FILE DATE: 11:30Z, 10 March, 1995.

FILED BY: Statham, Thomas, 1LT
     Long Range Surveillance
     Detachment Alpha
          102nd   Military   Intelligence
          Battalion
          2nd Infantry Division, US Army, North
          Korea.

FILED UPON COMPLETION OF: OPORD #4398.

(TS) OPORD MISSION: **Investigate rumors of North Korean Elite Soldier Initiative.**

(U) SUMMARY

(TS) In compliance with OPORD #4398, LRSD Team Alpha conducted thorough 65-day search for evidence of **North Korean Army "super-soldier"**

program. Suspected location: Changbai Mountains, NK.

(TS) Mission successfully accomplished. Reports of **"secret mountain base" housing elite soldier initiative** could not be substantiated. LRSD Team Alpha discovered zero evidence to corroborate prior intel.

                    Thomas Statham
                    1st Lieutenant
                    LRSD Alpha
                    102nd MI Bn, 2nd ID

        --TOP SECRET--

    ****

No. 238 is fighting today.

With steely focus, Colonel Pak stared straight ahead as he was pedaled through the concrete tunnel.

It had been a long day's journey from Pyongyang. The top-secret route to the mountain camp was a tortuous collection of winding back roads and ravines. It was a necessary inconvenience. The obscure route and frequent stops were designed to evade known satellite surveillance over Colonel Pak's beloved nation.

The Colonel didn't mind these laborious treks. He relished every opportunity to personally inspect the progress of his charges.

Especially now…when things were going so unexpectedly well.

No. 238.

The rickshaw reached the end of the tunnel. Five soldiers standing at attention smartly saluted their superior officer. As the

Colonel climbed down from his seat, one of the soldiers stepped forward to present Pak with a clipboard.

"Excellent to see you, Commander!" the soldier barked. "It is wonderful that you were able to come up here to personally witness--"

Colonel Pak interrupted the man's overture.

"Report!" he ordered.

"Y-yes, of course, Commander," the man apologized. "Food supply is adequate. Educational and combat initiatives proceed smoothly. Subject tests and eliminations are on schedule. There has been nothing to warrant special interest—except, of course, for No. 238, but obviously you're well are of—"

"Yes, yes, of course!" Colonel Pak impatiently waved his hand as he thumbed through the data on the clipboard. The Colonel looked at his subordinate. "Take me to the site—now!" he commanded. "I won't be staying long. Pyongyang wants an immediate report."

The soldier nodded, and stepped aside. Colonel Pak shoved the clipboard into the man's hands, strode past him out of the tunnel, and marched into the forest toward the camp. The five soldiers dutifully followed.

Hundreds of other soldiers moved about the concrete huts that dotted the forest floor. As the colonel approached, they snapped to attention.

As Pak continued along the forest trail, he also noticed other individuals.

Smaller than the soldiers, they wore white t-shirts, black drawstring pants, and black loafers. Beneath their shaved heads, hollow eyes stared blankly.

They were the lifeblood of the Crocodile Program.

They were the children.

The boys were all now 13 or 14, well-removed from their formative years. There was still plenty to teach, of course—about weaponry, electronics and infiltration techniques—but the basic elements of the Crocodile Program had been drilled into the boys long ago. Emphasis was no longer on learning. It was on surviving.

Colonel Pak halted at the center of the camp.

Several hundred feet farther was the Training House—the large concrete structure where the boys received their education. Between the

Colonel and the Training House, 15 wide, circular clearings had been meticulously created in the snow, each exposing the brown soil beneath. The clearings ranged from 30 to 70 feet in diameter.

Pak and his five-man entourage came to a stop at one of the smaller circles. The Colonel's eyes narrowed as he carefully surveyed the dirt circle.

"What will they be using?" he inquired.

"Knives, Commander. And, as you can see, we've placed three stone benches in the center to serve as obstacles."

"The other boy?"

"No. 1143, Commander. He's much taller than No. 238, with a longer reach. He hasn't used a knife thus far, but he has performed quite well with machetes. The boy is quite capable. As the Commander is aware, there aren't any weak subjects left..."

"Yes, obviously," Pak hurriedly replied. The Colonel briskly circled to a gray folding chair that had been set out in anticipation of his arrival. Pak quickly seated himself and nodded at the soldier with the clipboard.

"I'm ready. Begin."

The soldier turned and gestured to another soldier, who turned and disappeared into the trees. Minutes later, accompanied by their respective handlers, the boys emerged from the forest.

No. 1143 was the first to reach the clearing.

As Pak had earlier been told, he was a tall boy—5'7", at least—with a lithe, athletic build. No. 1143's face radiated dramatic intensity, his brown eyes blazing with focus. The boy was clearly a warrior. Colonel Pak knew that, in another life, this boy would have made a fine soldier in the beloved General's army. But that was not to be...

The three soldiers accompanying No. 1143 led him to the fringe of the dirt circle. One of them pulled a glistening silver knife with a long, razor-sharp blade from his pocket. The soldier handed the knife to No. 1143, who stared at the weapon and began to expertly maneuver the blade in his hands.

As the boy danced from side to side, familiarizing himself with the blade, No. 238 appeared at the clearing. Colonel Pak immediately glued his eyes to the new arrival.

This boy was everything.

Pak had received a packet of photographs of No. 238 over the preceding months. He had actually seen him fight several years earlier, prior to the boy's talents being truly recognized. The Colonel was struck by how small the child still was!

No. 238 stood just a half inch over five feet tall. The boy's frame wasn't weak, per se, but his bony body certainly wasn't imposing. If anything, No. 238's diminutive physique—capped by a pronounced pair of protruding ears—looked slightly comical.

Pak's jaw dropped slightly as he studied the tiny child. His dossier was so...unbelievable. As No. 238 was led to the side of the clearing opposite No. 1143, Pak addressed the soldier with the clipboard.

"What's the longest he's taken thus far?" the Colonel asked.

"Three minutes, ten seconds, Commander. But that was without weapons. And the other boy was trying to run away..."

Colonel Pak nodded slowly, and watched closely as one of No. 238's handlers gave him a knife of his own.

The boy's response to the gift was bizarre, to say the least. No. 238 didn't even glance at the weapon he had just been given. The boy held the knife loosely in his right hand, and blankly stared out at the clearing.

The child didn't seem tense or calm. He didn't seem human.

No. 238's relaxed eyes slowly stared around the dirt circle. They lingered for a few seconds on No. 1143 (who appeared ready to explode), then moved on. No. 238 seemed to pay as much attention to the three white, four-legged benches in the center of the clearing as he did to his opponent. Colonel Pak was puzzled.

What is he looking at? Is he going to use the benches to shield himself from his opponent? What advantage is he envisioning?

Seconds later, No. 238 concluded his inspection of the clearing. His eyes casually returned to the gaze of his fierce competitor. Forty feet apart, the two boys prepared for battle, their breath steaming.

Colonel Pak took a deep, slow breath and nodded to the soldier with the clipboard. The soldier returned the nod, looked out at the clearing, and shouted a single word.

"Begin!"

As soon the command was uttered, the two boys advanced to the center of the clearing.

To Colonel Pak's surprise, No. 238, who appeared so languid seconds earlier, moved with greater urgency. While No. 1143 assumed a measured combat stance and approached his opponent warily, No. 238 briskly loped toward his foe.

No. 238 was the first to reach the middle of the circle. He limply stood between the three weathered marble benches, awaiting No. 1143's arrival. The larger boy, his knife in his right hand and his legs spread in a wide defensive crouch, guardedly joined his combatant.

No. 238 struck first. At least, he appeared to strike first.

Standing directly in front of No. 1143 and to the immediate left of one of the stone benches, No. 238 suddenly slashed from left to right across No. 1143's body with his right, knife-holding hand. But it was a weak, sloppy, off-balance maneuver. No. 238 missed No. 1143 completely, and left his own abdomen completely exposed.

No. 1143 had been presented with a golden opportunity, and he wouldn't waste it. The tall boy lunged forward, plunging his blade into No. 238's left side.

As the blade ripped into the boy's flesh, Colonel Pak and his soldiers gasped in alarm. Even No. 1143 seemed shocked by the ease with which he had struck such a vicious blow.

The only person who wasn't surprised, apparently, was No. 238.

With the knife impaled to the left of his stomach, the tiny boy's expression scarcely changed. With lightening speed, he whipped his left arm toward his abdomen and clasped No. 1143's right wrist. Instead of attempting to push the knife out of his body, No. 238 actually pulled on the larger boy's arm, holding it in place! Colonel Pak's eyes went wide in realization.

Good God! He planned this!

As a startled No. 1143 attempted to pull his arm, and his knife, from his enemy's side, No. 238 suddenly dropped toward the ground. As he did so, the boy unleashed a series of moves that completely stunned the Colonel.

First, No. 238 rocketed his right leg into No. 1143's lower body. The larger boy, still confounded by his opponent's calm desire to leave a deadly weapon in his blood-soaked mid-section, lost his balance and plummeted.

As the two boys fell, No. 238 dropped his own knife. As soon as the blade left his right hand, the boy delivered a vicious punch—directly into one of the legs on the nearby stone bench.

As his fist impacted the white marble, the top of the leg shattered and the rest of the piece broke free. No. 238 grabbed the two-foot-long marble rectangle and, with breathtaking strength, swung it at his opponent.

No. 1143, now lying on top of No. 238, saw the blow coming. But there was little the bewildered teenager could do, other than raise his left arm to shield himself from the blow.

No. 238 had anticipated this. The arm was his target.

When the leg of the bench hit No. 1143's forearm, the larger boy's bones shattered immediately. As No. 1143 shrieked in pain, his mangled limb at his side, No. 238 raised the leg a second time.

No. 1143 was finally able to remove his right hand from the knife in his opponent's side. He tried to raise it in self-defense. It was too late.

The bench leg smashed into No. 1143's shaved skull, spewing blood and bone in all directions. As his opponent lost consciousness, No. 238 slowly and deliberately cocked his right arm again. With merciless precision, the tiny child swung the stone forward a final time.

Forty-five seconds after it had begun, the battle was over.

Colonel Pak watched in shock as No. 238 rolled out from beneath No. 1143's lifeless corpse. The boy methodically raised himself to a sitting position, and removed his blood-drenched t-shirt. He tightly balled up the shirt, pressed it against the gruesome wound in his left flank, and lay back down on the ground. Without a hint of emotion, he fixed his dark, penetrating eyes on Colonel Pak.

For a moment, the Colonel remained spellbound. Then he realized that the other soldiers, equally astonished, were milling about like idiots. Pak pulled his eyes away from No. 238.

"Well?" he bellowed to the soldiers. "What are you waiting for? Take care of him!"

The Colonel's directive shook the men from their collective trance, and they sprang forward to tend to the prostrate teenager. As No. 1143's body was carelessly dragged to the side and dumped in the snow, the five soldiers delicately picked up No. 238 and carried him back to the camp. Colonel Pak rose and headed back down the trail. The soldier with the clipboard hustled after him.

"Have a doctor look at him, now!" the Colonel demanded. "If his condition is in any way serious, phone Pyongyang immediately, and have them dispatch top physicians to treat him."

Pak wheeled back around and proceeded down the path alone.

As the Colonel approached the tunnel, his stern expression softened. Finally, assured that no one would see him, Pak allowed himself the rarest of luxuries: a tiny smile.

At last, after toiling for so many years on a seemingly dead-end assignment, Colonel Pak would return to Pyongyang with glorious news.

He had found his crocodile.

CHAPTER 31

The cargo truck lumbered up the dark mountain road through a light snowfall. A steady stream of snow crystals impacted and melted on No. 238's face and bald head.

He was seated cross-legged atop the shipping container, resolutely staring at the area illuminated by the truck's headlights. He was in "stand-by" mode, ready to instantly power-up into action. This was the way No. 238 traveled.

The air whipping through his black long-sleeve shirt and drawstring pants was numbingly cold, and no one would have begrudged him riding in the cab. But No. 238 preferred to avoid the company of others, and besides, the cold weather was just another form of pain he could easily ignore.

The two soldiers in the cab of the troop transport could barely make out the 29-year-old man, perched like a Buddhist Monk atop the vehicle ahead. They knew who he was, of course. All of the men did. They were strictly forbidden to talk about him, however.

No. 238's black eyes stared straight ahead as the cargo truck rolled toward the drug storing facility, a place he knew well.

Something is different.

As the truck came to a stop, No. 238 quickly scanned the area, immediately noting and mentally processing the presence of footprints and vehicle tracks in front of and beyond the gate.

A shipment truck and troop transport were stopped here, but for longer than usual. The troop transport vehicle was attacked. The attackers then ran to the barracks with no one in pursuit. Later, they drove the trucks into the hangar. There are no signs of their departure.

Dangerous intruders are inside the base.

No. 238 determined all this in seconds. He had encountered unexpected situations like this one hundreds of times before. His response was always the same: Do a quick visual assessment. Develop a plan of attack. Execute it. It was his gift.

If his military companions had a fraction of No. 238's acumen, they would have noticed the tracks in the snow and reached similar conclusions. But the men hadn't noticed anything amiss. And they weren't going to be receiving No.238's assistance.

Tonight, No. 238 would let his countrymen die.

No. 238 leapt from the roof of the shipping container with gravity-defying athletic grace, and silently vanished into the darkness of the adjacent forest.

Normally, upon arrival at the facility, No. 238 would sprint through the forest toward the tunnel, returning to the only place he had ever known as home. Today, however, he crouched near the perimeter fence and waited.

Soon, the cargo truck and the troop transport rumbled through the gate of the base. No. 238 tracked their headlights.

Any moment now...

The crackle of rifle fire suddenly erupted from within the base.

No. 238 listened expectantly as the North Korean soldiers were executed a hundred feet away. He studied the sound of the firing assault rifles.

Three—no, four rifles. American made. M-4s.

No. 238 bolted toward the gate.

Americans are here.

He flew through the entrance with mind-bending speed. An onlooker might have thought he was gliding above the snow rather than pushing through it. His silent steps left nearly-invisible footprints as No. 238 raced toward the sound of the gunshots. Then, suddenly, the rifles ceased firing. His comrades were now surely dead.

No. 238 didn't care. Right now, only information mattered. The sound of the rifles had told him everything he needed to know.

There are four highly-trained American soldiers here. Two to my right, near the fence. Another between the barracks and the hangar. The last is somewhere inside the hangar.

No. 238 quickly planned his attack. It was time to kill.

No. 238 had been born into killing, raised by it, and educated through it. Killing drove his existence.

First, the soldiers on the right.

No. 238 rocketed through the facility, pulling his menacing black combat knife from the sheath strapped to his leg. Gripping the weapon in his right hand, No. 238 studied the black abyss ahead of him. In the darkness thirty feet away, two scarcely visible shapes were crouching.

The Americans would be wearing night-vision scopes. If they turned around, No. 238 would appear as a bright, easily identifiable target. But the soldiers had no reason to turn around, and they wouldn't hear No. 238 coming. No one ever did.

Like a ghostly apparition, he descended on his foes.

The first American visibly tensed as he suddenly sensed that he and his partner were not alone. Before the soldier could react, No. 238 deftly pulled his blade across the man's jugular and let the blood-spattered body drop to the ground.

While the other American was distracted by his partner careening face-first into the snow, No. 238 circled behind and made the man his second victim.

No. 238 ran onward. Soldiers—good soldiers—were always in radio communication. The others would soon realize something was wrong. No. 238 had only seconds. The black-shirted assassin sped toward the barracks. To the right of the building, a third crouching black shape materialized.

Time was of the essence. There would be no circling behind this American; instead, No. 238 noiselessly charged directly at the man. When he was within ten feet, the American detected a moving shape, turned, and instinctively raised his weapon in self defense.

The move was futile. No. 238 was airborne, rocketing towards the American with his knife outstretched. The blade exploded into the man's Adam's apple, exiting through the back of his neck. No. 238 then kicked against the dead man's mid-section, propelling himself backward, while simultaneously removing his knife from the American's neck. In one continuous fluid motion he spun in mid-air, and sprinted toward the hangar.

No. 238 had covered half of the distance when the situation abruptly changed.

In the dim glow of the troop transport's headlights, the last American unexpectedly rolled into view. The soldier was dressed completely in white. A black night-vision scope poked out from the hood drawn tightly around his face, and his camouflaged rifle was raised and pointing directly at No. 238.

No. 238 reversed course in a flash, speeding back towards the barracks. The crack of rifle fire echoed in his ears as bullets flew past his body. In seconds, No. 238 was sheltered behind the barracks' rear wall.

Get to the forest.

The remaining soldier had been lucky, but his success would be short lived. Once No. 238 reached the pines, he would circle the facility, climb a tall tree, and jump over the section of fence nearest to the hangar. Then he would stealthily flank the unsuspecting soldier.

No. 238 sped along the back of the barracks, reached the end of the wall, and turned left. A moment later, he was in the open again, racing back toward the base's gate.

As he ran, No. 238 heard the pop of the M-4 rifle as the American tried in vain to bring him down. Then the rifle went silent.

He's out of ammunition.

No. 238 reached the gate, stopped, and stared at the American. As he watched the distant figure furiously slap another clip into his M-4, he calmly pondered...

What would bring the Americans here? How would they know how to get to this place, unless...

No. 238's uniform eyelids raised ever-so-slightly.

The tracks in the snow.

The troop transport tracks outside the gate had been shallower than the tracks of the other vehicles. They were shallower, No. 238 realized, because they had been filled in by the recent snow fall. This meant that the transport tracks were much older than the other tracks. The transport had stopped outside the gate long before the four Americans arrived.

The Americans hadn't attacked the troop transport. Someone else had. Someone the Americans were following...

No. 238 raced through the gate into the forest, descending deeper and deeper into the unlit wild. The last American could wait.

No. 238 had been raised and trained to be an unstoppable, remorseless killer. Deeply hidden within his robotic mind, however, was a single flaw that everyone in the Great General's Army had missed.

No. 238 had been trained to follow orders without question, which he did. But beyond every order, an unrelenting need coursed through his veins.

The need to fight.

Tonight, No. 238 had allowed a dozen Korean soldiers to die because he had wanted to fight the four well-trained American soldiers alone. The lives of his comrades meant nothing compared to combat against a worthy foe.

The battle was all that mattered.

As No. 238 raced through the woods, the barren mountain wilderness began to brighten with the arrival of dawn.

No. 238's greatest battle, like the sun, lay on the horizon.

CHAPTER 32

"It was called the Crocodile Program," Eric began. "And it was conducted right here."

Eric gestured grandly at the spacious room. Outside, the sun, which had been just rising when Tim first arrived, had now set. Tim sat spellbound, waiting to hear the next chapter in his brother's bizarre tale.

"In a totalitarian state like this one," Eric began, "where everyone lives in fear, no one will tell the Emperor if he isn't wearing any clothes. The Crocodile Program was a good example of this principle."

"One morning, decades ago," Eric continued, "Kim-Jong-Il's father, the late Kim-Il-Sung, woke up with an idea: to create the perfect soldier. He wanted one highly-trained, unflappable killer with fighting skills superior to all others, who demonstrated no feeling or remorse."

"The very idea was absurd. The cost of such a project would far exceed any real benefit. Really, what can you accomplish with a single fighter?"

"This was the sort of far-fetched idea that would be criticized and rejected by any reasonable government's military establishment. But this is North Korea. When Kim-Il-Sung demanded a perfect soldier, his underlings blindly accepted his vision and went to work."

"Ninety-nine percent of the resulting program was based on the teachings of Mr. Charles Darwin." Eric leaned toward his brother with a questioning stare.

"Tim," he inquired, "What do you know about crocodiles?"

"Uhh…" Tim wasn't sure exactly what kind of reply his brother was expecting. "They're big, their skin is like a suit of armor, and they tear apart many a poor unfortunate wildebeest?"

Eric rolled his eyes.

"Thanks, Professor. Apparently some North Korean zoologist knew a tad more about crocodiles than you do."

"Some of the most interesting facts about crocodiles," Eric continued, "deal with the way they grow and mature. A crocodile's journey from birth to adulthood is a classic Darwinistic trip."

Tim began to catch his brother's drift.

When baby crocodiles first entered the river, they were vulnerable to even the smallest predators, not to mention the likelihood of being swept downstream. As they matured, the stronger ones hogged the river's food supply and killed their weaker brethren.

Out of a hundred crocodile eggs, less than 10% developed into fully-grown adults. Those that did, however, dominated the river ecosystem. They sat on thrones at the top of the food chain, killing anything that came close, perpetuating a genetic line that dated back to the dinosaurs.

"I'm with you," Tim nodded.

"Well, what the North Koreans did," Eric explained, "Was impose this crocodilian process of natural selection on people."

"First, they grabbed several thousand male infants from their prison camps and carted them here under a tight veil of secrecy."

"All of the little huts you've passed," Eric continued, "Were homes. Each hut housed several babies, as well as the soldiers charged with raising them. As they grew, these boys received a very unique form of parenting."

Tim's face went white as Eric proceeded.

The Crocodile 'curriculum' had included hand-to-hand combat, the use of firearms, knives and explosives. There had also been a little reading and writing—mainly, however, the boys were simply taught how to kill. And eventually, they began to fight each other in life and death competitions!

The circles Tim had passed on his way through the camp were arenas, where the boys were pitted against each other in deadly combat! The loser's body was incinerated. The winner received more combat training followed by another battle in the quest to become the perfect soldier. This process was repeated until only a single child remained!

"Good God..." Tim mumbled.

"I know!" Eric exclaimed. "Fucking crazy, right? The whole premise plays out like some shitty action movie, but they really did this. They devoted thousands and thousands of man-hours and young boys' lives to an insane project."

"But," Eric asserted, "In the end, they hit the jackpot."

One of the boys, Eric explained, truly was exceptional.

His skills were unparalleled in both the arena and the classroom, and he could quickly memorize and remember everything he was taught. He responded automatically to any command, regardless of its nature, and he never expressed anger, fear, or fatigue. The boy was one in a million, and was eventually the last man standing in the Crocodile Program.

Kim-Il-Sung's insidious program had actually achieved its objective. Subsequently, the Koreans took their elite soldier, 18 or 19 at the time, and embedded him somewhere within their military machine, effectively ending the Crocodile Program. The mountain base became a ghost-town for several years, until Eric was handed the key to the castle.

"Now, consider the real problem with the Crocodile Project," Eric went on. "Once you've created this super-soldier, how do you use him? He's no substitute for an invading army. And he can't be used to train other soldiers because he isn't exactly 'leadership material.'"

"The kid left the Crocodile Program about 10 years ago. I'm not sure what he did during his first few years of service. But I can tell you what he's done for the past three years. He's had two main jobs."

"First," Eric listed, "he's ensured that drug deals occur without incident. Suffice it to say that, once his reputation spread, his mere appearance at a deal deterred any wrongdoing."

"Second," Eric continued, "He's guarded me."

"When our killer isn't tending to his drug duties, he's at or around this camp. I suppose, technically, part of his mission is to prevent me from escaping. In truth, he's more of a one-man defense. No one will get close to this place while that super-soldier is patrolling it."

"The fact that you're alive right now means he's not here. He must be riding along with one of our drug shipments. He'll be back here late tonight, when the shipment reaches the holding facility."

Eric frowned.

"Shit..." he muttered to himself. "And that means...we don't have much time."

"Time for what?" Tim exclaimed. "What are you talking about? I still don't have a clue!"

"I know, Tim, I know," Eric apologized. "You will in a second."

"The most important thing to recognize about this 'crocodile' is that he doesn't really do anything! When he's up here at the camp, he patrols the woods, guarding against an attack that will never come. When he's not here, he gets, at best, an opportunity to kill some dim-witted drug dealer who will never even see the attack coming."

"Remember," Eric proceeded. "This guy was raised on fighting. His whole childhood revolved around killing other children! The older he got, the tougher his opponents became, until, finally, there was no one left to fight. Battling and killing are his lifeblood. And he's just sitting up here in the woods doing nothing."

"Which brings us," Eric concluded, "to the watershed event for our North Korean super-soldier: the day he blew a fuse."

Eric shot his older brother a telling look. Tim responded with a puzzled shrug.

"When? What event?"

"Oh," Eric replied, "It's one you know quite well."

"You were there."

CHAPTER 33

On a cold night in February, No. 238 charged up the snow-covered hill.

The gently-sloping, treeless, completely frosted mound was the kind of place many people would have associated with the merry sled rides of their youth.

No. 238 hadn't had that kind of childhood. He focused on his current mission, the most important he had been assigned thus far.

No. 238 reached the crest of the snowy rise. Up ahead, bright white lights blinked intermittently from beyond a forbidding wall of barbed-wire fence.

The tiny North Korean carefully climbed the chain-link fence, wary of the possibility of attached vibration-detection security sensors. After expertly tip-toeing around the deadly-sharp razor wire at the top, he softly dropped to the ground with the grace of a ballet dancer.

Now No. 238 was on the run again. Before him was a vast, completely flat stretch of wide-open terrain. Off to his left, the flickering white landing lights had begun to grow brighter. As No. 238 sprinted through the snow-covered grass, he whipped his head to the left and stared back over his shoulder.

Overhead, blinking blue lights and a thunderous roar heralded Manchester Airport's latest arriving plane.

That's his aircraft. I must move quickly.

As the jet touched down on a runway 50 yards away, No. 238 moved rapidly toward the airport terminal. When his black shoes contacted the edge of the tarmac, he dropped into a crouch and waited.

No. 238 monitored the plane's approach.

Which gate?

The appearance of ground personnel with illuminated light sticks and the sudden movement of a nearby docking terminal answered his question.

As the jet came to a halt and the accordion-like docking tunnel began to extend from the terminal, No. 238 surveyed the area surrounding the arrival gate.

Four personnel: Three baggage handlers on the ground, and at least one individual operating the tunnel. The baggage hold door is on the far side of the aircraft. Passenger cabin door is on the near side.

With lightning speed, No. 238 silently bolted across the slick black asphalt toward the terminal gate. When he was within 20 yards of Flight 190, the assassin ducked behind a green Ford F-150 bearing an airport insignia. As his forehead and wide ears poked up over the hood of the vehicle, No. 238 eyed the three baggage handlers approaching the plane.

They're on the other side of the aircraft. They can no longer see me. Wait for the tunnel operator…

The motion of the docking tunnel ceased, and its operator quickly exited through a metallic door, descending a stairway that led down to the tarmac. He joined his co-workers on the far side of the plane.

Attack route is clear. Go.

No. 238 immediately launched himself toward the docking tunnel. He sped up the stairway and pressed his tiny frame against the tunnel's metal door. He carefully peered through the door's clear Plexiglas window.

No. 238 watched as Flight 190's cabin door sprung forward and slid to the side. Shortly thereafter, a man in a brightly-colored winter jacket exited the plane. The man was followed into the tunnel by three animated men wearing leather coats. A young girl clutching a bright pink novel was next.

Finally, a lanky, pale, blond-haired young man anxiously strode from the aircraft. He appeared to be the last deplaning passenger. A stroke of luck.

That's him.

Quietly opening the door, No. 238 noiselessly slid into the tunnel. He was now directly behind his target.

No. 238 glanced back at the plane. The voices of two flight attendants echoed from within the aircraft. They, as well as the pilot and co-pilot, would be in the tunnel soon. Since No. 238 had been told to avoid unnecessary bloodshed on this mission, he had to act quickly.

As he closed in on his target, No. 238 pulled his long black combat knife from the sheath hidden beneath his jacket. When he was within five feet of the young man, No. 238 slowed his approach and coolly maintained his distance.

Wait for the girl to leave the tunnel.

Up ahead, the young woman deposited a pink novel into her purse before disappearing around the corner. No. 238 and his target were the only ones left in the tunnel.

The blond man suddenly sensed No. 238's presence and began to turn...

Sprinting from behind, No. 238 unleashed two thunderous kicks, each landing directly behind one of his target's knees. The blond man fell to the floor, losing his grip on his suitcase. No. 238 wrapped his right hand around the man's face and forcefully clasped it over his mouth. With his left hand, No. 238 touched the knife's menacing blade to the front of his target's neck.

"Eric Sutton," he calmly instructed. "Do not attempt to speak or move. If you do, I will kill you."

No. 238 waited in silence. When he was confident that he had the total compliance of his target, the North Korean pivoted while keeping the knife pressed to the young man's throat.

"Stand up, Eric Sutton. You are coming with me."

Terrified, the young man stumbled to his feet. No. 238 pushed Sutton down the tunnel back toward the airplane, still brandishing his knife.

The flight attendants were still engaged in chatter within the airplane when the Korean soldier and his hostage reached the tunnel access door. No. 238 poked his head out the door. After making sure that no one was standing in or around the tunnel, he turned to his captive.

"Eric Sutton," No. 238 softly intoned, "Walk down these steps. I will follow you. If you attempt to run or call out, I will kill you." Sutton nodded.

No. 238 followed the frightened young man through the tunnel door and down the steps to the tarmac.

"This way," he commanded.

No. 238 roughly shoved his captive toward a nearby access door to the terminal building. A recently plowed snow bank lay between the two men and the doors. As Sutton waded through the snow, No. 238 expertly placed his shoes inside the larger man's footprints. To a casual observer, it would appear that one man, rather than two, had passed through the snow.

At No. 238's command, Sutton swung the door into the terminal, and the two men stepped inside.

They were near the end of a brightly lit, taupe-colored hallway that ran the length of the terminal. No. 238 had studied detailed blueprints of the building. He knew that a double swinging door 25 feet down the corridor led out to an employee parking lot. Once they reached the parking lot, No. 238 planned to break into a car and make his escape with Sutton in tow.

"What the fuck is going on here?"

Although he tried, Eric Sutton could not hide the fear in his voice.

"You're North Korean, right?" Sutton continued. "Are you kidnapping me?"

"Quiet!" No. 238 barked. He had heard the sound of voices.

No. 238 pressed his ear against the door he and Sutton had just passed through. Outside, near the snowdrift, two men were conversing loudly.

"Wait!" One of the men shouted. "There's a fresh set of tracks through the snow here leading to that door. It has to be him! Get on the radio and tell Hutchins to circle back in case the kid tries to escape through baggage claim…"

"Jeff, he went under the terminal," the second man intoned, apparently into a radio. "Get to baggage claim…"

No. 238 turned to face Eric.

"Someone else is chasing after you," the Korean stated.

"What?" Sutton replied, incredulous. "What, you mean besides you?"

"Walk that way, quickly," No. 238 ordered. "Go. Now."

As the confused young man backed away from his attacker and slowly moved down the hall, No. 238 pressed himself against the wall, a short distance from the hinged side of the door. Moments later, the door flew open, and two large muscular men in black suits charged ahead.

The first thing the men saw was a shocked Eric Sutton standing 20 feet away. They immediately raised their pistols.

"Eric Sutton!" one of the men yelled. "FBI, freeze! Freeze or we will…"

No. 238 stepped out from the wall behind the two agents.

The man closest turned in his direction and issued an exclamation.

"What the…freeze! Free…"

The man's sentence came to an abrupt halt as a blade raked his jugular and crimson blood spurted from his neck.

The second man tried to get off a shot, but the tiny assassin was moving far too quickly. Ducking under the man's outstretched arms, No. 238 jammed the dagger upward into his throat. The man's frame went limp, and he collapsed against the wall of the hallway.

No. 238 stared at the two blood-soaked bodies.

"United States Federal Agents," he stated evenly, rotating mechanically towards Sutton. "They were chasing you."

Sutton, completely stunned by the bloodbath he had just witnessed, staggered toward the side of the hallway.

"Wh-what?" he managed, weakly leaning against the wall. "Chasing me? Why?"

Sutton came to a sudden realization.

"They know about the money!" he exclaimed. "But how…"

"We are leaving." No. 238 interrupted.

He wiped his bloody knife on the sleeve of one of the dying men. No. 238 didn't know why Federal Agents were chasing his target, and he didn't care. But if there were more agents in the airport looking for Sutton, he needed to move quickly.

No. 238's head shot up.

Someone else was in the hallway.

A short, athletic, red-haired woman was sprinting down the corridor, clutching a long, silver knife in her right hand.

Another agent.

"Come here," No. 238 commanded, looking towards Sutton. "Stand behind me."

As his astonished captive circled behind him, the North Korean calmly advanced toward the red-haired woman. He would kill her quickly, then escape with Sutton before they were confronted by more agents. This mission had already taken too much time...

When he was within five feet, No. 238 lunged toward his next victim's throat, knife extended, prepared to unleash a blinding strike.

To his surprise, the red-haired woman attempted an almost identical combat maneuver!

Suddenly confronted with a body flying directly at him, No. 238 twisted and flew off to the left side of the hallway. The woman, who appeared equally surprised, mimicked No. 238's movements and dodged to the right. To arrest his momentum, No. 238 pressed his hand against the wall and turned back to face his opponent.

The tiny woman had already begun a second attack! Nimbly stepping forward, she executed a skillfully deceptive thrust towards the North Korean's head, before redirecting her blade to his mid-section.

No. 238 anticipated the second attack, blocked it with his right arm, and lunged forward with his own weapon. But the woman evaded the strike, spun smoothly into an attack stance, and slashed at him a third time. No. 238 again parried the assault with his right arm, powerfully swinging his left leg around toward the woman's abdomen.

The woman, to No. 238's surprise, immediately dropped to the ground, ducking under the kick. No. 238's momentum carried him beyond his opponent. Rather than attempting to stop himself, the killer continued to spin in the same direction. The result was a lightning-fast 360-degree rotation that returned him to his original position.

No. 238 immediately unleashed a knife strike, but discovered that, again, his opponent was attempting an almost identical move! As No. 238 blocked the red-haired woman's latest move, his own near perfect blow was also deflected. He recoiled from the failed attempt, jumping back into a defensive combat stance. The red-haired woman did the same.

The entire exchange had taken less than a minute.

No. 238, adept at assessing his opponents' capabilities, had seen more than enough.

The woman's physical prowess, combat skills and poise prompted his jarring conclusion.

This is the deadliest opponent I have ever faced!

The surprised assassin studied his foe with an unprecedented amount of care. The small red-haired woman's posture, balance, dexterity, and weapon handling were...perfect! For the first time in his life, No. 238 could detect no weakness. With nothing he could use to gain an advantage, it was as though he were staring at the mirror image of himself!

No. 238's robotic brain diverted every bit of its focus to his new opponent. The circumstances that had brought him to an airport in Manchester, New Hampshire quickly faded from his mind. Eric Sutton was forgotten, as was the need for a timely escape. In the face of what had inexplicably become the most challenging battle of No. 238's life, nothing else mattered.

No. 238 stared into the unblinking brown eyes of the freckle-faced woman standing across from him. She was collected, but radiated a focus that matched his own.

Then, at last, they each lunged a final time.

No. 238 assailed his enemy with a dazzling array of complex attacks and blistering knife strikes. But the red-haired woman returned fire with moves that tested the outer limits of his defense. Adrenaline flooded his circulatory system. The tiny North Korean, who had never confronted the possibility of death in any of his previous battles, was suddenly locked in a titanic struggle for survival!

No. 238 and his combatant darted back and forth along the hallway. No 238 tirelessly executed one maneuver after another, trying to bring her down...

The pop of a single gunshot abruptly echoed through the hallway.

The red-haired woman let out a high-pitched yelp, and dropped to the ground. As she fell, No. 238 could see the blood streaming from a bullet hole in her left thigh. The North Korean traced the apparent trajectory of the bullet back to its source.

Standing twenty feet away, Eric Sutton gripped one of the FBI Agents' pistols with trembling hands.

His face emotionless, No. 238 stared with wide eyes at the quivering blond man. Then he turned and looked down at the red-haired woman, who had pulled herself back against the opposite wall like a cornered animal. No. 238 dropped his knife wielding hand to his side.

This battle is not meant to end this way.

"I-I. . . didn't know...if she was going to kill you!" Sutton stammered. "I thought, maybe, she was here to kill me, too!"

Sutton's words drew No. 238 back on task.

I need to get Eric Sutton out of this airport, immediately.

His eyes glued to the bleeding woman at his feet, No. 238 called to his blond-haired captive.

"Eric Sutton," he barked, "Come here, immediately. We are leaving, now."

Sutton stumbled down the hallway to his diminutive kidnapper (and toward the woman he had just shot.) His mouth hung open in a combination of shock, fear, and emotional exhaustion. Sutton blankly presented No. 238 with the pistol he had just fired, as well as an FBI radio he had reflexively grabbed off of the hallway floor.

"J-just...get me out of here," he stuttered, "before the U.S. Government sends anyone else! Okay?"

"Drop the radio. Give me the gun."

No. 238 continued eyeing the red-haired woman as he grabbed the pistol, removed its ammunition, and let the weapon fall to the floor. He grabbed Sutton by the hand and pulled him down the hallway. The red-haired woman, her hands clasped tightly over her wound, silently watched them go.

When No. 238 reached the set of double-doors leading to the employee parking lot, he paused to cast a final glance back down the hall.

The red-haired woman had pulled herself into a standing position, and was nimbly hopping toward a door on the opposite side of the corridor. As she prepared to disappear inside, she slowly turned. In the unnatural light of the corridor, No 238 silently eyed the only opponent who had ever fought him and survived.

Then No. 238 whirled around, pushed open the double doors, and raced out into the cold.

CHAPTER 34

"Are you suggesting..." Tim began, stopping in mid-sentence. "No way..."

Eric didn't respond. He leapt up from the conference table and hustled across the room to his cluttered workstation, where he rummaged feverishly through different piles of printed material. After a few minutes, Eric retrieved a small stack of colorful glossy covers and plopped the stack down on the conference table.

"Here," he declared. "Any of these look familiar?"

Tim perused the stack. Neatly preserved in clear plastic sleeves was an assortment of first edition comic books. Appreciating their enormous value, Tim carefully thumbed through the classic collection. A few of these titles were displayed under his glass counter at Dragon Comics.

"First appearance of 'The Punisher'...First appearance of 'Wolverine'...First appearance of 'Spiderman'...Wow!" Tim exhaled. "Eric, this is valuable stuff!"

"I know," Eric concurred. "About a year ago, I waxed nostalgically about the days we used to spend together reading these. So I asked my North Korean minders to snag me a few. Of course, they assumed that I meant the original classics, so they brought back these gems, which they probably stole from some poor bastard's collection."

"Anyway," Eric went on, "Since my kidnapping, I've only seen our Crocodile super soldier a few times. Once, I caught a glimpse of him flying up a dirt trail above the tunnel. Another time, I thought I saw him hustling through the woods between the tunnel and this building."

"But one morning," Eric added, "I woke up stunned, to find him sitting in this room! Right over there." Eric pointed to his cluttered workspace across the room.

"I realized that he was reading all my comic books! This government-bred assassin was casually perusing those masterpieces as though he were a kid in your store!"

"I found myself wondering how many other times he had been in my room while I was sleeping! But I slowly got a grip, and seized the golden opportunity to interact with the guy. So I just start talking. I mentioned you owning a comic book store, and how you and I were avid readers of comics growing up."

"At the time," Eric continued, "I wasn't sure if any of what I said had registered. He didn't even look up. He just sat there and continued reading. Finally, after about twenty minutes, he neatly set the stack of comics next to one of my computers, got up, and walked out of the room."

"I mean, with everything in this room, he picked comic books! At first, I was totally baffled."

"But now I understand." Eric asserted. "It was the battles! All of these comics present titanic struggles between superheroes and villains! Every page depicts an epic clash!"

"He identifies himself with these characters. These comics mirror his own life, one shaped by formative years of combat. Battles like the ones depicted in these comics are the only experiences this guy knows or cares about."

"God..." Tim realized. "So at the airport..."

Eric nodded.

"He found his ultimate warrior. And she got away."

"As soon as we were out of the airport," Eric proceeded, "The little psychopath stuck a needle in my arm. I spent the next two weeks in a narcotic haze, until I finally arrived here in this camp. Since then, I haven't been able to totally sort out what I witnessed in Manchester that night."

"But now, looking back, I see how important it was to this guy. He shows up at the airport with orders to kidnap me. But suddenly, he finds himself locked in the epic battle he was destined to fight."

"But," Eric went on, "He doesn't get to finish it. Thanks to my unbelievably lucky shot, the fight is no longer fair. He steps back, regains his senses, remembers his mission, and yanks me out of the airport."

"But he never forgets about Sarah. He replays the battle over and over in his mind. The fact that he didn't get to finish his title bout eats at him. Finally, after a couple of years he's about ready to snap, so he puts his own plan into motion."

"Oh...my...God." The realization hit Tim. "He sent the comic to my store!"

"Exactly," Eric responded. "He remembers that you own a comic book store in New Hampshire. He finds the address, doctors a comic book, and sends it. What kind of comic did he use, anyway? I know he didn't steal one of mine..."

"It was a North Korean propaganda comic!" Tim replied. "But I still don't get it. Why me?"

"Maybe," Eric returned, "his whole scheme was simply based on a lucky guess. Think about what he knew. The U.S. Government was chasing me. Sarah was a part of that effort. You were my only sibling, with whom I had indicated having a strong emotional connection. You were the person I would mostly likely contact. And he figures that, if Sarah is still trying to find me, she is probably keeping an eye on you."

"Somehow, he finds out that Agent Hutchins was at the airport that night. So, almost three years to the day after leaving Manchester, he sends a coded message in a North Korean comic book. He tells you to save me."

"He clung to the hope," Eric continued, "that Sarah, at some point, would notice your actions. Or, that Hutchins would pass along what you gave him, and the U.S. Government would send Sarah over here. Either way, Sarah would attach herself to your voyage across the Pacific. When you finally arrived here in the mountains, so would she. And our Korean super-soldier would be waiting."

"So," Tim concluded in astonishment. "This is all about some fight?"

Eric nodded with a smile.

"The fight," he added, "that will soon take place." Eric pointed to the late night sky. "Right about now, our super-soldier is en route to the drug-holding facility. As soon as that convoy he's accompanying arrives, he'll head back here. When he does, he'll find Sarah, and by the time the sun comes up, I predict those two will be locked in battle!"

Tim slumped in his chair, emotionally drained, but at the same time somewhat relieved that the whole situation finally made sense. His epic journey had been engineered by a North Korean bent on settling an old score.

Tim's facial expression changed from relief to dismay as he pondered their current predicament. He slowly looked back at his little brother, who was still standing next him at the table.

"Eric, we're dead," Tim intoned with dread.

Eric, still smiling, didn't understand.

"What are you talking about?" he dismissed. "This thing has nothing to do with either of us!"

"Yes," Tim replied, his voice cracking, "It does."

When the Haihu docked in Dalian, Sarah had left Tim in the container and taken off. Tim hadn't had a clue where she was going or why. Now, he suspected it involved the U.S. Government in one of two possible scenarios.

One possibility was that the feds had sent Sarah to North Korea to get Eric. Unbeknownst to her bosses, however, Sarah had subsequently realized that a big fight with the super-soldier was now in the cards.

A second possibility was that Sarah had intercepted the message Tim had received in the manila envelope. Realizing who sent the message, Sarah had gone A.W.O.L.—the airport battle had had the same effect on her as it had on the super soldier. Sarah had then headed to North Korea for the fight of her life. If she survived, though, she would need something to get back into the good graces of her employers. That 'something' was Eric.

Tim explained all of this to his brother.

"If Sarah succeeds in killing the North Korean," Tim summed up, "She's going to come for you. She won't take you to a U.S. prison. You stole $20 million from the United States, and have intimate knowledge of dirty CIA dealings with a Malian warlord. If you are sent to a prison, it will be a secret one. More likely, you'll just wind up dead."

"As for me," Tim concluded, "No one but Jeff Hutchins knows I'm here. It's in the government's best interest to simply make me disappear."

Eric was no longer smiling.

"But, if the North Korean wins--" he protested.

"We're no better off," Tim interrupted.

The whole crazy plan, Tim explained, had been the super-soldier's idea. If his masters figured this out, they would conclude that he deliberately led Americans to this secure location. In so doing, he had jeopardized not only Eric's safety, but the entire illicit North Korean drug operation! In essence, the man had consciously betrayed his own country for the chance to finish his personal battle with Sarah.

It had probably occurred to the super-soldier that Tim and Eric would deduce all of this. If the Korean assassin killed Sarah, Tim doubted he would just ask Eric to keep quiet. The man was a killer. Killing was his only form of "discussion."

After the super-soldier executed Eric, he could easily claim that Sarah had done the killing when he was off on a convoy. His country's industry would encounter serious road-bumps, but what did he care? He would have finally concluded his long-awaited battle. Tim's inevitable death, of course, would be a mere afterthought.

"Eric," Tim concluded morbidly, "We are screwed."

Eric slumped in his own chair, his body language mirroring that of his older brother.

"Fuck," he whispered. "You're right. And there's no way we can escape. The only vehicles are the cargo trucks over at the holding facility, and there's no way that either of us could get one of those out of these mountains. And we wouldn't make it on foot."

For the first time in many years, Eric Sutton, the diabolical boy-genius, was fresh out of ideas. He anxiously turned to his only hope.

"Big Brother," Eric implored, "What do we do?"

Tim was silent for a minute. Finally, he turned to face his blond-haired sibling.

"I can only think of one thing," Tim began. "And it's a long-shot."

"OK," Eric eagerly returned, "What is it?"

Tim responded.

"These computers of yours have Internet access, right?"

CHAPTER 35

Percy Danielson anxiously paced back and forth across the penthouse's plush carpet.

"We should have heard from them by now..." he muttered to himself.

Jeff Archer, staring at the darkened Dalianwan Bay, said nothing.

It was after midnight in the Chinese port city. Twelve hours ago, Sergeant Jim Sariani and his team of Rangers had set out on their mission beyond the North Korean border, to retrieve the duffle bag full of drug money, and apprehend Sarah and Eric Sutton. Sariani hadn't radioed in a report in several hours, and this worried Danielson and Archer.

While the balding CIA agent and the grey-haired Ceiling Program Commander monitored their satellite radio system, Jeff Hutchins squeezed his tall frame into a nearby desk. The St. Paul's schoolteacher used a government computer with wireless access to check his email.

"Something's wrong..." Danielson fretted, beads of sweat dotting his forehead.

"I think those guys have run into trouble," he went on. "And I don't think their problem is the North Koreans!"

Archer turned from the window and glared at Danielson.

"Percy," he declared icily, "Don't presume to know what's going on up there. You never logged a day of combat in your life. And don't imply that Sarah is causing problems, just because you haven't heard the phone ring."

"Whatever," Danielson returned with scorn. "Just remember, if that redheaded psychopath turns on our boys, their blood will be on your hands!"

"Our boys?" Archer scoffed. "Don't pretend you have any relationship with Jim Sariani's team. And don't forget, they wouldn't even be up there if you hadn't allowed that kid to hijack $20 million in dirty money. You're just. . ."

Archer was interrupted by the squawk of the radio.

"Squirrel to Tree. Squirrel to Tree. Come in, over."

Danielson and Archer rushed over to the radio, where Archer grabbed a small microphone that sat on top of the device. Hutchins jumped up from the desk and hustled over.

"Squirrel, this is Tree," Archer returned into the microphone. "What's your situation?"

"Tree, it's...it's bad. I'm on emergency evac back to China with our Korean CIA operatives. We've suffered significant casualties, over."

Archer's face darkened.

"Squirrel, elaborate on the casualties."

"Tree, they're...my team is gone. We arrived at the target site about two hours ago and found a camp full of dead North Koreans, just as you predicted. We located the money, but were surprised by a drug convoy arriving from the east. We eliminated the enemy threat, but. . .were subsequently attacked by someone else. He, or she, killed my team. I was forced to scrap our initial plan and get the hell out of there. I'm inside a container with the money and the bodies of my team members, over."

When Archer responded, his voice was hollow and his tone, grave.

"Squirrel, I'm sorry about your casualties. Can you confirm the identity of the person who eliminated your team...was it Apple, over?"

"Tree...that appears to be a positive. I only saw the attacker through my infrared goggles, but the size and shape of the target matched Apple's description. I've also never seen anyone move like that. I suspect it was your operative, over."

Archer raised his right hand to his head and began to massage his temple. Casting a forlorn stare at the carpeted floor, the Commander readdressed Sergeant Sariani.

"Copy that. Proceed to Dalian and rendezvous with our personnel. Over."

"Roger that. Over and out."

Archer slowly let the microphone fall from his hands.

"I just...I don't understand," he murmured. "Why would she...I just don't understand."

Danielson was livid.

"Understand this, pal!" he vowed. "You're going to swing for this one! Your little Apple just massacred three U.S. Army Rangers! Whatever you thought she was doing here, you're obviously mistaken! Sarah's in league with Eric Sutton, the North Koreans, or both! You're going to hang; I'll see to it myself!"

Archer ignored Danielson's outburst.

"Why would she do any of this?" he asked himself, softly. "Why would she lead us way over here, and then kill some Rangers in North Korea? There's just...there's no way that could have been her...it doesn't make sense. . ."

"Oh, are you in denial now?" Danielson cut in. "Sariani just told you he saw her kill his men! In any case, 'why' isn't the point! The point is that you've created a female monster that you can't control!"

"And now," Danielson went on, "We've probably lost the only chance we had of apprehending Eric Sutton!"

Hutchins quietly retreated to his desk, away from Danielson's fury and Archer's grief. The lanky former FBI agent didn't know what to believe.

Had Sarah masterminded Tim Sutton's visit to Hutchins' classroom weeks earlier? Had she cooked up a fake story about Eric Sutton being in North Korea?

Exhausted and disillusioned, Hutchins collapsed in the armchair next to the desk and turned to the laptop. Hutchins caught something out of the corner of his eye.

In the bottom-left corner of the monitor, the email icon was flashing, indicating that he had a new message in his mailbox.

Hutchins was somewhat surprised. He had checked his email minutes earlier, so this new message must have arrived while he was at the radio with Danielson and Archer. Hutchins clicked on the icon.

As he began to read the message, his eyes went wide. Hutchins shot up in his chair as though he had received an electric shock, and leaned toward the monitor in earnest.

The email message extended far below the space allotted in the small window. Hutchins franticly scanned the visible section of the letter. Without bothering to scroll down any further, he whirled around.

"You're not going to believe this!" he announced. "I just got an email from Tim Sutton!"

****

"Wait, what?"

Tim stared down at the computer's microphone in confusion as the voice repeated itself.

"Do you have any details of Sarah's actions within the past 24 hours at the drug holding facility near your position? Do you know of any casualties?"

Tim leaned away from the microphone and flashed Eric a puzzled glance.

"Sarah's actions?" Tim questioned his brother. "Eric, do you know what he's talking about?"

Miraculously, after Tim had sent a desperate e-mail to Jeff Hutchins, he immediately received a response! Hutchins was in China with several US officials who had presumably set up a base of operations!

Tim and Hutchins had exchanged a few short email messages when Hutchins suggested switching to Skype, a free internet service that turned computers into long-distance telephones. Now, as Eric sat tensely nearby, Tim was talking to an unnamed agent who had apparently commandeered Hutchins' computer.

Eric reflected on the last question, his mouth broadening into a knowing smile. He pulled Tim away from the mike and covered it with his hand.

"Shit, Tim! They don't have a handle on their little super-agent!"

"What do you mean?" Tim replied, still confused.

"When Sarah freed you from the shipping container, what was the situation at the drug holding facility?"

"It was quiet," Tim offered. "The place was like a ghost town."

"It shouldn't have been," Eric leveled. "There are at least a dozen men at that base at all times. I'll bet Sarah slaughtered the whole lot before she opened up your box."

"You know," Tim returned, his eyes widening in recollection, "Last night I awoke to what I could have sworn were gunshots!"

"Right," Eric cut in. "That was probably Sarah at work. The point, though, is that the guy on the other end apparently doesn't know that. If Sarah's the point-woman on a secret mission, why isn't she constantly updating Hutchins and his CIA buddies on her progress?"

Tim nodded.

"Because," he deduced, "She isn't with them! She's operating on her own!"

"Exactly," Eric concurred. "And these guys are just trying to keep up with her. Shit, they don't have a clue about what's going on here!"

"But," Eric added quickly, "You better not keep this guy waiting."

"Yes, I'm aware of Sarah's recent actions at the base," Tim informed the man on the other end of the line. "Shortly before she released me from my shipping container, she killed the North Korean soldiers guarding the facility."

"And as far as you know," the voice immediately replied, "Are those the only casualties?"

Once again, Tim backed away from the microphone and cast a puzzled glance at Eric.

"Other casualties?"

"Oh, fuck!" Eric exclaimed. "I'll bet the United States sent soldiers up here chasing Sarah, and something went wrong! Now, they're trying to figure out whether or not she killed her own countrymen!"

"Well, if she didn't kill them," Tim muttered, "I've got a pretty good idea who did…"

"Exactly," Eric concurred.

Tim slowly returned his eyes to the computer screen. He rolled this latest information around, took a deep breath, and cast a determined look at the microphone.

"If that's true," he whispered, "then that's our leverage. I just pray that someone with a U.S. flag stitched to his uniform is still up in these mountains. If your North Korean super-soldier didn't kill all of them, we have a chance…"

Now it was Eric's turn to be puzzled. Before he could ask Tim exactly what he meant by "leverage", Tim began to speak into the microphone.

"Okay," he barked into the device authoritatively, "I can see that you don't have a clear picture of what's transpired up here. But I assure you, I have all of the answers you seek."

There was no reply from the other end of the line.

"I assume that you came here with two objectives," Tim continued. "To reel in your rogue agent Sarah, and to apprehend my brother."

Again, the voice on the other end was silent.

"Understand this," Tim finished. "You can find your rogue agent, get your questions answered and apprehend my brother. In exchange, however, we have a specific set of demands and instructions that must be met. We're running out of time. Do we have a deal?"

When Tim had finished, he stared down silently at the microphone. He could feel his younger brother's eyes piercing his back. Eric's surrender was not something the two brothers had discussed. Tim realized, however, that Americans, ironically, were the best chance they had to get out of this alive.

Before Tim could explain his motives to his younger brother, the voice on the other end issued a reply.

"I'm listening."

CHAPTER 36

Jeff Archer pushed away from the laptop, leaned back in his chair, and let out a low whistle.

"Goddamn it," he murmured to no one in particular. "The Crocodile Program…"

Archer was not a man to lose control of his emotions under pressure, but this particular rollercoaster ride was testing him to the limits.

Earlier, he had grudgingly considered the possibility that his highly skilled and prized female agent had killed the three U.S. Army Rangers. Now, after a lengthy internet conversation with Tim Sutton, he had learned that his soldiers had been executed by a North Korean super-soldier whom Sarah had traveled across the globe to fight in fatalistic hand-to-hand combat!

Archer had known that Sarah's instability was rooted in her desire to extend the boundaries of her own physical and psychological limits. In hindsight, it was obvious that she would go A.W.O.L. after an unexpected clash with the "Crocodile" in New Hampshire.

"You knew of this 'program'?"

The nervous words came from Percy Danielson who, having realized his earlier accusations were wrong, was attempting to weasel his way back into Archer's good graces.

"I'd heard rumors," Archer replied distractedly, without turning around to face Danielson. "A decade or so ago there was talk of some elite soldier initiative by the North Koreans. We tried to get meaningful intel, but hit a wall. I assumed the whole thing was a bunch of bullshit. I guess I was wrong."

"Well," Danielson offered, "I contacted Staff Sergeant Sariani and apprised him of these new developments. He immediately ordered his truck to turn around and head back up into the mountains. I have to say, I was surprised and impressed by his desire—"

"Of course you were," Archer dismissed, still staring at the laptop. "You have no idea how a soldier like Sariani thinks and operates. The risks, no matter how extreme, won't deter him. And once I radio that his target is a North Korean soldier who killed his buddies and intends to kill Sarah, he'll be damn near unstoppable."

Jeff Hutchins, sitting cross-legged on the king-sized bed, threw his two cents into the conversation.

"I'm sure Sergeant Sariani is one of our very best soldiers," he began, "But does he have a chance up there? According to Tim Sutton, Sariani's success depends entirely on his getting within range of Sarah and this 'Crocodile' while they're fighting each other."

"I don't know," Archer admitted. "The odds of Jim finding Sarah before the conclusion of the battle are remote. That said, I'm more worried about the result of the fight."

"If Sarah wins," Archer continued, "I'm pretty confidant that she'll come back to us. But this 'Crocodile' slaughtered three highly-trained Rangers without firing a single shot. If he kills Sarah before Sariani can reach them…Sariani and the Sutton brothers are as good as dead."

Danielson delicately attempted to remind everyone in the room of the CIA's interests.

"Let's say that Sergeant Sariani does reach those two," he speculated, "And he's able to incapacitate Sarah, kill this 'Crocodile' and escape with the Sutton boys. When Eric is in our custody, are we really going to capitulate to his demands?"

"It's your call," Archer dismissed. "My concern is Sarah. If you want to play ball with Sutton and offer up federal prison, that's up to you. My guess, though, is that you'll prefer to crucify him."

"I see no alternative!" Danielson admitted. "I want him taken to a dark corner of the earth and thoroughly 'interrogated'. I want to use every technique at our disposal to determine what he knows, and how much of that $20 million he's got left. If he's still alive, or sane, at that point, we'll reevaluate the situation. I've invested too damn much into this operation to see Eric Sutton do a short stint in Club Fed!"

"Cool your jets, Percy," Archer retorted, "You haven't put nearly as much effort into finding Sutton as some people have. Someone right here in this room lost his career in pursuit of that kid."

Archer turned toward Hutchins.

"You have a huge stake in this, Jeff," Archer offered. "What do you think we should do with Eric Sutton?"

Hutchins was caught off-guard. After a few moments of reflection, he slowly offered a cautious response.

"Well," Hutchins began, "I've wanted to get my hands on Sutton for as long as I can remember. But for me, it's not about revenge or money. It's about justice. I want to see that kid do time for the things he's done."

"But," Hutchins went on, "I've also come to realize, over the years, just how brilliant Eric Sutton is. Why waste that talent if we can use it to our advantage? Eric will know his options are limited. My guess is that he'll want to work with us. With his help, we could map out the entire North Korean drug network and construct an effective response to the proliferation of foreign narcotics!"

Danielson was unconvinced. He crossed his arms, turned away, and stared out the window at the black waters of the Pacific. Archer sighed, moved over to the satellite communication radio, and prepared to issue instructions to Sergeant Sariani. Before he began, the silver-haired Commander looked back toward the penthouse bed.

"Hell, Jeff," he stated. "Barring some sort of miracle, there's no way Sariani is going to make it up there in time."

* *

Tim stared reluctantly into his younger brother's eyes.

"I had to, Eric," he managed. "Without their help, we're both dead. Our only hope for escape is to make it back to the drug-holding facility and hop on a truck before Sarah and the super-soldier finish their fight. I know you don't trust the CIA to keep their word, but, we have no choice. I'm sure they'll realize you're a valuable resource. Who knows?

Maybe you'll only do a few years in federal prison and then go work for the guys who put you there."

Eric stepped forward, puts his hands on Eric's shoulders, and forced out a thin smile.

"Big Brother," he interjected in a tone that was soft but firm. "I'm not mad at you."

Tim grinned in obvious relief.

"Okay, then! Let's get the hell out of here! Are you sure about the fight location?"

Eric took a step back, dropping his arms to his side. His smile faded and he slowly nodded.

"Yes, I'm sure."

After he had spied the super-soldier scampering up the path above the tunnel, Eric explained, he had begun to wonder where the soldier had been going. One day, when Eric was sure the North Korean killing machine wasn't around, he had climbed up the path to take a look.

Eric had discovered that the mountain the tunnel passed through actually leveled into a forested plateau. In the midst of those isolated woods, Eric had found a dirt circle identical to the ones back down in the camp.

Tim understood immediately. The little psychopath had cut down trees and tilled enough soil to create a private arena! He obviously didn't want to risk fighting down in the camp, where soldiers could turn up at any time. So he had replicated an arena in a place he knew no one but Sarah could ever find.

Tim nodded, sufficiently convinced. He had turned toward the sliding wooden entrance when his brother resumed speaking.

"And Tim," Eric proceeded. "I'm not going with you."

Tim's jaw dropped.

"What?" he managed, his eyes bulging. "What the hell do you mean? You just admitted that this plan is the only chance we have!"

Eric nodded.

"It probably is. And if you go alone, it should almost certainly save your life. But I'll never willingly turn myself over to the U.S. Government."

"Eric!" Tim protested. "They're not going to kill or torture you! Those guys aren't idiots! Damn it, come on!"

Eric sighed and deliberately shook his head.

"Tim," he pleaded earnestly, "You know this is about more than the threat of torture, death, or a lengthy prison sentence. You know me."

For a second, Tim's mouth hung open as he futilely searched for a response. Finally, Tim's body slumped in dismayed defeat. His brother was right.

Even if things did work out for the best, and the government did put Eric to work—Eric would still be in the same kind of prison he had endured in Ruston.

Tim's brother had spent the past five years establishing the kind of life he had always wanted, achieving the "greatness" their mother had envisioned. Eric, Tim knew, would rather die than surrender the success he considered to be his birthright.

In his rush to secure his brother's safety, Tim had booked Eric a ticket back to the world in which he had never belonged.

Not knowing what to say, Tim pursed his lips and stared down at the floor.

"Tim," Eric consoled with a smile. "These are my problems, not yours. Get out of here. Get back to Ruston and enjoy a long, enjoyable and prosperous life selling comic books. You've done all you can here."

Eric reached past Tim and slid open the thick wooden door.

Tim, struggling to hold back tears, extended his right hand toward his brother.

"Hey," he offered, his eyes brightening slightly. "Remember 'Jeopardy'?"

Eric grinned as he reached out and grabbed Tim's hand.

"Of course! You know, I was always better than you. Mom knew it."

Tim managed to roll his glistening eyes.

"Whatever," he managed. "Maybe, someday, you'll get the chance to put your money where your mouth is."

"You're on," Eric returned. "Save me a spot on the couch."

The brothers released each other's hands.

"Good luck Tim."

"Same to you, Little Brother."

"See ya."

"Bye."

With that, the elder Sutton pulled away and hustled out of the building.

Eric watched as Tim pushed open the metal door beyond the structure's small front room and disappeared into the white forest. Then he weakly stumbled back toward the conference table. Eric collapsed into the nearest chair, put his elbows on the table, and dropped his head into his hands.

* *

As the pale light of dawn reflected off the tears streaming down his face, Tim sprinted along the snow-covered trail. He flew by the row of dirt circles, and past the scores of concrete huts scattered throughout the woods. When Tim finally emerged from the forest and reached the tarp that hung over the mouth of the concrete tunnel, he leaned forward to catch his breath. With one hand on his knee, he wiped his opposite arm across his tear-stained visage.

Less than 24 hours after reuniting with Eric, the two were again separated! And soon, Tim feared, his darkly brilliant brother would breathe his final breath! As the grief washed over him, Tim suddenly came to a realization.

Weeks ago, when he had first committed to undertaking this trip around the world, he had done it for a single reason. After sitting for days in the corner of a cold, dark container, reaching a secret camp in the North Korean wilderness, and finding his brother alive and content as a state-sponsored criminal, that reason hadn't changed.

Eric was still in danger.

Tim raised himself up and fixed a determined stare on the mountain that rose above the tunnel.

You didn't come all this way just to turn around and head back home.

Tim was going to save his little brother.

After taking several deep breaths, Tim charged past the entrance to the concrete tunnel and up onto the mountainous, snow-covered rock.

His first attempts to scramble up the slippery incline were unsuccessful. Gradually, however, he gained some footing, and managed a slow crawl up the mountain.

After a few minutes, Tim discovered a faint trail that wound upward. He carefully ascended the frozen path.

After thirty laborious minutes of climbing, the slope of the mountain began to gradually level off. Tim found himself stepping onto the plateau that Eric had described. As his footing became more secure, Tim switched to a jog and headed into the thick woodland in front of him. He was now running as fast as he could, wildly swatting tree limbs and brush out of his way as he flew across the powdery forest floor.

As Tim pushed onward he lost sight of the trail. Without knowing if he was even heading in the right direction, Tim plunged deeper into the thick white landscape. The world around him was a blur as Tim lost all sense of direction. Undeterred, he blindly pushed on.

And then, suddenly, after a full hour of climbing, hiking, sprinting, and stumbling, the robust vegetation that had swallowed Tim up vanished.

Taken aback by the sudden shift in the landscape, Tim attempted to grind his speeding frame to a halt. Instead, he careened across the icy ground, crashing into the trunk of a pine tree. For a few seconds, he lay dazed at the base of the tree. Then, realizing where he was, he shook the snow from his hair and hopped up onto his feet.

Tim stared at the forest opening in front of him. Fear and determination waged war for control of his spirit. Tim took a final deep breath, pushed his terror as far down into his stomach as he could, clenched his fists, and stepped into the center of the snow-covered arena.

For Eric.

CHAPTER 37

The first soft hints of dawn crept onto the remote highland and advanced over the frosted conifers. Slowly, the pale light illuminated the 50-foot-wide circle that had been meticulously carved out of the dense forest. When the light reached a particular pine at the edge of the snowy clearing, it ignited the fiery-red hair of a woman lying prone on one of the tree's largest branches.

Sarah was waiting.

It had been nearly 24 hours since she had left Tim Sutton at the mouth of the concrete tunnel. Since then, Sarah had painstakingly surveyed every inch of the wilderness that surrounded his brother's enclave.

Sarah had seen the dirt circles that lay adjacent to the building where Eric worked. She had found every trail, path, and route that her long-lost combatant might have taken as he patrolled this remote landscape.

Finally, in an isolated patch of forest high above the tunnel entrance, Sarah had discovered the clearing. She recognized its purpose immediately. This was a space that had been cleared in her name. This was where she would undertake the greatest test of her life.

And so, for nearly 12 hours, Sarah had waited. She didn't know where he was, but she knew that he would come. He had invited her here.

As the frigid wind battered her rosy cheeks, Sarah's acute senses, on high alert throughout the night, suddenly trumpeted a fierce warning.

Sarah clenched the tree limb in heightened anticipation, while staring with brown eyes blazing, toward the tree-line at the opposite end of the clearing. It was time.

Sarah swung her body off of the limb, gracefully descending to the base of the tree. Landing silently at the edge of the clearing, she deliberately stood tall.

Not once did Sarah take her unblinking eyes off the figure who emerged from the trees 50 feet away.

Sarah's pulse quickened as her hand slid down to the silver combat knife strapped to her leg. She slickly slid the blade from its sheath and gripped it firmly with her right hand. As white powder cascaded off of her icy hair, Sarah widened her stance, readied her weapon, and prepared for combat.

Her long wait was over.

* * * * * * * * * * * * * * * * * *

No. 238's black eyes peered through the dense, snowy forest, surveying the trees along the edge of the circular clearing that he had so carefully crafted. His unwavering search finally settled on the limb of a particular pine tree.

She is here.

Hours earlier, as No. 238 had watched the U.S. soldier reload his rifle, he had realized that his plan to lure the diminutive redhead to this remote mountain location might have succeeded.

Minutes after that realization, he had raced to the entrance of the concrete tunnel and discovered a minuscule set of footprints in the snow at the opening. That was when he knew his plan had worked.

In the hours since, No. 238 had doggedly stalked his prey.

He had surreptitiously followed the tiny footprints to the wooded plateau above the tunnel, then over to the building that housed Eric Sutton. There, No. 238 had seen Tim Sutton's set of tracks leading into Eric's hideout. But this meant little to No. 238. Tim Sutton was a mere pawn in his plan.

Finally, No. 238 returned to the place he had cleared for this moment.

Now, he could see her in the tree, her mop of red hair radiating in the light of dawn.

No. 238 pulled the long black dagger from its sheath. He stepped forward into the clearing and watched as his opponent swung off of her tree limb and dropped onto the snowy earth below. As she regained her balance and prepared for combat, the North Korean resolutely did the same.

At long last, the fight of No. 238's life would come to a conclusion.

****

The two warriors warily studied each other from opposite sides of the 50-foot circle. There would be no surprises this time.

Neither Sarah nor No. 238 had any notions of supremacy. Both Apple and the Crocodile knew that they could as easily perish as emerge victorious.

It wasn't that they were apprehensive. Neither had ever known fear. There was simply a mutual acceptance that this battle had two possible outcomes.

Sarah, who had once slain a grizzly bear to test her limits, could never rest until she killed the most dangerous beast of all. The need to continue her battle with No. 238 gnawed at her soul. Nothing else mattered.

For No. 238, it was simply a robotic need to finish the fight. To him, a battle did not end until someone was dead.

Now, the two warriors faced each other in the frozen ring. Within seconds, they were circling the arena like a pair of wild dogs, each waiting for a chance to tear the other apart.

And then, just over three years after Eric Sutton's bullet tore through Sarah's leg, the clash resumed.

Sarah struck first, lunging forward with a knife strike that would have punctured the throat of any other accomplished fighter. No. 238, however, narrowly escaped the thrust with an undetectable shift of his small frame. He immediately retaliated with a sweeping slash toward Sarah's chest, but the little redhead bent her torso backward in an eye-popping display of flexibility. She watched No. 238's weapon slide within centimeters of her flesh, then counterattacked with blade extended.

But the North Korean dropped under the thrust and responded with a jab toward Sarah's left thigh. Sarah avoided the attack by rocketing her left leg out to the side. She then attempted to pin No. 238's knife-holding arm to the ground by lunging with both of her hands.

No. 238 anticipated this move and rolled to his left, regaining his footing three feet from his opponent. Swiftly hopping back onto his feet, he drove toward Sarah like a creature possessed. No. 238 unleashed a bewildering combination of preprogrammed kicks and knife strikes at his tiny foe. But Sarah had an answer for each, expertly parrying the attacks and responding in kind.

For fifteen minutes, the battle raged. Both warriors threw every ounce of their souls into the contest, but neither could land a lethal blow. At this point, fatigue should have set in, but the two athletes were so superbly conditioned, and so adept at ignoring pain, that neither showed signs of tiring. Weariness would not be a factor in this fight.

The two warriors pressed on. Steam rose from No. 238's bald head as he continued to systematically search for a single flaw, a single weakness he could exploit to deliver his killing blow. For her part, Sarah pushed harder and harder with every passing minute, determined to overwhelm her enemy or collapse in the attempt.

And then, out of the blue, the battle flipped upside down.

****

Sarah and No. 238 picked their disheveled, disoriented bodies up off the snowy turf. As they shook the powder from their frames and regained their bearings, the two jumped back from each other and resumed combat stances. Their focus was so intense that, for a moment, they forgot what had just happened.

Seconds earlier, an unseen force had smashed into the pair, driving them across the frigid circle, down into the snow.

Five feet away, a pale-skinned, auburn-haired young man was dizzily wobbling to his feet.

Tim Sutton.

No. 238's brain immediately instructed him to dismiss what had just happened.

Tim Sutton is not a threat. Deal with your opponent.

Sarah found herself confused by Tim's sudden appearance, but was unwilling to divert any focus from the task at hand.

Tim Sutton doesn't matter. Finish the fight.

And so, the two fighters completely ignored the man who had bizarrely collided with them.

But as they closed ground on each other, Sarah and her opponent were sent flying again.

As the two rose up from the frosty earth a second time, they reluctantly acknowledged the intruder they had tried to ignore.

This is a problem.

****

His body quivering in terror, Tim spun back towards the center of the circle and pulled himself to his feet. Against every survival instinct, he staggered back towards the two smaller people he had just knocked to the ground a second time.

You have to get closer. If you don't, they'll just ignore you and keep fighting.

Tim's stomach churned as he stationed himself in the middle of the arena.

Three feet away, the two powder-covered figures were eyeing each other as if they didn't even realize he was there. But unlike the first time he had plowed into them, Sarah and the North Korean were no longer in a rush to resume fighting. This time, they simply stared into each other's unblinking eyes.

Tim took another step, so that he was now standing directly between the two fighters. He slowly raised his trembling arms and extended an open palm toward each, signaling for them to remain in place. He tried to think of something to say, but his brain, overwhelmed with fear, offered nothing.

As the howling wind whipped across the tops of the trees, the three figures stood motionless in the center of sphere: A U.S. Government super-agent, a North Korean death robot, and a mild-mannered young man who ran a comic-book store in Ruston, New Hampshire.

Tim was nauseated. Technically, his plan was working, but that didn't make him feel any better. Tim felt as though he were standing between two cocked pistols ready to fire. He wanted to vomit.

Five long minutes passed. The two fighters, who seemed to be staring through Tim at each other, did not move. Neither seemed willing to surrender the tiny amount of focus necessary to eliminate him.

After another 5 minutes, Tim visibly jumped as Sarah addressed him with a single word.

"Leave," she commanded, without moving any part of her body other than her lips.

Tim managed to summon a choked response.

"I-I can't leave, Sarah," he mumbled. "You guys can't do this! You have to stop!" Neither Sarah nor the North Korean replied to Tim's words.

For another ten minutes, the three continued their stalemate. Tim's outstretched arms grew heavy, and he let them slowly drop to his side. Exhausted emotionally and physically; Tim was close to passing out. Before he could, however, he was startled by movement to his left.

The North Korean slowly began to step backward. He continued his retreat all the way to the edge of the clearing before stopping.

Where is he going? Tim wondered. *Is he leaving?*

The super-soldier stood at attention, slowly lowered his knife to his side, and while maintaining that posture, nodded a single time at Sarah.

Tim whipped his head to his right. His eyes went wide with fright.

Oh no!

Sarah stared at the North Korean for a few more seconds. Then, for the first time, she shifted her cold brown eyes to Tim. As the redheaded agent resolutely eyed the lanky young man she had accompanied across the globe, she slowly raised her blade...

****

No. 238 watched as his opponent quickly sized-up Tim Sutton. Soon, she would slit the young man's throat, and their epic fight could continue.

As No. 238 waited for Sarah to act, the wilderness around him came back into focus, reemerging in the light of a rapidly rising sun.

No. 238's eyes moved beyond the clearing to roam the nearby forest. Something in the dense brush caught his attention.

What is that?

Tucked beneath a distant group of trees, a patch of snow-covered earth didn't look quite right...

No. 238's eyes opened wide.

No!

He whipped his body around and dove toward the trees.

****

Sarah had taken a single step toward Tim Sutton when a loud popping sound rang out from the forest. Then the bullet ripped through her right shoulder-blade.

The impact of the shot spun Sarah around and she dropped to the ground. Sarah tried to ignore the pain as well as the shock of the sudden attack. As she attempted to rise, Sarah spied something moving in the distant forest.

The redheaded agent locked her eyes on her newest target, but made no more attempts to move. Lying on her side in the deep snow, Sarah shifted her gaze to the side of the clearing where her North Korean foe had retreated. He had disappeared.

Sarah's emotions raged. For the second time, a gunshot had interrupted her ultimate challenge! How could she have come this far, only to be robbed again?

Sarah took small consolation in the knowledge that her opponent would almost certainly circle back through the woods to kill her shooter. She collapsed and slapped both hands against her pulsing wound. Once again, she waited.

****

Tim was so shocked by the sudden change in events that he simply stood in a stupor over the woman who had intended to kill him.

Regaining his senses, Tim spun to his left and saw that the super-soldier had vanished into the forest. He turned to Sarah and saw that she wasn't moving.

Tim's mind began to grasp what was happening. He scanned the surrounding forest, but couldn't see anything, other than trees. He noticed, however, that Sarah was fixated on a spot fifty feet beyond the clearing. Tim traced her gaze with his own eyes, but still saw nothing.

Tim exhaled. Had his plan actually worked? Tim looked back toward where the 'Crocodile' had just been standing. He glanced down at Sarah, then stared into the tree line.

No.

Tim closed his eyes in despair. The Crocodile had escaped. All of Tim's effort had been for naught. Right now, the little psychopath was probably racing through the forest towards Sarah's shooter, who would never see him coming. Then the North Korean assassin would shift his attention to Eric.

In the midst of his grief, Tim realized that he still had a chance to save the man who had just saved him. Tim took the deepest breath he could muster, and bellowed the words that had popped into his head.

"If you try to kill that soldier," Tim screamed. "We'll kill her! Do you hear me? If you advance one more step in his direction, he's going to put a bullet in the middle of her forehead! You might kill him, but she'll be dead! Do you understand? She'll be dead!"

Tim's bold words flew into the trees. Exhausted, he dropped to his knees and cast a forlorn glance at the surrounding trees. For several minutes, Tim knelt in silence beside Sarah. He was so mentally spent that it didn't even occur to him to slide from her reach.

Tim was roused from his trance by a rustling noise coming from the woods. Tim turned in the direction of the sound and there, amidst a clump of trees, Tim saw something oddly familiar, a ghostly white shape materializing out of the snow.

As the shape moved towards the clearing, the white cloak draped around it fell to the side, revealing a soldier clad entirely in white camouflage. The soldier advanced into the clearing, keeping his M-4 assault rifle keenly trained on the woman he had just shot.

The soldier reached the center of the arena. Without moving his eyes or his weapon away from Sarah, he addressed Tim with a surprisingly recognizable voice.

"Are you okay, Tim?" Staff Sergeant Sariani asked.

"Um...y-yes!" Tim stammered in shock. "I mean, I-I think so! Aren't you, aren't you?"

"Yup," Sariani grimly replied. "Small fuckin' world, ain't it?"

CHAPTER 38

Jim Sariani kept his rifle pointed squarely at Sarah's chest.

"Can you move?" he hurriedly asked Tim.

Tim nodded, shivering.

"Y-yes," he managed. "I'm okay."

"Then come here," Sariani commanded. "Open the cargo pocket on the outer left leg of my pants, and pull out the syringe."

Tim slowly rose to his feet and staggered over to the Ranger. Reaching down, he unzipped a flap on the cargo pocket, reached inside, and pulled out a small clear vile of fluid.

"Now," Sariani instructed, "Pull the syringe out of its protective case, and stick the needle into one of Sarah's arms, just below the shoulder."

"What?"

"Just do it!" Sariani snapped. "We don't have any time to dick around here!"

Tim reluctantly pulled the needle out of its case, and made his way to Sarah. His hand shaking with fear, he reached towards the female warrior.

Sarah didn't flinch as Tim jabbed the needle through the thin black jacket into her flesh. She remained focused on the soldier standing above her. A few seconds later, however, her gaze began to waver. Finally, her eyes rolled back into her head and her body went limp.

"Is she…dead?" Tim asked.

Sariani shook his head.

"No, just knocked out. By the time she comes to, we'll hopefully be way the fuck out of this place."

Sariani shifted his eyes to Tim.

"That was some quick thinking, telling that guy we were going to kill her," Sariani praised. "You probably saved my life. But what the fuck are you doing up here, anyway? You and your brother were supposed to head straight for the drug facility!"

Tim's eyes dropped in sorrow.

"I-I couldn't," he mumbled in reply. "Eric didn't...he wouldn't come with me. I thought that, maybe, if I came up here and stalled these two long enough, it might give you time..."

"I see," Sariani responded. Not offering anything further, the Ranger abruptly tossed his rifle towards a surprised Tim. Sariani hustled over to Sarah's sleeping frame, and produced a small first-aid kit from his snow-suit. After bandaging Sarah's shoulder wound as best as he could, Sariani lifted her and draped her over his shoulder.

"Follow me," he commanded. "We don't have much time. That Korean fucker is going to come after us again, to see if he can take us out without getting Sarah killed. Lucky for us, the first thing he'll probably do is head back down into camp to take care of your..."

Sariani paused.

"Anyway," he resumed, "That's going to buy us a little time. With any luck, the next thing he'll try do is move ahead of us through that tunnel to cut off our retreat. That will buy us even more time."

"W-what?" Tim stammered. "How will that buy us more time?"

Sariani responded by tilting his head down towards his right leg.

"My right cargo pocket," he indicated. "Open it up."

Tim ducked under the redheaded woman hanging from Sariani's right shoulder to open the pocket. He produced a tiny key, as well as something that looked like a remote for a radio-controlled car.

"Extend the antenna on the remote, and put the key in the keyhole," Sariani instructed. "Then turn the key to the right."

As Tim did so, a green light came on. Directly under the light was a circular red button.

"Now," Sariani commanded. "Push the button."

Tim pressed his left thumb against the remote. He removed his hand and looked back at Sariani.

"What did that do?" he inquired.

"On my way up here," Sariani returned, "I laced the mouth of the tunnel with plastic explosives. You just detonated them. Anyone who heads down that tunnel now is going to run into a dead end. I set the explosives as a back-up plan, in case I didn't make it up here in time, and that Korean fuck tried to catch up to you and your brother by running down the tunnel."

"What? But Eric's still at the camp!" Tim vainly protested. "How is he going to—"

"Tim," Sariani leveled forcefully. "That's not our problem. We are getting the fuck out of here, right now! Grab the detonator, my rifle, my C.F.B.I. blanket, and try to keep up."

With that, Sariani readjusted Sarah's limp body and jogged back into the woods. Tim ran over to pick up the insulated white blanket, then rushed to catch up.

For more than two hours, the men silently hustled through the dense forest. Tim knew that, at any second, the tiny North Korean could materialize out of the trees and kill them. But, at this late stage of his emotional rollercoaster ride, he was too exhausted to care. Tim's head drooped, his glazed-over eyes listlessly following Sariani's footprints. His only thoughts were morbid ones dealing with his younger brother's likely demise.

The two men finally reached the end of the wooded plateau and began to gingerly scramble down the steep, slippery mountain slope. It was late morning now, and under the bright sunlight, Tim could see a pile of rubble below him at the base of the mountain. Thanks to Sariani's plastic explosives, Eric's secret enclave was effectively closed off from the world.

If Eric hadn't somehow escaped by now, Tim realized, he never would.

After another half-hour descent, Tim, Sariani, and Sarah's comatose body reached the base of the mountain. As Tim stared in sorrow at the demolished tunnel entrance, Sariani pulled a tiny communication radio from his white jacket.

"Sang-Ki, Du-Ho, do you copy, over?"

"We read you, Sarge, over."

"I have the package," Sariani stated. "I've reached the base of the mountain, and we're heading out of the woods. Meet me at the same spot where you dropped me off, over."

"Copy that."

Sariani led Tim down the same winding trail that Sarah had guided Tim along a day earlier. For a final forty-five minutes, the focused Ranger and the somber comic book aficionado trudged through the last bit of snowy North Korean forest. Then, at last, the narrow mountain road came into view.

Tim stepped out of the wilderness and saw a large cargo truck idling in the road adjacent to the trailhead.

Sariani nodded at the two uniformed Korean men sitting in the front seat, then jogged toward the rear of the vehicle. He swung open the door to the shipping container, deposited Sarah's body inside, and turned back to Tim, who was still standing at the mouth of trail.

Tim was blankly staring into the forest—as if, through sheer power of will, he could force his younger brother to appear.

Sariani hopped down from the truck and sprinted across the frosty landscape. He roughly grabbed Tim by the shoulder and spun him around.

"Tim!" he ordered. "Let's go!"

But Tim, with nothing left to give, barely reacted to Sariani's urgent tone. Sariani sighed, and softened his grip on Tim's shoulder.

"Tim." Sariani leveled, in a soft, paternalistic voice, "He's gone."

Tim's tired eyes drooped. As a single tear rolled down his left cheek, he looked back up at Sariani.

"I know."

Sariani nodded, then pointed silently toward the container. Tim took a final sorrowful look back toward the forest, then wobbled out onto the road. Sariani led him around to the rear of the truck, and the two men hopped inside.

"Du-Ho," Sariani affirmed into his radio. "We're good to go back here. Come shut us in, and let's get the fuck out of these mountains."

A minute later, the door swung shut, and Tim and Sariani were plunged into darkness. Outside, the truck's deep engine growled, and the vehicle began a slow roll down from the mountains.

The drug-holding facility, Eric's secret mountain enclave and North Korea soon faded in the distance.

****

No. 238 flew through the trees with blinding, relentless speed.

Seconds earlier, as he had instinctively leapt from the clearing, a single bullet from an M-4 rifle had torn into his redheaded opponent's shoulder. For the second time in three years, No. 238's ultimate showdown had been ruined by a single gunshot!

The Korean warrior's synapse was in a state of chaotic upheaval. From the moment Tim Sutton had unexpectedly arrived in the clearing, No. 238's flawless plans had begun to unravel. And, predictably, the relentless assassin could see only one path toward making his world right.

He needed to kill.

The soldier who had shot his opponent, No. 238 knew, was almost certainly the same man he had left in the drug-holding facility hours earlier. No. 238 had no idea how this soldier had found his isolated arena, nor did he care. The bottom line was that these were his woods. No. 238 was invisible here. In this place, no one, not even a highly skilled American soldier, had a chance of escaping the blade of No. 238's knife...

"If you try to kill that soldier, we'll kill her! Do you hear me? If you advance one more step in his direction, he's going to put a bullet in the middle of her forehead! You might kill him, but she'll be dead! Do you understand? She'll be dead!"

Tim Sutton's words rang out across the frigid landscape, and brought No. 238 to a sudden halt.

For fifteen seconds, the North Korean stood motionless between the frozen trees. Like a computer program with an unfixable glitch, No. 238's mind vainly ping-ponged back and forth in search of a solution that did not exist.

Finally, the Crocodile abruptly abandoned his initial plan, and settled on a new, albeit unsatisfactory, course of action.

He would leave the plateau, return to the secret base, and kill Eric Sutton.

Eliminating Sutton, of course, had always been a part of No. 238's plan. It was inevitable that Sutton would figure out what No. 238 had done and why. No. 238 had to eliminate the blond-haired young American before he notified Pyongyang.

He would dispatch Sutton as quickly as possible, and then rush off to intercept Tim Sutton and the soldier.

The tunnel would be the quickest route, unless this smart American soldier had placed demolition charges at its entrance. The other path, back up and over the mountain plateau, would take much longer. It was unlikely that No. 238 would reach his targets before they returned to the drug-holding facility, grabbed a vehicle, and escaped...

As his mind spun in circles, No. 238 raced back across the wooded steppe. In 30 minutes, he reached the steep, rocky slope that led down to the former Crocodile base. No. 238 hurled himself off the plateau and flew down the side of the mountain. He skidded through the deep powder like an alpine skier, arriving at the mouth to the tunnel in mere minutes. From there, No. 238 transitioned from skid to sprint, madly dashing off toward the base.

He rocketed past the concrete huts where he had been raised. He glided past the dirt circles where he had once executed his fellow crocodiles, arriving finally at the site of his former schoolhouse, the building where No. 238 had first learned how to kill.

Swinging the metal door open, he hustled through the building's tiny outer room and slid open the heavy wooden door at the rear. No. 238 burst through the opening and entered the warm, cavernous space beyond.

Eric Sutton sat in a chair at the opposite end of the room. His blond head was resting on his pale arms, which were folded on the table in front of him.

As No. 238 entered the room, Sutton slowly raised his head, leaned back against his chair and wearily slid his arms off of the conference table. He inhaled deeply, let out a long, resigned sigh, and stared expectantly at No. 238.

The North Korean clenched his combat knife and charged across the room.

CHAPTER 39

"Percy," Jeff Archer assured, "Eric Sutton is dead."

Archer didn't bother to look across the Lear Jet's narrow aisle at Danielson as he spoke. Archer kept his eyes glued to Sarah, who, having been restrained, was resolutely staring out of the window directly to his right.

Danielson dismissed Archer's comment, and stared keenly at Jeff Hutchins.

"Despite what my esteemed colleague Mr. Archer may think, I'm not going to take any chances on this one."

"We'll pass intel to the North Koreans through backchannels. Sutton went rogue, killed a bunch of people, and stole drug money. It won't exactly be a hard sell, given the bodies that are piled up in those mountains and the millions missing in cash. I'll even throw this 'Crocodile' into the mix. I'll paint him as Sutton's mule, pin some of the killing on him, and hopefully, they'll eliminate him along with Sutton."

"I might be mad as hell," Danielson went on, "that I wasn't able to get my hands on Sutton, but I'm not stupid. I know that this trip still yielded a bevy of valuable information regarding the North Korean drug trade."

"And," Danielson concluded, "I'd like your help."

Hutchins blinked in surprise.

"What?"

"I figure," Danielson replied, "That your 'undercover' assignment at that New Hampshire boarding school has just about run its course. I think it's time that we brought you back into the fold."

"I'm sorry: 'undercover' assignment?'" Hutchins replied in confusion.

Danielson winked.

"You said yourself that you thought Eric Sutton was extremely valuable as a resource. Well, we don't have Sutton now. But we do have a foundation on which to build our drug-fighting efforts. That said, this will be an uphill climb without Sutton. If I'm going to do this thing, I need men who have a knack for following dirty money. I need men who find answers, and people, when no one else can. I need you, Jeff."

Hutchins was completely taken aback.

"W-well," he stammered, "I guess I don't really know what to say!"

Danielson nodded.

"You think about it," he returned. "In the mean time, I'm going to think about the best way to ensure that that blond-haired little bastard ends up in a pine--"

"Jesus Christ, Percy," Archer interrupted, his eyes still locked on his redheaded charge. "His goddamn brother is sitting five rows behind you."

Danielson glared at Archer.

"I don't need to do Tim Sutton any favors!" Danielson muttered. "He's getting off easy, as far as I'm concerned. How do we know that he wouldn't have tried to help his brother escape?"

"But he didn't," Hutchins cut in. "He tried to get Eric to turn himself in. Tim Sutton, despite all that he's been through in the past couple of weeks, did the right thing. He did everything he could to save his brother and still see justice done."

Surprised, Danielson wheeled around to face the man he had just offered to hire. Hutchins dropped his eyes.

"All I'm saying," he finished softly, "Is that Tim Sutton is a good guy."

Danielson shrugged.

"Maybe."

Danielson turned back toward Archer.

"In any case, Commander, you should be happy! Of all of the people on this damn plane, you're the only one whose week has turned up roses. You got your precious Ceiling agent back."

Archer finally turned toward Danielson. He stared hard at the baldheaded CIA agent for a few seconds, then shifted his gaze to the rear of the plane. Archer studied the two somber men who were sitting in silence at the back end of the cabin. The silver-haired Commander briefly looked back at Sarah, then to Danielson's round face.

"Percy," Archer sighed, dourly shaking his head, "There are no winners here."

Archer abruptly rose from his seat.

"I'm going to talk to Tim Sutton," he announced. Archer pointed at Sarah. "If she somehow frees herself while I'm gone," he advised, "You should...well, try not to scream too loudly when she jumps on you."

As Danielson squirmed uncomfortably in his seat, Archer made his way down the jet's cramped walkway. At the rear, Archer produced the warmest smile he could muster and looked down at the young man seated next to the right-rear-window.

"Do you mind if I sit down, Tim?" he gently inquired.

Tim, clearly depressed, had been staring out at the Pacific Ocean in trance. He wearily faced the Commander.

"Uh, sure," he mumbled. "Go ahead."

"Tim", Archer began, "I just wanted to extend...well, I guess I owe you an apology as well as a debt of gratitude."

Tim continued to gaze at the vast blue abyss beyond the thick plastic window. Archer continued.

"Sarah was my, well...I guess you could say that I'm principally responsible for molding her into the person she is today. She's a special woman, and I tried my best to take that potential and turn it into--"

Archer cut himself off.

"Anyway," he went on. "For whatever part I indirectly played in pulling you into this whole mess...I'm sorry. I also recognize the balls it took to go up there and stop that fight before it played out. I know you probably don't care, but you very well may have saved my program's most precious asset. You've been a big help to me, Tim, and I thank you."

Tim deliberately turned from the window and forced a charitable smile.

"Mr. Archer," he tiredly assured, "I don't hold any ill will toward you. I mean, I'll be honest: Sarah scares the hell out of me. If it weren't for Sergeant Sariani, she would have killed me. But, well...I'm sure that you trained Sarah with the best of intentions, and I'm sure she has done a lot of good work to protect the United States."

"But," Tim gravely continued, "The things I did...I didn't do them for Sarah, or you, or for anyone else on this plane. I went over to North Korea with one purpose—to save my brother. And I failed."

Archer shook his head.

"Failure, Tim," he disagreed, "is a relative term. For crying out loud, son, you run a little comic book store in New Hampshire! And yet, to save your brother, you were willing to cross the globe, travel to one of the most dangerous countries on earth, and put yourself directly between two trained killers! You did more than anyone could have ever imagined."

"That's not failure," Archer finished. "That's fate. You did everything you could do—but all the effort in the world wasn't going to make Eric follow you out of those mountains."

Tim shrugged.

"I guess," he murmured.

Tim looked toward the front of the plane.

"So," he quietly questioned, "What happens to Sarah now?"

Archer stared ahead at his shackled Ceiling agent.

"Honestly," he admitted. "I'm not quite sure. I suppose we'll try to break her down and see if we can retrain her. Maybe we'll succeed. In truth, though, I doubt I'll ever be able to put Sarah back into the field."

"Over the years," Archer continued, "I chose to ignore her faults because of her enormous capabilities."

"I suppose," Archer conceded, "That's the main thing this whole damn fiasco has forced me to recognize. You can take a person, polish him, hone his skills, maximize his potential...but you can't change who a person is."

"But I guess," Archer realized, "You already know that."

Tim turned back to the window.

"Yeah," he whispered in agreement. "I suppose I do."

Archer reached out his right hand and patted Tim on the shoulder.

"You're a heck of a guy, Tim. Those comic book kids are lucky to have you."

"Now," Archer added, hopping up from his seat, "I've got to go think of a way to explain to my son why I missed the biggest high-school basketball game of his career! Something tells me the prom party will be held at my house this year!"

Tim produced a thin but genuine smile. Archer grinned, winked, and moved away.

Instead of heading back up the aisle, however, Archer leaned into the pair of seats across the aisle from Tim. The Commander solemnly extended his right palm toward the short, dark-skinned man dressed in camouflage sitting alone next to the window.

"Sergeant," he stated.

Jim Sariani gruffly reached out and clasped his leathery mitt around Archer's hand.

"Commander," he firmly replied.

Archer gripped Sariani's hand tightly and earnestly addressed the soldier.

"Jim," he began, "I could tell you that your country is deeply sorry for the loss of your brave men. I could tell you that they died for the noblest of causes, and that America's children will rest on their pillows much more soundly tonight as a result…"

"But," Sariani knowingly finished, "We'd both know that that was a bunch of horseshit."

Archer nodded, his lips widening.

"You're a hell of soldier, Jim," he stated. "And so were your men. When you head out to the bar tonight, toast them once for me, will you?"

Sariani nodded. Archer released his grip, turned, and headed back to the front.

Sariani slumped in his seat and closed his exhausted eyes. Before he could doze off, however, his attempt at slumber was interrupted by the voice of Tim Sutton.

"Sergeant?" Tim called softly from the opposite side of the jet.

"What?"

"Yesterday," Tim ventured timidly, "in the back of the cargo container…those were your men?"

Sariani nodded.

"And, up in the mountains," Tim continued, "when you reached the clearing, you got there just before you shot Sarah, right?"

Again, Sariani raised and lowered his drowsy head.

"Yup. I got within sight of the clearing, dropped under my C.F.B.I. blanket, stared through the scope of my M-4, and the first thing I saw was Sarah moving in on you. I made a quick decision."

"But," Tim replied. "Going up to that clearing, you knew priorities were saving Sarah and capturing my brother, right? And you knew that that North Korean had killed three of your men..."

Sariani gruffly stared back across the aisle at Tim.

"Yeah, okay," he allowed. "So?"

"So..." Tim reluctantly proceeded, his eyes falling,. "Why didn't you shoot the North Korean guy instead of Sarah? I mean, if you had, you could have avenged the death of your men. Then you and Sarah could have grabbed Eric, together. You'd have Sarah and my brother right now-"

"You want to know," Sariani interrupted, "why I saved your life."

Tim inhaled deeply.

"Well," he managed. "I...I guess that's what I'm asking, yes."

Sariani eyed Tim for a few more seconds. Then the Ranger closed his eyes a second time.

"Let's just say," he growled with a small, fatigued smile, "That I didn't want to go up to the S.W.I.P.E. course next year, look Will Sutton in the eye, and know that I'd allowed his boy to get his throat slit. Fair enough?"

"Fair enough," Tim whispered.

As the tiny jet soared across the shimmering blue water, Sariani closed the conversation with a final pledge.

"By the way," the Ranger vowed as he drifted off to sleep. "Next year, I'm going to beat that fucking course."

CHAPTER 40

"Get down! Get down, now!"

The thunderous words tore through the stuffy air and slammed ferociously into the ears of the terrified recipient.

"I swear," Leon vowed, "If your chubby little fingers spill so much as a drop of that milkshake on our copy of 'Hellblazer #1', I'll do so much damage to your fat face that you'll have to drink all of your meals through a fucking straw!"

The stout, milkshake-holding middle-schooler managed to nod a single time before climbing down from one of Dragon Comics' display racks and scampering out the store's poster-covered door.

"Wonderful," Tim sighed sarcastically, looking up from a packing slip he was inspecting. "Another satisfied customer."

"Yeah, whatever," Leon scoffed. "I'm telling you, you're too soft on these little bastards. While you were gone, I ran this place like a boot camp. No one messed up the comics, no one put their hands on the display counter, no one even thought about swiping a trading-card pack…"

Tim grinned and rolled his eyes.

"Leon, why do you think I hired you as my full-time assistant? Your authoritarian customer-service techniques notwithstanding, you've proven yourself to be a capable right-hand man."

Leon stared in satisfaction at the pack of young-adults meandering up and down Dragon's narrow aisles.

"Whatever," he replied, gruffly attempting to mask his newfound sense of self-worth. "I think you just want some extra time to choke the chicken."

Tim sighed and refocused on the packing slip.

"Yup, Leon, you've got me pegged…but I'm also your boss now. Speaking of which…"

"Wait a second," Leon backpedaled. "Hold on…"

"I'm looking at today's UPS manifest," Tim continued, "And I notice that three of the boxes we received today have yet to be checked off. Since we're closing in 30 minutes, would you please go into the back room and make sure that we got everything that we ordered for this week?"

"Fuck you Tim, I don't even-"

Leon cut himself off in mid-sentence. He slowly turned back toward the display counter, and stared at Tim with a sheepish frown.

"Shit," he muttered.

As Leon glumly trudged back into Dragon's tiny storeroom, Tim struggled to suppress a chuckle.

It had been nearly two weeks since Tim had returned to his quiet New Hampshire town. Life in Ruston had not changed one iota in his absence.

It was still mid-winter, and the city was blanketed with the same mixture of gray snow and dirty-brown road-salt that had covered the roads before Tim embarked on his grand adventure. Half of the store-fronts on Main Street were still vacant, the roads were still warped and cracked, and kids of all ages still poured into Tim's humble store to get their comic fix.

Tim was home.

He had worried, initially, that the lingering trauma of his round-the-world odyssey would haunt him. Tim had even feared that he would no longer be satisfied with his simple existence as a comic book merchant.

Instead, Tim's small-town existence had welcomed him back with open arms, enveloping him like a warm blanket. The basic day-to-day routine of running Dragon Comics had buoyed Tim with much-needed normalcy. Tim's harrowing trip to North Korea and back might have shaken him to the core, but he slowly realized that—over the span of what would probably be an entire lifetime spent selling comic books—it would prove to be little more than a hiccup. Life went on.

Tim still thought, of course, about Sarah, and the North Korean 'Crocodile.' Sitting beside Dragon's cash register, or alone in his apartment, Tim would often remember T.C. Watson, Jeff Hutchins, and Jim Sariani. He would reflect on the times during his chaotic journey when he had somehow cheated death—and on the people who, wrapped up in the same mess, had not been so lucky.

But mostly, Tim would think about Eric.

Tim had ventured thousands of miles from home in a desperate attempt to keep his brother's dim light from being snuffed out—only to discover that in North Korea, Eric's candle was burning more brightly than it ever had.

And now, Eric—Tim's mental equal and greatest friend—was lost forever.

"Alright, asshole, I'm done."

Leon noisily re-announced his presence, tramping back into Dragon's main room. He carelessly flipped the packing slip in Tim's general direction before bluntly announcing his next course of action.

"I'm leaving."

Tim looked at his watch and saw that it was, indeed, closing time. He looked up and realized that, as he was lost in thought, the final few kids who had been perusing his wares had headed home for the night.

"Alright," Tim allowed. "Get out of here. I'll see you tomorrow, Leon."

"Yeah," Leon muttered. "We'll see..."

Tim watched in amusement as his first and only employee stamped his combat boots across Dragon's worn carpet, brazenly batted open the front door, and clomped off into the darkness.

Tim was now alone. He ducked into the back room, quickly tidied up (neatness, oddly enough, was not one of Leon's strong suits), and turned off the overhead light.

Tim performed a quick once-over of the premises. When he was satisfied that his stock of comic books were in sufficient order, Tim strode back behind the glass counter, removed the large bills from his register, and tucked the tray in a hidden spot in the back room. Tim was just about to shut off the rest of Dragon's lights and depart for the evening when a set of knuckles rapped against the front door.

Somewhat surprised, Tim headed back up to the front. He swung open the poster-strewn door, prepared to tell the unfortunate young man that Dragon, alas, had shut its doors for the night.

Instead, however, Tim discovered that the weathered hand tapping belonged to William Sutton.

"Hey, Pops!" Tim saluted in cheerful surprise. "I was just closing up! What brings you to this neck of the woods?"

"Evening, Boy!" Will merrily replied. "I just figured I'd swing by and catch you before you took off for the night!"

Tim held open Dragon's door as his father stepped inside. He locked the door behind Will, then leaned against the end of a row of tables in the center of his store.

"So, Old Man," he queried, "Any particular reason why you're gracing me with your presence on this fine frigid evening?"

"Well," Will returned. "I just figured, you know, since you and I hadn't really had the chance to talk since…"

Tim's smile slowly faded from his face.

"Right," he admitted softly. "You're right. I know."

Will leaned his aged frame against the table to Tim's left. For a few seconds, the two men stared ahead in silence, vacantly eyeing the racks of comics that flanked Dragon's front wall. Finally, Will began.

"Tim," he stated in a low, serious tone, "I've got to say, I was pretty darn relieved when you arrived back from…well, from wherever it was you went off to. And over the past two weeks, I've been happy to see that, physically, anyway, you don't seem any worse for wear."

"Now you know me," Will continued. "I'm not one to rock the boat. So I don't want to ask you anything that's going to stir up any grief, or interfere with your ability to run the best darn comic book store in New England. Okay?"

Tim nodded his head in understanding.

"It's fine, Dad," he quietly assured. "And I'll be completely honest with you. Ask me anything you want, and I'll tell you the truth."

"Well…" Will deliberately hemmed. "Then I guess…I guess I've only got three questions."

"Shoot, Pops."

Will turned and stared solemnly at his auburn-haired son.

"Tim," he slowly inquired, "Did you find what you were looking for?"

Tim looked back into his father's eyes and nodded a single time. "Yeah, Dad. I found him."

Will pursed his lips and stared down at the floor.

"And," he managed, his throat growing hoarse, "were you surprised by what you found?"

Tim stared straight ahead at his store's front door. He lifted his right hand and slowly ran it through his hair.

Then, slowly, Tim's mouth broadened into a smile that was fueled by both amusement and realization.

"You know," he remarked, as much to himself as to his father. "I wasn't. I wasn't surprised at all."

Will nodded slowly, and took a moment to compose himself. Then, as tears welled in his eyes, he forced out his final query.

"Tim," Will choked, "Was...was he happy?"

Tim, doing his best to keep from crying himself, nodded one last time.

"Yeah, Dad," he whispered. "He was happy."

Will nodded to himself.

"Good," he breathed.

Will brushed the tears from his eyes, and took a deep breath.

"Okay," he hurriedly declared to his son. "That's it on the questions! I'm heading home."

Coughing for effect as he regained control of his emotions , Will spun around toward the store's front door. He waited as Tim unlocked the door and swung it open, then stepped out into the freezing New England night.

"Take care, Tim."

"Take care, Pops."

Tim was closing the door when Will called to him a final time.

"Hey, Tim?"

"What, Dad?"

"How's that Leon kid working out as your Number 2?"

Tim shrugged his shoulders.

"Ah, he's alright. He's cheap, he knows where things go, and he maintains law and order. I suppose I can't complain."

Will nodded.

"Well," he cautioned. "You might want to tell him to be a little bit more thorough the next time you get your weekly shipment of comics."

Tim furrowed his eyebrows.

"What do you mean?"

Will bent over and reached down to the small pile of snow to the right of Dragon's door. Lifting himself back up, Will turned and tossed a small brown object toward Tim.

"Because it looks," Will assessed, "Like Leon missed a package today."

Tim looked down.

In his hands was a tiny manila envelope.

The envelope was addressed to "Tim Sutton, Dragon Comics."

There was no return address.

EPILOGUE
GHOSTS

The black Mercedes-Benz limousine sped down the snow-swept boulevard.

The spacious thoroughfare was almost completely devoid of traffic. It was early, not yet 8 o'clock in the morning—but neither the time of day nor the icy driving conditions had anything to do with the lack of traffic.

Pyongyang was always like this.

In the North Korean capital city, as in the rest of the country, privately-owned vehicles were rare. Few North Koreans had the connections necessary to secure a car, and almost no one could afford to buy one. And so, day or night, winter or summer, Pyongyang's grandiose roadways were, effectively, automotive ghost towns, except for a state-run fleet of roomy limousines. These hulking vehicles ferried North Korea's bureaucrats, administrators, and military officers about the city.

This particular black Mercedes was delivering Colonel Pak to his downtown office.

Pak's angular, aged face stared rigidly out the right-rear-window. He watched as the Mercedes headed west, onto the long Taedong Bridge that spanned the waterway of the same name. Looking to the north, Pak's cold black eyes followed the river as it wound its way through the center of Pyongyang. Packed tightly along the river's icy banks were the same nondescript concrete apartment towers that filled the rest of city.

The limo reached the end of the bridge and turned to the right. Off to the west, the pyramid-shaped shell of the Ryugyong Hotel soared high above the uniform skyscrapers that surrounded it. The towering, 105-story high-rise would become the world's tallest hotel—if it was ever finished. The North Korean populace had been led to believe that the hotel was in a continuous, gradual state of construction. But government insiders like Pak knew that the hotel had originally been scheduled to open in 1989—and that, by 1992, it had been essentially abandoned. Since then, Pyongyang's skyline had been dominated by an empty, windowless husk of steel and concrete.

The lonely boulevard veered away from the river and widened, magnifying its frosty emptiness. The Mercedes followed the road to the northwest, finally arriving at the circular roadway that ringed the deserted grounds of Pyongyang's Triumph Return Square.

One of the numerous spots dedicated to North Korea's deceased former leader, Kim-Il-sung, Triumph Return Square was centered around a concrete Arch of Triumph. The colossal arch, specifically designed to be a much larger version of the Parisian edifice, was outfitted with numerous staircases and observation decks. These decks were rarely used. Triumph Return Square was, effectively, a gaudy tourist attraction in a city that had no tourists.

The limo wound its way around the square, past another monument to Kim-Jong-Il's late father: The 100,000 seat Kim-Il-sung Stadium. Finally, to the north of the square, the Mercedes arrived at its destination--a long, gray, five-story stone office-building.

Ten soldiers in olive-green uniforms stood sentry at the front door. As the limo rolled to a stop, one of the men marched forward and opened Colonel Pak's car door. The soldiers saluted the stoic, white-haired officer as he exited the vehicle and strode into the building.

Once inside, Pak rode an elevator to the fifth floor. Exiting the elevator, he turned to his right and strode down the wide, red-carpeted hallway. Affixed to the unpainted walls on his left and right were framed photographs of various North Korean generals and war heroes, as well as numerous paintings of the country's two "Dear Leaders": Kim-Jong-Il and his late father, Kim-Il-sung.

Finally, Colonel Pak reached a thick wooden door, where a uniformed soldier snapped to attention, saluted, and swung the door open. Pak wheeled to his right, strode past the soldier, and entered his office.

The Colonel's sparse, low-ceilinged workplace was brightly illuminated by overhead track lighting. The office was clean and well-organized, but it was far from spacious. Pak's dark-brown work desk took up the rear half of the room. The office's remaining space contained a narrow walkway and a smaller desk at which Pak's secretary worked.

"Good morning, Colonel!" he announced, rising up from his desk and saluting his boss.

Pak nodded silently and proceeded toward his workspace.

"Colonel," the secretary noted. "You have a package waiting for you on the top of your desk. It was apparently forwarded to this office by some of our narcotics contacts in Dalian, China, and it is marked extremely urgent."

Pak frowned. Dalian? What connection did he have with Dalian? The Chinese city, Pak knew, was the main port through which North Korean drugs were exported. But Pak wasn't directly involved in any of that. He was only responsible for the secret base that housed Eric Sutton, the drug trade's coordinator. So why had this package been addressed to him?

Pak turned back toward his secretary.

"Call the top officials in our narcotics program," he ordered. "I want to know why this package was sent to me."

"I've already called them several times," Pak's secretary replied. "None of them are answering their phones. I was unable to get a response on any of the phone lines connected to any of the top narcotics officers. It could be that the phones in those buildings are experiencing technical difficulties…"

"Try again," Pak commanded. The grizzled Colonel circled around his desk, sat down in his cushioned leather chair, and reached for the thin brown envelope that was lying in front of him. Pak opened the envelope, stuck his hand inside, and pulled out a single sheet of white computer paper. He set the paper on the desk in front of him, leaned down, and examined the message.

As Pak's dark eyes scanned the communiqué, they opened wide with horror. The Colonel's wrinkled hands tightly gripped the arms of his chair.

This can't be possible!

According to the communiqué, millions in drug money had been stolen during a firefight at the drug-holding facility in the mountains! At the same time, the corresponding drug shipment had simply vanished off a dock in Dalian!

Subsequently, North Korean agents had determined that the mastermind of the theft was Colonel Pak's precious charge, Eric Sutton! Worse, Sutton had convinced Pak's beloved 'Crocodile' to do his dirty work for him!

Pak bolted out of his chair in shock, and spun toward his secretary.

"Have you gotten hold of the narcotics officials?" he bellowed.

The secretary, taken aback by the Colonel's sudden change in demeanor, timidly lowered the phone from his ear and shook his head.

"N-no, Colonel! Still nothing!"

Pak marched across his office.

"Call me a car! Now!" he ordered. "If I can't reach the narcotics offices by phone, I'm going to drive over there myself!"

The Colonel's head was spinning. How could the two most important men in his life have decided, out of the blue, to betray North Korea?

Perhaps it wasn't true. Perhaps the contacts sending this message simply had their facts wrong. Maybe this was all just a big misunderstanding…but until he could actually talk to the people who had forwarded the message, how could he know for sure?

"I'm going downstairs!" Pak announced. "By the time I step out of the elevator, that car had better be waiting at the front door!"

Pak's secretary nodded in fright as the Colonel flung open the door to his office. Before Colonel Pak took a single step, however, he was stopped in his tracks by an astonishing sight in the hallway.

On the floor to his left, the soldier who had been guarding the entrance was sprawled face-down. A pool of crimson blood soaked into the carpet beneath the man's neck.

As gruesome and shocking as this discovery was to Colonel Pak, it paled in comparison with the other surprise that confronted him.

A diminutive, bald, large-eared man stood in the middle of the hallway.

Colonel Pak staggered back into his office.

"Please!" he managed. "Please, wait! You don't--"

These were the Colonel's last words.

The small figure exploded toward Pak with blinding speed, clenching a black dagger which rocketed into the Colonel's jugular. As blood poured from the gaping wound in his neck, the aged officer careened back across his office, smashing into the side of his desk before finally collapsing to the floor in a lifeless heap.

The secretary, frozen in terror by the whole display, was next to die.

For a few seconds, No. 238 slowly surveyed the cramped office. Then he walked to the rear of the room and stared down at Colonel Pak's body.

This elderly officer was the man who had been chiefly responsible for No. 238's upbringing. From the very beginning, he had supervised No. 238's diet, education, combat training, and battles. In a way, Colonel Pak was the closest thing No. 238 had ever had to a father.

And maybe—if he had been capable of feeling pain, remorse, sorrow, grief, or love—No. 238 might have actually cared.

The assassin produced a tiny cellular phone from the pocket of his pants. He methodically dialed a number, then raised it to one of his ears.

"Hello?"

"Pak is dead," No. 238 casually declared into the phone.

There was a brief pause on the other end of the line before No. 238 heard a reply.

"That's it, then. That's all of them. Colonel Pak was the last one. In 24 hours, you've killed every top narcotics official, and every officer with any knowledge of the Crocodile Program. Every person with details of your existence or my presence in this country is dead. We're ghosts now."

No. 238 lowered the phone from his ear and tucked it back into his pocket. He whirled toward the front of the office, rocketed out into the hallway, and disappeared.

****

Eric raised his weary blond head from the surface of his conference table. He looked across the cavernous room at the killer who had just slid open the room's wooden door.

This is it. Time to die.

Eric's arms dropped to his sides. He stared at the assassin, sighed deeply, and hoped for a quick death.

But then, curiously, as his soon-to-be murderer scampered toward the conference table, Eric saw something.

Something was clearly out of place. It was a tiny anomaly where anomalies simply did not exist.

The North Korean super-soldier was frowning.

He's not happy...

Eric's eyes widened. His brain, which had shut down in anticipation of death, suddenly sprang to life. As the killer closed in with his menacing knife extended, Eric's mouth emitted a single question.

"You didn't kill her, did you?"

The bald-headed Korean ground to a sudden halt, as if he had just run into a brick wall. Frozen like a wax statue, he stared at Eric, his blade mere inches from the young man's throat.

For five seconds, Eric gazed at the fearsome dagger. Gradually, his eyes traveled up to meet those of his would-be killer.

With a wry hint of a smile, Eric queried No. 238 a final time.

"Do you want to?"

John Lacombe lives and works in Chicago.
Winter Games is his first novel.

Printed in the United States
109795LV00005B/211-333/P